CODE OF ETHICS

CIPHER SECURITY BOOK #3

APRIL WHITE

"Maybe love, at its essence, is being a mirror for another person—for the good parts and the bad. Perhaps love is simply finding that one person who sees you clearly, cares for you deeply, challenges you and supports you, and subsequently helps you see and be your true self."
— Penny Reid, *Capture*

I first learned of the Canadian residential school system during my research into the schools of the Yukon for a short story I wrote in 2017. When I decided to use that history as part of the backstory for this book, the mass graves of children who attended some of those schools had not yet been discovered. I send my deepest love and hopes for healing to the people who hold the memories and carry the legacy of that experience.

[1]

DALLAS

"My alone time is sometimes for your safety."

- DALLAS PROFEIT, SECURITY SPECIALIST

Finding a douchebag in Chicago did not take any special skill.

"Douchebag" was the day's target category for my Tracker Jack game, and was sponsored by a skipped lunch and a late meeting with a prospective client, both of which had resulted in my general grumpiness with the human race. Tracker Jack was my variation on a game called Following that some performance artists came up with as a way to see a city like a local—follow a random stranger wherever they go and let them lead you on their shortcuts, down paths, and into neighborhoods you might never have explored on your own. My personal version of the game went something like this: pick a target based on some criteria chosen depending on my mood, then, taking care not to be noticed, follow the chosen target until they entered some place I couldn't

1

legally follow them into or until they took me too far off my own track. If the target either saw me or seemed threatened by my presence, I broke off the tracking and found someone else to follow. I never followed women, because we got followed enough, but most days there remained plenty of targets to choose from.

Red baseball caps were sometimes a sign of douchebaggery, and there were three in my compartment on the L blue line. Canada Goose coats were another sign because *a:* they were lined with the sun, and not even my Yukon-bred bones needed to stay that warm, and *b:* they were the approximate cost of a month's rent.

I automatically eliminated one of the redcaps when I saw his wife. Another one had settled in with his *Wall Street Journal,* so he was probably bound for one of the later stops. Most likely Logan Square, because with his pressed khakis and expensive briefcase, he fit the leafy life profile. The third was a decent prospect though—he was totally nondescript in a creepy, forgettable way. He was of average height and build, with average Caucasian coloring. He was the kind of invisible man who would have to work extra hard to get someone's attention, which, I assumed, was the reason for the red hat. Without the hat, even my hunter-trained eyes would have just slid right past him.

As the train approached the Division station, the invisible-man redcap didn't shift or change his position, so I scanned the passengers for another possible target. If I couldn't find one on the train, I'd usually go up another stop to Damen and drop in at Myopic Books, a great used bookstore near the station. It was easy to find Tracker Jack targets there —I just picked a book genre and strolled down that aisle. Of course, a decent amount of literacy was suggested in the targets one found in a bookstore, but I'd met literate douchebags before in my life.

Then, just as the train pulled into Division, a young hipster guy wearing a Canada Goose bomber jacket stood up and moved toward the doors.

Bingo.

I studied him as I casually moved into place behind him at the door.

He wore a knit cap pushed back on his head, which revealed perfectly tousled hair a little lighter than my own dark brown. His beard was trimmed to a three-day-scruff length, and he wore a knit turtleneck sweater that I might have chosen for myself if I hadn't seen it on him. Between the sweater and the coat, the guy was either a vampire with no actual body heat or an android who didn't sweat.

The average temperature in Chicago in March was forty-five degrees, so in deference to the client meeting, I wore a tailored suit under a flea market cashmere topcoat. I'd left my dress boots at work and instead had on my favorite Chelsea boots with rubber soles, which made me quiet and able to blend. The hipster's work boots would have been functional on any of my cousins, but on him, with the laces hanging open as if he had just rolled out of someone's bed and slipped them on to sneak home, they were a fashion statement.

Just before the train doors opened, he flashed a grin at an attractive woman in her early fifties, and then bestowed a devastating smile on a young woman behind her.

He fit his charming flirt persona so well it was almost comical.

Hipsterman was one of those men whose place at the top of the food chain had resulted in the kind of confidence only someone with no natural predators had. He walked like he owned the street, and based on the startled smiles of the people who passed him, apparently grinned at everyone he saw. He was tall, with a loping gait, and he carried a battered leather duffle on a strap worn diagonally across his chest. The orangey tan leather had aged well, and I took a mental snapshot of it so I could look for it online later.

Mental snapshots were a trick I'd learned from my grandfather when he taught me to track game. Spruce trees in the Yukon Territory tended to look identical, so mental snapshots of an interesting rock or a particular animal trail could mean the difference between getting back to the house before dark or spending a cold night in the boreal forest.

I stayed far enough back from Hipsterman that he wouldn't catch my reflection in any shop window he passed. I also varied my position on the sidewalk, moving to the right as if to peer into a shoe store, or to the left to avoid people exiting a restaurant. He looked behind him to cross the street, and I studied my phone. He cut between cars in a bold move, and I kept walking toward the crosswalk, my eyes continually finding him and his easy stride until he turned and entered a small gourmet market in the middle of the block. I watched the market as I waited for the light, taking note of the people who went in and out. They carried their own cloth bags and seemed to emerge with just enough for a meal or two in them, which told me the place was probably full of overpriced specialty and organic foods—the kind I loved, but rarely indulged in.

The first thing I noticed upon entering the market was the smell of fresh bread. It was my kryptonite because it represented the ultimate comfort food. Bread was not something a person could easily make if survival was a daily consideration. It required time, heat, and the proper ingredients, all of which had felt like luxuries to me at one point or another.

I veered toward the bakery section while keeping my other senses tuned toward locating Hipsterman among the other hipstery shoppers. There were a couple of other Canada Goose jackets among them, which made spotting him slightly more challenging, but once I did find him, flirting with a woman in an expensive suit in the snacks aisle, he was the only one I could see. He was all smiles and charm as he reached a bag of gluten-free crackers on a top shelf for her, and after he'd added a pricey fruit and nut mix to his own basket and continued down the aisle, the woman walked away with a happy smile and a backward glance.

As he approached the bakery aisle where I stood guard over a basket of freshly baked bread, I could see that Hipsterman's basket contained the ingredients for a fancy steak dinner for two—not surprising at all given his apparently boundless charm. In addition to the steaks, it included five perfect gold potatoes, a head of garlic, European butter, a small bundle of chives, Brussels sprouts, the fruit and nut mix, and a package of bacon. When he reached past me for a baguette, I had to fight the urge to duck away, and instead, I let myself glance up at him.

The guy's eyes slid across my face as if I had the forgettable features of the redcap on the train. Despite my intended invisibility, I bristled with annoyance when he moved past me down the aisle with no acknowledgement that another person had shared space with him.

It made no sense for me to have wanted him to notice me. It flew directly in the face of my rules of Tracker Jack, and was actually pretty stupid for any woman who wanted to keep a low profile. I'd never been someone who liked any sort of spotlight, and I considered the fact that I could blend in with most ethnic groups a point in my favor. My long, straight dark hair, brown eyes, and high cheekbones could be found scattered among Indigenous people of North and South America, as well as several Pacific islands and Southeast Asian countries. Guesses as to my ethnicity included those, plus Middle Eastern, Mongolian, and South Asian, and I rarely corrected anyone or admitted to my Northern Tutchone heritage. It required far more conversation than I generally wanted to have with people.

But there, in the bakery section of an overpriced market, in the midst of a game of Tracker Jack that only I knew I was playing, I was annoyed to realize just how invisible I was.

I slipped into a checkout line with my own baguette before Hipsterman had finished his shopping, and then lingered at a table, savoring bites of bread as I watched him flirt with the cashier. Her laughter at something he'd said was like nails on a chalkboard to me, and I tore off another bite of bread as an antidote to the annoyance. Their hands touched as Hipsterman reached for his plastic tote full of groceries, and I scoffed, inhaled a crumb, and nearly missed his departure in my fit of silent coughing. He was nearly at the door when I slipped in behind him to leave the store.

Hipsterman's route took him up Milwaukee Avenue, the main restaurant and shopping street in Wicker Park. He paused to check out the window display at Volumes Book Café, and I caught a flash of red in the window of a hair salon when I turned to avoid his gaze. There were mirrors in the display, presumably to show passersby how desperately they needed the salon's services, which was how I saw the redhat hunched into his coat across Milwaukee Avenue. The back of my neck itched at the sight of him. One of the redhats from the train? That seemed unlikely, but I had learned long ago to trust instinct. It was a survival tool that was just as valuable as a knife or fire, so I listened to it and hurried after Hipsterman as he turned down an alley between buildings.

When I rounded the corner, my Canada Goose–wearing quarry had disappeared, and I nearly halted in surprise at the empty passage. The itch at the back of my neck persisted though, so I kept moving forward, away from Milwaukee Avenue and whatever had disquieted me.

The sound of traffic behind me was dulled by the tall brick buildings on either side of the narrow alley. I glanced behind me. No one had followed me in, and the tension in my chest eased slightly, right until the moment I turned back around and almost collided with Hipsterman.

"Why are you following me?" he demanded sharply.

My shock instantly quieted to cold calm, and I took a wary step backward.

His hand shot out to grab my arm. "Answer me, damn it! What do you want?"

I twisted out of his grasp, and he looked stunned at how easily I'd done it. But then his eyes flicked over my shoulder and went wide with fear.

I spun, then grabbed the Canada Goose jacket to jerk Hipsterman away as a redhat lunged. Redhat held a fixed blade, and I instinctively kicked at his knife hand as I reached for my own blade, which I wore in a sheath at my back. He dodged my foot and swung to face off with me just as my knife hand came up. I knocked his red baseball cap off as I sliced him across the forehead—a clean, shallow cut, just like Grandpop had taught me. *Blind them with their own blood*, he'd said. *It stings and barely leaves a mark, but head wounds are nasty bleeders.*

Redhat jumped back, snarling in a foreign language as blood streamed into his eyes. He swiped an arm across his face to clear the blood, then zeroed in on the knife I held defensively in front of me. He sent a glance over my shoulder, grabbed his hat off the ground, turned, and ran.

Adrenaline shot through me, and my feet were moving before my brain had a chance to catch up. This redhat *had* been the invisible one from the train, but I reached Milwaukee Avenue and discovered that even with blood running down his face, he had melted back into the scenery.

I didn't enjoy having been surprised, and I retreated back into the alley, now empty of both Hipsterman and Redhat, to wait out the adrenaline aftermath away from people. There was a doorway at the back of one of the Milwaukee Avenue–facing buildings, and I spotted Hipsterman's grocery bag sitting there. I waited, wondering how long it would take him to come back for his steaks, but based on the fear I'd seen in his eyes, I figured he'd probably gone home to hide in the closet. The steaks would be eaten by rats if nobody claimed them, so after the adrenaline crash, I picked up the grocery bag and continued down the alley in the direction he had run.

The alley emptied out into a neighborhood full of condos and parking structures, and there were no Canada Geese in sight. I turned left and continued up to West North Avenue, eyes peeled for my hipsterman in every window, but I saw no one resembling him or Redhat anywhere.

Well, that was the most interesting game of Tracker Jack I'd played in a long time.

I dissected the incident in the alley as I walked home to my Humboldt Park rental. Hipsterman had definitely seen me in the market. His sliding glance had been *too* disinterested. I knew I could blend into the background. It was a skill I'd practiced every summer I spent hunting, and I'd turned that skill into an asset for my close-protection work. But I wasn't invisible. Granted, I wasn't one of the big bodyguards people hired to intimidate and terrify. I was young and female and decent-looking enough to be a friend, or sister, or girlfriend—someone who actually belonged by the client's side. Hiding in plain sight meant I was seen but never really noticed, and that was why my invisibility to Hipsterman had bothered me so much.

It definitely wasn't because I'd wanted him to notice me.

His brand of pretty wasn't my type. His easy, charming smile at passersby definitely wasn't appealing to me. And flirting with every woman in range was so far off my list of desirable traits it might have been written in smoke.

I was two blocks from my destination and lost in uncomfortable thoughts when I heard the car. It was coming too fast for the yellow light above me, and my hands were already reaching for the woman in front of me at the curb. I grabbed her coat and yanked her backward as the car slid around the corner.

"Hey!" she said, and I couldn't tell if she was protesting the bumper's near miss or my grab.

"You okay?" I asked the woman. She wore smoky black eye makeup the way tutorials have never been able to teach me, and her long, straight hair was hot pink. The t-shirt she wore proclaimed "Feminist as f*ck," and it made me smile because my friend Anna had one just like it.

"Bloody hell," she said, tossing her head toward the departed car. Then she turned to me and stuck her hand out. "Thank you." She looked at me another second. "I've seen you walking here before. I'm Lynn."

"Dallas," I said as I shook her hand. I'd seen her too. The hair was unmistakable. "Nice shirt."

Her smile grew wider. "Nice reflexes."

The light changed and we crossed the street. When we got to the other side, Lynn turned right with a wave. "I owe you a save someday," she said as her bright pink hair bobbed away.

"No worries, it's my job," I said quietly, mostly to myself, as I continued on my way.

It *was* my job—saving lives, protecting people who were threatened, keeping people safe. Usually my clients were women, but sometimes having a female close protection agent on a man was the best way to stay under the radar. Which brought me right back to Hipsterman's radar and why he'd been so finely tuned to me and so immediately afraid of Redhat.

Was he expecting to be followed? Was that why he'd been so careful not to notice me? I should have realized that a guy with such an easy smile for everyone he saw wouldn't have gone so poker-faced at my presence unless he'd been aware of me tailing him. I didn't like giving the guy credit for that level of awareness, but it made sense.

I shifted his grocery bag to my other shoulder and felt momentarily bad that I'd be eating his steak. The moment of sympathy passed when I remembered there were two steaks in the bag. He'd have company tonight, and I definitely didn't wonder how she would console him on the loss of his groceries.

[2]

OLIVER

"Never in the history of calming down has anyone calmed down by being told to calm down."

- OLIVER CURRAN, TECH ENTREPRENEUR

I'd slept less than usual, which meant basically not at all, so the smile I flashed at the pretty Black woman behind the front desk took effort. "Hi, I'm Oliver Curran, here to see Quinn Sullivan."

"Do you have an appointment?" the woman, whose security badge read "Kendra Eze," asked in a British accent.

"Sterling Gray set it up for me this morning," I said, looking around the lobby with its general vibe of style, class, and understatement. The Cipher Security Systems building had an interesting look for an agency that specialized in corporate security with a side of bodyguards, and the young woman behind the desk with a textbook open in front of her added to the polish of the place.

"What are you studying?" I asked, looking over the desk at her book when she hung up the phone.

She wrinkled her nose. "Citizens United v. Federal Election Commission."

"Nothing like a little light reading before lunch," I said in sympathy.

She grimaced. "More like a political thriller meets a Shakespearean tragedy."

I laughed. "Law school?"

She nodded. "Studying for the bar exam. Mr. Sullivan will meet you on the third floor, Mr. Curran."

I shot her the wry smile that read as either charming or flirtatious, depending on the person's mood. "It's Oliver. Mr. Curran's my dad."

It was my classic line, always spoken with an easy grin so the distance I put between my famous philanthropist father and myself didn't sound like it was said through gritted teeth.

"Good luck with your meeting, Oliver," the woman said with a friendly but impersonal smile, which meant she wasn't in the mood for flirting. Too bad. Flirting was my favorite sport.

"Good luck with the bar, Miss Eze," I said, dialing the wattage of my grin back.

The elevator doors opened to the third floor, and the handsome white guy I knew from photos as Quinn Sullivan stood talking to another guy I identified as Darius Masoud based on the description Sterling had given of his girlfriend's brother-in-law—Iranian, nice suit, lean and fit. I had developed the habit of instantly classifying faces for skin tone, facial features, ethnicities, and unique elements because faces had become my life's work. Every app I'd designed and sold since college had been built around faces—recognizing them, altering them, enhancing them, and replacing them with animal heads and cartoon characters. It was maybe a strange way to view the world, but then again, everyone else did the same thing when they met someone new, they just weren't always aware of it like I was.

Darius saw me first and held out his hand. "Oliver, I'm Darius. Sterling told me you'd be in. May I present Quinn Sullivan, owner of Cipher Security."

"Thanks for meeting me," I said as I shook both guys' hands. Darius hit the elevator button to hold it. "You have my number," he said to me, then shifted his gaze to Quinn and said, "And I'm available if you want me to take a look at his place."

"I'll let you know after Mr. Curran and I speak." Quinn's voice was deep and sure, and he gave the impression that he was in total control of himself and everything around him. The guy wore king-of-the-world as confidently as he wore his custom-tailored suit. "Right this way," Quinn said, gesturing for me to walk with him.

The office setup was unexpected and reminded me of the Google campus in Palo Alto, or maybe the Snapchat offices in Venice Beach. There seemed to be private offices for those who wanted them, but there were also people working in various conference rooms and open spaces without a carpeted cubicle divider in sight.

"This place looks nothing like any security firm I could have imagined. It's way more like something a creative director designed," I said appreciatively.

"My Director of Information Technologies is married to a psychiatrist, and she gave me a long lecture about work environments and their effect on happiness and productivity," he said wryly.

I nodded. "Oh yeah, I worked in a room full of cubicles once. Each one of them was decorated like a museum to all the fun things people *used* to do, before they worked in cubicles. When I started my company I tried to do one big space, but you can't hire a bunch of gamers and expect office-hours productivity." I chuckled. "I ended up letting a lot of people work from home, and it was a shock to exactly no one how much work got done at one in the morning."

A striking white woman with long chestnut hair walked by with a cool waxed-canvas photojournalist's bag slung over one shoulder. "Nice bag," I called out to her.

"Thanks, it's my boyfriend's," she said with a gorgeous smile.

"Too bad," I said, the wry grin showing my disappointment. I wasn't really disappointed, but it was part of the game, and she knew it too, because she chuckled as she walked away.

Quinn's mouth twitched in what might have been a smirk, but since he was all hardwood and leather, it was hard to tell. "The biggest factor to the success of what we do here," he continued as if I'd never spoken to the hot brunette, "is collaboration, and while our agents are able to work from home, most prefer to come in for the water cooler conversation." He nodded over at an Asian man and a woman whose ethnicity could have been indigenous to North or South America sitting on low sofas with a long coffee table running between them. "Or the coffee table talk."

The woman looked up as we passed, and I stopped in my tracks.

What the fuck? "You."

Quinn must have sensed the tension in me, because his cold calm dropped to something arctic.

"Dallas, would you join us, please?"

The woman he'd called Dallas tore her eyes from me and met Quinn's implacable gaze. "Sure," she said, flipping the notebook in front of her shut. She closed a bag of spiced fruit and nut mix that stood open next to the notebook. I frowned, grabbed them from the coffee table without thinking, and held them tightly.

"These are mine," I said inanely.

She nodded, confirming that they were from the grocery bag I'd left behind after almost being knifed in a dark alley. "I'll replace what I ate last night."

Quinn looked at both of us with the kind of expression that indicated he wasn't thrilled not to understand what was going on. He led the way to a smallish room with a big window and a round table and took the seat facing the door. "Please have a seat, both of you."

I glared at Dallas. Her expression was unreadable, and she didn't flinch.

Quinn looked back and forth between us for a few long seconds until Dallas finally broke the silence.

"I followed him yesterday after work," she said on an exhale, like she'd been dreading saying the words. "It's a game I play. I didn't mean to scare him." She turned to face me directly. "I didn't mean to scare you. It's just something I do to stay sharp."

"To stay—" I stared at her. "You stalk people to stay sharp?" I turned to glare at Quinn, even as I was rising from my seat. "This is how you get clients? Send a stalker so people freak out and go looking for security?" I shook my head in disgust. "For fuck's sake."

"Mr. Curran," Quinn began, but Dallas shot him some sort of look and, oddly, he sat back. She stood to face me, her unreadable expression finally breaking to something a little bit less severe.

"It's not a tactic, Mr. Curran," she said. "It's a game I call Tracker Jack. I follow random people, ideally without being spotted, and they show me their world. I happened to be in the same L car as you and chose you because of your coat. I followed you to the food store, and you obviously saw me there. I didn't realize that the redhat, who was also on the train, was following us until he attacked."

"The redhat," I echoed, thinking, and trying not to freak out. "You mean the non-descript white guy who came at me with a knife? He was on the train?" She nodded, and I studied her for a moment, my heart pounding with the memory of his face and the damn knife. God, I *hated* being afraid.

"My question," she continued, fixing me with dark brown eyes, "is how you knew you were being followed."

"What, you think you're a ghost?" I shot back defensively. I fought past the pounding heart to take deep breaths. I'd rather be angry than afraid, because fear came with a side of helplessness, and I refused to be helpless.

The woman didn't even twitch. "I know I am."

Quinn watched us over the top of steepled fingers with a look of placid interest, and I glared at him. "If she's so good, how did the guy get the drop on us both?"

"*She*," the woman said pointedly, drawing my eyes back to hers, "made a mistake. Your acting skills are very good." She said it grudgingly, as if it cost her something to admit that I'd seen her. "It took me too long to realize you'd seen me in the market," she continued. "It's obvious now that you were looking for a tail, but I had no way of knowing that."

I scoffed. "You think you're so good that the only way for me to have seen you was if I was already looking for someone else?"

"Yes," she said simply.

"Ridiculous," I muttered.

"The question stands, Mr. Curran. You are here for a reason. Why did you believe you were being followed?"

The woman—Dallas, I amended mentally—was one of those suit-wearing, good-posture, sensible-shoes, hair-tied-back, professional women who'd probably had to be better than every man in every class she ever took. Women like that made me tired, and except for the sensible shoes, they reminded me of my mother. There was never any freedom to just *be* around them—everything had to have a purpose or a goal, and they were always ready to judge you if you didn't. It probably made her really good at her job, but it also sucked the fun right out of every room.

I sighed and finally sat down. Dallas hesitated just a moment, but another look must have passed between her and Quinn, because he gave a slight nod and then she sat across from me.

"I'm in talks with a couple of major corporations about some tech I'm developing," I said reluctantly. "Two weeks ago, someone broke into an office I sometimes use for meetings. They corrupted a bunch of operating system files trying to get into a computer."

"How did you determine it was a targeted attack?" Dallas asked.

My expression was bland, but my voice was *don't be an idiot*. "When your office is the only one in the whole building that's trashed, it's pretty clear who the target is." Her own expression didn't change at my snark, and I continued. "I mostly work from home since I sold my last company. Three days ago, someone broke into my car when it was parked outside my house and went through it like they were looking for something specific."

"The car break-in could be unrelated," Dallas said. Her voice was low-pitched and calm, but I wasn't in the mood for calm.

"I'd left this coat in the car, and they didn't steal it," I said holding up my Canada Goose bomber. "Do you know how much these damn things cost? The extra credit card I leave in the car for gas was still there too. They were looking for something specific."

I didn't miss the blink of judgment in Dallas's glance toward Quinn, and it annoyed the hell out of me. Annoyed was good though, because it beat the crap out of fear every time.

"Do you have any idea who it might be and what they're looking for?" Quinn asked in his deep rumble.

"Hard drives, obviously."

"Why hard drives, and why are you sure?" Dallas asked.

Annoyance was making me an asshole, and yet I couldn't seem to back it off with her. "Because I'm about to sell the rights to groundbreaking tech to the highest bidder, and no one keeps programs like that online."

"So, either someone wants to steal the program to sell themselves, or someone doesn't want you to sell it in the first place. Is that right?" she persisted, apparently unfazed by the asshole sitting in front of her.

"No one else can sell it because it's not finished yet. I'm offering exclusive rights to a program no one else has and everyone needs." My patience had frayed. I wasn't this guy. I never let anger and fear win, because then I lost. I made a conscious effort to calm down, and when I had my heartbeat back under control, I pulled a smile out of my back pocket and put it on. It felt false, but if I wore it long enough, the edges would blend in and they wouldn't spot the fake.

"So, possibly, someone is trying to prevent you from finishing the program?" Quinn asked, ignoring the mask I'd just pulled on. "That is significantly more serious. What is this product that no one has and everyone needs?"

"It's proprietary," I said bluntly.

The curiosity on Quinn's face shut down into politeness, and after a long, intense moment, he stood up. "Right, well, Mr. Curran, you have Darius Masoud's information if you'd like to have him look at security for your home. Otherwise, I don't see that we can help you."

"That's it?" I stared at Quinn in disbelief. "Sterling said this is the best security company in the city. What about the guy who attacked me?" I looked over at Dallas, frowned, and amended, "Us."

Quinn sighed, though not impatiently. "There are ethical concerns for us when we are not in full possession of the facts. I will not commit my people to the protection of anyone who might be engaged in illegal or illicit behavior, or whose business is in any way unethical or harmful."

"I'm not a criminal," I said.

He looked steadily at me. "Mr. Curran, background checks are easy. I know you've never been charged with a crime. What I don't know, because I haven't committed any resources to finding out, is whether you've done anything criminal."

"I haven't." I was starting to sound like a petulant child to my own ears, so I put the attitude away and replaced it with amiable self-efface-ment to cover my agitation. "Well, except for the underage drinking in high school. And ditching the nanny for a day in Port-au-Prince. Oh, and when I was, like, seven or eight, I thought it would be cool to light little fires in the mountains outside Kathmandu, but I stamped them out before they could do damage."

Dallas scowled at that, and I added a mental *uptight* to the list of her mother-like qualities, which was right up there with *judgmental* and *perfectionistic* in the *nope* category.

"When your life is worth more to you than whatever you stand to earn for your proprietary tech, feel free to come back to us to discuss close protection. In the meantime, Darius is willing to work with you if you'd like his help assessing the vulnerabilities of your home security." Quinn's tone was final, and he punctuated it by stepping out of the room. "Dallas will see you to the elevator, Mr. Curran," he said before he walked away.

I stared after him. "When my life is worth more than what I stand to earn?" I said incredulously. "He has no idea how much is at stake." Dallas ushered me out of the room before I had a chance to fully process that I'd just been insulted and dismissed. I stopped suddenly and she ran into me, and I had the instant impression of taut muscle and bone on a lean frame. She pulled away and gave me an icy look.

"Is there something else I can help you with, Mr. Curran?"

"Oliver," I said automatically, my eyes still looking in the direction Quinn had gone.

"Excuse me?"

"My name is Oliver," I said, my eyes finally meeting hers, and I dug for my nicest-guy-in-the-room default. "Yours is Dallas, right?"

"Correct."

She started walking toward the elevators again, and I couldn't think of a reason not to follow. I assumed it wouldn't get me anywhere to go after Quinn, and Dallas seemed to be the only one who cared that I was still in the building.

"Proprietary tech is the only game in the marketplace right now. If my code leaks, my program turns into the equivalent of generic drugs— worth pennies instead of millions."

We'd reached the elevators, and she turned to face me. I was surprised that she wasn't taller, because her vibe was all ferocity and overbearing disapproval. "You didn't ask for my opinion, but I'm going to give it to you anyway," she said.

Of course she would. Women like her couldn't help themselves. They had to be right—all the time—out loud. I sighed, too exhausted to bother to dig up more charm for her.

"Millions are just zeroes and ones in an account," she continued. "This is your life, and I think the Russian will do a lot worse than try to knife you if he manages to catch you alone."

I'd just hit the button, but I whipped around to face her. "The Russian? What are you, partners?"

The woman almost rolled her eyes at me, and I was glad to get a rise out of her. It was way more fun than panicking, which was my other option.

"I heard him swear in Russian," she said in a voice that was back to ice queen inflection.

"You speak Russian," I scoffed.

"Enough," she said. The elevator doors opened behind me, and Dallas reached a hand past me to hold them.

"What did he say, then?" I asked. She took a step forward, crowding me back into the elevator.

"*Ty moy, suchka.*"

"Which means?" I asked, taking a step forward when I realized that she'd managed to make me move with just her body language.

She let go of the elevator doors. "You're my bitch," she said, and I had to jump back as the doors closed between us.

[3]
DALLAS

"The fascination of shooting as a sport depends almost wholly on whether you are at the right or wrong end of the gun."

\- P.G. WODEHOUSE

"Tracker Jack?" Shane said as she swerved from her coffee maker trajectory to join me.

I sighed. "Quinn?"

"He asked Dan if he'd ever heard of it, then told him how you'd thwarted an attack on some guy because of a game you were playing." She grinned. "I didn't think you were a gamer."

"I'm not," I said as I unloaded the leather briefcase I kept at work into the backpack I used to get to and from the office. "It keeps me sharp."

"For following people, or being followed?"

"Both," I said simply.

She watched me for a moment. "Why do you do that?" She nodded at the bags. "Why not just take the briefcase to and from the office?"

"I like having my hands free"—I shrugged—"and my mom gave me the briefcase when I got the job here, so I like to keep it nice for work."

Shane frowned. "Your mom does know you're a bodyguard, right?"

I chuckled. "She knows I'm a close protection security specialist."

She waved the title away. "Same thing."

"You mean she should be worried for me and hate what I do for a living?"

Shane studied me, the frown still tugging at her forehead. "Yeah, I guess. I mean, isn't that what moms do, when, you know, they care?"

Huh. I filed away that interesting insight about Shane before moving on like she hadn't said anything revealing. "Do you know how I put myself through college?" I asked.

She shrugged. "I don't know, stripping?" I stared at her, and the slightest smile pulled up the corner of her mouth. "Didn't everyone?" she continued innocently, her eyes twinkling at the joke. At least I thought it was a joke. With Shane—tall, model-gorgeous, and super-fit—a person couldn't be too sure.

I shrugged. "My mom probably wishes I'd done that instead of guiding hunting expeditions for bored rich guys."

She stared at me open-mouthed. "You did what?"

I nodded and continued packing my backpack. "I started guiding when I was sixteen. Worked for a Yukon outfitter every summer through high school and college. I got paid to be outside, exploring nature, tracking game, camping, and riding horses." And catering to the whims of men who saw me as little more than a hired girl who could set up and run a camp. Worse were the ones who saw me as another trophy to bag in their hunt for the most elusive game.

"Aren't there bears in the Yukon?" Shane ventured when my words hung in the air.

I scoffed. "Moose are more dangerous than bears, but self-important clients are more dangerous than all the things that can kill you in the wild."

"Hmm," she said as she studied me. I looked away so I could pretend I wasn't under her microscope. "I've known you for more than a year, and somehow I think I don't really know you at all, do I?"

"I've been on assignment for a lot of that time, and you mostly work with Gabriel."

"You've been back in town for a month. I think it's time for a girls' night out, don't you?"

"I don't go to bars," I said reflexively.

"Neither do I," she said. "I meant on Darius's boat. Anna will drive."

Darius and I had partnered on a few jobs, so of all the Cipher agents, I knew him the best. His wife, Anna, was a bounty hunter, and I liked her. She made him laugh. He was only marginally more serious than I usually was at work, so by extension, she made me laugh too.

I raised an eyebrow. "Could be entertaining."

"It'll be *fun*," Shane said with certainty. "I'll call you."

I shot her a skeptical look. "Shane, it's March. Who goes out on the lake in March?"

"Yukoners, backpackers, and skydivers—and no one else. That's kind of the point. I mean, we have the gear, right?

I chuckled. "I have the gear."

"Good." She started off down the hall, then turned back. "Seriously? Hunting guide in the Yukon?"

I slung my backpack over my shoulder and deadpanned, "Seriously? Stripper?"

She grinned. "Swing by Quinn's office before you head out. He thinks the new client will be back."

I nodded, and she threw a wave over her shoulder as she walked away. Her new prosthetic leg must have been perfectly weighted, because even the tiny hitch the old one had given her step was gone.

I veered away toward the corner office my boss used to impress those clients who were impressed by things like corner offices. I thought that, given the choice, Quinn would probably rather work from home or wherever it was his wife happened to be. It wouldn't be obvious to most people who only saw a powerful man with a face carved from granite, but whenever I'd seen them together at office functions, something about the way Quinn looked at his wife made me think she was an oasis to a man who expected to spend his life in the desert. Janey Sullivan seemed oblivious to her husband's … thirst. It was probably why they were perfect together. His focus would overwhelm someone who was attuned to it, like looking directly at the sun would blind someone without shades.

I heard the distant thrum of the coffee machine in the boardroom where Shane and Gabriel preferred to work, and pictured him setting a cup in front of her as he'd done ever since she began working at Cipher. The faint sniff from the sofa where Saahil, a cybersecurity recruit from Berkeley, usually sat told me he'd been eating sugar again. It made his nose run worse than any cold ever had, and a glance in the bin next to him revealed the wrapper of a chocolate bar. At least it had been good chocolate.

Avalon, who used to be a stunt driver for the movies, saw my sympathetic wince as I passed Saahil's station, and she raised an eyebrow in question. Damn. She'd noticed me noticing. I always felt like I'd failed a little when people became aware of me, because so much of my job was about becoming the background. I let my gaze soften as if I were deep in thought, then schooled my expression into something carefully neutral as I tapped on Quinn's open door.

"Come," he said. His tone was distracted, and I caught the faint scent of Alex Greene's soap as I pushed the door open, so it wasn't a surprise to see him standing across the desk from Quinn.

"What's your impression of Curran?" Quinn asked without preamble.

"I haven't had time to form one yet," I answered, careful to keep the lie out of my voice. My impression had been a complete knee-jerk reaction to the flirtatious pseudo-charm he used on everyone but me. He was so reminiscent of my ex that I had to deliberately shove the memory of Ashton right back down into the putrid long-drop hole where it belonged.

He shook his head. "No, Alex will get me facts. I want your gut."

It was with effort that I didn't flinch. "My … gut?" Was my loathing of the guy obvious?

His eyes narrowed as he studied me. "You said you tracked him last night to stay sharp. That is the action of a hunter, and a successful hunter understands her prey."

It actually helped to think of Oliver Curran as prey, because Quinn was right, I was a hunter. I just hadn't known that anyone else realized that was how I operated.

I exhaled and turned to calm, cold logic. "He's an apex predator who just realized there's something out there more dangerous than he is, and it confuses him. Scares him too." His sudden anger when he saw me and thought he'd been set up exposed that fear. "He still believes he has options, which means he won't behave like a cornered animal yet. But he also thinks he has the upper hand, so he'll make stupid choices that'll get him hurt. He's resourceful under duress and isn't likely to freeze in panic, but he has no practice at it, so it's more instinct than skill."

My word-choice became instinctual as I finished. "He's an alpha hiding in the easy skin of someone unconcerned with pack hierarchy, which means he won't take direction well and will likely be a very big pain in the a— eye for whoever has to protect him." I stumbled over the invective, suddenly remembering that I was talking to my boss. He didn't seem to notice, but the corner of Alex's mouth twitched in what was, for him, probably the equivalent of a belly laugh.

I narrowed my eyes at Alex Greene, Cipher's Director of Information Technologies, which was the corporate title for hacker. "Wait, you know everything in the tech world. Do you know Oliver Curran?"

"I know his code," he said, as if that were an answer.

"Is he your friend?" I added, my stomach sinking a little at the prospect.

"I don't have friends," he said, expressionless. I nodded, unsurprised at his self-assessment. I didn't either. I had family and people I worked with, that was all.

Quinn was still, and I recognized the quiet thoughtfulness of another hunter. When he finally moved again, it was to hand me a business card. "Familiarize yourself with Oliver Curran while Alex looks into the IP that he's protecting. Somehow I doubt the interest in his health is personal."

"By the way," I said, tucking the card into my pocket, "the interested party speaks Russian."

Quinn's eyes narrowed. "Fascinating." He glanced at Alex, who nodded.

"On it."

Alex left the office with a brief tilt of the head at me, and I turned to follow him.

"Dallas," Quinn's voice stopped me. "When Curran comes back in, I'm going to put you on him. Will that be a problem?"

"Not for me," I said calmly, ignoring the flip of my stomach.

"You think it'll be one for him?" Quinn asked.

I considered for a moment. "It's clear he doesn't like me, so I imagine he would question the choice."

"You're the right person for the job, so if you think Curran needs to like you for you to effectively keep him alive, then by all means, court his favor."

"Court his favor?" I asked, eyebrows raised.

Quinn regarded me steadily. "My wife has been reading Regency romance novels to escape the news."

"As one does," I said with a nod. Either Janey had begun speaking like a nineteenth-century Englishwoman herself, or she'd been reading passages out loud to her husband.

I left before my boss could see how much I appreciated that mental image.

[4]

DALLAS

"Invisibility is a superpower."

- DALLAS

Oliver Curran surprised me. Not the significant social media presence, which I'd expected from such an annoyingly good-looking, Canada Goose–wearing hipster. Or that all his vacations were spent with beautiful people in exotic locations. Or even that he was never photographed with the same woman twice. No, the surprising thing about Oliver Curran was that I had to revise my expectations of his hipsterman status because besides being a card-carrying tech geek, he also fit the corporate wunderkind type.

He'd gone to Harvard, where his mom—a major activist for broad-spectrum environmental policy reform—was an alumna. He dropped out after cashing in on some software he created, and spent the last few years creating photo apps—everything from filters that changed your appearance to fit a cartoon character to something that inserted your picture into scenes from movies. And apparently, he'd made another boatload of money selling all the filter and face-swap tech. I knew Alex Greene would dig deeper into the money side, so my job was to figure out the *man* I'd be protecting.

Oliver's Instagram account was the most revealing in that regard. The photographs were all surprisingly well-shot and interesting, and his feed was full of surfing trips and island adventures with pretty people. The people were different in each location though, and I wondered if he traveled with friends or just made them wherever he went.

He was tagged in lots of photos with beautiful women, which fit the apparently charming flirt I'd met, but none of the women made it into his own feed. If I had a social media feed, there would have been no people in it at all—just wilderness and animals probably, or maybe some of my sister's food. Interestingly, there were a bunch of photographs of food in Oliver's Instagram feed too—mostly ramen dishes that looked complicated and homemade, which reminded me that I needed to replace the groceries he'd left behind.

I shoved my laptop inside my backpack and slung it over one shoulder. Darius was just stepping out of the paneled staircase door in the lobby ahead of me as I exited the elevator.

"Hold up," I said to get his attention. He waited for me to catch up, and we both nodded to Kendra, Gabriel's sister, who had taken a part-time job with us while she finished law school. Her nose was buried in a bar review textbook as usual, and she threw us a distracted wave as we walked toward the exit.

"Have you heard from Oliver Curran about doing a security assessment on his place?" I asked my sometime-partner whose wife called him her Disney prince. She wasn't wrong about his looks, and I had the sudden thought that his eyes would flash if he were ever angry and his teeth would probably gleam when he turned on the charm.

"I have. I'll be going there tomorrow." Darius had a way of speaking that told me his first language hadn't been English. My grandfather had the same slightly formal way with his own English.

"Any chance I could get his address from you? It didn't come up in the basic searches, and I need to return something to him." We all had security clearances on par with most military intelligence services, so I wasn't worried about the propriety of asking for it, but I did have a pang of conscience about not sharing exactly what I'd be returning.

Darius pulled out his phone. "Sure." He scrolled through his contacts and then shared Curran's info.

"Thanks," I said, as it popped into my messages. "What do you know about him? Quinn wants me to work with him if he comes back to us."

Darius shrugged. "I don't know him. His friend, Sterling Gray, is a client I know well enough as he's dating Anna's sister, so I can guess that Oliver Curran probably fits into Sterling's workaholic, play-hard, privileged set quite well. Apart from that, I haven't bothered to look. I expect that the examination of his home will tell me more, though. I'll let you know what I find."

"I appreciate it. Tell Anna I said hi," I said as I turned toward the L.

"Dallas?" he said, before I'd gone more than a few steps.

I turned back. "Yeah?"

"Is everything well?" He seemed to fumble for words, which was so unlike him I didn't immediately answer that yes, everything was fine. It always was, even if it wasn't. "You've been … distant." He exhaled, as if even that much prying was too much. It was, but he didn't need to know that.

"I was in Mexico with the political activist and her family, and before that I was in England with the diplomat. That's pretty distant."

He hesitated, and I made myself stay still while he figured out if he was going to dig deeper. I didn't want to evade his questions, because I genuinely liked Darius, but whatever instinct he'd had about me that had prompted his asking was not something I was inclined to examine out loud on the street … or at all.

He finally shrugged and gave me one of those blinding smiles he did so well. "Come have dinner with us soon, okay? Tell us about Mexico."

"Sure," I said with a smile I didn't feel. It seemed to be enough though, and this time he let me walk away.

It was nearly dark when I emerged from the train at Division station, and colder than usual as the lake-chilled wind snaked its way down wide boulevards. Chicagoans hunched into their parkas and walked with single-minded focus toward the warmth that beckoned from indoors, and even I could admit it was a welcome respite from the wind to step into the fancy market where Oliver had shopped the day before.

I pictured the contents of the grocery bag I'd rescued, and then filled my basket with two steaks, vegetables, fresh bread, and various snacks. I tried not to flinch when the cashier rang up the total, and consoled myself with the fact that at least he hadn't gotten wine.

Oliver Curran lived just around the corner from the alley where the Russian redhat had attacked us, and I was glad to see heavy-duty locks on the steel-reinforced front door. I was also impressed to note a high-end security camera aimed at the front, and therefore not surprised that it took so long for Oliver to answer the door. He had probably seen me and then debated with himself whether or not to acknowledge my presence.

"Hold on," he said. The wary expression on his face made it clear he hadn't decided if I was friend or foe. I stayed silent until he did.

Then I saw the wireless earbuds in his ears and realized he held his cell phone in his hand.

"Oh, you're on the phone," I said, embarrassed. The "hold on" hadn't been for me.

He was expressionless. "What do you want?"

I held out the bag. "Your groceries."

I'd surprised him, and he took the bag carefully, as though it were full of fish guts.

"I'm sorry about yesterday," I added. He still said nothing, so I took a step backward and prepared to go. "If anything's missing"—I nodded at the bag—"just leave a message for me at Cipher and I'll replace it. And, I'm sorry about your date last night."

Oliver frowned and looked at the grocery bag in his hand. "My date?"

"Dinner for two?" I caught a glimpse of confusion on his face, so I elaborated. "Two steaks?"

He shook his head. "One for dinner and one for lunch the next day. It's easier."

Huh. Not what I'd expected.

"Well," I said, turning to go. "Enjoy your dinner."

I walked away quickly, but not before I heard him resume his phone conversation. "Just some weird stalker chick who can't stay away from me."

Charming.

The vacation rental I'd found when I got back to Chicago from Mexico was part of a duplex in the Humboldt Park district near the actual park. I'd chosen it for its proximity to the outdoor space and because the owner, a former college professor named Sharon, lived in the other unit.

I was one of the few close protection agents at Cipher who didn't have a husband, wife, or partner, so I took all the out-of-town and live-in jobs. When I did need a place of my own, I booked a vacation rental on a weekly basis, which I could leave the next time a job came up. The apartments were always furnished, and each time I came back, I deliberately chose parts of the city and styles of architecture I hadn't experienced before.

This one was my favorite so far, probably because Sharon was an artist and she'd decorated it in a bohemian style that reminded me of the extravagance of the Orient Express or the inside of a pasha's tent. It felt like walking into a warm hug when I stepped inside and peeled off my coat.

The walls were white, and the floors were blond hardwood, but everything else, from the explosion of rugs on the floors, to the invitation of low cushions for living room seating, and even the hearty hand-thrown pottery, was a riot of color.

The apartment had been carved from a parlor and the butler's pantry of the original Victorian house. It was a studio with a front entrance, but it was more conveniently entered from the rear of the building. The pantry, with its built-in cupboards and shelves, had become the mudroom and kitchen, with more cupboards than I had things to keep in them. The large main room was both a sitting and sleeping place, and the big windows and tall ceilings allowed light to reach all but the far corners. When I'd moved in after spending two months in Mexico with my last client, Jennifer Jones, and her family, the light was gray and the mornings so cold I could see my breath. I had never been cold in this apartment though—there was just too much color to feel any chill.

I set my backpack on the low bench in the mudroom and kicked off my boots, shoving them against the wall with one foot. My auntie had knit the socks I wore, and I appreciated the thick, soft, orange wool most when I padded around my apartment after a long day.

I grabbed the computer from my bag, hit the electric kettle on my way through the kitchen, and then settled onto the big Turkish rug with the divan cushions at my back. I set my laptop up on the coffee table, opened it, and messaged my sister. She sent back a single word—*video*—and a moment later, a video call came through.

"Hey, Christi," I said when I answered the call.

She was in the kitchen of the Vancouver apartment she shared with three to five roommates at any given time. Her phone was propped against something on the counter, so I mostly had a view of her from the neck down as she stirred a pot on the stove.

"Hey. What's Grandpop's recipe for moose?" She dipped the wooden spoon into the pot and smelled its contents, then wrinkled her nose in concentration and grabbed a handful of something green from the counter and began tearing it into the pot.

"It's not moose season," I said with a frown.

She actually looked at me then, just long enough to make a face. "I know that. Robbie found some moose from last season in his freezer. Grandpop's recipe is better than anything I can find on the internet."

"You're going to have to ask him for it. I only know Mom's, and it's definitely not traditional."

She made another face, but this time it wasn't directed at me. "They must have just had a storm because the cell tower's down again. Give me Mom's and I'll try to figure his out."

I gave Christi the simple, slow cooker version of moose roast that our mom taught me to make in the mornings so there'd be hot food when we got home from the private school in Alberta where I was a student and where she worked in the admissions office so I could go there. Packaged onion soup as a dry rub for the meat, then put the meat in the slow cooker with a cup of apple juice until the meat fell apart with a fork. It definitely wasn't traditional, but it was easy enough for a six-year-old to make. My mom and Christi's dad had gotten married when I was eight, so Christi never had to learn Mom's shortcut recipes because I'd been there to make them for her.

The irony was that Christi was now a way better cook than any of us, and she would probably be able to figure out our grandpop's recipe on her own.

"Mom said I can't bring Robbie to fish camp this year," Christi said, annoyed.

"Is he the one?" I asked, looking around the kitchen behind Christi for clues to how she was living. This batch of roommates seemed to be pretty clean, but it looked like the Italian guy had moved out and taken his strings of garlic with him.

Christi made another face. "No," she said, as if that were obvious.

"You know the rule. No one goes to fish camp until it's time for a trial by fire."

Christi scoffed, but I could hear the affection in it. "Trial by fish guts and smoker, you mean. He's strong enough to be decent help."

"Fish camp is for family," I said automatically.

"You say that like it means something to you," she groused.

"Hey, that's not fair," I answered, knowing that it was but flinching anyway. "I'm there every year."

"I know," she said, "sorry. I just get stuck doing all the other stuff during the year when you're not there. But even when you are there to do most of the work, fish camp is hard," she whined.

"Suck it up, Buttercup," I said, guilt making my insides twist. But as Mom's baby, Christi had gotten away with doing the easy chores a lot longer than any of the rest of us had, at least until my cousin Rori was born. I'd never minded the hard work though, because it meant time spent learning skills from my grandfather. "When you reach Grandpop, tell him you want to learn his bear sausage recipe."

She wrinkled her nose adorably. "Ewww. No, thank you. The parasites are too hard to kill and the intestine casing is gross. I'll stick to moose."

I chuckled and looked again for whatever she wasn't saying. "You okay, Sis? What's the real reason for wanting Robbie at fish camp?"

She darted a quick glance at me as she concentrated on the pot she stirred. "I don't want to drive alone."

"Why would you drive? It's three days from Vancouver to Whitehorse."

She shrugged and avoided my eyes. "I might need to move my stuff out." Her door sounded and she looked up suddenly. "Talk to you later, Sis," she said as she reached over and shut off the phone before I could respond.

What the hell was that? I thought about calling her right back, but knew she'd send me straight to voicemail. I missed her. I missed my whole family.

But when you screw it up, you need to suck it up, Buttercup.

I sighed and got up to fix myself one of Oliver's steaks, then settled in to learn whatever else I could find on the internet about Oliver Curran.

[5]

OLIVER

"Show me your kitchen and I'll show you your soul."

\- - OLIVER

Darius Masoud was stupidly good-looking. He also had the kind of manners that Europeans and old-money people had—like they automatically knew which fork to use without getting a raised eyebrow from whichever parent might have been home.

"Good morning, Mr. Curran." His breath fogged the frigid morning air, and I shivered in my jeans, sweater, and bare feet.

"Thanks for coming," I said with a friendly smile, stepping back from my open door. "And it's Oliver."

He ignored the smile and looked pointedly up at the camera. "That records to a hard drive, I presume?"

I nodded. "The system came with the place when I bought it."

He followed me into the living room, which was also my home office. I didn't see the point in hiding my work from myself, since I lived

35

alone and pretty much worked all the time anyway. My desk faced the windows to the back patio, and bookshelves filled the walls behind it. I'd turned the dining room into a TV lounge, and I slept upstairs in a room that took up the whole floor. I bought the place for its kitchen, which was huge and had been updated right before I moved in, but the bedroom with its big skylight was a bonus.

"Nice place," Darius said, his eyes going straight to the bookshelves. "Have you lived here long?"

"I moved in a couple of months ago. I used to work with the guy I bought it from. He put in most of the security system. You want coffee?" I asked, as I went into the kitchen to refill my own cup.

"No, thank you," he said.

Everything about Darius Masoud seemed precise and automatic, like he hadn't even bothered to check in with himself to see if he actually wanted that cup of coffee before declining it. My impression that he would make a decent android was confirmed with his next words. "I'm going to suggest, Mr. Curran, that you remove the old system entirely."

I sighed. "It's Oliver." I tried the smile again to soften my tone. It had been a rough night of programming until I was too tired to keep my eyes open, and then I'd slept just enough to keep from going totally nuts. In other words, the usual.

He gave me a direct look. "Physical security is remarkably similar to cybersecurity," he said. "Unless you build your own system from the ground up, you have to assume someone left a back door open." And then he smiled, and the android became a stupidly good-looking human again. "And it is my strong recommendation that you close the back door and build your security from scratch."

I sighed and rubbed my jaw with the hand that wasn't holding coffee. "Right," I finally said. "How long will that take?"

"A day to remove the existing system. For an installation estimate, I need to see the whole place."

I gestured around. "Help yourself. Bedroom's upstairs. I'm going to stay down here, drink my coffee, and attempt consciousness. It's not a guarantee until I'm about three cups in."

He smiled. "I'll make a note of my questions," he said as he pulled a little Field Notes book out of his pocket. The android was an analog note-taker. Classic.

Darius wandered around the main floor as I settled in at my desk. He wasn't wrong about cybersecurity, and therefore, security in general, which was annoying. I had state-of-the-art encryption on every computing device I used, from my phone to the data drives where I stored my work. The cloud was not an option, so everything was on drives, and it was hardware someone clearly wanted. I just couldn't believe they'd actually sent someone to get it.

The doorbell sounded, and I glanced at the front door camera. A pretty, blonde white woman with long, curly hair stood outside. She wore motorcycle leathers and carried a helmet under one arm. I stood up just as Darius popped his head back into the room.

"Stunning blonde in leathers?"

I grinned. "Yeah. She with you?"

His answering smile was proud. "She is. Mind if I let her in? She's a B and E specialist and can identify the weaknesses in nearly any system she encounters."

I waved my hand in the direction of the door. "I'll make more coffee."

I dropped a capsule into my machine and put a clean cup underneath as I heard the distinct sound of a kiss before Darius showed the blonde in.

"Anna, this is Oliver Curran. Oliver, Anna Collins Masoud."

She held her hand out in a way that reminded me of how men greet each other. "Good to meet you."

"You too," I said with a smile. "How do you take your coffee?"

She looked past me as the coffee maker shut off. "Black, please."

I handed her the mug and raised an eyebrow at Darius. "Change your mind?"

He shook his head, and Anna answered for him. "He's a control freak. He decides a thing and nothing except a T-rex suit can change his mind."

I spluttered a laugh and glanced at Darius, whose expression of fond pride hadn't shifted one bit. Then I raised my mug to Anna in a salute. "Here's to T-rex suits and five-cup days." I was pretty much an equal-opportunity flirt—guys, girls, kids, dogs—it didn't matter. Everyone, especially pretty blondes, got the smile and friendly chatter. Well, almost everyone. That Dallas chick was a piece of work and inspired the opposite of flirting from me.

"Cheers," Anna said with a grin, obviously unable to read my thoughts about her colleague. Anna turned to Darius. "Give me the tour and let's figure out how to break in."

I raised an eyebrow. "That's what you meant by 'B and E'? Break and enter?"

"Of course," Darius said.

"Of course." I watched the pair of them leave, and wondered if Quinn Sullivan had a radar for beautiful people. These two looked like they'd stepped out of the pages of a European fashion magazine spread, except in my imagination, she was the gorgeous thief and he was the handsome insurance investigator sent to track her down. Of course, Quinn was ridiculously good-looking himself, Kendra at the desk had been lovely, the model-tall brunette was a knockout, and even Dallas …

I turned on my computer and navigated to the security footage from my front door. I entered the time code from the Cipher agent's visit the night before when she'd handed me my groceries and walked away. She was surly, all business, and nothing about her was even friendly, which might have been why I hadn't paid real attention to her appearance. My first impression had just been about identification—she wasn't tall or short, and she could have been one of about ten different ethnicities, but I was leaning toward Indigenous North American. I studied the video and tried to focus on finding the one thing that set her apart, but nothing stood out about her clothes or her features. She had dark hair, dark eyes, wore dark-colored clothes, and seemed about my age—late-twenties more or less. The only thing different about her from every other person who hunched down in their coat against the wind was that she didn't. She didn't hunch, or brace herself, or anything else that said she was affected by the cold. And once I'd seen that, I noticed everything about how she moved. And that's when I freaked out.

Dallas moved like a predator.

Even as she'd walked away from my front door, it was like watching something lithe and deadly assessing the shadows for threats or prey.

Dallas was dangerous.

The generosity from someone so unfriendly had surprised me, and I backed up the footage to watch a couple more times, oddly compelled. But since being compelled by dangerous women wasn't the way I operated, I shook thoughts of the grumpy bodyguard out of my head and tried to focus on my next steps. Securing my house was a big one since someone was after my work, but was it enough?

Darius and Anna startled me when they returned downstairs. I was buried in a piece of machine learning code, and I'd forgotten they were still in my house. From the frown on Darius's face, whatever he had to tell me wasn't good.

"Your security company is McCallum?" he asked.

"That sounds like the name I get a bill from every month."

"We have some … concerns about them," he said, like every word had been carefully chosen not to offend.

"Why?" I looked from Darius to Anna, and I was surprised to see that his somber mood had infected her. She seemed like the last person who would ever be serious.

"McCallum's been on our radar for the last year, since they undercut Cipher on a job and then failed to deliver," Darius said quietly.

"Failed to deliver." Anna snorted. "I broke into one of their jobs too easily," she added. "Security's what they failed to deliver."

I shrugged, looking back and forth between them. "Okay, well, they're your competition, so whatever. No one has succeeded in breaking in here yet—"

"I found six possible points of entry just on the second floor," Anna interrupted.

"Six …" I frowned.

"My real concern," Darius said, before I could finish figuring out what that meant for me, "has to do with the ownership of McCallum."

I closed my mouth and waited while he marshalled all his careful words.

"We have found evidence of a connection to a man named Alex Karpov through both the start-up money McCallum used and the tech they're selling under their own label."

"Who is Alex Karpov?" I asked.

"Doctor Evil." Anna snorted again, and I smiled. Her snort-laughs were contagious.

Darius was apparently the long-answer guy, and less prone to snorting. "He was one of the partners in a company that folded under federal investigation for illegal data mining and conspiracy to commit murder. He escaped to Russia and has been lying low since then. The connection to McCallum was discovered a few months ago through a Russian shell company."

Coincidences, even random ones, made me twitchy. "Karpov is Russian?"

"Yeah, ethnically anyway. High school and college here in the States, but his family came from the western part of Russia near Lake Peipus in the nineties." Darius looked searchingly at me. "Dallas mentioned that your attacker spoke Russian."

I scoffed, "Russia's huge. A connection between my guy and yours would be epically coincidental."

"Epic coincidences are kind of our specialty," said Anna, with a little smile at Darius. It was the kind of shared look that made me almost miss having a girlfriend, which meant it was definitely time to find a hookup to cure myself of that thought. I did not do girlfriends. They invariably expected to spend the night, and I definitely didn't do sleepovers. I'd spent too many years never really sure where I'd wake up or who would be there when I did. Now, the only way I got any sleep at all was making sure it was in *my* house and that I was alone. No surprises.

I'd missed whatever sidebar thing Anna and Darius had said to each other, and tuned back into the conversation in time to hear Darius say, "Even if Alex Karpov isn't a direct threat to you personally, the fact exists that there are significant vulnerabilities in your current security system, and as I mentioned before, I strongly recommend a complete overhaul."

I stood up with that *it's your cue to leave* energy that let me keep wearing the charming smile without looking like a dick, and stuck my hand out to shake Darius's. "Right. Cool. You've given me a lot to think about, and I'll definitely get back to you."

He met my eyes with a *sure you will* look, and then Anna grabbed my hand with a solid handshake. "Listen, I have a date on a boat with some girls, or I'd give you a proper lecture, because despite the fact that you're a friend of Sterling Gray, you seem like a nice, only mildly shady guy."

I couldn't help the bark of laughter, but I realized Anna was actually serious. "That should go on my letterhead. Oliver Curran, Nice Guy, Mildly Shady," I said. "Sterling know what you think of him?"

She hadn't let go of my hand and her gaze was intent. "My sister's dating the guy, so there are no illusions. My point is that you're vulnerable here. Be smart about this, Oliver, and protect yourself. Get a dog if you won't upgrade your security, but, dude, I could break in here in under a minute."

I couldn't let that opening go by, and I flashed her one of my best smiles. "If only all the thieves were as cool as you, I'd welcome the break-in."

She shrugged. "I'm an original." She turned and held her hand out to Darius. "Shall we?" she asked him with a huge grin, like they'd just shared the best secret and now they were leaving to indulge in each other. Apparently this woman was immune to me too.

Flirting was a game I usually won. I had natural skills, and I'd also worked at it, so catching people's interest was easy. Anna seemed impervious to my charms—she only had eyes for Darius, and for that matter, he only had eyes for her. It was vaguely unsettling to realize that everyone I'd encountered at Cipher Security had flirtation immunity.

I followed them to the door and threw the deadbolt behind them, but not before I heard Anna say something about closing barn doors after all the horses had already escaped.

[6]

DALLAS

"The Wild still lingered in him, and the wolf in him merely slept."

- JACK LONDON, *WHITE FANG*

"Normal people don't take boats out on Lake Michigan in winter weather," I said with an eyebrow raised at the hand-crocheted, green Baby Yoda hat Anna wore over her long, crazy blonde curls.

"Normal is boring," Shane said with a shrug as she tossed the mooring line into the 1950s wooden party cruiser that Anna expertly maneuvered out of its slip and into the waterway.

"Fair point."

"Dallas," Anna said from her place at the wheel, "pull up the bumpers and watch for sea lions until we're out of the harbor?"

"Sea lions don't live in fresh water," Shane said as she coiled the lines on the deck. She was wearing a heavy, knit turtleneck sweater and a black watchman's cap, and somehow managed to look elegant despite the cold red nose.

43

"A sea lion broke out of the Lincoln Park Zoo in the late 1800s," Anna declared. "It could have had babies. Also, there's a whole species of freshwater seals that lives in Lake Baikal in Russia … hey, speaking of Russia, I met your pretty client Oliver this morning," she added, nodding at me.

"There are so many problems with that statement, I almost don't know where to begin," I said with a shake of my head, "starting with how you know about seals in Russia. But I'll restrain myself and go with the most obvious. He's not my client."

Anna shrugged with a smirk. "Given the state of his security system, he probably will be soon."

"Oh, that's right, I saw him at Cipher. He *was* pretty," Shane said as she dropped into a seat in the cockpit, "and flirty. Darius was going over there today to check out his house."

"Guess who designed his security?" Anna said as she navigated past the markers.

Shane shrugged. "Not us, presumably."

"McCallum." Anna sounded pleased, or maybe smug. I wasn't sure which.

"Mmm, I don't like coincidences like that," Shane said. "Any connection to Alex Karpov, no matter how tenuous, is bad news."

"You and Alex Greene connected Karpov to McCallum after the T-rex incident, right?" I asked with a straight face. Shane had actually seen Anna in her safe room break-in costume, and she laughed as she nodded. Anna merely concentrated on navigating away from the harbor.

The boat picked up speed, and I retreated from the wind, dropping into the cockpit with them. "By the way," I added to Anna, "no sea lion sightings."

The giant, floppy green Yoda ears on Anna's hat bobbed ridiculously in the wind as she shrugged. "It's okay. I just didn't want to take a chance on hitting one. Darius usually drives, so I'm the spotter."

Shane and I sat facing Anna at the wheel, and Shane was the one who turned to me to continue the conversation. "Karpov had his fingers in politics, big data, micro-targeting, blackmail, and murder. He could have snuck back into the U.S. anytime in the last six months. It makes me nervous to have his name and tech tied to any company that operates in our territory."

I looked at Anna. "Did Curran have the McCallum system installed on purpose?"

She shook her head. "He inherited it."

"Like everything else," I muttered.

"'Splain," Anna said with a glance at me.

"It's plain, or explain?" Shane raised an eyebrow at Anna.

"Both, obviously," she said with a grin.

"It's plain," I answered, "because he's a privileged, hipster-handsome, top-of-the-food-chain guy whose parents are, like, philanthropy superheroes who have raised more money for the environment than the GDP of small countries. He's a Harvard legacy, spent his youth living all around the world, travels to exotic locales with beautiful friends, makes pointless photo apps and sells them for a bazillion dollars, and believes he's God's gift to womankind."

Shane stared at me with an open mouth, and Anna sputtered in laughter. "Tell us how you really feel," she said.

"Quinn told me to research him as a potential client," I said a little defensively.

Shane nodded. "Yeah, he's trying to cut down on the private clients, so he's being rigorous about ethics."

"I don't think Curran will hire us anyway," I said. "He thinks he's immortal."

"I think I am too," Anna said with a grin, "and I'd hire us."

Shane laughed. "Yeah, but you're special. What other grown woman would wear that hat?"

"It's cool, right?" Anna said proudly. "Darius asked his friend Amy to crochet it for me. It makes him laugh every time I wear it, so I make sure he catches me in it when I'm naked."

Shane burst out laughing. "Naked Baby Yodanna!"

Anna flapped her Yoda ears. "When I can make Darius laugh, he looks at me like I'm chocolate and movie night and browned butter all rolled up in one."

I shook my head. "Until you came along, I never saw Darius laugh. It's good that you married him."

"You're welcome," she said with a grin. "I mostly married him for his mom, but also for browned-butter looks. And Baby Yoda hats." Anna looked at Shane. "What does Gabriel do best?"

Shane looked a little dreamy-eyed, and a pinprick of jealously stabbed my back. "He talks to me. His voice is like a thick, creamy salve you put on sunburns when you don't want to be touched, and when I get sunburny like that, his voice feels like fingers running through my hair—which he does too, by the way."

"So, you're saying he's like a wolf whisperer. You get mad, which is usually fear-based, and he talks you down, petting you to calm you out of whatever fear made you mad," I said, a little surprised at myself for speaking so intimately to her. Shane looked surprised too, but not at me.

"I never thought of it that way, but you're totally right. He calms me out of my fear, and I stop being angry," she said with a hint of wonder.

"What about you, Dallas?" Anna asked. She stood at the wheel of the wooden cruiser, looking a little like a geeky little Norse warrior withstanding the onslaught of wind chill. "What's your equivalent of a browned-butter look?"

I turned away from her gaze to look out at the choppy water.

"It's okay—" Shane began.

I didn't let her give me an out, though, maybe because I wanted the out too badly. "I picked up my grandfather's habit of talking about people like they're wolves, maybe because it's the best way to understand them. Like, people are confusing, but wolves have clear rules of behavior."

I thought about late-night conversations with Grandpop, and tried to reconstruct one that had landed with me. "The hierarchy in a wolf pack is all about survival. The elders lead, the young learn from everyone, and dominance is just a personality trait, not a gender thing. Pack is protection and warmth and food and family, and without it, wolves die." I inhaled, trying to pretend it was the cold air and not memory that ached in my chest. "Lone dominants are tolerated, but not really welcome, so they have to leave to find their mates and start their own packs, because pack is everything." I shrugged, and let the cold wind be my excuse for watery eyes. "I guess my version of browned butter is … pack." I exhaled. "Family."

"You want kids?" Anna asked.

I shoved the wave of longing back firmly. "You know I was just in Mexico for a couple of months, right?" They both nodded. "My client was dealing with all kinds of threats from the worst of the bottom-feeders. It was scary for her, and there were a lot of times I felt like a really expensive babysitter—not just for her, but for her two little ones." I shook my head, trying to clear the images out. "They hired regular security for their new place, so they didn't need me after Mexico. Leaving that baby and her brother was way harder than it should have been." I shrugged. "It just makes me think about some of the choices I've made, and what I might do differently now."

I blinked the wind away and turned back to the two women with a faint grimace. "Sorry for the overshare."

Anna's Yoda ears flopped in the wind as she waved away my embarrassment. "Nah. This is just sharing. It's what friends do."

I didn't have friends, I had co-workers, but Anna seemed determined to ignore my silence. Her gaze darted to mine, then back out over the water. "You don't usually say a lot when I'm around," she said, "and I'm pretty sure it's because I fill up all the space. Just tell me to shut up when you have something to say."

Shane shivered violently. "Okay, seriously, I'm turning into an icicle. How are you not freezing cold?"

Anna pulled something out of the inside pocket of her coat and held it up for us to see. "Pocket warmers," she said happily. "They're my secret weapon whenever we take the boat out. Darius and his brother think I'm made of steel. But you're right, it's getting colder. We can hook up the heater and have a glass of wine below deck when we get back to the slip."

"Sounds perfect." Shane's teeth chattered, and she rubbed her gloved hands together as she looked at me. "Any secret pocket warmers for you?"

I shrugged. "I've used them, but only when I need accurate aim. It's not cold enough here, and I don't need to shoot anything today."

"Today." Anna snorted.

I shrugged again. "It's still early."

[7]

DALLAS

"Monsters don't like kitchens. They're allergic to all the love in them."

The boat rocked in the slip as someone boarded it.

"Hi, honey, you're home!" Anna called out.

I slipped off the bench seat in the small galley kitchen and reached for my knife. "That's not Darius," I whispered.

The hatch opened, and a tall man stood in the entry. I tensed, ready to launch at the first sign of concern from either Anna or Shane.

"Reza!" Anna welcomed the man gleefully. "Come in. Join us." She turned her gaze to us. "Reza lives three boats over. He's Darius's brother."

The man stepped down the short staircase with easy grace. "I'm clearly interrupting something important," he said as Anna scooted over to let him onto the bench beside her.

"Dallas was just about to explain how she knew you weren't your brother," Shane said, eyeing the knife I was tucking into its sheath at my back.

"He's heavier by about twenty pounds. And Darius used to run, so his step is different." I turned my gaze briefly to Reza. "You played hockey," I said, perusing his upper body musculature and the way he stood, "and now you row."

I ignored his startled expression as I turned my attention back to Anna. I'd only accepted a short pour of wine, which I finished with a final sip. "I need to get going. Thank you for inviting me today. I had fun."

"Did you?" Anna said, tilting her head to the side as she studied me. "Because I'm kind of intimidated by you most of the time, and I'm never really sure."

I huffed a surprised laugh. "I'm pretty much the opposite of intimidating. If anything, I'm intimidated by both of you." I included Shane in my gaze. "You," I said to Reza with a slight smirk, "not so much. Not when you board boats without calling out a greeting first."

"Guilty," he said with a grin.

I slung my backpack over my shoulder and started up the steps.

"The second floor of Oliver Curran's house is the most vulnerable," Anna said, in the *non sequitur* of the century. "And ten bucks says the bathroom window's unlocked."

I turned to stare at her. "And you felt the need to tell me this now because …?"

She shrugged. "Because if someone doesn't break in there, he'll never change the whole system, and whatever it is he's working on is clearly interesting to at least one Russian." She waved airily. "I'll be by to break in tomorrow if you can't do it tonight."

"Good to know," I said, shaking my head as I left.

I practiced walking silently down the dock. A few of the boats I passed had lights on inside, but most were dark and closed up for the winter.

It was dark, but not late, and I debated stopping by Oliver's market for another baguette on my way home, but Anna's words were still running through my head when I stepped off the train at Division. My steps took me away from the commercial district, and a few minutes later, I stood in front of Oliver Curran's door, wondering what the hell I was doing there.

I reached toward the doorbell, then pulled my hand back and looked up at the camera that hung above it. I gave it a count of ten, and just as I was about to turn and leave, the door opened.

"What do you want?" Oliver said gruffly.

"Anna Masoud told me to break in."

He raised an eyebrow, which made his too-handsome hipsterman face look snarky and interesting. "This is you breaking in?"

The corner of my mouth quirked up in the approximation of a smile. "This is me telling you that if you don't change your security, someone else will break in."

He stared at me for a longer minute than would be comfortable to most people. I stared back because discomfort didn't bother me, but a part of my brain still wondered why I was there. Then he opened the door wider. "You better come in, then."

"Why?" I asked, startled into an inane question.

He sighed. "Because I'm about to eat and my food's getting cold. There's enough for you if you want some."

I was suddenly aware of the food scents wafting through the open door, and my stomach growled embarrassingly.

Oliver turned and walked away, leaving the door open behind him.

And because conscious and rational choice seemed to have fled the playing field, I followed him inside.

If McCallum had installed the deadbolt on the door, it would have to be changed, I catalogued mentally as I turned it behind me. The main floor of the house was up a short staircase from the front door. It encompassed a large office, some sort of TV lounge, and a kitchen that was nearly as big as the office. Oliver was in the kitchen dishing a bowl of something that smelled like ramen but looked like an Instagram photo.

"There's pork in it."

"I'm a carnivore," I said, staring at the shimmery broth filled with braised pork, greens, a soft-boiled egg, pickled ginger, soba noodles, and topped with sesame seeds and a piece of nori.

Oliver set the bowl on the island, tossed a cloth napkin next to it, handed me a spoon, and indicated the stool. "*A table, s'il vous plaît*," he said as he sat at his own spot down the island.

"*Merci*," I answered automatically. My private school education had been bi-lingual, as it usually was in Canada, but I wondered about Oliver's perfectly accented French. The question must have shown on my face.

"French nanny," he explained tersely, apparently waiting for me to take a spoonful of soup before he resumed eating.

"In Haiti?" I asked, remembering his strange recitation of his sins in the Cipher office.

He grunted agreement, and then I did taste the soup, and I nearly moaned with pleasure.

The flavors of the broth were unbelievably complex and perfectly balanced. If I hadn't seen the big stock pot on the stove, I might have assumed he'd ordered takeout from a Michelin-starred ramen restaurant.

I opened my mouth to say so, but Oliver was concentrating on his food, so I filled it with another delicious bite instead. We ate in silence, and it was remarkably companionable for being so awkward. He was deliberately not looking at me, so I found my gaze wandering around the kitchen with interest.

The spice rack was prominent and filled with small jars with handwritten labels. The pans were the kind professional chefs used with bare metal handles, and the stove was big and looked like it cost more than my last car had. A bookshelf at the entrance to the kitchen held several bookmarked cookbooks, and I wanted to pick through the titles to see which recipes each book fell open to.

We finished at the same time, so I stood and picked up both bowls. "Are you done?" I asked. Oliver seemed almost startled that I was still there.

"Yeah."

I took the bowls to the sink and washed them. When I turned off the water, I was surprised to see him waiting with a hand towel. "That was the best ramen I've ever had," I said as I dried my hands.

He stepped back and leaned against the counter, watching me.

"Why are you here?" His tone wasn't exactly suspicious, but it definitely wasn't friendly.

I hung up the towel. "I don't really know. You haven't hired us, so you're not a client." His expression was stony, and I let my gaze drift out to the room behind him as I spoke. "I genuinely am worried about the holes in your home security. I think you should let Darius and Anna set you up with a new system."

"You don't know me. Why would you care about my security?"

I sighed. The question was one I'd been asking myself, and the only answer I could come up with barely made sense. "I was there when the Russian attacked you."

"So? You didn't make him do it, did you?"

I scoffed. "Clearly not."

"It's not your responsibility, then, is it?" He sounded angry, which made me defensive.

"I shouldn't have come. I don't know why I'm here, or for that matter, why you fed me." I moved past him and out into the office, which was really more of a living room dominated by a big desk.

I was almost to the steps down to the front door when he sighed behind me. "Hang on."

I stopped and turned to face him. My own expression was as stony as his had been, and I crossed my arms in front of me.

"Could you show me—" He hesitated, as though the words hurt him to say. "What do I need to do to secure this place until Darius can come in and build a new system?"

Something loosened in my shoulders, and I nodded. I didn't like feeling responsible for him. "Anna said something about upstairs."

He winced self-deprecatingly. "She said there were at least six ways in. I've only found one."

"Lead the way," I said.

Oliver's house was long and narrow, so it felt like it was really only three rooms big. The bedroom upstairs took up the whole floor, with a walk-in closet and large bathroom at one end and two big, gabled windows at the other. Those windows were at the front of the house and looked like eyes from the street. They were also a point of vulnerability from the roof, as gables were easy to climb down onto.

"I wasn't up here with Darius and Anna, but I can tell you those windows are alarmed," Oliver said confidently.

I looked out the windows. "You have above-ground power. It's easy to cut, which renders the alarms useless and the cameras blind."

"Okay, so that's two," he said grudgingly. "What else?"

I poked my head into the bathroom. It was strangely spotless for a guy living alone, with big white towels on a heated rack. I pointed to the window. "Alarmed?"

He shook his head. "No. Why would it be? I couldn't fit through it."

"I could," I said.

Some product he used in the bathroom smelled kind of outdoorsy and nice, and I left before I could figure out which one. I did not need to be sniffing Oliver Curran's skin products. The same-sized window existed in the walk-in closet, and this time I merely pointed to it. He sighed and rolled his eyes.

"That's four," he said.

"Staircase is five," I said. "No motion sensors inside that I could see."

He stared at me. "People do that? Wire the inside of their houses with motion sensors? That seems … excessive."

"Fear is a powerful motivator," I answered.

While he contemplated whether that tidbit about humanity applied to him, I looked at the clothes hanging around the small space. He had more clothes than my sister and I put together, and everything was hung neatly —even jeans and khakis hung on the lower bars as if it were a retail store. And it smelled good too, not like sweaty running shoes or old socks. I had to get out of there before I started sniffing his shirts.

I moved back into the bedroom and looked around at the furnishings —a big bed, positioned nearly in the middle of one wall, a television mounted on the wall above a mid-century modern credenza, and a leather chair near a guitar stand between the windows. Then I looked up and pointed at the skylight positioned right over the bed.

"Number six."

He sighed. "It doesn't open."

"It breaks. That's enough."

"How do I protect myself from that? If someone's up on my roof willing to break my skylight to get to me, I'm pretty much screwed." He sounded exasperated.

"Pretty much," I agreed. "That's why I have a job, I guess."

He looked startled. "Because of skylights?"

I smirked. "Because most people don't live in bunkers."

He scrubbed his hands through his hair, which mussed it into something resembling artful bedhead. "I don't want to live in a bunker, and I don't want a bodyguard."

I shrugged. "Well, I guess you could give them what they want."

He looked sharply at me. "Them?"

"Whoever sent the Russian. I presume they want whatever is worth the millions. Maybe if you give it to them and ask nicely, they'll leave you alone." I could see his temper tighten his shoulders. I enjoyed putting him on edge, which probably made me a bad person, but I could live with that.

"Are you good at your job?" he said suddenly. I rolled with it.

"Very."

"I guess you'd have to be, because I can't imagine any other reason to keep you around."

"Right," I said, heading straight for the stairs so I didn't pick the fight he so richly deserved. "Put 911 on speed dial, don't bother trying to use your home phone because they'll have cut the power, and I recommend a baseball bat next to the bed. Good luck, Mr. Curran."

I was down the stairs and at the door before I even heard him move upstairs. I gave it a fifty-fifty chance that Cipher would see him the next day.

[8]

OLIVER

"Fear changes everything."

- - OLIVER

I was still working at three a.m. when I heard the crash.

Whether it was too much coffee or leftover annoyance from the weird visit by the bossy security chick, my fast twitch reflexes were *fast*. Everything I'd been working on was stored on external drives, and I swept the critical ones into my bag, grabbed my laptop, phone, and my coat, and I was out the door in fifteen seconds.

I slung the bag over one shoulder and tightened the strap like a bike messenger so I could run. I didn't even stop to wonder whether someone was stationed on the street waiting for me to scurry out like a rat. I just bolted.

Blind panic overtook me, and I let my slamming heartbeat set the pace for my feet to follow.

I ran straight for Milwaukee Avenue because it was the most public place I could think to go. Five blocks away from my house. I ducked into an alley and pulled out my phone. I hit the Cipher Security number before I'd even had a chance to consider an alternative, and after two rings, a deep male voice picked up.

"Cipher," he said gruffly, as though he was as surprised as I was to find himself still at work.

"This is Oliver Curran," I panted. My heart was pounding so hard I couldn't catch my breath. "Someone just broke into my house. I need—"

"You're ten blocks away from Dallas. I'll text you the address. Go there now," he interrupted. I realized the voice belonged to Quinn Sullivan, and before I could say another word, he hung up. A second later, a text message came through with an address. The map showed that it was over by Humboldt Park, and I was running before I was even conscious of the way.

I kept my phone on, checking it at every intersection until I was a block away. I was sweating in my down coat, and breathing was hard to do through all the panic. I slowed when I turned the corner in a feeble attempt to get myself under control, but then I saw Dallas standing on the sidewalk, one hand at her back, waiting for me.

My eyes suddenly burned, and I was horrified that I was about to cry. She didn't seem to notice though, because she was scanning the silent street behind me as she walked toward me.

"Door's unlocked. Get inside," she said curtly, her eyes never leaving the street.

I bounded up the steps of the Victorian row house she'd indicated and turned to see her prowling down the block, the hand at her back gripping the handle of a big knife she wore tucked into the waistband at the back of her jeans.

I closed the front door quietly behind me and leaned back against the wall of a dark hallway. I couldn't catch my breath, and I scrubbed at my eyes with the heels of my hands. They came away wet.

"*Fuck*," I whispered into the dark as I tried to wipe my face dry. Whether it was sweat or tears, I didn't know and didn't really care. My legs gave way, and I slid down the wall and cradled my face in my hands while I swallowed the gasps of fear.

The door opened, and I almost leapt to my feet. "Fuck," I said again, louder when I saw it was Dallas. My voice was wet, and I scrubbed my face again.

"Are you hurt?" she asked in a semi-whisper.

I shook my head, and then said, "No," in case she couldn't see in the dark.

Apparently she could, because she reached a hand down to help me up. Her grip was surprisingly strong as she hauled me to my feet. "Come on," she said as she shot the deadbolt behind her and started off down the hall.

I followed her through another door, which opened into a big room that seemed to be a living room/bedroom combo. There was a lamp lit on a low table at the corner of two long couches, one of which had been made out into a bed that had clearly been left in a hurry. Dallas closed the second door and shot the second deadbolt behind me before looking me over.

I felt like she was cataloging all my parts, looking for damage. She registered my sweat, my messenger bag, and the fact that I was still sucking air. She seemed to decide I was whole, because she nodded and then finally looked me in the eye.

"Go wash your face. I'll get you some water." She indicated a closed door that I assumed led to the bathroom. Her calm officiousness was oddly more comforting than "are you okay?" would have been, and I felt my breath come more easily.

I didn't take off my bag and coat until the bathroom door was closed and locked behind me. When I finally looked at my reflection in the old mirror that hung over the pedestal sink, the reality of the last thirty minutes stared back at me. I'd been hunted, and this tiny Victorian bathroom had just become my refuge.

"Fucking hell," I whispered to myself, then bent to the task of washing my face and blowing my nose. My eyes were bloodshot and I was pale, but that was pretty par for the course after working all night.

This was more than that, though. I felt like I was nine years old, terrified of things I couldn't see in the dark, and the fear just *erased* all my carefully crafted confidence. I felt like a train wreck, and at the moment, it was as good as I was going to get.

Dallas had turned her bed back into a couch and sat on the rug with her back to it, writing something on her laptop. She looked up when I emerged from the bathroom, and then gestured to the other couch.

"Have a seat," she said as she closed her laptop.

I dropped my bag and coat on the couch and sat on the rug. A glass of water stood on the coffee table. I downed it, vaguely surprised that my hand was steady enough to hold it.

"Quinn said someone broke into your house," Dallas said quietly, as though she were coaxing a story out of a little kid.

I nodded. "Something crashed upstairs, like glass breaking. I was still up working, so I got out before I saw who it was."

She glanced over at my messenger bag. "Is that what they're after?"

I swallowed thickly. "I guess so."

She nodded again. "Think you were followed?"

I mentally replayed everything I'd done since the moment I heard the crash, every sound I'd heard on my run through Wicker Park, but I didn't think I'd heard the slap of any feet other than my own.

I shook my head, and something in Dallas's shoulders seemed to fractionally let go.

"Quinn called the police and is having Darius and Anna meet them at your house. Since they were just in it, they can tell, more or less, what's been disturbed."

I nodded again mutely, strangely unsurprised at the efficiency of everything. My gaze had been wandering over the patterns and colors in the room, muted in the dim light, but when I realized she'd stopped talking, I returned my attention to Dallas. She seemed to have been waiting for me to notice her again.

"I know you aren't officially a Cipher client, and you haven't actually hired me to protect you, but I'm going to tell you what I believe you should do."

I waited, oddly unbothered by the bossiness. My silence must have surprised her, because she left space between her words for an argument. When she didn't get one, she raised an eyebrow, then continued.

"I think you need to come clean with Cipher about what you think is going on here so we can start to work on who hired your assailant. That information will also help us determine the level of security you need beyond a home system upgrade, and, for the moment at least, a close protection agent."

I still said nothing, and her eyes narrowed as she studied my face.

"I also don't think you can go back to your house. Quinn has a secure building we call The Vault where he reserves a couple of suites for high-profile clients. He is working on finding availability for you while we attempt to neutralize the threat."

I played with the empty water glass in my hands as the silence stretched between us. It was a soft silence, without noticeable tension, and it allowed me to breathe as I watched the light refract through the glass.

I felt … numb. The panic that had fueled my ten-block sprint had eaten adrenaline and spit out fear, but even that had sunk back in under my skin and become invisible again. I finally looked up from my hands and found Dallas watching me with some kind of weirdly sympathetic expression. It looked foreign to her face, like it didn't quite fit, and I waited for her to drop it and go back to the sharp angles and planes that I expected.

The softness melted away as she got to her feet and moved to an armoire against one wall. She opened it and pulled out a down pillow and an old quilt. She laid them on the couch behind me.

"Try to get some sleep if you can, and we'll go downtown together in a couple of hours when Quinn and Darius get in."

She opened the lid of her laptop and then turned off the table lamp behind her. The white glow from the screen of her computer made the planes of her face look like line drawings. She looked up from the screen and met my eyes.

"Sleep, Oliver. The blanks will fill in when you've gotten some rest."

That was exactly how I felt—blank. Every muscle groaned as I climbed to my feet. I kicked my shoes off and left them near the door, then dropped my messenger bag on the floor near the pillow. I wanted my bag close, so I covered it with my coat and made sure both were in easy reach.

"I don't sleep," I murmured as I stretched out on the couch and pulled the quilt over myself. The last thing I remembered hearing was the click of her fingers on the keyboard.

[9]
OLIVER

"It's hard to go wrong with rainbows and hand knits."

- DALLAS

Strong black coffee steamed on the table next to my head. As an alarm clock, the scent of coffee didn't suck, and it went a long way toward normalizing the view that assaulted my eyeballs when I opened them.

There were so many colors and patterns in the room that my eyes didn't know quite where to land. Then I remembered where I was and why I was there, and I rolled onto my back to stare at the ceiling as a wave of adrenaline crashed through me.

"There's a clean towel in the bathroom for you if you want to shower before we head downtown," Dallas said quietly. I turned my head and saw her leaning against the doorway to what must have been the kitchen, nursing her own cup. Even her mug was too bright, but it somehow fit her hands.

I nodded and scrubbed my hands over my eyes and through my hair as I sat up. Shockingly, I had managed to put away … I checked my phone … three hours of sleep. "Thanks," I croaked, surprised at the roughness of my voice. I reached for the bright rainbow hand-thrown mug. "Colorful," I said.

"My host collects them," she said. "That one's my favorite."

I sipped the strong coffee and contemplated the woman who had given me her favorite mug. "Your host?"

She indicated the room. "Vacation rental. I'm not usually in town long enough for a proper apartment." Her eyes wandered around the color explosion. "I think it's the best one so far."

I followed her gaze. The single room was hardly someplace I'd rent for a vacation. It was more like crashing on the couch of someone's crafty, color-blind aunt.

The edge came back into her expression, like she'd heard my thoughts. "Is half an hour enough?"

I couldn't tell if she was being bitchy about how long it might take me to get ready, and I wasn't sure how I felt about talking to Cipher at all. I drained my mug and stood up, slightly surprised to feel the ache of muscles not used to panic-sprinting. "I'll be ready to go in ten," I said.

She nodded, turned, and left the room.

I didn't think I'd ever heard a woman talk less than Dallas did, and most of the words she did say were laced with judgment. And yet … I set the rainbow mug on the table and pointedly shoved away thoughts about a woman who'd *protected* me.

I didn't get protected.

I got left behind, or forgotten, or overlooked, until finally I grew up and made myself into someone who got noticed. I was charming, I smiled, people liked me. I didn't need protection because I was the nicest guy in every room, and everyone knew *that* guy had it all handled. Except now I had to admit that maybe I didn't, and that wasn't a conversation I looked forward to having with anyone.

I was finally able to shut off my brain in the shower, probably because the botanical scent of her shampoo invaded my senses and pushed everything else out. Also, her soap was handmade—because of course it was. Even though I could have spent half an hour under the water, I refused to give Dallas anything to snipe at, so I was dressed and ready to go in ten minutes. That my speed inspired the barest lift of one of her eyebrows in surprise was oddly satisfying.

We left through the kitchen and emerged onto the street three buildings away from the Victorian. Dallas walked casually next to me, but I had the sense that she was coiled and ready to throw a hand out to pull me out of the way or something equally protective at a moment's notice.

It was still early enough for most of the traffic to be commuter, but I found myself scanning the people on the sidewalk for red hats. Dallas fit into the office crowd with her practical suit and topcoat, but I couldn't shake the predator vibe I got from her whenever she moved. We didn't speak until we arrived at the Cipher building. She turned to me just before we entered, and her gaze collided with mine. "You can trust them," she said, as though she was willing me to believe her.

"Just them?" I asked before I could stop myself.

Her eyes searched mine. "Not just them," she said with a frown before she turned back toward the door. She reached to open it for me, but I got there first and held it. The frown deepened, and I front-loaded my smile with shiny teeth, glad I'd irritated her.

I hadn't been nice to her since the day she'd saved me from the Russian. I wasn't charming or flirty or even friendly. My default nice guy just didn't kick in around her, and yet she'd protected me anyway.

The pretty young law student, Kendra, was at the desk again. She said Quinn was waiting for us in a conference room on the fourth floor. I asked Kendra about her legal studies, I told her I liked her sweater, I turned the charm on, and got what I wanted: a genuine smile. Her smile grounded me and restored the confidence I needed to get on the elevator.

Dallas said nothing on the elevator ride, and whatever calm I'd been able to generate with my Kendra-charming act was starting to stiffen into something that felt tight and itchy. Just off the elevator I stopped to unsling my bag so I could strip off my coat. I was fidgety and trying to cover it with actual motion.

"Ridiculous," Dallas whispered under her breath.

"I'm ridiculous?" I asked incredulously as I pulled the messenger bag back over my shoulder and tightened the strap across my chest.

"No," she said sharply, then added, "Well, yeah. But really it's your coat."

I scowled. Honestly, woman. "What's wrong with my coat?"

"Are you an Arctic explorer?" she shot back.

I rolled my eyes. "Really?"

"If you're an Arctic explorer, polar scientist, or ice road trucker, you can wear a Canada Goose parka, otherwise, you're ridiculous. And the bomber jacket version? If it doesn't cover your ass, what good is it?"

I just stared at her, momentarily speechless. And just when I opened my mouth to deliver some scathing set down I had yet to come up with, she raised an eyebrow. "Righteous indignation as an antidote to nerves. Works every time."

She opened the conference room door and pointedly held it for me to enter first. The itchy tightness in my skin turned to annoyance at her look of smug satisfaction. Damn it.

Quinn, Darius, and another guy were already in the room, and all three looked up at our entrance. The seriousness of their expressions promptly killed off both my irritation and my default smile, and I greeted Quinn with a solemn handshake.

"Thank you for taking my call last night," I said.

"You did well to get out," he said. "Darius and Anna reported the theft of all your office electronics and the destruction of your work station setup."

My stomach churned at that, and Darius held my handshake a few moments longer than necessary. "It looked like a methodical search that turned violent. As though the searcher didn't find what he was looking for."

"He didn't," I said. My hand went automatically to the strap of my messenger bag, and Darius nodded his understanding.

"Good."

"Oliver Curran, this is Alex Greene. He's our Director of Information Technologies, and I asked him to sit in."

I shook Alex's hand and gave him the once-over most guys give other guys. Weirdly, he didn't give it back. My quick glance showed me a tall white guy with stupidly broad shoulders, black-framed nerd glasses that only made him better-looking, and the distracted air of someone who had a million other things to be doing.

"Good to meet you, Alex," I said with the default smile.

The look he gave me was devoid of greeting. "I know who you are."

And with chilling calm, he sat at an open laptop on the table and proceeded to type something.

I sat down next to the seat Dallas chose, not quite sure why I'd decided she was an ally.

Quinn took charge of the meeting. "I'm sorry for what you experienced last night, Oliver, and I was glad to be able to offer assistance in the moment. I'm sure you can appreciate, however, that there are some things that need to be addressed if we're to continue helping you."

I sighed. Dallas leaned back in her chair, and I could feel her gaze land on my face. I wanted to inch away so she couldn't see me so clearly, but I forced myself to sit still and breathe.

"You might as well start with your version of the DeepFace program," Alex said, matter-of-factly.

I was surprised enough to let the friendly mask slip. "Information Technologies? Really?"

"I alternate between red and white hats," he said simply.

A hacker. It made sense for a security firm to use a hacker's skill set. A white-hat hacker was a "good guy" who hacked into systems to find their vulnerabilities. The red-hat hacker's objective was to find the black hats and put a stop to their mayhem.

"Right," I said, deliberately looking away from Alex to Dallas and Darius, with occasional glances at Quinn, who, I was sure, had already heard it from the hacker. "Are you familiar with DeepFace?" I asked them.

Dallas shook her head, but Darius raised an eyebrow. "It's Facebook's AI facial recognition program."

"Like the Next Generation Identification program the FBI uses?" Dallas's gaze swung between Darius and me.

I scoffed. "NextGen has an eighty-five percent success rate on LFW data sets."

"LFW data sets?" Dallas asked, with a raised eyebrow indicating her annoyance. "In non-cyber-nerd-speak, please."

I didn't bother to hide that I enjoyed annoying her. Maybe annoying Dallas had the same effect on my confidence as my nice-guy routine did. "LFW is 'Labeled Faces in the Wild,' otherwise known as tagged photos. DeepFace learned how to recognize people using a data set of four million images uploaded by Facebook users."

She frowned. "So, every time someone tags a photo on Facebook, they're potentially feeding its facial recognition AI."

"Basically," I said. "Just like the prove-you're-a-human thing on Google that wants you to click on all the stoplights. They're using humans—us—to teach their artificial intelligence how to recognize … us. DeepFace uses a nine-layer neural network to identify people's faces with an accuracy rate of 97.35%."

I paused dramatically to let my words sink in. Showmanship—the kind that sells start-up companies to big buyers—came so naturally I was barely aware of doing it anymore. "We humans have a 97.53% accuracy rate. That means DeepFace is sometimes better at deciding who's who than people are."

"Google's FaceNet got to 99.65% accuracy on the same data set," Alex said.

"My version of DeepFace got to 99.67." I looked at Alex, knowing he would get the significance of what I'd just said.

He arched one eyebrow. I arched one back. He gave an infinitesimal nod. I gave one back. A whole, unspoken conversation: *Really? Yes, really. Impressive. I know.*

"And then you sold the technology," he said out loud.

I sighed. "It's how I financed my first start-up."

My gaze returned to Dallas and Darius. "I developed the program when I was at Harvard, and dropped out when a company called ADDATA made me an offer on it—"

Dallas flinched and Darius sat forward. "What?" Darius's exclamation seemed involuntary.

"You were associated with ADDATA?" Quinn demanded. He turned to Alex. "Did we know this?" Alex said nothing, but his expression told me that yeah, he'd suspected at least.

"I sold them my code, was *idiotic* enough to sign a massive NDA and non-compete"—I looked pointedly at Quinn—"and was contracted to hang out there anonymously for three months answering questions about AI." I hated talking about this. "Three months was long enough to know I'd fu— screwed up selling it to them."

"You think?" Alex said.

I glared at the hacker. "I didn't know. They were a start-up, acquiring tech from unknown developers for ridiculous money and then putting their name on it. Lots of companies were doing it."

"And it didn't occur to you to wonder what possible use they could have for facial recognition software?" Alex growled.

"I was twenty-one and had invented something someone wanted to buy for what I thought was a shit-ton of money. Twenty-one-year-old guys don't usually ask why."

Dallas narrowed her eyes in her judgmental way. "One of ADDATA's partners was Alex Karpov," she said quietly. "The same guy involved in providing the start-up funds for McCallum Security. A Russian."

I flinched then. "Shit. The guy I dealt with was Dane … something. Smarmy dude who knew eff-all about programming, but could sell you the shirt off your own back."

Quinn leaned forward. "When was the last time you had contact with anyone at ADDATA?"

"About a year ago. One of their programmers, a guy named Greg Morris who I'd partied with when I worked there and a few times over the years since then, reached out to me. The owner"—I glared at Alex— "I thought he meant the smarmy one, had acquired some face-swapping tech from a small start-up out of MIT, and this guy reached out to ask me about integration options."

Alex snapped the lid of his laptop shut so fast Dallas flinched again. He sat forward, and we had another non-verbal exchange of eyebrows and nods that said, N*o shit? No shit. That's bad. Yeah, really bad.*

"Out loud, please?" Dallas said wryly.

"Adding sophisticated facial recognition software to a solid face-swap program is the next step toward being able to create almost undetectable fake images. These images, called deepfakes, can't be discerned by the human eye, or *by machines*," Alex said ominously.

"It's already happening," I added. "When you see Tom Cruise's face on dancing bodies, for example, or the remaster the guys at Derpfake did of the shit CGI Princess Leia in *Rogue One*." I wore my charming smile to see if it worked as well as annoying her did.

Dallas glared at me. "I'm very familiar with deepfakes. I just spent two months protecting a woman in Mexico because a political 'news' site ran deepfakes of her face on some other woman's body in a sex tape. She got the kind of rape and death threats I haven't seen since Gamergate."

I held up my hands to ward off her evil death glare. Apparently even my charm annoyed her. "Hey, I get it. But I'm not the one doing the deepfakes."

"Your program gave ADDATA a powerful tool, which likely explains some of the QAnon deepfakes that have been perpetuated on the dark web for the past several years," Alex said.

"Like the video showing people burning ballots that were actually just sample ballots?" Dallas said with a snort of disgust.

"I was twenty-one and they wanted my tech and they gave me a lot of money," I ground out through gritted teeth.

"Ever heard of an ethical conscience?" Dallas said in that judgmental voice that grated on every last nerve I had.

"Ever heard that capitalism beats ethics every time when you're hungry?" I shot back.

She scoffed. "So, you were pretty hungry at Harvard, then?"

"Yeah, actually, I was, since I was paying my own way." It was my turn to glare. It wasn't public knowledge that I'd broken up with my parents, legally and emotionally, when I was eighteen. It wasn't good for their benevolent activist image, and they were just famous enough that I didn't need the press.

Quinn intervened and redirected us away from the argument that was brewing. "We saw to it that ADDATA was dissolved, so they're not a concern anymore. But Karpov, or perhaps a new player, is out there, and they want something from you. What is it?"

I took a breath to calm my temper while I figured out how to answer the question.

"There could be any number of black hats playing the game by now," Alex said, his eyes narrowing at me. "But you have an idea what's behind all this, don't you?"

I met his gaze. "I'd been cocky and naïve when I sold them my program, and yes"—I shot a pointed look at Dallas—"it pissed me off that I hadn't thought beyond the money they paid me. So, I started working on a program to reverse engineer my own facial recognition code."

The room was silent, as if everyone was waiting for the punchline.

"And?" Quinn finally prompted.

"I think it'll beat deepfakes."

[10]

DALLAS

"Anything less than your continued safety is an unacceptable outcome."

- DALLAS

He hired us, but only if I would be his bodyguard.

I refused to show how much he'd surprised me, because my job was to anticipate surprises, but I'd been pretty certain he couldn't stand me. So when he requested my close protection, it took me a second to agree.

Our new client and Alex Greene then spent the next five hours in the basement with Cipher's resident MIT genius, Jorge, discussing true cyber-nerd stuff, while I worked with Quinn, Darius, and Shane on a plan to keep Oliver safe until we could find and neutralize the threat that may or not be Alexander Karpov.

Karpov was the owner of ADDATA that Cipher *hadn't* been able to bring down. His partner, Dane Quimby, was currently rotting away in federal prison for killing a judge, courtesy of Shane and Gabriel—the rotting part, not the killing part. Karpov had disappeared when the feds confiscated his luxury yacht.

"We traced Karpov via Canada to St. Petersburg," Shane said, "and we know he still has family in Russia." She shrugged. "He's on federal watch lists, so he can't come back into the U.S. on his current passport."

Quinn's tone was matter-of-fact. "Passports are simply a matter of funds, and Karpov was not without resources when he ran." He thought for a moment, then addressed Shane directly. "You and Gabriel, take the Karpov angle. Hand off any extant cases and put your resources toward tracing all known associates and business dealings. The information that they've been hiding the acquisition of sophisticated tech for several years is unwelcome, and I suspect you'll need to warm up the programmer you used to know there to find out what else they acquired."

Shane nodded as she tapped notes in her phone. "I'll try to find Oliver's programmer contact too."

"Greg Morris," I said, remembering the name he'd used.

Then Quinn turned to Darius. "You and Anna track down whatever you can on McCallum, starting with the system in Oliver's house. Find out who sold the house to him and determine the degree to which surveillance could have been done on him while he lived there. I suspect that the McCallum security system is the leak for the program he's been developing, and if you follow that stream to its source, we may find Karpov directly involved."

Darius wrote in a small notebook he carried everywhere he went. I loved the little water-resistant notebooks and had introduced him to them the first time we partnered on a job. I suspected he used his as a journal as much as a notebook for work, and I approved. He looked up at Quinn. "There's a good chance the house is being watched. Do we need a cover to go in?"

Quinn shook his head. "No, it's already blown. Your interactions with Chicago PD this morning will have alerted McCallum to the presence of private security." He included me in his gaze. "No matter who goes in, it's always in pairs. I want no one to be caught unaware in that house."

We both nodded, and Quinn's attention remained on me. "Dallas, you're on Curran personally. I'll have a suite at The Vault cleared for his use on Sunday, so we need to sort out his housing for the next three nights."

"Hotels are too public, especially for an adversary with security skills," Darius said. "If he wants to stay in town, you guys are welcome to my boat."

I shook my head. "Thanks, but my place is easier to secure. I'll talk to him and see what he's comfortable with, but in the absence of a solid plan, I'll stash him in my rental until the apartment is ready."

I turned to Darius. "If you guys do get the go-ahead to change out his security system, can you build in an audio/visual loop that lets McCallum believe they still have eyes on his place? That might buy us some options."

Quinn nodded. "Good idea. Let me know if you want backup outside your house. And we can find office space for him to work here when you need a break."

"Thanks. It's just a couple of days, though. I'm fine." I'd been trained by my guiding days to stay with clients twenty-four seven, and I only ever needed a break from them when they were truly jerks. This one was just another annoying party boy. Nothing I wasn't used to.

Quinn looked at all three of us, and his expression was grave. "I won't bring in outside agencies on this one unless it gets away from us. There's no proof yet of any crime other than the attacks on Curran, and he'd have to be willing to hand over his files as evidence if a government agency were in on an arrest."

"I'm not willing," Oliver said as he strode into the room behind Alex. "That'll kill off all the deals I'm trying to make."

Alex snorted quietly, and I couldn't tell if it was a sound of laughter or derision.

If Quinn was bothered by their abrupt entrance, he betrayed nothing as his eyes met Oliver's. "What, then, is your plan?"

Oliver flopped into a chair almost like a teenager. "I need time with a dedicated rig to work on my deepfake buster. Oh, hey. You're the stunner with the nice bag," he said noticing Shane. "I'm Oliver." He flashed her a blinding smile, and I barely restrained the eye-roll.

Shane nodded with a pleasant smile in return. "Shane." Then she returned her attention to Quinn, who was looking at Alex for confirmation of what Oliver had said.

"We're working on it," Alex said. "We're looking for a computer system and data sets that will give the machine time to learn what it needs to so it can utilize his code."

"The sooner it does, the sooner I can sell it," Oliver added.

"Which means?" I asked.

He answered with a shrug and a boyish grin. "I'll be millions richer, and the program will be someone else's problem."

God, this guy annoyed me.

"What's a dedicated rig?" I asked Shane. I was done talking to Oliver.

Shane's eyes narrowed at Oliver, who was still trying to work his charm on her, and she turned to me. "A powerful computing system dedicated to a single task."

He directed his question to Shane as well. "Since you seem to be the go-to person in the room, any chance we can find enough drives to download data sets?"

My eyebrows rose at the clear flirtation in his tone. Shane ignored him and explained his question to me. "Elaborate internet security—the kind that can protect the contents of someone's laptop from someone like him"—Shane nodded at Alex—"is too time-consuming to set up every time you need to work. The most paranoid programmers I know work on bricks, computers with disabled internet. My guess is that Oliver, for all of his easygoing, happy hipster persona, is about as paranoid as they come about his code, especially after discovering what Karpov is possibly doing with it. Therefore, having his data sets downloaded to drives means he can brick his rig."

The interesting thing about the range of emotions that played across Oliver's features was that they didn't end in an explosion of temper, as I'd suspected they would, but rather in a wry, self-deprecating humor. I seemed to be the only person he was a moody jerk with.

"Being called paranoid is pretty bad news. Deserving it is even worse," Oliver said with a smiling wince. The charm he'd turned on with Shane disappeared when he spoke to me. "The program I've written needs data sets to learn from. That machine learning takes time, and while the data sets process, the code is running, learning what to look for and how to recognize the *real* human. Like she said"—he looked at Shane, and a small part of my brain was intrigued that he didn't seem to have logged the most beautiful woman in the room's name—"the code is vulnerable while the machine is online."

I shrugged. "Makes sense. Thanks for explaining."

A line appeared between his eyebrows for just a moment, and then was gone, even as he looked like he wanted to say something else.

I stood up and stretched. "If there are any personal documents or meds, or anything you can't immediately buy, give Darius a list and he'll get them from your house. It has to be small enough to fit in his briefcase though, because anything larger will invite a tail."

Oliver looked startled, and then thoughtful. "My passport is in the top right drawer of the credenza by the front door."

I nodded. "Good. Now, if you'll give me a list of sizes and brands you prefer for socks, underwear, sweats, and t-shirts, I can make sure you have enough to last until we can get you into the suite at The Vault."

He looked even more surprised at that. "Okay ..."

"Also," I added, turning my laptop to face him, "here's the website for the drugstore around the corner from me. Order a toothbrush, deodorant, razors, and whatever else you need. I'll pick it up."

He started to pull out his wallet, but I shook my head. "We'll add it to your bill. From this moment on, the only things that get charged to your cards are whatever you've got on auto-pay. There can be no other financial activity from you online or anywhere else until this thing is finished. Cool?"

Oliver looked a little stunned, but he nodded. "Yeah, cool. Okay." He turned the computer toward him and typed a search, then looked back at me. "The drugstore is around the corner from your place? Is that where I'm staying?"

Shane and Darius had gotten up to discuss Karpov, and Quinn and Alex were having a quiet talk about hard drives and AI, so for the moment, Oliver and I were alone in the conversation.

"The suite won't be available until Sunday, so we need to find housing for you for three days. Hotels are too public, travel by anything other than a car is traceable, and unless you have another suggestion, a private home is pretty much your best option for lying low. Mine is too small, and you won't be comfortable, but it's defensible, and unless you were followed by an actual ghost last night, it's unknown to your assailant." I remembered his accusation that I thought I was a ghost. It would be hard to find another tracker of my skill in this city.

He scowled as he looked around the room at my co-workers. "Is that normal? Do other bodyguards invite clients into their homes?"

"We prefer 'close protection agents,' and it doesn't happen often, but this isn't the first time a client has slept on my couch in an emergency."

"Doesn't seem very professional," he said, still frowning.

I bristled. "The security of our clients takes precedence over personal concerns, which makes it nothing but professional. Anything less than your continued safety is an unacceptable outcome."

"What if I don't want to sleep on your couch?" he said, his eyes rising slowly to meet mine.

I wasn't sure what it was that heated my face, but my own reaction to his words annoyed me, so my tone was more emotional than I was comfortable showing. "Right now, the easy options are my place or Darius's 1950s wooden boat. I understand you and Sterling Gray are friends, so if you ask him for a room, please make sure there's a cot or a piece of floor for me. If you're on speaking terms with your parents, that's another option." I was intrigued to notice that the growing outrage on his face shuttered tight at the mention of his parents. Between that and the comment about paying for his own education, I thought there might be gaps in what the internet knew about his family.

"Anyone else you ask," I continued, "will need to be vetted for security risks before it's safe to stay with them, and I wouldn't recommend anyone with kids or pets, because that just invites a hostage-exchange opportunity." I shrugged to allow myself the time to calm my voice back into tonelessness. "Bearing in mind those caveats, you're welcome to make other arrangements."

I let my eyes meet his again, and I was startled to see he'd gone pale.

"Christ. Hostage exchange? People do that, in real life?"

"Yes," I said simply, "they do."

He stared blankly at the screen of my laptop, then typed something in and finished his order. He turned the computer back to me and finally met my eyes again.

"I'll stay at your place." He suddenly looked tired. "I'll make you dinner to make up for it."

I searched his face for insincerity, but he seemed to be perfectly serious. "I have some pork chops brining in the fridge. Can you do anything with them?"

A smile tilted the corners of his mouth, and I realized it was the first one I'd ever seen directed at me. "I think I can manage something."

Ignoring the flush of irritation the smile gave me, I stood, closed my laptop, and started packing my bag. "Good. I'm suddenly hungry for something I don't have to cook myself."

Avalon drove us back to my place in one of the Cipher SUVs based on a route I gave her that doubled back on itself a few times. She dropped us off across Humboldt Park from my place, and we wove our way down paths and through trees, accessing the back entrance to my rental through the narrow gap between houses. Oliver was quiet on both the drive and the walk, and it wasn't until we hung our coats in the kitchen that he finally spoke.

"You've spent a lot of time mapping out different routes through the city."

"You learn a lot about a place when you explore it on foot," I said, as I kicked off my boots and pushed them under the bench.

"Those are good socks," Oliver noted, as he kicked off his own boots to do the same.

"Thank you. My auntie knits everyone a pair for Christmas, and they're indestructible, so I have about fifteen years' worth of fancy socks. I can loan you a pair if you'd like," I said.

The look of delight on his face was unexpected and therefore strange. "That'd be cool."

I turned away so Oliver didn't see my surprise, and then I got him the most rainbow pair I owned. He chuckled as he pulled the socks on. "These are awesome."

I started a load of laundry and loaned him one of my sleep t-shirts so I could wash his socks and shirt with my stuff. Then I showed him where I kept food staples and spices and went into the sitting room to work while he puttered around the kitchen.

My phone showed a missed video chat from my sister, but when I tried her back, it just rang. I texted her to try again when she could, then opened my computer to follow up on communications with Shane and Darius.

Half an hour later, delicious smells began wafting from my kitchen. I climbed to my feet and padded into the kitchen to investigate.

Music played from the phone on the counter—a spare from the office that Oliver's calls had been routed to so his own phone could stay secure at the Cipher building—and he swayed in time to it, unaware I'd come in.

The sight of Oliver dancing in my kitchen, wearing handmade rainbow socks with a dishcloth tied around his waist, was such a departure from the Canada Goose–wearing hipsterman on the train that I almost laughed out loud. I quelled the urge and schooled my voice to something neutral. "Smells good," I said, indicating the pork chops frying in a cast iron pan on the stove.

"How do you have a freezer full of salmon?" he asked, nodding toward the refrigerator.

I shrugged. "I fish in the summer." I stood at the stove and peered over his shoulder.

"Of course you do," he muttered, and I wondered how it was possible that I could annoy him so fast.

I pulled out two plates as he removed a baking dish from the oven. He spooned spiced coconut-milk rice into the center of the plate, rimmed it with roasted green beans, then placed a spice-crusted pork chop on top.

"It looks good," I said, as we sat on tall stools at the tiny café table in the kitchen that I used for dining.

He waited until I'd taken a bite before he took his own.

"This is amazing," I said through flavors of sweet, savory, and spicy pork.

"Vanilla-brined spice-rubbed pork chops," he said. "I charmed the recipe out of a camp cook in Laos."

"Of course you did," I said, echoing his own grumpy tone. I could imagine how good the spice rub would taste on salmon, and thought I might make a batch to send to my sister.

We ate in silence, just like the last time. He was a client sharing my personal space, which was awkward, but not fatal. I didn't respect him— he was too much like every entitled hunting client I'd ever had—and didn't much like him, but the laughter and jokes and charm that he used with other people were background noise, and his general annoyance with me was becoming so familiar it was almost comfortable.

"So, where do you fish in the summer?" Oliver finally broke the silence. I wasn't sure if he was just making small talk or if he was genuinely interested, so I didn't elaborate.

"With my family," I said, not looking up.

After a few uncomfortable minutes of silence, I finally met his eyes.

"When were you in Laos?"

He shrugged. "The first time was when I was a kid. I went back a couple of years ago to test my memory."

"To test your memory?" I asked.

His expression seemed conflicted, and he ate a few more bites of food before finally meeting my eyes again. "My parents dragged me around the world with them when I was young. There were so many different apartments and houses and cities and nannies, I wasn't really sure what was real and what I'd made up. A couple of years ago I went back to test my memory."

"To Laos," I said.

"To a lot of places," he said, looking back at his food.

"So, Haiti?" I asked, since that was the only other place he'd mentioned.

"No." The sharp tone was so unexpected that I flinched. He looked away and seemed to take a deep breath to calm himself.

We finished the food on our plates in silence. I could do silence. I'd spent hours in hunting blinds not talking, not moving, not even thinking too loud, so some asshole rich guy could take the shot.

"You said you were playing a game when you followed me the other day," Oliver finally said, startling me out of my bitter memories.

It was an interesting swerve. "Yeah, Tracker Jack."

"What is that? You follow people, yeah, I get that, but how do you choose them, and … why?"

I looked at him over the rim of my water glass. The silence between the words was getting too thick and soupy, and if I was feeling itchy, Oliver must have been positively claustrophobic being stuck with someone he barely tolerated just to feel safe.

I checked my watch. It would be dark soon. "I have to go pick up your drugstore order," I said.

He stood up immediately. "Can I come?"

My mouth was open to say no. The word had already been thought and said in my mind—it was too dangerous, he was too visible, it wasn't worth the risk to him or to my professional reputation—and then I really looked at him. Oliver Curran, pretty boy with playboy charisma and a tech genius brain was seriously anxious. His usual cocky confidence was somewhere down around his ankles, and his uncertainty was weirdly … off-putting.

I sighed and looked out the window at the darkening sky. "Yeah. Put the hood up on your coat and we'll go. The park is right across the street from the drugstore, so you can wait there for me while I grab your stuff." There were enough trees to keep him hidden from view if anyone was watching, but I thought the chances of that were pretty slim. Humboldt Park was a totally different neighborhood than Wicker Park, and there was nothing to tie him to the area unless he'd been followed the night before. And if he *had* been followed, I'd rather meet whatever was coming out in the open anyway.

As we left my place I shook my head at myself, wondering if I was going to regret this. "And afterwards, if you promise to stick with me, I'll show you how to get a stranger to show you their city."

[11]

DALLAS

"Listen to silence, it has so much to say."

- RUMI

The park was beautiful in the spring, but its lingering winter dormancy made it a perfect place to practice stalking. I joined Oliver there after I made the drugstore pickup, hoping to burn off some of his nervous energy so he didn't go insane for three days in my cramped rental.

For once, the Canada Goose jacket made sense, if only to keep him from complaining as night fell and the chill in the air turned bitter, because I was relentless in my drills for silence.

I taught him to take slow, measured breaths through his nose, to always look for the next step, to roll his foot from heel to toe, and to walk on dirt or fresh grass whenever it was available. I also taught him to roll his step from the outside to the inside, listening for the crackle of dried leaves before he committed his weight to it. And I taught him the small, tight fox steps, the glacial stealth of stalking, and to run on the balls of his feet. City stalking was different than in the forest, and in Chicago, the best way to follow someone silently was to match the cadence of their stride.

I made him lead me through the trees, following him silently as he wove his way down paths and through fields of grass gone brown with the cold. He finally stopped at the edge of the marsh and shivered when I came to stand beside him.

"You're right, you *are* that good," he said.

I shrugged my agreement.

"Don't do that," he said, sounding annoyed. "Don't shrug off a compliment."

I raised an eyebrow as I looked at him. The habit of silence always left me slowly, so what he mistook as shrugging off the compliment was really me accepting it as my due. I *was* that good. It was the compliment from him that was weird.

He seemed to exhale whatever had annoyed him and then turned his gaze back out across the marsh. "Sorry. Things don't usually get to me."

I wondered if he actually was impervious to the things that should get to him, or if he just had surprising self-control, because I had just put him through intensive drilling in bushcraft stalking techniques, and he was tired. Doubly so because he'd barely slept. I touched his arm, maybe as a gesture of understanding, but I didn't have time to contemplate my motive because there, on the back of my hand, was a red dot.

"Gun!" I shoved him away from me, hard, just as a rifle shot tore through the night.

Oliver bolted for the trees with me at his back. In the split second before I followed him, I'd calculated the trajectory of the shot that had hit the marsh just past the place where my client had stood, and figured the shooter had been fifty to seventy-five yards away—far enough that we could make it to safety. Oliver ran toward the street, and I stayed right behind him to shield him from another shot. I'd been running on the balls of my feet and he must not have heard me, because he almost jumped in front of oncoming traffic when I appeared at his side after we cleared the park.

"Shit!" he gasped when I pulled him back up on the sidewalk.

"Keep running," I urged, trying to listen for pounding footsteps behind us.

A small hybrid car passed us and then suddenly screeched to a stop in front of us. The passenger window rolled down, and I half-expected a rifle to nose out, but instead, a familiar voice yelled, "Get in!"

Oliver balked. "What the hell are you doing?" he snarled at me as I grabbed the door handle.

I'd seen the hot pink hair, so I knew it was a friend. "Lynn! You're a lifesaver," I said as I tried to shove Oliver into the back seat. He fought me with body weight and resistance, which I knew was panic, but it pissed me off nonetheless.

"Oliver!" I said sharply. "Get in."

My tone of voice must have finally registered, because he didn't push back when I shoved him into the back seat and fell in next to him.

"Go!" I said to Lynn.

She did, and a moment later the park was out of sight.

"Told you I owed you a save," she said with a look in her rearview mirror. "Saw you come tearing out of the park like death was on your heels." Her tires squealed as she rounded a corner. "Where to?"

I directed her to the street behind mine, and then caught a glimpse of Oliver's face. He looked angry and tense.

"We're fine," I murmured. "She's a friend."

He said nothing and turned back to look out the window.

When Lynn dropped us near my place a few minutes later, she opened her window. "Are you going to be okay?" Her sharp-eyed gaze went to Oliver.

"Thanks to you," I said, ignoring Oliver's frown as I handed her my card. "Call me the next time you're near the Fairbanks building. I'll take you to lunch and tell you the story."

The suspicion in her eyes let go. "Sure thing."

I caught a glimpse of her t-shirt. It read, "She needed a hero, so that's what she became." "Nice shirt," I said, and then threw her a wave as we stepped back from the car.

Oliver stood, stiff and angry on the sidewalk, but I grabbed his hand and pulled him with me. "Follow my lead," I said, determined to appear as if I were just out for a walk with my boyfriend.

He managed to pull off his usual easy loping stride as I led him to the alley that ran between the houses. I finally spoke the words that had been whispered through my brain.

"Are you okay?" I asked quietly, without looking at him.

He hesitated for a beat too long before answering. "I'm not hurt." His voice was still taut.

I exhaled and nodded. "Right."

"That was him, wasn't it?" Oliver asked, as his grip on my hand tightened reflexively.

"Probably." I'd stopped to listen to the street noises, and when I was sure we hadn't been followed, pulled him into the alley.

I turned to face him. His normal hipsterman dishevelment looked ragged and wild.

"We're going in to grab our stuff, and then we're getting a car to the office," I squeezed his hand. "You have to trust me."

Oliver practically vibrated with tension. "I just got shot at in a park around the corner from your house, and you want me to trust you?"

My first instinct was to tell him to shove it, but a long history with unreasonable clients had taught me to take a breath first, and in that brief moment, I saw the fear. It was just like what I'd told Shane that day on the boat about fear and anger. To get him through this, I had to become a wolf whisperer.

I reached behind me to the sheath at my back and took out the knife I always wore. He flinched at the sight of it in my hand, the fear becoming palpable. I turned it hilt first, and held it out to him.

"You didn't hear me running behind you in the park, did you?" I asked. His glare was his confirmation. "I positioned myself directly at your back, to take any bullet meant for you," I continued, "and now I need you to watch *my* back." That last bit was a lie that I hoped he would accept.

He didn't hear the lie because his fear was too loud, so he took the knife without meeting my eyes. I hoped I wouldn't get stabbed between my shoulder blades for trying to help.

I led the way down the alley and made him wait outside the kitchen door, knife at the ready, while I did a quick sweep of my rental. It was empty, just as we'd left it.

When I called him inside, he set the knife down on the kitchen table without a word, and I was glad to see that his hunched shoulders had somewhat relaxed.

"Get your stuff together," I said, as I handed him the bag from the drugstore that I'd stashed in my coat. Then I started to get my own things together and texted Darius for a ride.

I was pulling the clean clothes out of the dryer when Oliver called from the sitting room. "Dallas, someone named Christi is trying to reach you." His voice sounded more normal. Not friendly, but I'd come to accept that with me, not friendly was normal.

"Accept the call. I'll be right there," I called back.

Oliver stood in front of the screen of my laptop, bewildered. "She's crying."

I rushed to his side, and he stepped out of the way so I could talk to my sister. "Christi, what's wrong?"

She was sobbing, but I couldn't hear her until I unmuted us both. "Christi!"

Her words nearly got lost behind gasps. "You need to go home. Grandpop's dying."

[12]

OLIVER

"Send not your foolish and feeble; send me your strong and your sane."

- ROBERT W. SERVICE, *THE LAW OF THE YUKON*

They gave me a choice. Dallas was going home to the Yukon. I could be reassigned to another bodyguard and stay in a locked hotel room until space at The Vault was available, or I could go with her to the almost actual ends of the earth and lie low while they figured out who was trying to kill me.

Someone was trying to fucking kill me.

I chose the Yukon.

We landed in Whitehorse, the capital of the Yukon Territory, fifteen hours and two plane changes after being shot at in Chicago. I had my passport, the clothes I'd been wearing, two cases full of hard drives, and a bodyguard named Dallas who hadn't said more than ten words to me since we'd departed the city.

I'd left whatever remained of my nice-guy persona back in Humboldt

Park impaled to a tree by a bullet. I'd panicked, lashed out, and then, for some strange reason, I'd actually chosen to flee the country with a person who was totally immune to me.

It made no sense at all. None of it.

I hadn't felt true panic since the first night I'd been left alone in an empty house a very long time ago. I hadn't lashed out at anyone since I discovered the perks of being nice, and I definitely didn't spend time with people who didn't like me.

And yet, I'd chosen her to be my bodyguard. Clearly, I was losing my shit.

Dallas seemed to rouse herself from her silence when the wheels touched down, and she looked past me out the window at the snow-covered forest beyond the edges of the tarmac.

"It's going to snow tonight," she said, then met my eyes. "We'll probably get caught in it."

Oh good. More stuff not to freak out about.

A couple of the ten words she'd said to me earlier were that we had a six-hour drive in front of us. I nodded and tried to sound normal. "Whatever. It's fine."

She frowned, but I ignored her and looked out the window at a landscape of mountains and snow and spindly spruce trees, and I realized just how far outside my comfort zone I'd actually stepped.

We disembarked the plane down a staircase to the tarmac, the icy wind ripping the breath right out of my lungs. By the time we'd made it inside the gate, I was shivering.

The single luggage carousel disgorged the bags from our flight, and Dallas reached for her bright yellow North Face duffel. Until she'd pulled the big duffel out of the wardrobe at her bohemian rental and started filling it, I hadn't realized that she was leaving that place for good. A couple more of the ten words she'd said were about finding something new when she got back. *If she went back*, my mind supplied at the memory of the stricken look on her face when her sister had given her the news about her grandfather.

I tried to be a gentleman. "Do you need any help?"

She scowled so fiercely that I stepped back. "I hate that question. Of course I don't need help. You wouldn't ask a guy to help with his bag." Then she picked up the bag and slung it across her chest as if it weighed nothing.

Her reaction pissed me off. I couldn't even be polite to this woman without her biting my head off. No wonder the nicest guy in the room disappeared whenever she was around.

I figured we'd grab a taxi at the curb when we stepped outside the airport, but I clearly knew nothing about this place. I watched a couple of people from our flight get into something called the Husky Bus, which I was actually game to try, but Dallas marched past the van and out to the parking lot just beyond the terminal. She scanned the parked vehicles quickly, then headed toward a beat-up white Chevy SUV, reached under the rear bumper, and pulled out a magnetic key holder.

"You left a car here?" I still chafed from her grumpiness, but I controlled my irritation for the sake of peace.

"My cousin dropped it off for me this morning. He keeps it running when I'm not here." She unlocked the driver's side, hit the master lock, threw her duffle into the back seat, and did a Vanna White gesture presenting the vehicle to me. "Oliver, meet Polar Bear."

I got in and was greeted by a small toy polar bear stuck to the dashboard with Velcro and one of those new-agey dreamcatchers hanging from the rearview mirror. My hand went automatically to the feathers dangling from leather strips.

"A friend of mine is Ojibwe," she said, as though it explained the dreamcatcher.

"I don't know what that means," I responded, sounding like an asshole even to my own ears. I needed to get the urge to fight with her under control or she was going to kill me before the Russian did.

She darted a glance at me, as if weighing the same thought. Her self-control was better than mine though, because she gave me a real answer, not a bitchy one. "The spider woman of the Ojibwe is the protector of children, and women weave these spiderwebs to protect people they care about who travel beyond the spider woman's reach," she said as she maneuvered the SUV out of the parking lot and past a couple of two-story hotels.

"I thought they were just hippie decorations, like macramé and bundles of sage." My words were still aggressive, but at least I'd gotten my tone of voice under control.

"Sage is about the farthest thing from 'just decoration' as things get," she said sharply as she navigated to a two-lane highway. "You can line your boots with sage leaves in the summer to help with sore feet. It's antimicrobial, antibilious, and makes a decent skin salve for healing cuts and blisters."

The way she rattled off the plant medicine facts like she was giving directions to the store pushed its way past my mood, and I wasn't digging at her when I said, "You're a little bit terrifying, you know that?"

Whatever stress had been easing since we landed in the Yukon slammed back into place as her expression shuttered. "So I've been told."

"Wait, what did I say?" I mentally replayed my statement. "That you're terrifying? You're a damn bodyguard. Isn't that a good thing?"

She stared straight ahead at the nearly deserted highway. The sky was beginning to darken with the storm she'd predicted, and I tried not to feel the worry that was creeping up my spine.

"Close protection specialist," she muttered.

I sighed and rubbed my eyes. I hadn't had nearly enough sleep—in my lifetime—to be having this conversation. "Dallas, I don't know you. I know nothing about you except that you've probably saved my life two, maybe three times. Do I find that terrifying? Yes, I do. Am I intimidated by how capable you seem to be? You bet your ass. Am I glad you have those skills? With every fiber of my being. Your confidence and capability are keeping me alive, and I'll admit to selfishly wanting to stay that way. So, if I find you a little terrifying, believe me when I say that under the circumstances, that's a big damn compliment."

I couldn't tell how my exhaustion-fueled tirade had landed, since her eyes never left the road, but if I had to guess, I'd say she wasn't impressed. I stared straight ahead at the highway, which was really just a strip of pavement big enough for two cars to pass, and tried not to think.

"Thank you," she said quietly.

I didn't believe her "thank you." Even if she had been susceptible to my usual routine of charm and smiles, my compliments to her fell flat. I ran on empty where she was concerned.

"It's weird that you're bringing a client home with you," I finally said, "isn't it?"

She shrugged. "It's not normal. But my family's fringe five percent."

I looked over at her. "Fringe … what?"

She exhaled. "Every population is ninety-five percent normal. The rest are the oddballs, eccentrics, and nutjobs—the colorful five percent. And in the Yukon Territory, that's *very* colorful. My family is considered on the fringe of the five-percenters. We're not quite far enough outside normal to be truly colorful, but there are enough fallow fields of fucks in our family tree to put us firmly on the fringe."

I stared at her, waiting for the accompanying grin that alliteration deserved, but I got nothing. Either she was completely without a sense of humor, or she had the best poker face I'd ever seen. I burst out laughing, and the sound shocked both of us.

I tried a different tack. "Tell me about them. What am I walking into?"

The tiniest smile played at the corner of her mouth, and I had the sense that it was motivated by affection.

"My grandpop Isaac is Northern Tutchone Wolf Clan, originally from Pelly Crossing. He married my grandmother Araminta, who was white, and they had two girls, my mom and my auntie Rikki. But they had them later in life because Grandma Minty refused to have kids until the last residential school in the Yukon was finally closed."

"Why would a boarding school matter?" I asked.

The line of her jaw hardened, but her voice stayed neutral. "Not a boarding school. Residential schools were a government-funded assimilation tool. The idea was that if you remove and isolate First Nations and Métis kids—Métis are mixed Indigenous and Euro-Canadians—from their families, teach them English and the Bible, and forbid them their own language and traditions, eventually they just might be able to find their proper place in Canadian society."

Her tone was too mild, and I wondered what kind of control it took not to give in to the pure sarcasm of the words.

"I thought that was, like, late 1800s stuff. Westward expansion and all that."

"It's not. The last Yukon residential school closed in 1971, and the last one in Canada didn't shut down until 1996."

"That's disturbing," I said, more than a little surprised.

She shot me a quick glance. "You're interested?" She asked in a way that told me she didn't believe I could be.

"I'm bored, tired, and I've never heard about this stuff, so sure, call it interested."

She barked a humorless laugh but didn't shut down like I half-expected her to.

"My grandfather escaped from the residential school in Carcross when he was young," she began, "and they 'accidentally' shot him when they tried to bring him back. My grandmother saved his life, and her dad hid him until Grandpop was well enough for them to run away together."

"That sounds like a movie."

"Fringe five-percenters, remember?"

She watched the road in silence for a few minutes. A forest of spruce trees marched alongside the road and up into the hills. Dallas exhaled, and the edge of her anger seemed to ride the breath out. She glanced over, maybe to see if I was still awake.

"My grandma went to the regular public school in Dawson City—one school, kindergarten through high school. My grandparents inherited her dad's house in town after they were married, so they survived the Sixties Scoop, and my mom and aunt went to school there too."

"The Sixties Scoop?" I asked, back to being annoyed because she'd said it like I should know what she was talking about.

She heard my annoyance, but she answered anyway. "When the government began closing down the residential schools, they compensated for all that assimilation they were missing out on by doing poverty checks on First Nations and Métis families. Anyone clinging to traditional ways and living off the land could be determined to be living in poverty, and anyone living in 'poverty' was at risk for losing their kids. A friend of my mom's was living off-grid with her parents, hunting and fishing and growing their food, but because they didn't have electricity or running water, the government social workers took the kids and put them in foster homes."

"Christ," I muttered. "The Sixties Scoop sounds like every kid's nightmare dressed up as ice cream."

Dallas looked at me for a moment, then returned her gaze to the road. "My mom moved us to Alberta after she and my dad split up. She worked in a private school so I could get a college prep education, but even there, living in the relative safety of the city, she was very strict about the condition of my clothes—everything was always clean, pressed, and in good condition. If it couldn't be repaired, it was instantly retired. The Sixties Scoop policies actually ended in the eighties, but not in our house. I still can't go out in sweats without hearing her voice in my head telling me not to look like a wild thing."

That put a whole new spin on the buttoned-up professional look she wore in Chicago, and I found I didn't hate it quite so much with that story filling in the blanks.

"I like wild things," I said quietly, as snow began to fall on the windshield in barely visible flakes.

"Me too," she murmured, maybe not even aware that she had spoken. The light had done interesting things to her face, and there was a little bit of peace in her expression which hadn't been there before.

[13]

DALLAS

"…The snows that are older than history,
   The woods where the weird shadows slant;
   The stillness, the moonlight, the mystery,
   I've bade 'em good-by—but I can't…"

- ROBERT W. SERVICE, *THE SPELL OF THE YUKON*

It was close to midnight when we arrived at the land just south of Dawson City where my grandparents had created a family compound after their daughters had gone off to college. Grandpop had missed living off the land, and even though it took work, I'd always loved my summers there. He'd given all of us a plot to build our own place somewhere on the property, but he was the only one who still lived there full-time.

My mom and her husband, George, stayed in the two-bedroom cabin my dad had built there before I was born. George's car was parked in the cleared area we used as a parking lot, and so were Aunt Rikki's and my cousin Reed's. The light was still on in the old-fashioned sod-roofed cabin Grandpop had shared with Grandma Minty until she died a decade ago. It was a spectacular-looking two-room, stacked-log construction, with moose antlers gracing the peak of the roof and a horn handle on the heavy wood door.

Oliver woke up when I stopped the car. He had drifted off to sleep watching the snow fall, and I realized he'd only gotten a few hours of naps in the past forty-eight. He rubbed his eyes, and in the same motion, scrubbed his fingers through his hair. It was cute in a Calvin and Hobbes little boy sort of way, and I must have scowled at the thought.

"What's wrong?" he asked.

"Nothing, sorry. Just tired," I said, having zero interest in explaining that noticing cuteness about him annoyed me.

He looked around at the various cars and abodes on the property. "Are we here?"

"Yeah. It's late though. I'll show you where to sleep, and I'll give you the tour tomorrow."

He nodded, distracted by the view outside the car windows, and I tried to see it through his eyes. Grandpop was forever tinkering, and to someone who didn't know that Isaac could bring a parts-yard Pinto back to life, the place might look more like a junkyard than a homestead.

I left my bag in the car, and Oliver slung his bags over his shoulder as he crunched through the snow to follow me. I took him to the camper that was parked near my cabin. "Guest quarters," I whispered as I tugged on the sticky door and prayed no one had stashed a random hitchhiker in the camper. I didn't have to see his face to sense that he was not excited about the accommodations option.

Mercifully, the camper was empty of human habitation, and I used the flashlight on my phone to find the candles and a box of matches. I lit one and then checked to make sure the bed was intact. The upholstery on the foam mattress had been re-covered sometime in the last year—probably Mom's work—and the camper was clean.

"I'll get you a pillow and a sleeping bag," I said. "We don't keep the generator running at night, so there's no heater, but my bags are rated below zero. You should be fine."

He turned to me in surprise. "There's no heat *or* electricity?"

I tried not to laugh at his dumbfounded expression and shrugged. "Trust me, you'll be fine in the sleeping bag. And Grandpop never cared about putting in wires. We're just far enough out of town that it was going to take paperwork to get a pole."

"How am I going to finish my program?" His tone had gotten sharp in a way I was too tired to deal with.

"Sometimes there's internet, if it hasn't just snowed, and we're on generator power during the day. I'll be happy to drop you off at a hotel in town if that's what you want, but for tonight, suck it up, Buttercup." I turned to go.

"Wait, where are you going?" he said with an edge of uncertainty.

I stifled a yawn. "My place is next door. You'll be safe enough here unless you have to pee anytime after dawn. Then you're screwed."

His eyes got wide. "Bears?"

"No. Grandpop's dogs," I said. "They know my car, which is why they didn't go crazy when we drove in. But they'll need an introduction to you, so I'll come and get you in the morning."

"Oh. Okay."

I could almost hear a question mark in his tone, and I had to suppress a smirk. I set a hurricane glass around the candle and headed for the door. "Come on, I'll show you the long drop and where to wash."

He followed me out of the camper, and I took him to the wash block next. Grandpop had bought the wash block from a production that had filmed a gold mining show near Dawson a few years back, and it was his pride and joy. Each side of the structure had a shower stall and a small sink, and when the generator was running, we could usually get a decent lukewarm shower. "Don't shower tonight though," I told Oliver, as I explained the hot water heater and the slow drip of the sink and shower. "If you drain whatever's left of the hot water, the pipes will freeze overnight."

He nodded silently, and I wondered if he was shocked by how we lived. I waited while he brushed his teeth and then led him to the long wooden structure we called the long drop. It was a British term that

George had used when he first saw it, and it stuck. "If you just have to pee, go find a tree—it helps keep the deer away. If you need more privacy, use the long drop. It's a glorified outhouse, but it serves its purpose."

Oliver stared uncomprehendingly at the long wooden structure with its collection of hubcaps that hung on the outside. "*That's* an outhouse?"

"My grandfather bought it from Joe Boyle's Bear Creek compound. It's where they made all the dredges in the Yukon, so old Joe kept a big crew."

Oliver just nodded. His eyes were glazed, and I had the sense that exhaustion was starting to take over.

"Okay, well, that's my cabin," I said, pointing to the small structure just beyond his camper. "I'm going to go get your bedding, and I'll meet you back at the camper."

"Cool. I'll go do my part to keep some deer away," he said.

"Don't go far," I said. More than one city-dweller had gotten lost in the woods because of modesty.

He huffed. "I won't."

I left him and went to open up my cabin and grab my spare sleeping bag, a sheet, a pillow, and a towel. He was already back in the camper when I got there, sitting on the bed in a haze of exhaustion.

"Move," I said. He moved like an automaton, and I quickly made up his bed as he stood behind me in the small space. "Blow out the candle before you fall asleep, but memorize where the matches are so you can light it again if you need to."

The last thing I saw as I left the camper was him pulling off the Canada Goose and unbuttoning his jeans. I ducked my head and closed the door behind me.

I grabbed my bag out of the truck, tossed it into my cabin, then trudged up to Grandpop's place. I could hear hard coughing coming from inside, and the dogs were already at the door when Grandpop's voice wheezed, "That you, Sis?"

"It's me. You awake?" I half-whispered through the door.

"Come in. Damn dogs are making too much noise."

I pushed open the door and waded through three large beasts and one small one, all of whom swirled around my legs in greeting.

The light from an oil lantern was just bright enough to see Grandpop struggle to sit up in bed. I had to tamp down my instinct to rush to help him. He wouldn't appreciate it, and the dogs would have tripped me anyway, so I bent down to give them my attention while Grandpop got himself situated.

"You get in okay?" he asked. His deep voice, usually so strong and gruff, was too breathy and thin, and I thought there might be an edge of pain in it.

"Yeah. Snow started just outside Whitehorse, but it settled down." I gave Wolf, who probably had some actual wolf in her, a final ear scratch and then moved to sit on the edge of the bed. Grandpop had moved his bed out to the sitting room after Grandma died. He said her ghost took up too much space in the bedroom. All her things were still there, and I had the sense he wanted to keep a place that felt like her that he could visit when he missed her.

"How about you? How are you feeling?" I gave him a surreptitious once-over. His breathing was shallow, and the pulse in his neck beat too quickly, but that could have been from the effort of sitting upright.

"Oh, you know. Getting old isn't for puppies. Takes an old dog like me to do it right."

"Really, Pop? Christi made it sound pretty dire."

His hand fluttered dismissively. "She gets her news from your mother, and Charli never could read me like Araminta could—or you. You tell me, Sis. How'm I doing?"

I took his hand in mine and held it, assessing. His skin was cool to the touch, and rough from so many years of hard work. My grandfather had never gone back to school after he escaped from Carcross, and though Grandma Minty had taught him everything she learned in high school and college, his heart was always with the wild things that lived in the forest rather than the things painted with words on a page.

His joints were inflamed with arthritis, and his pulse wasn't strong. I studied his face in the dim lamplight, and he submitted with scowling brows and twinkling eyes. The cataracts were getting thicker, but his eyes were otherwise clear. More worrisome was the pallor under the deeply wrinkled brown skin. His breathing was too shallow, and there was a definite wheeze in his chest.

"Anyone get you oxygen?"

He chuckled, and it set off a fit of coughing. "They tried. The damn things tickle my nose and I start coughing something fierce."

"How about X-rays? They do those at the clinic?"

He gave me the ghost of a smile. "You know it's time, Sis. Been time for a while. I'm not feeling up to all those treatments and whatnot. My lungs are giving out, and a day more or less isn't going to mean too much without the breath to talk."

I swallowed the tears down and appealed to my grandfather. "What if I can get you to fish camp this summer with all the voice you need to hurl directions and give orders? Will you let me give you oxygen, maybe run a test or two and get you some meds?"

Grandpop held my gaze for a long moment as Squirrel, the dachs-hund mix, jumped up on the bed and turned in a circle to lie down. My grandfather's hand went automatically to the dog's head as he considered me. "If you can get me to one last fish camp with enough voice left to tell Araminta its stories when I get back, then yeah, I'll let you do a couple things. One or two," he scolded sternly, but his eyes sparkled like stars.

"Or three," I said, with the matching tone I learned from him. "Now, where's your green medicine?" There was an herbalist in Whitehorse who made a healing salve from plants foraged in the boreal forest that could be used on everything from bug bites to swollen joints, and we all kept tins of it in stock.

He gestured to the shelf next to his bed. I retrieved a tin, scooped out a few fingers-full, and proceeded to rub it into his hands. He tipped his head back and closed his eyes with a slight smile. "Hurts pretty good," he said. "You've got hands like your grandmother. She could heal me with a touch."

I looked down at my hands rubbing his big gnarled ones. They were lethal hands; hands I'd trained to hunt, injure, and kill.

"Tell me about your guest," Grandpop said quietly.

"You heard us?"

"The dogs did. They don't much care for being shut up when there's a stranger on the property." His eyes were open again, but they weren't judgmental—just questioning.

"He's a client. A guy from Chicago. Someone's after him there—took a shot at him when I was with him. Christi called me about you"—Grandpop snorted, and I smiled faintly, but with no real humor—"and it seemed like a good idea to leave town. We won't be in your way."

"He deserve the shot?"

I took my time answering. My grandfather would know if I didn't believe my own words, so I said ones I believed. "I think life's been pretty easy on him. He's smart, rich, good-looking, and the easy way things happen for him makes him believe his own hype. He's not especially deep, but I think there's more to him than he tells himself there is. If there were a line of people who needed shooting, he'd probably be somewhere in the middle. Maybe even toward the back."

Grandpop laid his head back against the headboard again as I finished rubbing his hands. He smiled, and the deep lines at the corners of his eyes told stories of a lifetime of smiles. "Bring him by to meet the dogs in the morning. They'll tell me where he lands in that line."

I leaned over and kissed his cheek, and tried not to hear the wheeze in his chest. "Love you, Pop."

"Love you too, Sis."

Otter and Badger had retired to the couch, Wolf was at her usual position by the door, and Squirrel was snoring like an old man on my grandfather's bed. I turned down the lamp on my way to the door, and then closed it softly behind me.

I waited until I was safely in my own cabin before I let the tears come.

[14]

OLIVER

"Shit happens."

- CONNIE EBLE, *UNC-CH SLANG*

The swim up to consciousness was long and dark, and tangled with tree limbs that grabbed my clothes and held me under the snow. When I finally got my eyes open, it was with a gasp for air, as if the avalanche had been real and sleeping had been the dream. I rarely slept long enough to reach a dream state, but when I did, my dreams were inconveniently vivid and full of all the stress I didn't show during the day.

The Cipher phone in my coat pocket read noon and had zero bars. Not a shock considering that we were at the ass end of civilization and I'd slept in a camper that wasn't even dignified enough to be called a trailer. Also not a shock that it was my bowels that woke me up. I pulled on my jeans, slipped my feet into my unlaced boots, grabbed my coat, and opened the camper door. I stood in the open doorway blinking at the blinding white of reflected light, the frigid morning air burning my lungs. Christ, it was cold. It had snowed again during the night, apparently, because there were no tracks in the snow outside the camper door. Which meant Dallas had abandoned me to the dogs.

I sighed, tucked my laces into my boots so they didn't get wet, and stepped out into the snow. It wasn't deep, just a fresh dusting on top of harder-packed ice and snow, and I was reasonably sure I could make it thirty feet to the big outhouse without losing my way.

I shielded my eyes from the light as well as I could and crunched across the snow to what Dallas had called the long drop. It was a rustic-looking, long, rectangular building—bigger than any outhouse I could imagine. But not one bit of overactive imagination could have prepared me for the interior.

The door was in the center of the building, and the first thing I noticed when I opened it was that the room didn't stink, which was either a feat of engineering, or, what … cleaning? Did outhouses get cleaned? How? A spray bottle of bleach? A flamethrower? But the thing that made me stop in my tracks was that the interior of the building was just one long, narrow room with a single boxed-in bench running the length of it that had *eight holes the size of a human butt* cut into the top at regular intervals.

A few of the holes were ringed by a toilet seat of some variety—two were porcelain, one was plastic, and two were wood. The one directly in front of the door had no seat at all, and there was a crude, handwritten note nailed to the wall behind it that told me to *GO PISS IN THE GRASS*. I was inclined to follow its direction, except I was reasonably certain my balls would freeze off if I attempted to shit in the woods. One of the other seatless holes actually had a footpad on either side of the hole. I hadn't seen that since Laos.

Even more unnerving was that almost every hole had its own … personality. There was no other word to describe it, and the need to choose one was suddenly as paralyzing as it was pressing.

I pointedly did not choose the one in the far corner with a porcelain seat where someone had mounted a magazine rack on the wall next to it, with *People* and *Us* magazines that looked several years out of date. The magazines weren't the deterrent though. It was the air freshener and the small vase containing a silk flower that sat on the box next to the seat.

A flower. In an outhouse.

There was a ledge running down the length of the wall in front of the seats, holding variously sized rolls of toilet paper and packages of wipes. My indecision about which shitter to park myself on was getting ridiculous, so I finally chose the other porcelain seat with a tattered paperback of *The Stand* and a reasonably full roll of TP in front of it. It was two holes away from the door, and the floor creaked ominously underfoot. I'd just settled in and debated picking up the book when the door flew open.

And because my day could only get stranger, a wolverine came in.

"Aahhh!" I couldn't help it, and predictably, the shit was scared right out of me.

My exclamation startled the Indigenous guy wearing the wolverine … hat?

"Who the fuck are you?" he said, and then understanding seemed to dawn and he nodded. "Oh right. The client." He started forward with his hand out to shake. "How's it going? I'm Dallas's cousin Reed."

And because I couldn't think of a way not to, I shook the guy's hand. With my jeans around my knees and my ass hanging in the frigid air over a long drop. *Ah, of course, that's why it was called the long drop.*

"Oliver Curran," I said, like it wasn't the most mortifying position I'd ever found myself in.

"Dallas was looking for you," he said, as he flung the door open and yelled, "He's in here!" Then Reed, wearing an actual wolverine pelt on his head, dropped his jeans and parked himself on one of the wooden seats three holes away.

And there ensued the most awkward two minutes of my life.

"Guns, gold, or *Gourmet*?" Reed asked, nonsensically.

"Uh …" I was forced to look at him to understand. He held out three magazines for my perusal. "*Gourmet*?"

The wolverine face grinned at me from above Reed's own as he handed me the cooking magazine. The other two appeared to be about gun collecting and gold mining, which were apparently hot topics this far north.

I opened the three-year-old magazine to a "chipped beef on toast" recipe, and then had to wrestle incredulous laughter into submission when I remembered that chipped beef on toast is otherwise known as shit on a shingle, which was a good description of my current situation, crapping in the woods on a bench next to another guy, trying to decide if it was worse to stay and finish my business with all the noise that went along with a successful shit, or to wipe my ass in front of him and attempt a dignified exit.

Pounding on the door settled it. "Oliver, are you in there?" Dallas called.

I've never wiped my ass so fast in my life.

Reed looked up from his magazine and laughed at my bewildered expression as I considered my hands and the lack of running water in the room.

"That's what the wipes are for," he said cheerfully.

"Oliver?" Dallas called again.

"Give the man a minute, Dal!" Reed called back, and I was grateful.

There was yet another moment of confusion as I held the soiled wipe and looked for a trash bin. Reed nodded toward the drop. "Throw it down there. It'll freeze with everything else. This one's a ten-year hole, and it's got another five years left on it."

I had so many questions, but asking them of a man in an outhouse required more fortitude than I had on an empty stomach, so I did what he said, then handed him back his magazine. "Thanks."

"Anytime," Reed said as I left the long drop, and I sincerely hoped not.

Dallas wore a vaguely smirkish expression that on other people would be hysterical laughter. "You met my cousin, I see."

"Memorable introductions seem to run in the family," I said with as neutral an expression as I could manage.

Then she did laugh, and I was captivated. Laughter made her interesting face arresting. I had absolutely no idea what to do with that observation, or with the flush of heat it provoked, so I shoved it away and pretended I hadn't noticed.

"Come on, let's see how you handle meeting my grandpop." She started walking toward a cabin that looked like it had horns sprouting from it. I pulled back.

"Can I go wash my hands and brush my teeth first, please? Something died in my mouth last night, and I'm terrified enough as it is without worrying about killing the man with my breath."

She chuckled again. "Sure. I'll walk you though, just in case the dogs are out."

"Right. The dogs. Which you left me to this morning. Thanks for that," I grumbled.

"Sorry I didn't leave a wake-up call with the concierge," she said with absolutely none of the snark that statement deserved. I refused to forgive her though. She hadn't warned me I'd be staying in a glorified trailer park when she said I could go with her.

Go home with her. To her dying grandfather. We crunched through the snow in silence for a few steps before I let go of my annoyance. "You've already seen him?" I asked. She knew who "him" was.

"Yeah." That was all she said for another few silent steps. When we were almost to the camper door, she finally spoke again. "He'll let me get some tests run and said he'll try oxygen again, but whatever it is has settled in. He says he's not going to outrun the bullet this time."

"That's rough," I said, actually meaning it.

She met my eyes and nodded. "Yeah." Then she tossed her head toward the camper door. "Get your stuff. I'll wait."

"Any chance I can get some coffee?" I asked, trying to pull some charm on for the cause.

She regarded me dispassionately. "Only if you brought some with you."

I grumbled something unintelligible and left her standing outside. Ten minutes later, after a brisk washing of my hands, face, and teeth, we were headed toward the antler cabin.

My first impression of Dallas's family compound was that it was about a step and a half up from an equipment yard that happened to be situated deep in the boreal forest. But in the midday sun, with a fresh coat of powder dusting a couple of trailers, three log cabins, a small backhoe, and several trucks in various states of repair, it seemed more like a haphazard settlement full of different personalities.

Again with that impression of personalities, except my only experience with them so far was a bodyguard, a wolverine, and an outhouse.

There was a path worn in the snow to the antler cabin door, and the building itself was ringed by paw prints of various sizes. The cabin's roof was planted with sod, and the antlers that sprouted from the peak of its roof were massive.

"What kind of antlers are those?" I asked Dallas as we stepped up onto the porch. My voice was the trigger for a symphony of barking behind the heavy front door, which let most of northern Canada know we'd arrived.

"Bull moose. He was trying to kill Grandpop."

"Wow. I didn't know moose … mooses … meece …?" I paused hopefully and got another brief smile from Dallas.

"Moose," she said, apparently amused by my idiocy.

"I didn't know moose were predators."

"They're not predators, they're protectors. The forest is their home. It's where they raise their young, find their mates, and spend their lives. In the spring, the mama moose will kill to protect her calf, and in the fall it's the males that are most dangerous. Mating season."

"Ah, right. Probably not a good idea to get between a moose and his mate."

Dallas looked up at the massive antlers over our heads. "See that stain on the right side—the biggest prong?"

"Yeah?" The prong she indicated was tipped darker than the others on the rack.

"That's Grandpop's blood. He hung the rack to remind him that he only lived because his luck was better that day, but it won't always be. He says that moose reminded him to love like it was the only thing in life that mattered, because even a moose knows love is worth putting your life on the line for."

She ducked her head away from my gaze as she knocked on the door. I was still staring up at the brown-stained prong when a voice called out for us to come in.

The dogs—four or forty of them, it was hard to tell—came rushing out to the porch to tell me they had my number and if I put a step wrong, they'd have more than that. I, however, had a secret weapon. I was unintentionally, irrationally fearless of animals. Basically, although I respected the dogs' right to defend their territory, my body language and scent told them in no uncertain terms that I was not their problem.

From the time I was a kid, I'd been a dog and cat and bird whisperer. I had a pet crow that I'd saved from a dog when I was eleven, and it hung around my house even after its wing had healed until it finally disappeared when I was thirteen. I named him Raven because it sounded more majestic than Crow, and I went through a period of Edgar Allen Poe idolatry while he was around, just for the literary connection to my obsession with a bird who thought I was mildly useful for a time.

I crouched down and held my hands out. "Hello, beauties," I said as they sniffed my hands with varying degrees of suspicion. The little dachshund came first with an enthusiastic wiggle as she stood up to kiss my face.

"The fresh one's Squirrel. She thinks she's Grandpop's favorite," Dallas said. I could hear the smile in her voice.

I reached out a hand to a boxer mix. "And who's this handsome boy?" He came toward me no less enthusiastically than Squirrel had, butting his head under my hand for an ear rub.

"That one's Otter, and this is Badger," she said, as a smaller mix of something street with something stray, with colors ranging from pure white to beige, charged in for attention.

I had my hands full with three dogs, demanding whatever fingers I'd scrub through their fur. One dog hung back after her initial charge out the door. She stood just inside the cabin, feet spread and body rigid as she watched me with her man.

The man in question gave a short, sharp whistle, and the three dogs swarming me fell back to give me room to stand. "Take your boots off and come inside where I can get a look at you," he said in a gruff voice that would have been commanding if a fit of juicy coughing hadn't racked him as he spoke.

I stood and brushed my hands off on my jeans before kicking off my boots in the small mudroom entrance and stepping inside the cabin. My eyes were focused on the man in the bed, but I was peripherally aware that the space, though not large, was comfortable and warm. A wood stove burned in one corner, and hand-knit throws covered the couch and chairs in colorful patterns.

A full-sized bed fit into an area that had probably held a dining table at one time, and the man in it was sitting against the headboard, propped up on pillows. He was remarkable-looking. I saw echoes of his broad cheekbones in Dallas's. Reed, who I realized in retrospect was so handsome he was practically beautiful, looked even more like his Indigenous grandfather, with a strong jaw, and the same broad cheekbones. But deep lines etched this man's bronze skin, even though his long, thick, white hair still had some black strands woven through it. My fingers itched to snap his photo, but a healthy sense of self-preservation and a crappy burner phone knocked the impulse into submission.

"Someone wants you dead, huh?" he said, his gaze sharp even if his voice wasn't. "You deserve it?"

I shrugged and knew he'd see right past something as insubstantial as words. "Not for the reasons they think."

He grunted, and I couldn't tell what his expression meant, so I stayed quiet. I may have been unfazed by animals, but certain people could scare the crap out of me. Dallas's grandfather was one of them. Come to think of it, Dallas was another one.

"You going to get my granddaughter killed?" he finally asked.

"No, sir," I said automatically. "I sincerely doubt anyone could."

"Hmph. Haven't met many stupid people, have you? They're the ones who get other people killed."

So, he'd been asking if I was stupid. Good to know.

"Pop," Dallas said, before I could think up a reply, "I'm going to take Oliver into Dawson to get a couple things. Will you come with us? I'd like to get you a chest X-ray and maybe see about getting some oxygen."

The old man snorted. "I told you, the oxygen makes the cough worse." As if to punctuate the statement, he had a coughing fit so hard it made him breathless. Dallas rushed to the kitchen to fill a glass of water, and while she was gone I leaned in so she couldn't hear my words.

"Stupid people don't just get *other* people killed."

The look he shot me was loaded with something lethal, and it took every ounce of self-control I had not to flinch. Dallas returned with water, and her glance at me was full of the promise of pain if I'd upset her grandfather. I sat in one of the chairs near the bed and said in my most casual tone, "I'd appreciate any insight you have about how to keep my stupidity from hurting Dallas."

He glanced at me and then turned his gaze to his granddaughter. "I told you I'd let you do one or two things to keep me alive. I'll give you this one, but I don't want to see anyone I know."

She scoffed. "So, what? Should we borrow one of Rori's superhero masks to hide your face? You know everyone in Dawson, Pop. The only thing I can promise is that we won't actively search for your friends."

He shot me another glare and then huffed a sigh that almost started another coughing fit. "Fine. Go get your truck warm, and this one will help me out."

"I can—" Dallas started.

"Leave an old man his dignity, Sis," Isaac grumbled.

Dallas swallowed the smile his grumpy tone provoked, and got up to leave. "Five minutes," she said to me.

I saluted, and she rolled her eyes as she left.

"Surprised it's taken them so long to take a shot at you," he murmured to me when the door had closed behind her.

"Me too," I said as I stood. "How can I help you?" I'd worked on the phrasing of that question ever since Dallas had bit my head off about asking someone if they needed help, and it seemed to mollify the older man into giving me an answer.

Six minutes later, Isaac had a cane in one hand and my arm in the other, and we were making our way down the path to Dallas's truck. I helped her get him situated in the front seat, then climbed in the back seat to find the big shepherd mix already seated behind the driver's seat, presumably so she could keep an eye on her pack.

"That's Wolf, by the way," Isaac said by way of introduction.

"Is she one?" I asked.

"They all are in spirit. Some are just less shit at it than others," he said, as Dallas climbed in.

I turned to Wolf. "You're not a shit wolf."

She gave me a look that said *clearly not*, and we left it at that.

The drive into town was about twenty minutes, and I was only a little bit surprised to discover that the place looked like a movie set for an old Western. Only one road—the main highway which turned to follow the Klondike River—was paved, and what sidewalks there were in the commercial district were wooden boardwalks. There was also zero cell service to be found. I wasn't sure if it was the crappy burner phone's fault or if we were genuinely off-grid in the frozen North. It wasn't an optimal condition for doing the kind of business that would get me out of there, but I let myself indulge in the novelty of it for a day. I was pretty sure I'd be climbing the walls to escape after that.

Dallas walked me into the Raven's Nook, which had sort of a Colorado-outfitter's vibe. I liked the name of the place even before I kicked the snow off my shoes with a boot brush, and when Dallas told Ekaterina, the pretty cashier from someplace in Eastern Europe, to put my purchases on her tab, I liked it even better.

"Get yourself a knife too," Dallas said with a glance at the glass case full of pocket knives.

"What if I'm not feeling stabby?" I said innocently.

"There's a word for a guy without a knife in the North," she said drily.

"Dull? Unarmed? A … spoon?" I answered tentatively, with the most charming smile in my arsenal aimed at Ekaterina, who giggled.

Dallas, still obviously immune, pivoted with a sigh. "I'll meet you at the Day Pit when I'm done at the hospital. Kat can tell you how to get there."

She handed me Canadian cash, just in case, and left to take Isaac to the hospital for a chest X-ray. I had all the questions. *Was it an actual pit? Was there a Night Pit? An Armpit?* But first I had clothes to buy.

I was one of those strange species of male who actually liked shopping for clothes. Not the trying-on part, because boots and jeans and tiny cubicles were a shit-show waiting to happen, but choosing colors, fabrics, and styles entertained me. The Raven's Nook seemed to be sort of a one-stop-shop emporium for men's and women's clothing, and everything was functional, practical, and warm. The full rack of Canada Goose parkas drew me like a moth to a flame, and suddenly my own bomber-style jacket seemed lame and insubstantial. There were fixed-blade knives and pocket knives, boots showcased on their shoeboxes, every sort of Carhartt coverall and plaid shirt, and a remarkable selection of high-visibility vests, shirts, and jackets. There was even a black dress shirt with high-vis piping that I briefly considered buying as a nightclub shirt for when I got back to civilization, but I wasn't actually spending my own money until I got billed for it all, so it seemed like a little too much.

"It's for the gold miners," Ekaterina informed me. "Safety first."

"Do you sell gold pans too?" I asked, only a little cheekily.

"No." She gave me a look like I was an idiot. "You get those at the hardware store."

Of course you did. The old days of the outfitters and storekeepers mining the miners weren't so old after all.

I wandered around the shop, and Ekaterina trailed after me commenting on the types of people who had bought each item. "The tourists love those wolf shirts," she said, as I held up a particularly vivid, heavy cotton shirt with a wolf's head tie-dyed on the front. "And Wolf Wednesday was a thing a couple of years back, so even a few of the summer locals got them."

"Summer locals?" I asked, feeling up a bright blue Henley shirt for softness. Ekaterina's eyes were locked on my hand, and I gave the fabric a little extra stroke just to mess with her.

"Uh, yeah." She seemed to remember I'd asked a question. "Just over a thousand people live here year-round, but a bunch of people come up after spring breakup—like the population doubles because of tourists and music and art stuff."

"Spring break*up*?" I asked.

She nodded. "The river's an ice road to West Dawson during the winter. People bet on the exact date it'll break up every year." She leaned in close like she was telling me a secret. "Spring is also the time when people who chose their winter warmer poorly break up with them, so things start to get interesting in town too."

A winter warmer was an odd designation for what I assumed was a relationship, and it made seasonal sex sound about as exciting as a hot water bottle.

I tried on a few things while Ekaterina continued to regale me from outside the dressing room with anecdotes about some of the summer residents she'd known. And by known, she meant *known*. I smiled at the naughtiness of her tone. Not being able to see me must have made her brave, which was cute. I thought that if I were a summer tourist to this small river town to the north of everywhere, I might be enticed into a one-night hookup with someone like Ekaterina—pretty, curvy in all the right places, friendly, and clearly interested. But I wasn't a summer tourist, or even a winter warmer, and I didn't really need locals thinking too hard about who I was or why I was there.

I added a large pocket knife to the small pile of items on the counter when I checked out, along with a much-needed pair of gloves, a few pairs of socks and underwear that we hadn't had time to get in Chicago, and the blue Henley. I wouldn't admit to Dallas that she was right, of course, but carrying a knife felt good in a place that sold gold pans in the hardware store.

"I know Dallas told you to meet her at the Pit, but the Downtown is just across the street. Everyone who comes to Dawson has to get the toe. It's practically a tradition."

I detected a hint of mischief in Ekaterina's voice, but I decided to play along. "Practically a tradition, huh? I probably shouldn't ignore something so monumental."

"Oh, the toe isn't something that can be ignored," she said with a spark of playfulness.

I wondered if Dallas was ever playful. Except for one brilliant moment of laughter, I didn't think I'd ever seen a spark of anything more than the slightest smirk on her face. The realization made me want to do something outrageous, just to see if I could make her play with me.

"You'll tell Dallas where I went?" I asked Ekaterina as I tore the tags off my new gloves and put them on.

"Sure thing. It's just right across the street," she said as she handed me my bags. "Just remember to ask for *the toe*."

The Downtown Hotel was a big, red, two-story building with a white-painted balcony that added to its distinctly Western flavor. Pushing open the saloon doors to the bar was like stepping back in time.

Inside, I was assaulted by red flocked wallpaper, moose antlers—plural—and the ubiquitous brass footrest in demand at hotel bars the world round. The bartender, a big white guy with grizzled gray hair, looked up when I came in and raised an eyebrow when he didn't recognize me.

"Hey, how's it going? Ekaterina told me I needed to order the toe. That mean anything to you?"

"Kat sent you? You sleeping with her?" he asked, with an interesting tone of curiosity.

"Uh, no?" I wasn't sure why I was questioning it. "I just bought some stuff at the Raven's Nook, and she said I should come here."

He grunted something and then smacked an empty shot glass on the bar.

"Hey, Client!" a man's voice called across the room, and I turned to see Dallas's cousin saunter in.

"Hey, Wolverine." I smiled back. Reed's wolverine hat was kind of growing on me as a fashion statement.

Reed joined me at the bar and looked down at the glass the bartender had filled while I was admiring a dead animal. "Your first toe?"

I looked at the glass, now filled with a shot of something that looked like whisky, in which floated a very brown, presumably preserved human toe. "Well, that's something," I said, because really, what else could a guy say when a mummified toe floated in his drink?

"I'm about a foot in, myself," he said with a grin. "I'll take a beer. Thanks, Si."

Si, the bartender, looked sideways at me as he got Reed's beer. "No putting it in your mouth. Last guy did that swallowed it."

"It was weeks until they got it back," Reed added solemnly.

"Got it …" I tried not to think too hard about the toe's provenance, and just focused on the fact that it had been pickled in enough alcohol to kill a germ at fifty paces.

Si continued with his recitation of the rule as if Reed hadn't spoken. "You swallow it, you pay twenty-five hundred. Had to up it from five hundred after some damn tourist swallowed it, slapped the money on the bar, and said it was worth it. Toes are too hard to come by. Not enough frostbite these days."

I was nodding along as if to say yeah, *sucks there aren't more people losing toes these days,* when really, I was debating my odds of keeping my dignity without drinking the damn thing.

"Just touch your lips to it and call it done," Si concluded.

"Kiss the toe," Reed added with a grin. "That's in your wheelhouse, isn't it, Client?"

Si narrowed his gaze at me. "Dallas taking on clients again?" he asked Reed while his eyes never left my face.

"Not your business, Si," said a female voice at my shoulder. Dallas reached past me to the shot glass, which she downed in one smooth move. She winced at the taste presumably, because the toe remained in the otherwise empty glass.

"Ugh, serving from the bottom shelf now?" she said with a shudder.

I must have looked as dumbstruck as I felt, because she raised an eyebrow at my expression. "I did you a favor. Now you can back out with your manliness unquestioned, or you can ask for a shot of the good stuff to distract you from the evil that lies within," she said, indicating the blackened toe.

"I'll have a shot of Lagavulin 16," I said, spotting the high-end Scotch on the shelf, and then added with mock seriousness, "With the toe." My manliness was not to be questioned.

I turned to Dallas. "How'd the X-ray go?"

She shot me a glare with edges, and Si raised an eyebrow. "You sick, Dal?"

"Nah, it's a chick thing. Nothing to see here," Dallas lied as smoothly as glass. She met my eyes. "Just came to see if you wanted to ride back with me or stay and drink with your new friends?"

I'd pissed her off talking in front of other people. "Let's go." I stood up, downed my whisky, kissed the toe, and slapped two Canadian twenties on the bar. Then I grabbed my coat and bags, shot Reed a wry grin, and followed her out.

[15]

DALLAS

"This is the Law of the Yukon, that only the Strong shall thrive;
That surely the Weak shall perish, and only the Fit survive."

- ROBERT W. SERVICE, *THE LAW OF THE YUKON*

Grandpop was asleep in the truck when we got back to it, which wasn't surprising given the fight he'd put up with the doctor, so the ride home was silent. Oliver helped me get him back to bed, where Squirrel promptly curled up next to him. Old man and tiny dog were asleep before we even left the cabin.

"You haven't eaten anything, have you?" I said, so I could focus on anything else besides my own feeling of helplessness where my grandfather was concerned.

He shook his head, just as his stomach gave a mighty growl.

"And that shot's hitting you right about now. Twenty-minute lag time?"

"Yep. Pretty much."

He looked a little glassy-eyed, so I propelled him toward my cabin. "Come on. I'll feed you before I take you to meet my mom and George."

"Oh goody. More people to alienate," he said, but without the joking tone I'd been expecting.

I scowled at him. "What's wrong with you?"

He scowled back. "Nothing. What's wrong with you?"

I didn't dignify that with a response, and instead grabbed the bag of groceries from my truck that I'd picked up in town and led him to my cabin. I didn't have to lock it when family was at the compound because we were too far off the main road, and I'd left the fire banked in the wood stove so it was warm enough inside to leave our coats in the mudroom with our boots.

"Very nice," Oliver said, looking around at the 15'x15' room. It wasn't big, but I'd built, made, or salvaged everything in it, so it was mine.

"Thank you," I said brusquely. I busied myself making a sandwich, which I shoved in his hands as soon as it was done. "Eat. We'll talk when you have something in your stomach."

He ate while I chopped vegetables for a chicken soup. When he'd finished, he wandered over to the table I used for cooking prep. "Tell me about Isaac's X-ray," he said.

I handed him a cutting board, carrots, and a knife, and while I was pulling spices from the plastic bins where I stored them, I told him the words that had been burning themselves into my brain. "The doctor said he has TB," I said without looking at him.

His knife stopped moving for a few seconds, and when he finally began chopping again, he said, "That's actually not terrible news. There's a four-drug cocktail for tuberculosis that'll knock it out, especially if it's an old case from before the drug-resistant strains."

I looked up and stared at him. "Yeah, I know, but how do you know all of that?"

"I had TB when I was in college."

"You … what?"

He shrugged. "I'd just finished finals and was wiped out when I went to visit my grandmother, who was dying of lung cancer. Turns out she'd been exposed to tuberculosis when she was young, and it went dormant in her. The lung cancer probably knocked her immune system out, activating the TB, and because I was in a weakened state, I picked it up from her. It took them a couple months to diagnose it in me because I didn't fit the profile."

"What, you weren't homeless or an IV drug user?" I was mostly joking.

"Pretty much." He frowned because he might have caught the edge of a real question in my joke. "Anyway, my treatment was six months of meds, and after two months, I was basically fine. It sounds all dire and Victorian, but TB's totally treatable."

"The doctor wanted to check him into the hospital in Whitehorse right away, but Pop told him to go to hell," I said.

"Shocker." Oliver scraped the chopped carrots into the pot I had on the wood stove.

I allowed myself a small smile when his back was turned. "Yeah, well, the policy is to supervise the meds in the hospital so people don't stop taking them when they feel better. He gave Pop his first dose right there, and said I need to bring him back tomorrow for another."

"They're trying to prevent drug resistance," he said. "It's the same in Boston. I had to convince the department of health that I could take my own meds without someone watching me do it."

I watched him chop more carrots and forgot to look away when he met my eyes. "Will you help me convince the doc to let me give Pop the meds?"

"Yeah, of course," he said, without hesitation.

A weight shifted off my chest, and I smiled with relief. "Thank you."

His eyes widened in surprise, but he covered it with a casual shrug. "Sure. No problem. I can do whatever needs to be done."

"Thanks." I looked away, then bent my head to pull an onion from the bag. I waited until I'd cut away the outside before I let myself let go of some of the tension that I'd been carrying.

He didn't speak again, except to ask if I wanted oil or butter for the pot. He stood at the stove and stirred the vegetables. I added stock and a package of chicken thighs, then dumped a mix of sweet curry, salt, smoked paprika, and thyme into the pot. I clapped a lid on it and then pulled a cup of water out of the bucket of ice I'd melted from the river that morning. I dunked a washcloth in it and tossed it to Oliver. "Here, for your hands and the knife." I did the same for my own with another cloth, then rinsed them and hung both on a small line I kept strung behind the stove.

Oliver sat on a futon I'd fixed and re-covered. He looked around, and I tried to see my cabin through his eyes. The futon was pushed up against a wall, and I threw big pillows and a rug on it during the day to turn it into seating. I'd built shelves on one wall that held books and my collection of the rocks I brought back from my trips into the mountains. The kitchen corner of the room was really just my dining table, a bench, and more shelves. Those held the herbs and medicines I foraged, dishes I'd made and fired at the art center, and my knives. I'd also had a trapdoor cut into the floor so I could dig down into the permafrost to create a small cold cellar for food storage.

There were bundles of last summer's herbs and flowers hanging from the ceiling waiting to be made into medicines or stripped and stored in jars, and the only color in the room came from the bright quilt I'd sewn when I was in high school. My grandma Minty was a quilter, and it was the last big project we finished together before she died.

"What's the deal with this place?" Oliver said.

I met his eyes and tried to answer the question without getting personal. "My grandparents bought the land after my mom and Aunt Rikki left home. You saw Dawson City—the lots are just big enough for a house and a bit of yard, and I guess Grandpop missed the traditional ways of living he'd grown up with. He built their cabin, and later, when my mom was pregnant with me and my aunt was pregnant with Reed, the sisters wanted to raise their families here together. So, my dad built a two-room cabin here for us, and he brought in the ATCO trailer and converted it to a bunkhouse for Aunt Rikki's family."

"Impressive. Is your dad in construction?"

I shook my head. "He's a long-haul and ice road trucker, so Mom basically raised me here alone, even before they split up."

I had been three years old then, but at that point my dad was just a guy who showed up for a night or two every few months.

"You didn't go to school here though," Oliver said. I was surprised he remembered that. I didn't really think he'd been listening.

I shook my head. "Mom moved us to take a job at a private school in Alberta. She met George there, and they got married and had Christi. But we spent every summer here. I started building this place when I was sixteen."

The main window in my cabin looked out onto spruce trees and had no view of the buildings I'd described, but Oliver's attention had moved between it and my face. His gaze finally settled on me when he spoke. "That was the barest list of facts I've ever heard."

I got up and grabbed a wooden spoon to stir the pot on the stove. "You asked, I answered."

"You read off a grocery list."

I stared at him. "Really? You're picking a fight because I didn't give you my life's story?"

He held my stare. "Yeah, I guess I am." He rubbed the back of his neck and squeezed his eyes shut for a second. "Sorry. You don't owe me anything."

I put the lid back on the soup and balanced the spoon on top of the pot. "Actually, I do," I said. "You're willing to help me with Grandpop, and that means everything." I faced the window and looked out at the view I'd so carefully chosen when I planned my cabin. "I don't usually talk about myself, and it's hard to do without feeling like …" I sighed. "I don't know. I'm just used to being the only one."

"The only one who what?" he asked quietly.

I shrugged, still not meeting his eyes. "Who takes care of things?"

He watched me in silence, and I could feel his gaze. Then he stood and pulled on his coat. "Come on, introduce me to your mom, and then I'll leave you alone." He was smiling the way he did with other people who weren't me, and I thought he must have pulled on the nice-guy routine in anticipation of meeting Mom.

"I warn you now, she's nothing like me."

He chuckled. "Then we'll get along perfectly."

I couldn't help laughing too, and his smile got even bigger as he followed me out the door.

[16]
OLIVER

Dallas's mom was cool. She was shorter than Dallas, and her Indigenous heritage was more obvious. She also had an easy, funky style—a blend of vintage and handmade that contrasted with her daughter's usual starch. She smiled at me easily and reached her hand out to draw me inside her cabin.

"You're Oliver the client. Pop said you're an asshole."

I barked a startled laugh and looked at Dallas to see if her mom was serious. Apparently she was, because I caught the twitch of a smile at the corner of Dallas's mouth.

"It's nice to meet you, Mrs. … I'm sorry, I don't know your last name," I said.

"It's Thorpe, but call me Charli," she said. "And this"—she gestured to a tall, dark-haired white man seated at the table—"is my husband, George."

I walked over to shake his hand. "Good to meet you, sir."

Charli met her daughter's eyes and mouthed something that I didn't catch. Based on Dallas's frown, it was something that annoyed her, which meant it was probably about me. Why annoying Dallas had become a sport for me was a mystery, but it had, and I was good at it.

"I'm glad you got your grandfather to go in for tests," Charli said to Dallas, when we were all seated around the table. Charli had put out crackers and cheese, and I reached for them automatically as Charli turned her gaze to me and explained. "My dad wouldn't even let my sister take him to the hospital when she found him on the floor of his cabin. That's why Christi called Dallas. She's the only one of us who can get him to do things. She's had him wrapped around her finger since she was born."

Dallas's eyebrows drew together. "I just wanted to learn what he had to teach," she said to me.

"What kind of stuff did you learn from him?" I asked, well aware that I was playing "annoy Dallas." And if she didn't want to answer, I was pretty sure her mother would. Dallas seemed to know it too, because she answered the question with the frown that added points to my score. "Mostly he just taught me how to survive."

"Did Dallas tell you that she used to guide hunting parties into the mountains in the summers during high school and college?" Charli asked me.

I stared at Dallas. "Hunting parties? You mean like big-game hunts?"
She nodded silently.

"Wow. I've heard about those. A lot of the guys in big tech come back from Alaska and Canada bragging about all the things they killed." Which wasn't that much different than the trips I'd gone on with my friends, except we bragged about the waves we rode.

"Yeah, my clients were all just like you." She said it in a curiously flat tone, almost as if she wanted to spit, but swallowed instead. I sensed that questions about her clients would do more than just annoy her, so I changed the subject.

"Do you guys live here full-time?" I asked Charli and George.

Charli told me a detailed story about their lives in Alberta, George's work as a teacher, her work as an admin at the school where she met him, and their daughter Christi, who had moved to Vancouver to go to culinary school. Charli was a great storyteller, and from the animation in her expression, I could tell she loved her life. George watched his wife with pride, and though he answered direct questions, he seemed content to let her do all the talking.

I glanced at Dallas and saw a similar expression on her face. She loved her mom and was glad that she was happy. Dallas caught me looking and raised an eyebrow. I raised mine back.

Charli directed a question to Dallas. "Speaking of your sister, when is she coming?"

"She gets into Whitehorse tomorrow morning, and then she's riding up with a friend," Dallas said.

"Which friend?" It wasn't a casual question. Charli sounded concerned.

"A guy named Max she went to summer school here with."

"Oh." Charli seemed relieved. "I know Max's mom. That's okay, then."

I glanced at Dallas to gauge her reaction to her mother's overprotectiveness, but it seemed normal to her.

Charli invited us to eat dinner with them, but Dallas said she had soup that we needed to get back to, but maybe we'd see them later at the fire pit.

"I know you're sleeping in the camper, and that you're a client," Charli said to me as she walked us to the door, "but we don't cater to people who stay here on the compound, so you're not a guest. Treat it like a home and take responsibility for yourself." And with that interesting comment, she squeezed my hand and closed the door behind us.

"I like your mom," I said, as we headed back toward Dallas's cabin, "and your stepdad seems like a nice guy."

"He thinks the sun rises and sets on her. It's my favorite thing about him," she said.

We walked in silence for the few minutes it took to cross the compound. The sun was getting low in the sky, and it had gotten significantly colder, which was saying something.

"How old is your sister?" I asked as she pushed open the door to her cabin. The scent of chicken soup filled the air, and I was suddenly ravenously hungry.

"Christi?" she asked, surprised. "She's twenty."

"Was it weird that your mom was so worried about who she'd be driving from Whitehorse with? I mean, she talked about you guiding hunting parties as a sixteen-year-old with pride, but she seemed freaked out about a twenty-year-old getting a ride with a friend."

The caring, involved mom was strange enough in my world. Overprotectiveness was a completely foreign concept.

Dallas used a towel to pull the heavy cast iron pot off the wood stove. She set it down on a metal trivet, grabbed a ladle, and spooned out two bowls. "It's not weird if you're First Nations," she said. "Indigenous women are targets. It's a significant problem. As for why she doesn't worry about me?" she said wryly as she blew on a spoonful of soup. "I'm always armed."

I stared at her. "You say that like it's the most normal thing in the world."

She raised an eyebrow as she took a bite of soup. "What, to be armed, or that the National Inquiry into Missing and Murdered Indigenous Women and Girls is an actual thing?"

"That's fucked up," I said.

"You think?" she said casually, over another bit of soup.

I looked at her for a moment, then shook my head and took a bite of my food. "I don't know how you can sit there eating soup like what you just said is ... *normal*."

"What?" she asked, narrowing her eyes in judgment. "You think I should be an activist like your parents, or out protesting in the street?"

Dallas studied my reaction like she was just waiting for me to push her.

So I did, because she brought up my parents. "Yeah," I said. "I do."

She didn't rise to the bait. She just arched an eyebrow as she blew on the hot soup. "I've been angry," she said, "totally, justifiably, righteously furious. And you know the only thing that affected?" She concentrated on cooling a bite of her soup. "My mood. I'm just too tired to be as angry as I could be, because I'd rather put all that energy into something I can actually do something about."

I frowned. "So, it's not worth your anger?"

Her gaze sharpened. "Not if I'm not willing to step out in front of it, it isn't."

"What does that mean, to step out in front of it?" I challenged.

"I'm not going to take on the RCMP, or the government, or the legal system. Culture is too big for one person to affect alone."

"But you're not alone. Being a woman is belonging to a group. First Nations is a group. Canadian is a group, hell, *human* is a group." I didn't know why I was pushing so hard. It had nothing to do with me, but my "annoy Dallas" sport had become something more. Something personal.

"Why is it *my* fight?" she said. "Why is it wrong for me to sit this one out?"

"It should be someone's fight," I muttered, angrier than this conversation warranted, but I didn't care. It felt like leftover anger from everything I hadn't said. "You crawled all over me for selling my tech to ADDATA without caring about their intentions or having a—what'd you call it?—ethical conscience? How is sitting out a fight like this ethical?"

"Why don't you take it on, then?" she shot back. "It isn't enough that I have to battle the issue in my personal life? You're human too. Sitting on top of the food chain makes you *responsible* for the condition of the ecosystem."

She was flushed, and the heat of her own anger made her eyes spark, and suddenly I wanted to kiss her.

Shit. I pushed back from the table and walked across the room to stare out the window and get myself under control. This woman was the opposite of my type. She was too serious, too capable, too fierce, too intelligent, far too deadly, and my life was literally in her hands. I had every reason to stay very far away from her, and yet here I was, battling an attraction that had nothing to do with anything even remotely normal for me.

I made myself turn to study her. She was still annoyed, probably at herself for having shown any emotion, and she forced herself to meet my eyes. I could tell she didn't want to, but she would have tied herself to her seat rather than be the one to leave the room. She glared, and with that glare, she defied me to defend myself.

"You're fucking magnificent," I finally said. Apparently, my words were an adequate self-defense, because the woman who had an answer for everything was speechless.

And then, because I didn't know what else to do, I left.

[17]

DALLAS

"The social structure of the Northern Tutchone people is historically led by women and Elders. We are matrilineal, and the 'word' of the Elders is law—they are our knowledge keepers. But as they pass, a lot of valuable knowledge goes with them. Residential schools broke up the social structure of communities and families and led to major gaps in knowledge. Now there is a great effort to practice our traditions to keep them alive and to revitalize our language, which in itself will never be the same."

\- DARCIE PROFEIT

What the hell?

I stared at the closed door of my cabin as if Oliver were going to walk back in with his usual charming smirk and tell me it had all been a joke. Whatever *it* was—he was only pushing my buttons to get a rise. He was bored, and provoking me took the edge off the fact that he was stuck in the middle of nowhere with only a grumpy "bodyguard" for company.

I needed to get outside. I needed to breathe air so cold it hurt my lungs, and to do whatever it took to focus my mind on something other than my client and his damn words. *Fucking magnificent* indeed.

I pulled on extra layers and grabbed a headlamp and a bucket. Hauling water from the river was a hand-numbing, muscle-burning chore that was perfect for taking my mind off of stupidly charming, dangerously good-looking clients.

The Klondike River ran through the property, but Grandpop had built the main compound far enough away from its banks that the occasional spring flood wouldn't swamp the buildings. The path had been cleared of brush and lined with river stones, and during the early summer, the fire-weed burned with beautiful fuchsia flowers on both sides. But on a cold winter night, the only way to determine the path was to follow the dirty boot prints in the snow.

I'd never minded doing the chores a compound or a camp required to remain functional. There was always water to be hauled, wood to be chopped, fires to be tended, and meat or fish to be killed, cleaned, and smoked. I was an obsessive audiobook listener when I was driving or doing something repetitive indoors, but when I was outside, my ears were tuned to the world around me. Never silent, the sounds told me about predators, prey, other people, changes in the weather, and had even warned me once of an angry swarm of bees well before they descended on the rosehips I'd been harvesting.

The sounds and scents of the night told me that Reed had built the campfire already, the dogs were wrestling in the yard, and the new snow was coming in a day or two. As I approached the river, it was harder to hear anything but the water flowing over stones, until the lightest footsteps in the snow behind me made my skin prickle. I turned slowly as my hand went to the knife I always wore at my back.

The dark shape of Wolf stood out against the white landscape behind her. She was calm and alert, not anxious or insistent, and I exhaled in relief. I knew Wolf would come for me if something had happened to Grandpop, but this wasn't her getting me, this was her accompanying me. I gestured silently, and she came to my side to accept the rubbed fur that was her due.

I appreciated her company, and she gave me the excuse to say out loud the words that had been running on a loop through my brain. "Why did he have to do that? Why couldn't he just let me keep him in his client box where I didn't have to think about anything other than threat assessments? Why the hell did he have to open his mouth and mess with my head?"

Wolf continued her silent company while I muttered to myself as I stood over the hole someone, probably Reed, had cut in the ice. I filled my five-gallon bucket with the icy river water, and I had the sense that she stood guard so I didn't have to. Her presence gave me leave to mutter and rant all I wanted, because for once, I wasn't totally responsible for my own safety. It was a gift that I was barely conscious of, lost as I was in my tirade of nonsense. And then, as I hauled forty pounds of water back to my cabin, I was suddenly tired of my self-indulgence and stopped the muttering. Whatever was going on in Oliver Curran's head was not my problem. My job was to keep him safe and alive, and none of that required anything other than my vigilance.

I got the water into my cabin without significant waste and put a pot of it on the wood stove to heat before heading over to check on Grandpop. Wolf was waiting for me when I stepped outside my cabin.

"I'm fine now. You don't need to watch my back anymore," I said to her. Her steady gaze told me that she heard me, but she'd be doing what she liked regardless of my feelings on the matter. On the whole, I could respect that.

She walked with me to Pop's cabin, and I heard Reed's laughter at the fire pit beyond it. My cousin had been my best friend growing up, and our family always joked that I got his dose of serious, and he got mine of charm. It didn't matter to us—we always knew who we were.

I wondered if Oliver had made his way over there and if he'd be as charmed by Reed as everyone else always was, and then I told myself I didn't care. I knocked lightly on the cabin door, and when I'd kicked off my shoes and was properly greeted by the other dogs, I found Grandpop sitting up in bed, listening to music on the iPod we got him for Christmas last year.

"Sea shanties, Pop? Really?" I said as I closed the door behind Wolf, who padded in to settle on the rug next to Grandpop's bed. His hand went automatically to her head, and she accepted his attention for just a moment before lying down.

"Your mother came by with dinner for me earlier, and she said the same thing. Your client, on the other hand, told me he'd download new ones for me if he can find some internet the next time he goes to town."

That surprised me. "He was here?"

"He came by to set a time for meds, starting tomorrow if you'll go get them." Grandpop had a smug expression on his face.

"He tell you he had TB?" I said, trying to imagine Oliver and my grandfather having a civil conversation.

"He said his grandmother spent a year in Arizona on the res while her father recovered from TB, and she went to school with Navajo kids. Her best friend was Navajo, and she spent more time with them than at her own home. He tell you that?"

I shook my head. No, he hadn't told me that, and it surprised me. When people found out about my Indigenous heritage, they usually came back with their own percentage, and how they just missed having enough "Indian" in them to get that scholarship or whatever.

"Your client misses his grandmother."

"His name's Oliver, Pop." I sighed. It was hard to stay detached when I heard things like *he misses his grandmother*.

"I know what his name is, Sis. I also know that as long as he's a client, you won't cross that line. Too dangerous mixing your business with anything else. And you're damn good at your business."

I reached for his hand, and his gnarled fingers gripped mine tightly.

"I need you to get better, Pop."

He smiled wanly. "Well, we'll see about this medicine you've been going on about. If it takes, I figure I'll stick around for a little longer."

The tears that had been gathering in my eyelids let go, and I laughed and reached for a tissue from the bedside table.

"It's good to see you laugh, Sis. You don't do it enough anymore."

"Hasn't been much to laugh about, I guess."

His eyebrows furrowed as he shook his head. "Find things. It can't be all work, or what are you doing it for? To everything there's a season, and when it's darkest, that's the time to find laughter."

The fire in the wood stove popped and crackled, and I shifted over to scratch Otter's belly.

Grandpop broke the long silence. "You had a fever once, when you were a baby. A bad one. Your dad was off on the road, and your mom was doing it all alone."

I looked over to see his eyes a little unfocused, like he was looking inside himself for the memories. I'd always loved the sound of his voice as he spoke.

"She came to us one night, scared to death because you were so hot you were listless and couldn't even hold your head up. It just lolled on your neck like a doll," Grandpop continued. "I went and got the doctor— old Doc Turner—and he looked you over, and then he blew a raspberry on your belly that made you giggle right out loud. He turned to your mom and said, 'If she can laugh, she'll always be okay.'"

A smile crossed his face and spread into his voice. "And do you know, ever since then, your laughter is one of the sweetest sounds I know."

I brought his hand up to my mouth and kissed the back of it. "I love you, Pop."

"Love you too, Sis. Now get out so I can go back to my sea shanties. And get those meds first thing in the morning, because I have a date with your client at one o'clock."

I chuckled and stood to go. Wolf got to her feet to walk me to the door, and I turned back to my grandfather. "Thanks for sending Wolf to find me earlier. She's good at watching my back."

He raised his eyebrows and looked at Wolf. "I didn't send her. She must've thought you needed it."

"Hmm, maybe I did." I reached down and gave her ears a scratch, which she tolerated for a moment before heading to the door in a not-subtle-at-all hint.

When I opened the door to leave, Wolf escorted me out.

[18]

OLIVER

*"No man is an island, entire of itself; every man is a piece of the
continent, a part of the main."*

- JOHN DONNE

The night around the campfire with Reed, his mom, Rikki, and
twelve-year-old Rori reminded me of beach bonfires when I was
in high school, complete with a bottle of whisky, someone's acoustic
guitar, and a bag of marshmallows. Rori was in charge of roasting marshmallows to order, Reed was the self-proclaimed bartender, and Rikki
handed off a beat-up guitar for me to pick at while she kept us laughing
with stories of her cosplay adventures in the early days of Comic Con.

I stumbled to bed in my little camper and tried not to notice that
lamplight still flickered in the window of Dallas's cabin.

The knock on my door came too early the next morning, but I
didn't even care too much about the thunder god hammering away in
my skull, because for the first time in a very long time, I'd actually

141

slept a full night through. From about midnight until eight a.m. I'd been dead to the world, and the novelty of it was almost overwhelming.

"Yeah," I croaked, when the knocking came again. "Come in."

The camper door opened and Dallas poked her head in, hair still wet on the ends from being washed. "You awake?"

"Getting there."

"Good. There's still hot water in the shower block if you can get there before Reed runs it cold."

I sat up and pulled on a sweater. "Excellent. Thank you," I said, as I slid out of my sleeping bag and reached for my jeans. Dallas looked away, and I looked down to see if I'd embarrassed myself with morning wood. Nope. Too cold.

"I made coffee. You can grab a cup from my cabin. I want to get to town early enough to pick up some things before we grab Christi from Max's mom's place."

I buttoned my jeans, slid my feet into boots, and grabbed the towel. "Cool. See you in a few."

We parted ways outside. She went to her mom's cabin to see what they needed from town, trailed by her grandfather's dog, Wolf, and I had my first, very short, very cramped shower in two days.

I knocked on her cabin door, feeling like a human again in my new blue shirt, and was a little surprised to see Wolf inside with Dallas.

"She started trailing me last night and hasn't left me alone since then," Dallas said, when I asked.

I studied her as she poured a cup of coffee into a travel mug for me and then refilled her own. She was wearing jeans tucked into Sorel boots, a big, blue-green wool sweater that looked handmade, and a knit cap over hair which she wore in a single braid. The business suit she wore in Chicago had matched her buttoned-up attitude, but now, in these clothes and in this place, she seemed to be more … herself. If not exactly free-spirited, then at least a little less careful.

She caught me looking and raised an eyebrow.

"Nice sweater," I said instead of *you're surprisingly pretty*, because as compliments went, it would have been as backhanded as probably unwelcome.

She gave me the ghost of a smile. "Thanks. Aunt Rikki is a knitter, and her sweaters are pretty legendary in our family." She looked at me oddly. "You okay?"

I shook myself to stop staring. She was starting to relax around me, and it was disconcerting. "Sorry. I met Rikki last night. Her Comic Con experiences in the eighties were epic to hear about. I can't even imagine only 6,500 people at one now."

She handed me my coffee and pulled on a parka. Wolf followed us out and jumped into the back seat of Polar Bear.

"Apparently she's along for the ride?" I said, looking back at her from the passenger seat. The shepherd mix was looking especially wolflike with her tongue hanging out, and a smile that said *one wrong move and you answer to me, buddy.*

Dallas shrugged. "Like I said, she hasn't left me alone since last night."

The road out to the main highway was in decent shape for being unpaved, but I was happy to get back on the highway. The landscape became somewhat lunar, with wave after wave of snow-covered mounds on either side of the highway giving it the texture of desert sand dunes.

"What are those hills?" I asked after a mile of them.

"Dredge tailings," she said with a quick glance at where I looked. At my confused face, she explained. "Gold mining in the Yukon didn't start to get really profitable until they brought in big floating bucket dredges. They'd dig up the bottoms of the rivers, wash the buckets of dirt through an internal sluice, and after all the gold fell down into the riffles, all the clean gravel would be left behind them in big piles."

"It's pretty eerie-looking, covered in snow like this. What's it like in the summer?"

"Like a lunar landscape with random patches of fireweed growing in the gravel. A lot of people hate it, which is why they stopped dredge mining in the 1950s." She shrugged. "I have some friends who are buying up big tracts of dredge tailings land to reclaim it. They plant clover the first summer, then stone fruit seedlings, and after seven years, they have agricultural land to sell off at a big profit."

"That's the kind of enterprise that venture capitalists are always looking for," I said, the wheels starting to spin in my brain.

She scoffed. "They're not looking in the Yukon. The people who create things here—businesses, opportunities, art, music—do it with no expectation of help from anyone else. It's hard enough to survive up here. Being creative on top of that takes a force of will."

We turned off the paved road onto a long, straight dirt road that led past one- and two-story clapboard houses to a tall, modern building. Dallas parked the truck, but left it running. "So Wolf has heat," she explained as we got out.

"You want me to wait in the car with her?" I asked, a little freaked out that she left a car running in the parking lot.

She shrugged. "Who's going to get past Wolf to steal it?"

"Fair point," I said as we entered the hospital.

We met with the doctor, a young, good-looking Black guy from Vancouver who was doing his residency there, and I explained my history in hopes he would let me administer Isaac's TB meds. Dr. Ibrahim's expression was serious and concerned as he explained all the reasons it was against policy to let us take the meds home, right before he handed us a bag with a week's worth of pills. Dallas gave him a dazzling smile, and I was caught completely off guard.

I must have twitched or something, because Dallas shot me a strange look, then turned back to the doctor. "Is the Riverwest Café open yet?"

"Not yet," he said. "April first. I think Cheechakos Bakeshop just reopened though."

"Perfect. Can we get you anything?"

"No, thanks, I'm good. Just bring Isaac back in to see me in a week, and I'll make sure not to get you another week's worth of meds." He winked, and her answering smile was genuine.

It shook me to see her smile so easily.

I pasted on my go-to smile as I shook Dr. Ibrahim's hand, and we left the hospital.

"You okay?" Dallas murmured to me as we stepped outside.

"Do you usually offer to get food for random strangers?"

She studied me, her breath escaping her mouth as puffs of steam.

"In this town, doctors are not random strangers. They're sometimes the only thing between you and certain death, considering the next closest medical facility is six hours away. The government has to offer major financial incentives just to get doctors to consider living in the Territory."

Wolf gave Dallas a nuzzle when we got back into the truck. I got a show of teeth.

"Sorry. I've never lived in a small town. I don't know the rules," I said.

"One of the rules is that whenever you go into town, you do the errands. In this case, it's groceries from Bonanza Market, with a stop at Cheechakos for coffee and bread."

She drove back out toward the highway but turned left on a little residential street before we got to it. On the right-hand side was an overgrown double lot with an old log cabin sitting in the middle of it. The cabin looked as though it was one good storm away from tumbling down.

"What's this?" I asked. She was looking past me at the cabin, and I thought I could see longing in her expression.

She seemed to shake herself, then pulled into the driveway of a trailer across the street to turn around. "Nothing really. I just check on the cabin whenever I'm in town. I used to dream about buying it and fixing it up for myself. Full-time electricity and regular internet seem like luxuries when you spend a week out at Grandpop's."

"Oh, right," I said, pulling the burner phone out of my pocket and powering it up, "speaking of internet." Finally, a cell signal. When my messages finally populated, it was an explosion of texts and emails. "Crap," I said, looking at all the little red circles.

"Plug in." She reached for a power cord in her center console. "You can sit in the car with Wolf and do your business. Do not"—she glared at me, and for a moment, suit-wearing, stuffy, security-person Dallas was back—"give any indication that you're not in Chicago. Not in email, text, or message. And definitely do not go on social media. The tracking cookies alone will give you away."

I didn't bother to hide my smirk at the sternness in her tone. "Yes, ma'am. Hide my digital tracks. I might know a little something about how to do that, but I'll be sure to ask you if I get into trouble."

She sighed. "Ass."

"Yep." I was already scrolling through the messages and barely looked up when she parked and got out to do her errands.

I was only three emails in when my sense of humor disappeared completely.

[19]
DALLAS

"Fireweed, with its bright magenta flowers, is the follower of boreal forest fires and the official flower of the Yukon. The flowers, leaves, and shoots are edible and anti-inflammatory, and its extract can be used in medicinal creams and salves. It is considered a pioneer species."

- BEVERLEY GRAY, *THE BOREAL HERBAL: WILD FOOD AND MEDICINE PLANTS OF THE NORTH*

"Hey, beautiful," said a voice behind me. As always, even with snow still on the ground, there was a line at Cheechakos, and I'd been engrossed in deciding what kind of breakfast sandwich Oliver might like. I turned in surprise at the compliment, and then threw my arms around Mark Zeke, my cousin's best friend.

"Hey, handsome," I said as I hugged him. "Last time I saw you, you were headed for a life in the U.S. stock market."

He grimaced comically. "Too many big dicks swinging around the trading floor. I'm not cut out for the swagger."

Mark and Reed had always seemed bigger than Dawson City, and I was surprised that they'd both come back. "What are you doing now?" It was my turn to order, and I asked for two egg and sausage sandwiches, two black coffees, and two baguettes for later.

When I'd paid for my order, Mark and I grabbed a seat in the window to wait for our food. He leaned over and spoke in a low voice. "I'm mining for bitcoin."

I turned to stare at him, my face about three inches from his. "Bitcoin? Here?"

We were in one of the old gold mining capitals of North America, but bitcoin wasn't something that came out of the ground. Mark grinned, and I was reminded that despite his good looks, or maybe because of them, he was a total rascal. On the surface, there didn't seem to be much difference between Mark and my client, but I was beginning to see depths in Oliver Curran that I hadn't anticipated.

"No place better, actually," Mark said. "Weirdly, the cost of the electricity to run my rig is offset by how much heat it puts out. I made a couple of mods, and now my house has crypto-heat."

I laughed at the expression of pure mischief on his face. "Well, aren't you fancy. Any luck with the bitcoin?"

He shrugged. "A little, but it's not so very different from the old days of gold mining. A little luck and a lot of right place/right time is all you need to strike it rich."

I squeezed his shoulder as my name was called. "Reed's out at the compound. Come visit us?"

"I'll bring the tequila," he said with a grin.

I wrinkled my nose at that and leaned in to kiss his cheek. "See you later."

When I got out to the truck, I found Oliver staring through the front windshield at the window where Mark and I had been sitting. He looked strange—a little pale, and taut as a fishing line with a king salmon on the hook.

"What's wrong?" I asked him when I'd shut the truck's door. I handed him his coffee and breakfast sandwich, which he took automatically and put down. Then he handed me his phone.

"We have to call Cipher," he said woodenly.

I zoomed in on the image on his screen. It was a photo of me handing a phone to Jennifer Jones, the political activist I'd spent two months in Mexico protecting from rape and death threats. Below the photo was the headline, *Bodyguard Colluded with Deepfake Mastermind in Sex Tape of Voting Rights Activist.*

I stared at Oliver in shock. "What is this?"

"Scroll down," he said grimly.

I rolled down the article without reading sentences, just seeing words, until I got to another photo of myself walking in the park with Oliver the night someone took a shot at us. I looked up at him. "So?"

"So, they've twisted facts and planted 'evidence' to make it seem that you and I knew each other before you went to Mexico. Because she was a previous client of Cipher, they're saying that we colluded to create the sex tape and the trolling to give her a reason to rehire Cipher. Kind of like what I accused you of doing to me—scaring me into hiring you. You, me, and Cipher are being called criminals."

"Shit." I just stared at him in bewilderment as I tried to make sense of the words my brain refused to process.

Mark left Cheechakos and threw me a wave and a smile. I waved back automatically, but without the smile.

"Who's that?" Oliver said in a voice that was a little too casual.

"Huh?" I needed a moment to process his shift in focus. "Oh, him? That's Reed's best friend, Mark."

"You know him pretty well?"

I nodded vaguely, but his words didn't really register. My brain was spinning on the implications of the photos that connected me and Cipher to Oliver and his deepfake technology. I started the truck and drove out to the Visitor Center. It was still closed for the season, so I parked in front and powered up my cell phone.

"Why are we here?" Oliver asked.

"Free Wi-Fi," I answered, as I put a Wi-Fi call through a VPN to the

Cipher offices. I put my phone on speaker and placed it on the jockey box between us. I finally unwrapped my breakfast sandwich and said to Oliver as the phone rang, "Eat. They're better hot."

It almost seemed like he wanted to argue with me, but then Darius's cultured tones answered with a single word. "Dallas." He said my name with relief, and because I half-expected recrimination, I was startled into silence.

"We're both here," Oliver said, filling the gap in conversation.

"Good. Hold on and I'll add Shane. Quinn is in Texas," Darius said.

I looked at Oliver, and he understood the subtext as well as I did. Quinn was in Texas reassuring Jennifer that we'd had nothing to do with the faked sex tape of her with a guy who is *not* her husband that blew up her credibility and blasted a firestorm of rape, dismemberment, and death threats her way. The horror had sent her running to Mexico with me as her bodyguard—and now Quinn was trying to avoid a very expensive lawsuit.

"Dallas, Oliver, are you both safe?" Shane's voice was a calming influence on the panic that kept threatening to bubble up, and I was finally able to breathe.

"Yes, we're fine," I said. "How big is the story?"

Darius answered. "Quinn is using his influence to kill it, but it's enough for mumblings of extradition."

I exhaled. "We'll stay put here. We're far enough off-grid that we're not in immediate danger of being found. It seems pretty obvious they're trying to either smoke Oliver out or make it impossible for him to sell his program."

"So, your Russian?" Shane asked.

"Maybe," I said, eyeing Oliver, who appeared to be deep in thought

He suddenly burst out, "Is Alex Greene available?"

"Yes. Shall I have him call you?" Darius said.

"Please," Oliver said, distracted.

"You have what you need, Dallas?" Shane asked, the concern evident in her voice.

The feeling of having screwed up was making me nauseous, even though the whole scenario was completely fabricated—but by whom? "If the time is ever right, would you please tell Jennifer that I'm so sorry she got dragged back into the press?"

"It'll be fine, and you can tell her yourself when you get back."

"Thanks, Shane," I said quietly.

"Stay safe." And with that, the connection ended.

I looked over at Oliver to gauge what he was thinking, but he was still deep in his own thoughts. His phone rang, and he answered it up to his ear. "Greene? Yeah."

I took my coffee and left the car, whistling for Wolf to come out with me. She and I crossed Front Street to the riverside, where an old paddle-wheel boat, the Klondike Spirit, sat on the shore, beckoning tourists to imagine life in the days of the gold rush.

The ice bridge on the Yukon River was still frozen and would likely not be breaking up until sometime in April or May, so the off-grid community of West Dawson still had access to the goods available in Dawson City. There were several months each year, in early winter and late spring, when the people who lived on the other side of the river were completely on their own. It was a kind of lonely self-sufficiency that even I had never been drawn to.

It had been years since I'd spent a winter in the Yukon, and walking along the bank of the frozen river reminded me just how lonely it could get. The cold was oppressive, the darkness in the dead of winter even worse. Alcohol and drug abuse were real problems as connections between whoever hadn't run away to winter down south waned, and mental health issues seemed to flourish in the ever-present *sameness*.

In my family, winter was the time for crafting. It was when quilts were sewn, clothing was made and decorated, leather was worked, and warm things were knit. But my mom and I had moved away, and Aunt Rikki lived in town with her family. I never considered what winters must have been like for Grandpop and Grandma Minty when it was just the two of them at the compound. After my grandmother died, I was too busy trying to find my way in life to give much thought to Pop's winters alone, and guilt made the loneliness of the landscape seem even bleaker.

"You and your wolf look like you've always been here." Oliver's voice came from behind me. Wolf had told me he was coming in the relaxed alertness of her posture, and I felt his presence like a body of warmth. "Like it could be a hundred years ago, and you fit into the landscape the same way you do now." He came up and stood beside me, with gloved hands in his pockets and a knit fisherman's cap on his head.

"I'm sorry you're trapped here," I said without meaning to.

He turned to look at me, and his gaze held mine for long, silent seconds before he finally said, "I'm not."

Something electric passed between us, and I stepped back to quell the instinct to touch him. "I need to shop and then go get Christi," I said, for the excuse to take another step back.

He nodded and seemed to exhale. "Yeah."

"Everything okay with Alex?" I asked as we walked back to the truck.

"Just bouncing some ideas off him," he said cryptically.

"Anything I can help with?"

He shrugged. "Know anyone up here with a whole lot of computers?"

I held the back door open for Wolf to jump in and looked at Oliver across the roof of my truck.

"As a matter of fact, I think I might."

We got through the shopping list at the Bonanza Market and were just loading bags into the car when Christi called my cell phone. I answered it while Oliver finished with the bags.

"Max just dropped me at Cheechakos so I could eat while I wait for you. When are you coming?" she said.

"Grab your stuff to go, we'll be right there," I said before hanging up. "Well," I said to Oliver, "she's here."

"Cool. I need to give Isaac his meds and get my drives. Should I see if Reed can bring me back to town and make an introduction to his friend?" Oliver had been enthusiastic when I'd told him about Mark's bitcoin mining rig. I still had only the vaguest idea what they were talking about, but my expertise wasn't necessary to their operation, so I didn't dig deeper.

"I'm happy to bring you back to town, but I leave it to you." I'd just turned the corner on Front Street as my beautiful sister stepped out of the bakery wearing a hot pink parka and a giant smile. She had a hard-sided roller bag in one hand, carried a paper to-go bag in the other, and she looked way too glamorous to be on a Dawson City sidewalk.

"That's your sister?" Oliver asked with a note of awe in his voice.

"That's Christi, named for yet another city in Texas."

"Let me guess, if she'd been a boy she would have been Austin?" he asked as he jumped out of the passenger seat to help Christi with her bag. "Hi, Christi. I'm Oliver," I heard him say through the open door. He tossed her roller bag into the back with the groceries and then made her take the front seat.

I leaned over and kissed her cheek. "Any problems?"

She shook her head. "Max was a sweetheart." Then she looked back at Oliver. "So you're the client."

"So you're the sister," he said, beaming the full wattage of his smile at her.

My sister was objectively beautiful. She had Grandpop's dark hair and eyes that my mom had given us both, but where my face was all broad cheekbones and strong jaw, hers was heart-shaped and feminine. She was slim where I was strong, and her curves were suggestive where mine just said here I am, take it or leave it. I'd been eight years old when Christi was born, and I sometimes felt more like her mom than her sister, but I loved her fiercely and was so proud of everything she'd accomplished in her twenty years.

"Tell me about the restaurant," I said to her. "What have you been making?"

Christi launched into a story about shrimp scampi and a large party that had Oliver laughing out loud and hanging on her every word. Christi had always been amazing with an audience, and she loved being the center of attention. It was clear she'd captured Oliver's attention, and I thought she was probably exactly the kind of beautiful, intelligent, sparkly girl he usually dated.

They were still talking when we pulled into the compound, and he gallantly carried her suitcase to Mom and George's cabin where she'd stay. Wolf watched me unload the groceries first into my house, then to Aunt Rikki's. Oliver was waiting for me back at the car.

"I have Isaac's meds. Which bag goes to him?" he asked.

"It's okay, I can do it. Would you mind taking that bag of groceries to my mom?"

"Sure, I mean, I'll take the bag to your mom, but I promised Isaac I'd see him today with the dose of his meds." He gave me a look I couldn't decipher. "Are you alright?"

I shrugged. "I'm fine." I turned to pick up my mom's groceries. "Come find me if you want a ride in to meet Mark. I'm going to see if I can persuade Christi to make dinner tonight."

He picked up Grandpop's bag with a grin. "She sounds like someone I could actually learn something from."

I remembered the amazing pot of ramen he'd made and thought they'd probably be pretty well matched. I walked away thinking there was a lot about Christi that matched things Oliver liked. I didn't want to think about my client at all, much less as a possible match for my little sister.

Wolf followed me inside Mom's cabin and curled up to lie on the rug while Mom and Christi chattered in the kitchen unpacking groceries.

George sat in a chair by the window, reading a paperback, so I went over to him and kissed his cheek. "What are you reading?" I asked, perching on the arm of his chair.

He turned his book over to show me the title.

"*Call of the Wild*? Haven't you read it, like, a million times?"

He smiled. "More or less. Winter in the North brings it out in me."

"Brings what out?" I asked. I'd liked George from the first time Mom brought him home to meet me. He was a kind man, and thoughtful in the way lifelong readers often were.

"The desire for mastery. It's not enough to just survive the elements, especially in the winter. Sometimes a man has to master them to feel worthy."

"You're the worthiest of men," I said with a smile as I stood to join Mom and Christi in the kitchen.

"So," Christi said with a verbal pounce, "tell us about the Client." The way she said "client" made the word sound like a proper noun, as if it were Duke or Prince.

"Someone took a shot at him in Chicago after attacking him in an alley and breaking into his house," I said, looking over the food arrayed on the counter. "What're you making and how can I help?"

"I'm thinking cassoulet with ham hock, sausage, and duck fat. Want to start on the mirepoix?" she said, rolling an onion across the counter to me. "And p.s., that wasn't you telling us about your client, that was a threat-assessment report. What's he *like*?"

"Knows he's smart, entitled because he had early success, overconfident, too charming, flirts shamelessly with almost everyone he meets, so yeah, pretty standard for a young, rich, good-looking guy with enemies. Kind of like every client I ever had." The last bit slipped past the recitation I'd tried to keep toneless, but this was Christi and Mom. They knew I'd compared him to the clients from my guiding days, but as usual, they didn't let me dwell there.

"In other words, he annoys the crap out of you?" Mom said sweetly.

"Basically, yes."

"Except," Mom added, "your grandfather talks to him."

Christi stared at her with wide eyes. "On purpose? I mean, not just to bark at him?"

I chuckled. "Oh, there's plenty of barking." I finished chopping the onion and moved on to celery. "But to his credit, Oliver helped convince the new doctor to let us give Pop his meds, which counts for a lot. He was so tired after our trip to the hospital yesterday that I was worried about having to take him in every day just so someone could watch him take pills."

I described Grandpop's course of treatment, including once-a-week visits to the hospital so Dr. Ibrahim could keep tabs on his liver function and replenish the four-drug cocktail. As scary as tuberculosis sounded out loud, as long as it was managed with meds and didn't scar his lungs too badly, he would recover.

Then conversation turned to Christi and her life in Vancouver. "How are things going with Robbie?" Mom asked her.

She shrugged. "I'm thinking of not going back for a while."

"Back to him, or back to the city?" Mom wielded a neutral tone of voice like a master, but I could see concern vibrating off her.

"He's okay, but he's just not really ... focused. He wants to work just enough to pay the bills, but I want my work to matter." She exhaled. "I'm good at food, and I want to keep moving forward in my career."

"I thought that's why you were in Vancouver," I said. I didn't like the edge of frustration I heard in her voice.

"Being there without family is ... well"—she exhaled—"sometimes I don't feel safe. Robbie's just doing what Robbie does, and my room-mates would only notice that I was gone if it was time for the rent. It's a big city, and one girl alone more or less ..." Her voice trailed off.

I hated that my sister didn't feel safe, and I hated even more what that said about the levels of fear she lived with on a daily basis. I wasn't being dramatic when I told Oliver that Indigenous women were at risk, and added to the fact that Christi was pretty and young, she must have felt like she walked around with a bullseye painted on her back.

We spent the rest of the prep and cooking time talking through possible work options for Christi, both in Alberta and in the Yukon where she could be near family. It was nearly dark by the time the stew was done.

"Rikki's doing a campfire tonight for Reed and his friends," Mom said to us. "Will you guys join us?"

Christi was scooping cassoulet into a plastic container that she handed me. "Here. For you and the Client," she said with a knowing smile.

"He's going to want to talk food with you," I warned her. "You guys have that in common." Wolf got to her feet and followed me to the door. "Thank you for dinner," I said. "We'll probably see you over there."

"I'll walk you out," Christi said.

Since that involved putting on boots and a coat, I didn't take it lightly. Christi wanted to talk, and whatever it was would worry Mom.

She walked beside me in silence until I finally asked, "What's up?"

"I broke up with Robbie," she said.

"I figured from the way you were talking about him. Any particular reason?" I linked my arm with hers like we used to do when she was little, and she leaned into me, her slight frame almost as tall as mine.

She took a deep breath. "I thought I might have been pregnant last month."

"Christ," I whispered, suddenly ambushed by a rush of emotions I'd thought were long-since gone.

"I'm not," she said quickly, "but it made me realize that I wouldn't actually want Robbie to be the father of my kid."

I squeezed her arm. "I'm sorry."

"That I'm not pregnant?" she asked.

I felt her words deep in my heart, but I shook them away. "Only if you wanted to be."

"I don't know if I wanted to be," she said. "I'm just glad it wasn't with Robbie."

"Me too," I whispered. "You'll find the right guy, and you'll be a great mom. And in the meantime, you're a pretty cool chick all by yourself."

"Thanks, Dallas," she said, and I realized there were tears shining in her eyes. I pulled her in for a hug and held on for a long time.

[20]

OLIVER

"It is better to fail in originality than to succeed in imitation."

- HERMAN MELVILLE

Reed found me as I was leaving Isaac's cabin. "Hey, want another chance to kiss the toe?" he asked with a smirk.

"Actually, I was on my way to find you after I talk to Dallas," I said, heading toward her cabin.

The old man was still coughing so much that his skin tone was a little ashen, and I wanted Dallas to look in on him. My own cough, when I'd had TB, had virtually disappeared after two weeks of taking the meds, but Isaac was much older, and it would probably take longer for him.

Reed fell into step with me. "How can I be of service, Client?"

I bristled at the name, which, coming from him, sounded like a slur. In this case though, I did need the help in relation to the reason I was Cipher's client. "Dallas said your friend Mark is mining bitcoin. I have a favor to ask him, and I need an introduction."

Reed shrugged. "Yeah, sure. I'll text him when we get into cell range and he can meet us at the Downtown."

"Ask him if we can meet him at his place. The favor involves his mining rig."

I knocked on Dallas's cabin door, but there was no sound inside. "She's probably at her mom's gabbing with her sister," Reed said. "They're all pretty close."

"Okay, let me grab my bag and let's go. As long as we're not gone too long, it can wait."

Reed's truck was a beat-up Dodge that he drove like a race car. "So," I began, to distract myself from his driving, "do you live out at Isaac's compound full-time?"

"Nah, I live wherever I happen to be working. The compound's too far away from everything. Only time it's fun is when everyone's there. We almost never see Dallas anymore, so anytime she's home, it's a thing." Reed had a kicked-back way about him that was at complete odds with his recklessness in a vehicle.

"You know she'll kill you if you kill me," I said, not even a little bit joking.

That seemed to make him realize he was driving too fast, and he slowed down to something less nail-biting. "Sorry. Yeah, you're right. She would. So, are you into her?"

His directness was disarming because it was as easygoing as the rest of his manner. "I hired her company to keep me alive," I said in a non-answer worthy of Dallas herself.

Reed chuckled. "You sound like my cousin. Saying words without answering the question. But since she's always taking care of everyone else, I figure someone's gotta step up for her every once in a while, so I'll repeat. Are. You. Into. Her?"

"You're kind of an asshole, aren't you?" I said. It should have been easy to say *of course not, she's my bodyguard*, but somehow, it wasn't.

"When it counts," he agreed. He pulled over in front of a newish-looking one-story house. "This is Mark's." He turned to face me, and the easy jocularity left his expression. "Don't fuck around with Dallas.

She might be all tough and capable, and she could find six ways to kill you herself if she wanted to, but she's too good for you and anyone else I've ever met. And by good, I mean decent and kind with a heart three times bigger than the rest of us have. So don't fuck with her, man."

So much for easygoing.

With that dire statement hanging in the air, we left the truck and pretended the whole conversation never happened.

Mark's house was spare in that way of guys who need only a big TV, a videogame console, a couch, and a coffee table. It was also warm, and remarkably, I didn't want my coat for the first time in days. I shoved my gloves into my coat pockets and shook Mark's hand when Reed introduced me as Dallas's client.

Mark looked at Reed. "She guiding again?"

I shot him a quick look, but he just shrugged at Mark's question. "Something like that."

"Actually," I said to the guy who looked like a ski instructor the resort hired to bring in the ladies, "she's my bodyguard."

"No shit?" he asked. "What'd you do?"

I looked from Mark to Reed and back. These two were Dallas's age, but they seemed younger, maybe because life had put the experience in her eyes. Reed was her family though, and he'd just taken me on, for which I gave him props.

"I wrote a code to bust deepfakes, and someone wants to keep me from releasing it."

"No shit," Mark said again, with all the conversational diversity of a piece of fruit.

"That's why I'm here. I need your help. The guy who's after me has tried to frame Dallas for creating a deepfake video that caused a lot of trouble." Both men's expressions hardened, and I was glad she had such a fan club. "With enough time, I could bust that particular deepfake on my own, but that's not going to stop him from going after her—or me— again. I need to borrow your mining rig for about a week to teach the AI how to spot the fakes in the wild."

"You mean like TikTok has an algorithm so you don't post composites?" Reed asked.

"Sort of, only more complex. The TikTok and Facebook algorithms deal with simple facial recognition. This program expands on those and will, when the machine has time to learn from a big enough data set, be able to bust the fakes in complex videos."

"No shit," Mark said, and I grinned at the awe in those two words.

"What's the data set?" Reed asked, surprising me with his attention. Frankly, I thought he hadn't been listening.

"YouTube," I said. "Their user agreement on the public videos allows for informed consent."

"You mean not like the Stanford Brainwash data set?" Reed asked.

I was impressed. "You followed that?"

"What is it?" Mark asked Reed.

"Stanford had to take down a data set it had scraped from the live video feed of customers going in and out of a café called Brainwash in the lower Haight district in San Francisco," Reed said.

I filled in the details. "There's a Creative Commons photo reuse license for academic use, which is how Stanford got access to the feed, but none of the Brainwash customers knew they were being studied for facial recognition."

It was almost sad that Mark's only response to that was, "Damn!"

"So you've written a program that uses facial recognition tools to bust deepfakes?" Reed asked me.

I nodded. "It does one better. It'll identify the fake, then peel back the layer and mark the digital signatures. So, unless the deepfaker took time to scrub their signature, my program will find it and identify the source."

"That's badass," Reed said. "Who are you going to sell it to when it's fully functional?"

"That is the question, now, isn't it?" I said quietly, trying hard to ignore the itch in my conscience.

[21]

DALLAS

"There are strange things done in the midnight sun..."

- ROBERT W. SERVICE, *THE CREMATION OF SAM MCGEE*

Oliver and Reed arrived at the fire pit together, and Mark tagged along behind them in his own car. The three guys were in high spirits, and it looked like Oliver and Reed had become friends.

Oliver came and sat down next to me. "Have you checked on Isaac?" he asked quietly.

"I just came from there. He's sleeping now." I pulled a big Thermos out of the bag at my feet.

"Is he breathing okay? The coughing fits were wearing him out when I saw him earlier."

"I gave him some propolis in juice. It tastes nasty, but it helps with the cough." I handed him the Thermos and a spoon. "Thanks for checking on him. I saved you some dinner."

I'd reheated the cassoulet before putting it in the Thermos, so it was still hot. Reed looked over at us as Oliver inhaled the rich fragrance of pork, white beans, herbs, and wine. "How come he gets the good stuff, and we just get chili?" Reed whined, even as he and Mark ladled big portions of Rikki's famous chili into bowls.

"Because he's Dallas's Client," Christi shot back, with the same emphasis on "client" as before.

"That's right," Oliver said with a grin at Christi. Then he put a big spoonful in his mouth and deliberately moaned his appreciation. "Mmm, oh yeah, baby. This is the best thing I've put in my mouth all day," he said with a wink at my sister.

She giggled, and I worked very hard to keep my expression bland. Reed laughed out loud. "You have no idea the fire you're playing with, my man. Keep it up, though, I'm all about seeing fireworks tonight."

Aunt Rikki changed the subject to the Thaw-Di-Gras Spring Carnival that was coming up, and while Reed and Mark plotted their strategy for the dog team races, Oliver finished his stew and sat back with a contented sigh. His crossed leg rested against mine, and the contact felt intimate in a way that had nothing to do with our professional relationship.

"Did you find what you needed at Mark's?" I asked, trying not to pay attention to the heat of taut leg muscles.

Oliver chuckled and spoke in a low tone that I felt rather than heard. "Surprisingly, a dude-bro at the ass-end of nowhere had exactly the setup my code needs to learn how to do its job. He was cool to put his bitcoin mining op on pause, of course I'll make it worth his while, and I figure it'll take about a week or two for the machine to learn what we need."

"What then?" I whispered. He leaned closer, as if we were sharing confidences.

"Then we break open the layers on the deepfake video of your activist client, and we expose the signature the guy left behind," he said quietly, with the kind of confidence that made me believe he could actually do it.

"Guy?" I asked.

He shrugged. "I'm not trying to be sexist, it's just not usually a woman thing to fake a sex tape."

My eyebrows went up.

"What?" he asked. "You disagree?"

"No. You're right. You just surprised me with the 'I'm not trying to be sexist' comment. I didn't think you were that self-aware." I was being bitchy, but some part of me was bothered by Oliver's budding friendship with people I considered mine.

His voice hardened. "It must be exhausting to know everything all the time."

I sighed, baiting him was pointless. It was also beneath me, so I added a little drama to the sigh. "You have no idea."

That earned me a bark of laughter. Reed looked across the fire at us with a little too much interest in our conversation, or maybe in our body language and relative ease with each other. I ignored my cousin and turned to look at the man next to me.

The firelight made his skin glow bronze and his eyes sparkle. Oliver Curran, like my sister, was an objectively beautiful human. But while I'd always seen Christi's beauty because I knew her soul, Oliver's good looks, though aesthetically pleasing, had never made a deep impression on me before because he'd only ever let me see the top one or two layers.

He must have been able to feel my gaze on him, because he met my eyes. "So how about you teach me some of this stuff you know."

"Like what?" I asked, suspicious of his motives.

He shrugged. "Sewing, knitting, pottery. Whatever chicks in the North do."

I narrowed my eyes at him. "Chicks in the North chop wood, haul water, hunt, fish, and forage. We also build cabins, weld, fix cars, and drive heavy equipment. So much for 'I'm not trying to be sexist.'"

He grinned. "God, you're easy."

I took a deep breath, closed my eyes, and then got up from my seat. "I'm going for a walk," I said.

Oliver looked up at me. "I was teasing. Can't you take a joke?"

"Was that funny?" I asked. "Or was it just part of the 'be a dick to

Dallas' game you've been playing since I met you? Never mind," I said, holding up a hand as he started to respond. "I don't care."

I turned and walked away, and Wolf surged to her feet to follow me. I heard Oliver's footsteps behind us when I turned toward the path to the river, but I ignored him and kept walking.

"Where does this trail go?" Oliver finally asked when a snow-laden branch whacked him in the face.

"To the river," I answered automatically.

"Oh," he said as another branch whacked his shins. "Dallas, stop," he said, and then didn't seem to know what to say next.

I turned to face him. "What do you want, Oliver?" I asked, more tired than I'd felt in days. Tired of the bickering, tired of worrying about my family, tired of all the little ways I was becoming attracted to this client, and tired of fighting that attraction.

He smiled, and in the faint light of the moon his beauty took my breath away. "I was teasing," he said gently. "I'm not that guy. I'm the guy who cries at commercials and flirts with old ladies. I was teasing you with things I knew would get a rise out of you, and I *have* been a dick to you. I'm sorry."

It was the gentleness, the apology, the kindness to Grandpop, the friendship he was developing with my cousin, the fact that he liked my family—that's what sent me over the edge.

"I don't like who I'm becoming around you," I said angrily. "You push and push and push, until I finally push back, and then I'm the defensive and bitchy one and you're everybody's best friend." I sighed. "Thank you for your help with my grandfather, but I think maybe it's best if I do take you to a hotel in town."

I avoided his eyes as he watched me, and in the corner of my field of vision I saw Wolf go rigid.

"Well, this is awkward." Oliver exhaled, but I shushed him.

My eyes were riveted to Wolf's posture. Oliver opened his mouth again, but I gave a quick jerk of my head, put my finger to my lips. His eyes widened, and he nodded his understanding.

We both stood absolutely still as I let my senses open up. The spruce trees around us rustled in the slight wind that had picked up from the south. It carried the barest hint of warmth on it, as though winter had finally decided to loosen its grip on us.

Wolf's hackles had risen down the length of her spine as she peered past us and back toward camp. She put one foot forward, sniffed the air, and then another. Something was out there, something she recognized as *danger*.

A heartbeat passed, then two, and on the third heartbeat, Wolf growled, low and menacingly, and my skin bristled with gooseflesh. Oliver just barely shifted his position, but it allowed his arm to touch mine, and the contact comforted us both.

His intake of breath warned me of the whisper that would have come next if Wolf hadn't suddenly bolted toward the lower edge of the compound in the deep run of a predator. I broke into a sprint and ran after her, with Oliver only a step or two behind me.

The dog's tracks took her past the long drop and toward the camper where Oliver had been sleeping. I saw her ahead of us, circling the camper once, her nose to the ground. Then she bolted again, and when we reached my cabin, I finally stopped, breathless, outside my door.

I tried to listen past the pounding of my heart, but my senses were dulled by the blood rushing in my ears. Oliver stopped behind me, and he stepped up so his body shielded my back. "What is it?" he whispered in my ear.

I don't know, my mind said to him as my eyes scanned the woods beyond my cabin. The breeze still ruffled the spruce trees, but the wind carried only the scent of old snow. Oliver's hands had gone to my shoulders, and I was just barely conscious that I'd leaned back into his chest, almost as if I could muffle the sound of my own heartbeat against him.

Nothing moved in the woods, and I became aware of the faraway sounds of laughter from the fire pit clearing near the ATCO. Tension seeped out of me, and I accepted more of Oliver's support.

"Dallas?" His whisper in my ear sent a shiver across my skin.

I turned to face him and said nothing, as only inches separated us. His eyes searched mine, and then focused on my mouth.

"What are you doing?" I whispered. This wasn't about Wolf anymore, but danger absolutely lurked in the air between us.

"I don't know," he whispered back.

I closed my eyes. I wanted to laugh. I wanted to run away, deep into the woods until I couldn't breathe, couldn't think, couldn't feel. But I made myself hold still, very still, until the only things I knew were the sounds of his breath and my heartbeat.

And when I opened my eyes again, he kissed me.

[22]

OLIVER

"...THE ARCTIC TRAILS HAVE THEIR SECRET TALES

That would make your blood run cold;..."

- ROBERT W. SERVICE, *THE CREMATION OF SAM MCGEE*

I kissed her, a tentative touch of lips. A little bit of torture with a side of bliss, and the promise of so much more. And then the night exploded.

A gunshot. And then a second blast quickly followed the first. I heard a horrific non-human yelp, and then the shouts of men and women filled the air.

Dallas pushed me inside her cabin. "Stay away from the window!" she hissed fiercely.

In the near dark of the cabin, Dallas moved with certainty and confidence, grabbing things from shelves and filling a bag with them. As my eyes gradually grew used to the minimal light, I could see her shove what looked like a sleeping bag into a backpack. She pulled on ski pants, grabbed knives from the kitchen drawer, and picked up a lighter and a small hand ax from the wood stove. As I watched her, I tried to tell myself that whoever was shooting at us, whoever had shot Wolf, wasn't there for me. The lie made it possible to move, to think, to breathe without gasping in panic, but it was still a lie.

In less than two minutes, Dallas had a rucksack packed and closed. She gave me a fur-lined bomber hat, threw a knit scarf around my neck, and handed me the rucksack. "Put this on and follow me. Silently." Her whisper came out on a breath in the dark, and I did exactly as she said.

She slipped out the door and waited for several breaths, both of us pressed up against the wall. As my eyes adjusted to the new darkness, I saw hers shift focus to Polar Bear, parked ten feet away from the front door. "Crap," she whispered. "Tires."

She was right. The truck sat low in the snow on flattened tires. This guy was serious. And I knew for sure in that moment I was his target, though I couldn't begin to imagine how he'd found me.

"Grandpop's cabin," she whispered again, "in three, two, one …." She broke from the shelter of her own cabin, and I followed directly on her heels. We ran low, like the commandos in war movies, using the corpses of dead vehicles to cover us whenever possible.

The rest of the dogs were howling madly from inside Isaac's cabin, and only when Dallas whispered, "It's me," did they quiet enough for us to hear Isaac's voice.

"Don't let them out," he warned from his bed as we slipped inside the cabin.

His cabin, too, was in darkness, but when Isaac moved, I could see the glint of something metal in his hands. "Wolf?" he asked.

Dallas exhaled shakily. "He shot her, I think. I'm sorry." She moved swiftly to the side of his bed and reached for his hand. "She heard him. We were by the river when she went after him."

"You think it's the one who's after him?" Isaac said with a nod in my direction.

"It's the only thing that makes sense." Dallas's voice was strong and steady, and I found comfort in her tone despite her words.

Isaac reached into the drawer of the table next to his bed and handed

Dallas something that sounded vaguely metallic. "Take a rifle from the gun cabinet. Get enough rounds to last a week or two. Snow machine's in the shed behind the house, and there's fuel in it to get you out to fish camp."

"I'm not leaving you—"

"You're leaving," he interrupted with force. "We can take care of ourselves"—he nodded at me—"but he needs you to keep him safe. If he's here, we all have to keep an eye on him."

Those words landed like a slap, and I took a step backward.

Dallas didn't notice. She'd been ready to dump me at a hotel anyway, and suddenly, I didn't want to be useless.

The dogs tensed, and I heard a soft whisper at the door. "It's me."

"Christi," Dallas said to her grandfather just as her sister slipped inside.

Christi took in the scene, her eyes landing finally on her grandfather. "I'm sleeping here tonight."

Dallas exhaled in what I realized was relief. "Thanks," she said as she squeezed Isaac's hands and slipped into the second room of the cabin where I assumed the gun cabinet was. Christi went to the window, where she stood to the side and peered out into the darkness.

Isaac looked up at me, and I saw what looked like an old Winchester rifle across his lap.

"You listen to her. Do exactly as she says. She will keep you alive, but you've got to watch her back while she does it." His voice was stern and afraid and full of fierce love for his granddaughter.

"You take your meds and get well," I said in my own version of his tone. "She needs you."

"I'll make sure he gets them," Christi said softly.

Dallas returned carrying a small sling bag across her body, plus a long, slim rifle that she carried by its stock. "Christi, get his meds from Dr. Ibrahim next week if we're not back," she said to her sister as she hugged her quickly.

"There's fish under the ice—burbot runs up there now. Kit's on the shelf," Isaac said gruffly, reaching his hand out to hold Dallas's.

"Love you, Pop," she whispered.

"Love you too, Sis," he murmured back.

Then Christi moved to his side, and we slipped out of the cabin.

The snow machine Isaac talked about was a Ski-Doo snowmobile he kept in the woodshed behind the cabin. Dallas fixed the rifle to the back of the rucksack I wore, and then we pushed the Ski-Doo out to the snow. She climbed on board and gestured for me to sit behind her. "Hold on tight," she whispered, right before she fired up the engine and we shot out of camp.

As we blew past the big trailer thing they called the ATCO, I caught the barest glimpse of a Wolverine cap perched in the snow just above the long barrel of a rifle that tracked us until we were out of sight.

[23]

DALLAS

"When the snows fall and the white winds blow, the lone wolf dies but the pack survives."

- GEORGE R.R. MARTIN, *A GAME OF THRONES*

There'd been no further shots as we left the compound, and I knew Grandpop, Reed, and probably Mark would be up all night with their safeties off. I hated leaving them to deal with the shooter, and with Wolf—I swallowed hard, trying to push the pain way down—but Grandpop was right. They would all be safer if my client was gone.

My job was to keep Oliver Curran alive. Kissing him again was not part of the plan.

Reed and I used to take snowmobiles out to fish camp to escape our moms during the few Christmas holidays when we came up from Alberta, but it had been a long time since I'd driven there in the snow, and I'd never done it in the dark. Not much changed about the winter landscape in the Yukon, though. There hadn't been a fire in this part of the boreal forest in about a decade, so even the trees remained the same.

Oliver was clutching his arms around my middle and squeezing his thighs against my hips like the Ski-Doo was going to buck him off. I had expected pushback from him when I went into operational mode, but he'd been surprisingly cooperative considering we'd just fled in the night like refugees from a war zone.

The bastard shot Wolf. The surge of grief was instantaneous and brought sharp edges to my vision as we bounced over the snow-covered landscape toward my family's cabin on the river. I tried to put as much distance between us and the shooter as fast as I safely could, but neither of us was wearing a helmet, so it still took two hours over terrain that would be impassible except with another snowmobile. The gamble was that the shooter hadn't expected a chase through the wilderness and would need to wait until the next day to get a snowmobile if he wanted to follow us. Of course we'd left tracks, but the night air smelled like snow, and a ring surrounded the moon in a way that often foretold an incoming storm.

Fish camp was a summer salmon fishing camp, but over the years we'd built the cabin to accommodate a winter traveler too. Behind the single-room space was the smokehouse and a woodshed similar to the one Grandpop had built on the back of his own cabin. I drove the Ski-Doo right up to the door of that shed, and the silence, when I finally turned the engine off, was startling.

I heard the groan in my back when Oliver unpeeled his arms from around my waist and stood. I felt the loss of them as though a layer of clothing had been taken off, leaving me cold and unprotected. My own hands were clenched so tightly around the hand grips that it took conscious effort to open them. Standing required its own willpower, and straightening my back was almost a herculean feat.

"Are you okay?" I croaked, before clearing my throat to try again.

Oliver had removed the rucksack and set it down on the seat of the Ski-Doo so he could stretch.

"I can't move my toes. Is that a problem?" His tone sounded ironic, but my own feet were cold, so I knew he wasn't joking.

"Help me push this into the shed, and we'll get inside and get you warm."

His teeth had begun to chatter by the time the snowmobile was safely out of sight. The smoking chimney of the wood stove would give us away if someone tracked us out here, but I could tell he was more than just superficially cold, so I didn't have a choice but to light it.

I found the key to the cabin exactly where I'd left it the previous summer—hanging from moose antlers in the smokehouse. I brought in an armful of kindling and wood too, and within five minutes, I had a fire started in the wood stove.

I turned to find Oliver gingerly pulling off his boots.

"Wait," I said. "Let me help."

His boots were leather, and they'd taken a near-constant barrage of wet snow on the ride. The leather laces had swollen, and my fingers, stiff as they were, fumbled with them longer than they should have. "Sorry," I mumbled, then looked up to see Oliver watching me with an expression I couldn't read. I finally pulled the laces loose enough to peel back the wet tongue and carefully slide the first boot off. The sock underneath was soaking wet, and when I peeled that back, the skin of his foot looked dangerously pale.

"Crap," I muttered.

"I know it's a foot, but is it that awful?" Oliver said, his voice so tired it sounded weak.

I lifted my sweater and untucked my t-shirt from my snow pants. "Keep this one here," I said, placing his foot under my shirt on my bare stomach and trying not to flinch from the bitter cold of it. I covered it back up with my sweater and went back to work on the other set of laces.

"My God," Oliver whispered, eyes closed against the pain of defrosting flesh, "you're a better man than I'll ever be."

"A better woman, that's for sure," I said, not even bothering to add a snarky tone. "Body heat concentrates in the midsection. And naked skin against skin is the best way to reheat someone quickly." I got the other boot and sock off and placed the second chilled bare foot against my stomach too. "Damn, you're cold."

He chuckled weakly. "That's supposed to be my line." His eyes were closed again as he leaned back on the bench, shivering occasionally. He tucked his hands inside his coat, under his arms, and I realized it wasn't just his feet that had frozen.

The fire in the wood stove was beginning to warm the room, so I took off my parka and wrapped it around Oliver's feet. "I'm going to dig up some blankets. Be right back."

He didn't even open his eyes, and that worried me. When hypothermia set in, it caused lethargy and could lead to the kind of hallucinations that sent someone out into the snow in their underwear. And I was much too tired to be chasing someone down in the snow in the middle of the night.

The cabin had been built as a refuge for Grandpop and Minty when my grandmother's cancer had weakened her to the point we all knew it was her last year. Pop had rented a barge and brought in everything he'd needed to build his wife a comfortable room to sleep in during her last fish camp summer. Two wooden benches served as couches with foam pads on the seats, and the foam could be pushed together to make a double mattress, which was what I planned to do to make sure Oliver got warm. I put the foam from one bench on the floor next to the wood stove.

"Hey," I said, waking him from the doze he'd fallen into. "There's a foam pad on the floor. Lie down on that while I get you into bed."

He smiled sleepily, and cracked an eyelid. "Promises, promises."

"You sound drunk," I said, frowning with concern.

"I wish. Then I'd be warm."

"No you wouldn't. Alcohol makes too much body heat go to the surface of your skin, and you lose it even faster."

"You know too much," he slurred, but he did as I asked. I moved the pad he'd been sitting on down and pushed the pads together, then pulled the sleeping bag out of my rucksack.

"Take off the damn coat," I said, as I pulled the bag up over his bare feet.

"You don't like the Canada Goose?" he mumbled.

I helped him pull his arms out of the sleeves, and he shivered in his sweater. I tucked the coat up into a ball and shoved it under his head. He smiled dreamily. "Mmm. A pillow. Thanks."

Then I took my own boots, socks, and snow pants off, bunched my own parka up as a pillow, and, wearing a heavy knit sweater, my t-shirt, and underwear, I climbed into the sleeping bag with him.

"What are you doing?" Oliver said vaguely. That he didn't seem to have noticed my bare legs was either worrisome or insulting.

"Saving your hands and feet," I said, as I wrapped my bare feet around his and placed his icy hands under my sweater on my bare back. We were face to face, and I tried to wrap my limbs around as much of him as I could.

"Mmm. Warm." He sighed and seemed to snuggle in. "Thank you." The last words were said on an exhale, and I let myself sleep only after his shivering finally ceased.

[24]

OLIVER

"As if you were on fire from within.
The moon lives in the lining of your skin."

- PABLO NERUDA, *ODE TO A BEAUTIFUL NUDE*

I woke to a warm woman and a raging hard-on.

First impressions were everything, and the day had begun in the best possible way. Then reality crashed in. I opened my eyes slowly so I only had to deal with one piece of input at a time. Bright sun seeped around the edges of closed shutters, dimly illuminating the interior of an unfamiliar cabin. A wood stove that smelled like fire squatted on the floor next to my side of a bed that wasn't exactly a bed. More like a thick foam pad directly on the floor. I was fully dressed, though my feet were bare inside the warm down cocoon of a single sleeping bag. And, in my arms, with her back pressed against my stomach, her ass nestled against my insistent erection, lay a woman.

Not just any woman, my brain told me as I registered the long dark hair that smelled of something botanical, and the strong sinewy muscle of the thigh over which my leg was draped.

Dallas.

My dick jumped at that, and I just barely resisted the urge to pull her even closer. She must have sensed my alertness though, because she pulled away and rolled to face me.

"Wiggle your toes," she said.

And that woke me right up.

"What?"

"Wiggle your toes," she said insistently. "If you can do it without pain, you might not have gotten frost-nipped."

"Frost nip?" I tried to understand, but my brain did not seem to be able to grasp anything other than mourning the loss of Dallas's ass pressed against me. I wiggled my toes and rotated my feet. "No pain," I confirmed.

She must have been holding her breath, because she exhaled in relief. "Good. Now your hands. Is the skin warm? Can you press on the pads of your fingertips without tingling or discomfort?"

I did a very cheeky thing and slid my hands up under her sweater and pressed my fingertips against her back. "No discomfort. Are they warm enough?"

Her expression didn't change, and I was pretty much in awe of her self-control. "Normal. How's your head?"

I almost pressed my dick against her again, but decided to take a page from her self-control manual instead. "No headache, if that's what you mean."

"Fogginess? Cloudy thinking?" she asked.

Only from the blood rushing to other parts of my body. Out loud I said, "I have only vague memories of trying to untie my boots last night. Wait," I said as an image came clear, "did you put my bare feet on your stomach?"

My hands were still on the naked skin of her back, and I reveled in the feeling of woman in them—this woman, who spoke so matter-of-factly to the man whose hard-on had woken her up and still jumped at the idea of her.

"Like I told you last night, the warmest part of any body is the midsection, where all the vital organs are. Under arms and between thighs are also good for defrosting extremities and preventing frostbite."

Between thighs. I must have smiled out loud at that, because she glanced at my mouth, and that made the smile even bigger. But instead of kissing me, which is what I hoped would happen, she spoke again.

"We need to talk about what happened last night."

Damn.

"A lot of things happened last night," I said warily.

"My biggest concern," she said, and I braced myself, "is how your Russian found us."

I exhaled, more relieved and … disturbed than made sense. "*My* Russian."

"Clearly, I'm making an assumption. But it's a reasonably logical one to make, given the fact that you were most recently shot at in Chicago, and a shooter came to camp last night. Wolf must have tracked the shooter to wherever he was hiding—waiting for you—and he shot her to avoid being attacked."

My hands tightened reflexively on her back. "Definitely not a shit wolf," I whispered.

She was silent a moment, and to distract myself from thinking about Wolf, I reveled in the softness of her skin under my hands. I didn't move them because I didn't want to remind her they were there. I was certain she'd pull away, get up, do whatever put distance between us, and I wanted to stay there, in that moment.

"I guess there is a possibility that the shooter was someone completely different, a woman Reed or Mark pissed off, for example, or even less likely, a random hunter poaching on private land. But if it was your Russian"—her eyes met mine—"he was in hiding, waiting for you to return to your camper where he could take you out without bringing down the whole compound on his head."

That was a chilling thought. "You don't think he would have just tried to steal the hard drives and get away?"

"No. Even if he succeeds in stealing them, the only way to stop you from rewriting the code is to kill you."

The air whooshed out of my lungs. "Oh."

She moved her arm to mine and gripped it in a gesture of sympathy. "Yeah."

"Would you …" I struggled for the words because I was trying to figure them out, and then because I was afraid. "Would you mind if I … held you for a minute?"

My heart hammered, and I couldn't separate the fear that someone was trying to kill me from the fear that she'd say no.

She didn't say no. Instead she wrapped her arm around my waist and let me pull her in. My heartbeat was faster and harder than hers, until I felt myself calming to match her pulse and her breath. Maybe it was a minute, maybe it was five, but holding her felt like the only thing to do in the wide world of doing things.

When I began to be aware of the smell of her skin and the feeling of her body pressed against mine, she pulled her arm back and I let go.

"I'm going to add wood to the fire and go out to the woods to pee. When I get back, we'll take stock of the situation and figure out our next steps, okay?"

I nodded, already missing her presence five inches away from me.

"Oliver," she said solemnly, looking into my eyes. "We'll get through this."

My heartbeat had picked up again as I lost myself in her long black eyelashes and in pools of deep brown irises. "Dallas," I said, in the same solemn tone she'd used. My skin tightened, and my breath came faster. "I really want to kiss you right now."

She seemed to search my eyes for something. "I can't," she whispered. Then she turned, unzipped the sleeping bag, and slid out, leaving a void of rapidly fading warmth behind.

I watched her crouch in front of the wood stove, feeding it pieces of wood from the stack behind it, seemingly unconscious of the effect her beautiful bare legs and simple black cotton underwear had on me. Then she sat on the foam pad and pulled on ridiculously colorful hand-knit socks, before grabbing her ski pants and stepping into them. I had dated models, always tall and skinny, and I'd dated actresses, slender and curvy, but I'd never been with an athlete. Dallas was an athlete—graceful, strong, capable, rounder of hip than some, smaller of breast than others—but she wasn't just long legs or well-defined arms. Her body was useful. It moved well, it did what she asked it to do and it did so without obvious effort. She was healthy and capable, and I had the sense that she enjoyed what her body could do.

I had never looked at a woman's body with anything other than aesthetics in mind before, but as I watched Dallas run her fingers through her hair to untangle it, then quickly twist it into a single braid, I saw a woman—a whole person—not just the sum of her parts.

She caught me looking when she opened the shutters and let the blinding sunlight into the room. A half-smile, somehow softer than others she'd reluctantly given me, lifted the corner of her mouth. "See you in a bit," she said, as she grabbed a large pot from a shelf near the door and headed to the entrance for her boots.

A blast of icy air shot through the cabin, and I suddenly realized how very toasty it was to have slept next to the wood stove. My body ached in ways I didn't understand, until I remembered the long ride spent clinging to the woman and the machine with arms and legs gripping both tightly. I stood, stretched, and surveyed the room. My socks and boots had been set out near the stove, and the socks were warm and dry. Those went on, and I replaced the foam pads on the two benches, then draped the sleeping bag over the back of one of them. Finally, I let myself look out the window.

The view was spectacular.

The little cabin seemed to be perched on the edge of a vast flat field of crystalline snow. Mountains rose up from the far side of the flat plain, and they were covered with powder-dusted spruce trees.

As I watched, Dallas waded out through several inches of fresh snow to a pristine spot and scooped a potful of it. She took a moment to look around her, to breathe in the air, and to feel the sun on her face. This was a woman who embraced small moments of being alive, and watching her made me realize how often I forgot to look at anything other than the computer screen in front of me.

Suddenly, I wanted to be outside, standing next to her, hearing what she heard, seeing what she saw. I grabbed my parka off the bench, and something sharp jabbed my palm. I had picked the coat up from the hem instead of the collar, and whatever it was that stabbed me was inside the seam.

Looking at it more closely, I could see where the stitching had been messed with. My pocket knife made quick work of the seam, and I eased out a tiny square metal chip the size of the nail on my pinky finger. The cabin door opened, and Dallas knocked the snow off her boots before kicking them off to haul the pot of fresh snow to the wood stove.

"What's that?" she asked, eyeing the chip I held up to the light.

"I think," I said as I turned it in my fingers, "I know how the Russian found us."

[25]
DALLAS

"I saw them standing there pretending to be just friends,
when all the time in the world could not pry them apart."

\- BRIAN ANDREAS

A tracking device. Cipher Security had them, of course—not quite this size or configuration, but close enough for me to recognize it for what it was. "Well, that explains how he found you, here and also in Humboldt Park," I said, relieved that it hadn't been my carelessness that had led the Russian to us in Chicago. I photographed both sides of it with my phone, and wished we could keep it to send back to Cipher, but the Russian could place us in this cabin for the past eight hours, so it was time for Oliver to go.

"What do we do with it?" Oliver asked, the note of distaste clear in his voice. "I'd like to take a rock to it, personally."

I had an idea, and I dug around in my rucksack until I found the roll of duct tape I carried with me. I smiled when I held it up, and Oliver

185

laughed out loud. "Only you would carry duct tape. What are you thinking?"

I sliced off a piece of tape and carefully wrapped it around the chip, rendering it more or less waterproof. Then I tucked it in my pocket and grabbed a box from the shelf by the door. "Want to go ice fishing?"

Grandpop had a hand-held auger in the shed that he used to set the support beams for hanging salmon in the smokehouse, and Reed and I had discovered that it was perfect for drilling holes in the ice. I grabbed the augur, handed Oliver a shovel, and led us out onto the river.

"How can we fish in a field?" he asked in obvious confusion.

I took the shovel from him and started clearing a spot. "It's not a field," I said. When I looked over at him, I was surprised to see him standing with his face to the sun, taking deep breaths of the icy air. The expression on his face was blissful, and I realized I'd never seen him look … happy. He'd been angry, afraid, snarky, wry, charming, and vaguely irresistible, but this smile was serene, his expression peaceful, and he looked happy.

Oliver's eyes opened and focused on mine. "It's beautiful here. What is this place?"

"We call it fish camp, because our whole family comes here for two weeks every summer when the salmon are running."

He looked around, confused again. "Don't you need a river to catch fish?"

I smirked. "You're standing on it."

He looked down to realize the ice under his feet where I'd cleared the snow was colored the deep blue of the water beneath it. He almost jumped backward, but held himself still with considerable effort. I smiled at that. "Here," I said, handing him the shovel, "clear more snow so I can drill a hole."

The startled look on his face turned to wonder, and a strange glow of pride hit me. But why should it matter if he liked it here? Or for that matter, why should anything in my world appeal to Oliver Curran, entrepreneur and tech genius? And yet, it apparently did.

I bent to my task of drilling a hole into the ice, and within a few minutes, I was pulling small chunks out to clear the hole of debris.

"Okay, hand me that box, please?" I said, pointing to Grandpop's fishing tackle. He passed it over and I selected a heavy fishing line, several large hooks, and a couple of fluorescent yellow jiggly worms.

I explained as I tied the hooks on the line. "We're fishing for burbot, which is a prehistoric fish with tiny eyes, so any bait that moves or flashes is going to get its attention."

When the line was ready and a heavy weight was attached to the bottom of it, I tied it around the handle of the shovel. Then I dropped the line into the hole and laid the shovel across it. "Here," I said to Oliver as I handed him the shovel, "you can feel the current of the river."

Again, a look of wonder crossed his face, and another wave of pride washed over me.

"What would happen if a person fell in?" he asked, peering down into the hole as if he could see into the river's depths.

"First of all, this ice is too thick and won't break up until probably late spring, so you'd have to really try to break through it here. But," I said, squatting across the hole from him, "if someone did go through the ice, the first thing, obviously, is to get them out."

Oliver tested the line. "How do you do that if the ice is that thin?" he asked.

"Usually people break through at the edges of a river or lake, because that's where it's thinnest, so the obvious answer is, just stand up. But if it's deep, try to throw them a line or grab on to a piece of wood or something. If that doesn't work and you have to get them out yourself, lie down on the ice to distribute your weight and keep backing yourself up as you pull them out, so you don't put too much stress on the fragile ice."

"And then what?" he asked.

I shrugged. "Get them warm. Fingers and toes are in danger from frostbite, internal organs from hypothermia. Strip the wet clothes off and get the person dry. Snow is actually decent at drying off a wet person if that's the only option."

He stared at me like I was crazy. "You dry them off with snow?"

I smiled at the expression of horror on his face. "Snow is only wet when it melts. If someone's just come out of the freezing water, their skin isn't warm enough to melt snow."

He shivered violently, and I took pity and changed the subject. "Feel anything in the line yet?"

He handed me the shovel. "Is that just the drag of the river, or is there something on it?"

I dunked the line a couple of times and something yanked. I grinned at Oliver as I handed the shovel back. "Pull it out. Let's see."

He stood and carefully pulled the line out of the water. Two long, slimy fish—one on the top hook and one on the second hook from the bottom—thrashed on the line. They looked like eels sporting goatees, and they came out of the hole looking utterly furious at having been removed from their ice bath. "Pick one," I said, indicating the fish.

He blinked, maybe in surprise that I'd given him the choice, then pointed to the top fish, which was the bigger of the two. "That's dinner," I said, as I unhooked it from the line and tossed it onto the snow.

"What's this one?" Oliver held the bottom fish up.

I pulled off one slimy glove and reached into the pocket where I'd stashed the duct-taped chip. Then I shoved the chip deep into the throat of the angry burbot.

"That's Oliver," I said with a grin as I dropped the fish back into the hole in the ice.

I'd never heard a man laugh so hard as when the burbot named Oliver wiggled his tail and darted away. Hopefully that would keep the Russian busy for a while.

Cleaning, fileting, and cooking the fish was actually fun with Oliver. He wanted to do everything, so each step was a matter of explaining, showing, and then handing it off. Burbot was sort of a freshwater cod that could be made to taste a little like lobster. The easiest way to cook it with the supplies we had on hand was to cut it into bite-sized chunks and fry it in a cast iron pan on the wood stove. We kept oil and spices in the cabin, and I found some onions and potatoes in the cold cellar under the floorboards.

We ate our meal right out of the pan, which we then cleaned with a scrubber and some snow. We both sat back on the bench closest to the stove and warmed our feet.

"The thing about survival in the North," I said, enjoying the warmth and the full belly, "is that all your effort goes into shelter, heat, and food. If one of those things fails, you die, and that sort of puts things that matter into perspective."

Oliver leaned back and stretched his arm behind me on the bench. It was companionable to be there with him, and I almost leaned my head onto his chest. I resisted the impulse.

"What matters to you, Dallas?" he asked quietly.

"My family," I said immediately. "My job."

"What is it about your job that matters?" He didn't sound judgmental, just curious.

I thought for a minute about how to put into words something that had only ever been a feeling. "I've always been kind of a caretaker. When it was just me and my mom, she took care of me, but I took care of her too—making dinners, cleaning up, taking responsibility for things whenever I could. When Christi was born, that baby became mine. I was basically her second mom, and she's always looked to me for protection and advice. My mom taught me how to care for someone, and Grandpop taught me how to actually *take care*. I can hunt, fish, cook, ride, clean a gun, build a camp, chop wood, build a trap—basically anything a person needs to do to survive, I can do it."

Oliver's fingers had found their way to my braid and were twisting it idly. It was comforting, in a way, and I decided to pretend I hadn't noticed.

"When I left the Yukon, I didn't really need to use all those skills to survive anymore. Survival in a city uses different muscles, and although I had an advantage because of my wilderness survival experience, I never learned how to charm a landlord into fixing a broken window—I just fixed it myself."

He chuckled, and I felt the rumble of his chest in my arm, which had somehow gotten close enough to touch him.

"Self-sufficiency can be pretty lonely sometimes, because you convince yourself you don't need anything from anyone, so you don't ask for help, and then people forget to offer help, and then you're just alone."

Oliver's arm came down off the back of the bench to my shoulder, and he gathered me into his side. My head went automatically to his chest, and the sound of his heartbeat calmed my own.

"And at your job," he said quietly, "people need you. They need your skills, they need your protection, they need your brain and your eyes and your instincts."

"Yes," I whispered.

"I get it." He picked up my hand and studied it, turning it one way, then another, tracing the scars on my knuckles, the tendons in my fingers, and the veins on the back. Then he laced his fingers through mine and said, "I'm one of those people."

[26]

OLIVER

"Our culture is our inheritance. When we live our culture we are keeping it alive, we are sustaining it. You don't know traditional knowledge, you have to live it. You have to be a First Nations person to understand—the way we grow up, the way we hunt, the way we live on the land. The land is our university and our church. We went to school out on the land. That's our university."

- TR'ONDËK HWËCHIN ELDER, TH HERITAGE ACT 2016

"We left your family with an active shooter to deal with, and it kind of feels like we're taking a break from all my problems while you're teaching me this stuff." I took the ax for my turn at the wood splitting.

Dallas brushed sawdust off her face as she studied me. "This stuff"— she waved a hand around her to indicate the wood we'd been splitting— "is not 'taking a break,' it's survival. We would have to do it if there was a shooter or not."

"But he's there, and we're here. What are we doing?"

Dallas nodded at the ax. "Keep chopping, it'll keep you warm," she said, as she bent to pick up another piece of wood for the stack. She spoke while we worked.

"Here's my thought. Presuming it was the Russian who tracked you to my family's compound because of the chip he planted in your coat—probably when he broke into your car, by the way—"

I grimaced. Her feelings about me owning a thousand-dollar coat, much less leaving it in the car, had been made painfully clear.

She continued, unaware that I'd apparently begun growing a conscience. "You're his target. And since he's most likely an assassin, not a suicide-by-cop mass shooter, I assume he'd like to survive the experience. He is now aware that would be unlikely in a place full of people with guns and dogs."

My wince this time was for Wolf. Dallas seemed to have put away whatever she felt about the loss of Wolf, but I hadn't even really begun to process those feelings. I set up another piece of wood and swung the ax for a near-perfect split.

"Good," she said with a nod. "Later, when your arm is good and tired, I'll teach you how to throw that ax."

I scoffed. "Why when my arm is tired?"

She shrugged. "Somehow, the only time you ever need to throw a knife or an ax is when you're already exhausted."

"I'm sorry," I said with genuine bafflement, "when will I ever need to throw a knife or an ax?"

She shrugged. "Sometimes you just do," she said cryptically before changing the subject. "The Russian had about eight hours of tracker to follow through the densely wooded forest. He probably had a truck parked out near the highway, or we would have heard him drive in, so he was on foot. My guess is that he waited for daylight—because remember, it snowed last night too—and when the tracker began to move again, hopefully swimming far downstream"—her smile was pure mischief and it was totally contagious—"he either left to follow it, or he's camped out near the compound, waiting for us to return."

"That's the part that worries me," I said, swinging the ax over my head and down onto the upright piece of wood. "I really don't like the idea of a trained killer hanging out around your family while we're up here having a winter vacation."

She scoffed. "First of all, he deserves what he gets if he takes on my family. And second, winter is never a vacation in the North. Let's say, for the sake of covering all bases, that the Russian's tracking skills are close enough to mine that he actually does make it up here. My job is literally to keep you alive, and if I get taken out, you have to know how to survive."

I did not like the sound of that. "What do you mean, if you get taken out? You're not the Secret Service. You don't step in front of bullets for people."

Her eyebrows rose as if the comment wasn't worth answering. I sank the ax head into the chopping block and turned Dallas to face me. "Don't get me wrong, I want to learn everything you're willing to teach me, even ax throwing, but you don't put your life on the line for me, Dallas."

She met my serious gaze with her own. "You don't decide what I do, Oliver."

We stared at each other for much longer than was comfortable, but I wasn't going to look away, and neither was she.

A light crack that sounded like the snapping of a snow-laden branch came from the woods behind the shed. "Hold on," Dallas whispered.

My flight instinct kicked in hard. "The Russian?" I exhaled.

She shook her head. "I smell an animal." Dallas spun to face the sound, reaching out a hand to hold me in place.

She signaled silence, I nodded, and then I followed her slow, precise footsteps around the side of the shed. It was exactly the excruciatingly slow tracking walk she'd taught me in Humboldt Park, and I was ridiculously proud that I remembered what to do.

I was concentrating so hard on silence that I almost collided with her when she stopped. Her stance was tense, and she looked ready to bolt. "What is it?" I breathed into her ear.

She stepped to the side just enough to let me move up next to her, and I slowly peered around the side of the shed.

Then I stopped breathing entirely. Not even ten feet away from us stood a bull moose, stock-still, its nose in the air, maybe trying to catch our scent or maybe just searching for food. The creature was massive, like a Salvador Dali elephant. It stood taller than a horse, with long, knobby legs, a rough patchy coat, and a rack of antlers that rivaled the ones hanging on Isaac's cabin.

Dallas never took her eyes off the beast as her hand reached for mine and she pulled me back—slowly, so slowly my muscles protested—until we reached the front door to the cabin.

"Inside," she whispered, holding the door for me. She didn't even pause to knock the snow from her boots—just kicked them off in the vestibule and pulled me in after her.

When the door was closed behind us, she finally seemed to breathe.

The fire in the wood stove crackled, and I peeled off my coat, then took Dallas's coat from her to drape over the back of the bench. I watched her, worried, and when she still didn't speak, I finally asked, "Are you okay?"

Her eyes met mine, and she seemed to relax a little more. "I told you moose are dangerous."

"Yeah, during calving and rutting seasons. Has calving season already started?"

She shook her head. "Kind of like everything else in the Yukon, it starts around mid-May." She inhaled deeply and sat on the bench closest to the fire to warm her hands. She didn't look at me as she spoke. "I'm a little superstitious about moose sightings."

"Good or bad?"

She met my gaze and gave me a half-smile. It was something. "Not great," she said.

I settled in beside her and put my arm around her shoulder, hoping that the tacit permission I'd been granted earlier hadn't been revoked.

She put her head on my chest and looked up at me. "We're not doing this," she gestured between us. "This isn't a thing."

"Not a thing. Got it," I said with a smile.

She sighed and rolled her eyes. "Your charming smile should come with a warning label."

"You think I'm charming?" I batted my eyelashes and grinned at her.

"It's not a compliment," she said, shaking her head. "You've met my cousin. *He's* charming."

I huffed a laugh. "It should be illegal for a man to be that beautiful. Seriously, if I were gay, I'd be all over him."

She chuckled. "If I were gay, I would be too."

"Wait," I pretended to be confused, "you're—"

She elbowed me. "Don't say it."

I laughed and hugged her closer to my side. She allowed it, and I pretended I hadn't noticed. The silence settled back in, broken only by the crackle of the fire until she spoke again.

"I was twenty-one and had just graduated from college the fall I guided my last moose hunt." She looked angry. "The client was one of those entitled rich guys who'd hunted around the world putting a bullet into every big-game animal he could find. He hated the fact that I knew more about the bush than he ever would."

I smirked at her matter-of-fact tone. I knew it wasn't a boast.

"He was determined to be the big alpha hunter," she continued, "and if he could have gotten me fired, he would have. I never did find out if he tried, because it was my last guide job, and I left the Yukon right after."

I wanted to ruin the guy's credit and frame him for fraud, and I didn't even know his name.

It was getting dark, and Dallas picked up a poker to open the wood stove door. The heat and light from the stove warmed my feet and cast a glow over the woman by my side. She was the boss while I was still her client, but she had no say over what I felt when she shared small pieces of herself with me.

She nestled back into my side, and I was glad she couldn't see my smile. She probably would have distanced herself just to make a point. "The guy was determined to take down a prize-winning rack, and every bull moose I saw with antlers over fifty inches was deemed 'too small' because I was the one to spot it. But then, just as the light was going, he spotted a young male standing across a river. I'd already seen and dismissed the moose as illegal, but the client insisted he was a full-grown bull. He shouldered his rifle, and I pushed it away. Then he turned it on me."

I sucked in a breath. "Bastard," I murmured.

Then her voice got a faraway sound, like memory was the only thing backing it. "*You shoot it*, he said. *Use your Indian hunting rights to get me my moose.*" She seemed to come back to herself then. "He had a calculating look on his face, like he was trying to decide if he could get away with shooting me."

I didn't just want to ruin the guy then, I wanted to put him in prison.

"And then he said, *Never mind, I'll just put it on your tag anyway,* and he turned the gun on the young male and shot him."

Fury pumped through me as Dallas took a steadying breath and continued.

"Moose go to water when they're wounded, as this one did. He was bellowing in rage and pain, and he thrashed himself right out into the middle of the rapid where he got stuck in a beaver dam."

Her voice seemed distant, as though she was reliving the moment in her mind. "He was in so much pain, and he couldn't get free, and he was dying … I grabbed a hank of rope and stripped down to go, I don't know … help him, while the bastard who shot him stood there, smirking, as if seeing me in my underwear was exactly the humiliation he'd been hoping for."

Dallas ground the words out. "And then the moose drowned, and I was just *so angry*. I didn't even feel the cold when I went in after him. You can't leave a dead moose in the river because it'll foul the water. I was furious and sobbing as I swam out to him, and the asshole client was *laughing*."

I heard the tears in her voice. The asshole client. No wonder the word *client* was so charged for her.

"The current was really strong, and I finally began to feel the cold

…" She gasped with the memory. "And I heard a voice say, as clear as day, *If you do this, you will die.*"

I could feel the pounding of her heart, and I wanted to gather her into my arms.

"I'd never heard voices before, and haven't heard one since, but I listened that day. I left the moose where it was, trapped in the beaver dam, and I swam back to shore. The client was screaming at me to go get his rack, and I threw the rope at him and told him to get it himself. Then I picked up my clothes, got on my horse, and rode away."

She watched the fire in silence for a long time before she spoke again.

"There were northern lights that night, and I felt like it was the universe marking a turning point. Like nature was saying 'pay attention, don't forget this moment. It matters.' And when I got back to base camp, I knew what I had to do. I sent another guide out to find the client, and I never guided another hunt again."

She exhaled deeply, and the tension seemed to ease out of her body with the breath.

"The moose out there today knew we were close—we'd just been talking and chopping wood—but it didn't charge us."

My fingers played idly with her hair. "Do you need the moose to forgive you for its brother?"

She went still. "No," she finally said, "but I might need to forgive myself."

"Why?" I asked.

But she'd turned inward again. I could hear it in her voice. "We have complex Indigenous harvest rights that my parents' and grandparents' generations fought hard for. I knew the outfitters used my First Nations hunting privilege as a selling point to clients. I never stopped them because I figured the shots were mine to take or not. But that client felt *entitled* to my rights, as if he'd bought me, so my hunting privilege was his too."

She shuddered. "I worked for them for five years, telling myself I was doing a job and it didn't mean anything …"

Her voice trailed off, and I kept mine quiet enough that she could let it go unheard if she wanted to. "What did you make it mean?"

She didn't say anything for a few minutes, and then she did. "I took my Northern Tutchone heritage for granted because it was who my grandfather was. And even though he had moved away from his family, they taught him the survival skills he taught me, so being his grand-daughter connected me to his … *my* First Nations heritage. Working for the outfitter, allowing him to exploit something I valued about myself, made me complicit. I betrayed myself by staying, and worse, I betrayed my grandfather and the significance of everything he taught me." She inhaled deeply. "I wasn't worthy of my heritage if I could sell it out so cheaply, so I left, everything. And yeah, I come back to visit every summer, but I haven't really come *back* … until now."

She looked up and met my eyes, searching them as though to under-stand her own words. And then she looked past me out the cabin window, and a smile slowly lit her face. There were green and gold lights reflecting in her eyes, and I followed her gaze to see the northern lights dancing across the horizon.

"What do you think the universe is saying this time?" I asked quietly, watching the play of light on her skin. She breathed deeply, and then nestled her head against my chest as she watched the lights.

"Welcome home," she whispered to herself.

[27]

DALLAS

"Our women have always voted, held office, been an equal part of governance and leadership and because all people come from their mothers, we call your mother your 'first teacher.'"

— OJIBWE CULTURAL HISTORIAN

We watched the northern lights through the window for a while, even though the place we both really wanted to be was on the river, lying on our backs in the snow. Oliver made a joke about snow angels calling our names, but he didn't push, and I didn't have to remind him that the bull moose could be deadly if humans ventured too far into his territory.

Survival is exhausting, and I was trying to cram a couple decades' worth of learning into a few days so Oliver would have the skills he might need to stay alive if something happened to me. I didn't really believe I was going to die, but seeing that moose had knocked something loose in me—something that I'd held tightly for so many years—something that felt like fear.

I wasn't afraid of the moose exactly, although a healthy sense of fear where moose were concerned was generally a smart thing to hang on to. No, the fear that had been slowly creeping around the edges of my self-control was not for myself. I knew I could survive just about anything.

Except losing someone I loved.

I shut that thought down as soon as it formed into a sentence in my mind and busied myself with getting ready for bed. I banked the fire so the coals would be ready to re-light in the morning while Oliver pulled both cushions to the floor.

"There's no other bedding here that I could find," I said. "I'm sorry if it makes things awkward."

He flipped the lone sleeping bag out on the foam, and shrugged. "I'm sorry if my boner in your back all night makes things awkward."

I laughed, until I saw he hadn't cracked a smile. "You're serious."

"That I have a hard-on for you? Yep."

He said it so matter-of-factly that I was at a momentary loss for words.

"But—"

"I know, this"—he indicated himself and me—"isn't a thing while I'm your client. Despite what you may think about me, I'm capable of behaving myself."

What I'd actually been protesting was the idea that he would be attracted to me at all. I wasn't his type. I wasn't leggy, blonde, skinny, busty, or classically pretty. My eyes were too hooded, my cheekbones too broad, my lips were too big. I was too capable, too strong, too serious, and just too … different. I wasn't insecure about my looks, and when I put some effort into them, I'd been called striking. But I wasn't Oliver Curran striking, I was just … me.

"I can't sleep in my jeans again for another night though," he continued, clearly not a mind reader, "so I apologize in advance if my legs are too hairy or my feet are cold."

I laughed outright. "Nothing could top your feet from last night. I think I can deal." And strangely, maybe because he'd been so straightforward, it was okay to strip off our socks and pants and heavy sweaters, and crawl, shivering, into the chilly sleeping bag wearing only our underwear and long-sleeved shirts.

I turned my back to him, and he slid one arm under my coat-pillow and wrapped the other one around my ribs, settling on my chest between my breasts. He pulled me tightly against him and threw his top leg over my bottom leg so we were as spooned as we could be. And indeed his legs were hairy, and his feet were cold, and his dick was hard, and none of it mattered—and all of it mattered, because I felt the disquiet slipping away.

"Good night," I whispered.

"Sweet dreams," he whispered back.

And the pounding of my heart gradually calmed as our limbs warmed and the rhythm of our breath matched, and I felt him twitch that twitch of falling to sleep, and I smiled.

I'd left the shutters open, and the morning sunlight hit my face quite rudely. I buried it in Oliver's chest with a groan of protest, and he tightened his arms around me.

"Shhh," he whispered. "If it doesn't see us, it'll go away."

"It's late. We should get up," I mumbled, already wondering what we'd eat that day.

"Don't wanna." He sounded five.

"Well, I don't know about you, but I'm feeling kind of grungy, and I might know where a little geothermal pond is kind of near here."

"Really?!" Both eyes opened wide, and he grinned.

"Turn the wattage down, you'll burn the cabin with that smile," I said, but it was infectious, and I couldn't help smiling too.

He wiggled out of the sleeping bag. "Hmm, what to wear to a bath in the frozen North," he mused. "Oh, I know. The same thing I've worn for the last two days. Pretty hot, huh?"

He pulled his big sweater on over his head, and I took the opportunity to steal a glance at the rest of him.

Oliver had the shape of a surfer, with lean hips, long, strong legs, and broad shoulders. He had the impossibly flat stomach of a guy who didn't eat carbs, and yet I'd seen him eat bread and he enjoyed food, so maybe it was just excellent genes.

He caught me looking, of course, because I'd gotten distracted by the V-shape that dipped down below the waistband of his boxer briefs. He sat to put on socks and jeans and grinned mischievously. "Now you."

He didn't even pretend not to look as I got out of the sleeping bag and pulled on my clothes. "You're beautiful," he said, as I twisted my hair into a braid.

I shot him a look, expecting to see smirking, but instead he looked thoughtful and earnest.

"Thank you," I said, because I couldn't think of anything else.

"I'd like to photograph you," he added.

I scowled at that, and he stepped forward to touch the lines between my brows. "Even these. Maybe especially these, because you say so much with them." He smoothed the scowl away with his finger and then moved to pick up the sleeping bag and drape it over the bench.

"You're serious." Not a question.

"My world is very visual," he said, as he picked up the foam cushions. "I work with a visual language when I code, and when I'm not programming, I look for visual patterns in everything else. Some people absorb the world through sound, others, like I suspect your sister does, absorb it through smell and taste."

"You have that too," I protested, though I wasn't really sure why I thought the observation was a protest.

He shook his head. "Good food for me is still visual. It's still about how the colors and textures go together in a bowl or on a plate. I actually like the story of food more than the taste of it."

I thought about the ramen he'd made, how every element in the bowl seemed perfectly placed. I'd thought it was about balancing the flavors, but apparently, Oliver just had a really good eye.

"Please, Dallas. Let me tell the story of these days here through images. I've been trying to store them all mentally, but I'm running out of space." He smiled self-deprecatingly, and I shook my head at him.

"I keep the images?" I asked.

"Your phone, your photos," he said.

I sighed and pulled my phone from my pocket. "Don't lose it."

He opened the photo app and snapped a picture of me, probably scowling again, because it's what I felt like doing whenever a camera was pointed my way. "Thank you," he said with a grin.

He tucked the phone into his coat pocket, and we got ready to go out. I brought fishing line and a rifle, and I added a towel from the cabin's supply to my rucksack, which already held a first aid kit, some hand warmers, a box of shells, a change of socks for each of us, and a change of underwear for me.

I carried the rifle and Oliver carried the rucksack as we first set our fishing line at the hole we'd made in the ice and then continued walking down the middle of the river. It was like a wide, flat runway edged on either side with row after row of snow-covered gravel mounds resembling dramatic dunes higher than a person's head—a landscape feature left over from the days of dredging the river for gold.

The day was sunny, and the Yukon sky was showing off for Oliver.

"I never realized how big the sky is here," he said, as he snapped a photo of a beautiful stack of puffy white cumulus clouds.

"Have you ever been to Alaska?" I asked, and he shook his head no. "Haines is a small town just inland from Juneau, and about a three-and-a-half-hour drive from Whitehorse. I worked on a friend's gold mine there one year."

"You worked on a gold mine? Doing what?"

I shrugged. "Driving the excavator and a backhoe loader, whatever he needed. My point is that I expected the sky there to be the same—it's all the Yukon, just not the Yukon Territory."

He aimed the phone at me and snapped photos as I talked. I tried not to be self-conscious as I continued. "But this sky is so much bigger. Haines is surrounded by these spectacular, jagged mountains, and the trees there are all really majestic white spruce and paper aspen, not like the rounded mountains and scrubby black spruce here," I said, waving my hand toward the mountains on the far side of the river.

I turned in toward the bank where the thermal pool was that Reed and I had found one winter.

"Do you know, there's a road that runs right by the river just east of Haines, and during salmon season in August, tourists drive up and down that road looking for bear. Fishermen are standing five across in the river casting lines for coho salmon, and I once saw a mama bear teaching her cubs to fish not twenty feet away from the nearest fisherman."

"Did you get a photo?" Oliver asked.

I grinned at the excitement in his face. "Of course I did."

He held out my phone. "Where is it? Can I see?"

I climbed up the bank where it wasn't steep, and Oliver followed in my footprints. I kept walking as I scrolled through photos from two years before. "While I was watching the bear cubs eat the fish their mama had just caught, some idiot pulled up in his car and parked next to where I was standing. Then he rolled down his car window and took a big bite of a hamburger. Mama bear suddenly lifted her head and sniffed the air. I nearly turned and ran. She must have realized her salmon was way better than the guy's burger, because she went back into the water for another one. Meanwhile, the idiot had no idea he'd almost had competition for his lunch from a bear. Ah," I said, handing him the phone, "here it is."

Oliver grabbed for the phone, but it slipped from his glove and went sliding onto the ice at the edge of the river. "Ah! Shit!" he said. "I'll get it."

"No!" I grabbed his arm before he could head down the embankment after it. "You're too heavy. I'll get it."

I took the rifle off my shoulder and handed it to him before starting down the embankment.

"Shit, I'm sorry, Dallas. The one thing you told me not to do." He looked so anxious up on the embankment that I shook my head.

"Don't sweat it. If we weren't in the middle of nowhere, I'd leave it. It's just a phone."

"Unfortunately," he said, "we are in the middle of nowhere—because of me—and now we might be out one communication device, dodgy as the reception might be—because of me."

"Not everything is about you, Charmer."

He huffed a laugh at that, but it wasn't convincing. I got down to the edge of the river and wiped away the snow to get a look at the ice beneath. It was crystal clear and almost dark blue.

"Huh," I said unhappily.

"What?"

I took off my parka and tossed it up to him. "Hold that for me?"

"What? Why? You said the ice on the river wasn't a problem." He tucked my parka under his arm and looked, if possible, even more worried.

"We're so close to the thermal spring there might be a warm current that thins the ice. This river was dredged, which is why the banks are full of tailing mounds, and it's pretty deep here. Hopefully the ice is still thick enough."

I slid down to my stomach, a little annoyed that my sweater would have to dry out, but not willing to risk my parka. I inched across the ice, listening for the telltale pops and cracks that indicated weak spots.

"Dallas," Oliver said urgently from the bank above me, "if the ice breaks, what do I do?"

"I'll get myself out, but you have to get me warm. If I'm remembering right, the thermal pool is just over the next mound. If I'm not remembering right, then get me back to the cabin."

I stretched my arm out and drew the phone to me with my fingertips. It slid easily on the ice, which was not a good sign because slick ice meant thin ice. And then the ice popped under my chest. "Oliver— CATCH!" I rolled to my back and hurled the phone as high and as hard as I could. He snagged it out of the air just as the ice beneath me let go.

"Dallas!"

The expletive that came out of my mouth was not very inventive, but it was utterly appropriate as I hit the freezing cold river. Shock surged through me, and my muscles went rigid. My chest locked up and I fought for breath as I tried to stand, but I couldn't unlock the muscles in my legs as my boots filled with water. The icy cold felt like knives carving my skin as the current began drawing me downriver.

I was dimly aware of Oliver rushing down the embankment, but the cold had sucked all the air from my lungs, and I couldn't muster the breath to tell him not to. I tried to grab on to the broken edge of the ice, but my hands kept slipping and my legs were beginning to drag under the unbroken ice.

"Grab this!" he yelled, as a branch hovered near my face. I reached for it, slipped, reached again, and caught it under my arm.

"Both hands. Grip with both hands, Dallas." I couldn't feel the bite of the wood under my hands, but I felt it tug, and slowly, inch by excruciating inch, Oliver pulled me from the river.

He was holding a tree stump with one arm and the branch with the other, and he got me out over the top of the unbroken ice and onto the embankment. My teeth were chattering so hard I could barely speak when he pulled me into his chest, but I got two words out. "Up," I said, as he carried me, stumbling, falling, up the embankment, and "naked" once we were off the river.

"Now?" he said, aghast.

"N-n-n-ow," I said, trying to pull the wet sweater over my head and failing.

I tried not to let my own efforts at disrobing get in the way of his much more effective technique, which basically involved a lot of tugging and a little tearing. When I was finally stripped bare, I tried another word. "P-p-p-p-arka."

He understood immediately and wrapped me in my coat, which he had discarded along with the rucksack and rifle on top of the embankment to get me. Then he grabbed them, left my clothes, picked me up in his arms, and ran.

[28]

OLIVER

"A great photograph is one that fully expresses what one feels, in the deepest sense, about what is being photographed."

- ANSEL ADAMS

No, *no, no, no, no, no, no!*

The words were like a drumbeat in my head.

Dallas's body was shaking with constant tremors, her teeth chattering so hard I thought they'd break. Against my arm, her bare legs felt like an ice block, and I stumbled over the tailings mound with single-minded determination—get her into warm water.

"Th-th-th-th-ere," she stammered through her shivers. Next to the frozen river was a small pool, an inlet near a jumble of small boulders. I picked my way carefully down to the rocks.

"I'm going to put you down for a minute, and then I'll get you into the water. Just hang on, okay?"

She nodded, or maybe just shivered in agreement, and I set her gingerly on a rock. I leaned over and stuck my hand in the water. It was lukewarm, like bathwater, and clear. I wasn't going to risk her going in there alone though, so I set down the rucksack and rifle, kicked off my boots and jeans, and pulled off my sweater and shirt.

The air was absolutely frigid, and if my teeth were chattering this hard, I couldn't imagine how cold Dallas was. I stepped into the water and immediately felt icicles stab my feet. A few seconds later, the pain was gone and it was just tingly. I climbed back out and immediately my feet were stabbed with freezing pain again.

Dallas's body was wracked with shivering, but I thought that was a good sign because it meant her body was still trying to rewarm itself. "Dallas, honey, I'm going to put you in the water now. It's going to hurt like hell," I said, as I peeled her parka from her naked body and picked her up in my arms. My skin was cold, but hers was colder as I clutched her to me and stepped back into the water.

Icicle pain stabbed my legs as I walked in deeper, and when the water was to my waist, I ducked down. Dallas stiffened the moment her skin hit the water, and she struggled to get away as I submerged her body. Only her head had stayed above water in the freezing river, so I didn't dunk her head in the warm pool—I just held on as she struggled and cried out in my arms.

"It's okay, honey, it's okay. It's going to be okay," I crooned over and over as she thrashed against me, trying to escape the pain.

Finally, finally, she stopped trying to twist away from me, and she lay still with her eyes closed, twitching with discomfort, or maybe exhaustion.

"Dallas?" I murmured, as I tested the temperature of her face with my lips. I let her float then, barely supported by my arms and legs under her, her head against my shoulder.

"Felt stabby," she whispered, eyes still closed.

"Move your fingers and toes," I whispered back.

She smiled at that. "They move, see?" She reached for me under the water and petted the skin on my thigh. "Hairy legs."

I chuckled and kissed her hair. "I'm so sorry."

"You got me out," she said, looking over at me.

I scoffed, but she smiled, and my heart thumped deeply beneath her palm.

We floated like that for more than an hour, talking sometimes, at other times silent and listening to the sounds of the boreal forest. As her temperature stabilized, the time in the thermal pool became something personal.

I stroked her skin idly as we talked. She described other thermal pools she'd discovered on guiding expeditions through the Yukon, harvesting spruce tips in the late spring to eat along the way. She described an amazing meal Christi once made with spruce tips, smoked salmon, cream, and pasta, and our stomachs rumbled loudly.

"Think we caught any fish?" I asked her hopefully.

"You're going to be pretty sick of burbot if we stay up here much longer," she said. "I may have to teach you the much more complex skills of hunting and dressing caribou."

She was submerged from the neck down, semi-floating on her back. She looked up at me when I didn't say anything, and I was struck with a wave of awe.

She raised an eyebrow. "What?"

"I don't know," I said, unable to find the words. "Don't move."

She smiled. "This is me, not moving." She closed her eyes, and a half-smile played on her full, beautiful lips. I resisted kissing them by the barest thread of self-control, and instead, moved back toward the rocks where I'd left my clothes.

The water chilled on my arm when I reached for my coat, but there was enough heat in my skin for it not to freeze. I fumbled for the phone I'd shoved into my pocket and swore softly at my clumsy fingers.

"What are you doing?" she asked quietly.

"Something very stupid probably, but it's the only way I can describe … this." I opened the photo program on her phone, and her eyebrow went up even higher.

"Do you think that's wise?"

"I think it's probably colossally unwise, but what can I say?" I shrugged. "I'm either a genius or an idiot."

She laughed, and I took the photo. "There's a very fine line between the two in your case, I think." And yet she remained in her semi-submerged float, not trying to cover herself with more than the water.

I took another photo.

"You realize you're taking your life into your hands right now," she said. "Like, it's literally in your hands, hovering over water, and not only will I not save you this time if you drop it, I will actually be the one doing the killing." The smile remained on her face, and I took another photo.

"You know, you're kinda hot for a trained killer," I said, moving for a better angle to capture the length of her nude body in the frame.

She barked a laugh, and I took a photo. "Are you actually trying to be funny, or is it just part of your legendary charm?"

"That you're hot?" I shrugged. "Empirical evidence backs me up."

She scowled, and I took another photo. "You do mean submerged-in-a-thermal-pool hot."

"I mean face-to-launch-a-thousand-ships and body-to-worship hot," I said.

Her scowl deepened. "I'm not beautiful," she said.

I took another photo and then turned the camera for a selfie with her. Then I replaced the phone in my coat pocket and came back to where she still floated.

"I believe," I said, looking very intently into her eyes, "that beauty cannot be quantified scientifically. We've already established that I can usually be found walking the thin line between genius and idiot, so feel free to judge my opinions accordingly."

I inhaled, trying to find the words to express the images in my head. "I've written beautiful code that does exactly what it set out to do without a single missed or extra step. I've made beautiful meals that satisfy every craving and appeal to every sense equally. I've had beautiful connections with animals that trusted me when no one else would.

I've seen beauty in crowded cities where laughing kids played in the streets and dandelions pushed up through cracks in the sidewalks. The beauty right here, right now, is bigger than words. It needs all five senses to describe, and I don't have enough experience to do it justice."

Her eyes hadn't left mine, and my face inched closer as I darted a glance to her perfect lips. "I didn't see you when I first met you. I saw a suit, a scowl, and an air of competence that intimidated me." I searched her face for her thoughts, but she guarded them, so I took a breath and forged on. "Then you saved me, and you protected me, and that competence became a lifeline and armor *for me*."

Finding the words to match the images in my brain became easier. "But then we got to the Yukon, and I started noticing things about you that had nothing to do with me. The way your mouth quirks up just a little when you're laughing. The sound of your laughter with your sister, your mother, your cousin. The fierceness of your love for them, and for Isaac, whose stubbornness rivals your own."

She smiled at that, and suddenly all I wanted to be in the world was someone worthy of that stubbornness and ferocity. So I tried to pour that yearning into words that made sense. "Your capability and competence are like a siren song to me, and when you teach me the things you know, I feel … useful. Like maybe I could be worthy and you could possibly learn to trust me. It would be a heady thing to earn your trust, even if it's just when we're splitting wood."

Her eyes searched mine as though she were trying to trust my words, and just maybe succeeding a little.

"You've let me see pieces of yourself, and the person in front of me gets more beautiful with every bit that's revealed. I am in awe of just how beautiful you are," I said quietly.

Her gaze dropped to my mouth then, and my self-control snapped. "I'm going to kiss you now unless you stop me," I whispered, as I closed the distance between our lips. I hesitated just for a moment, just long enough to let her push me away if she wanted to, but instead, she reached her hand up behind my head and pulled me to her.

[29]

DALLAS

"Show me a man with a tattoo and I'll show you a man with an interesting past."

- JACK LONDON

His kiss was gentle, testing, tasting, letting me take the lead. So I led, softly at first, and then with more pressure, pulling his head closer, drawing myself to him. And then his kiss deepened, and he began to lead, probing, tasting, taking.

There was nothing tentative, nothing measured. He didn't hold himself back from me, and he took as much as he gave. And when our mouths weren't enough, his hands began to trace paths over my arms, my collarbones, my neck—cupping my face, drawing me even closer until I was cradled against him.

My heart pounded, and I ached with something more than physical desire, something deeper than longing. I *wanted*, and it was so much more than I'd felt in a very long time.

"Dallas." He whispered my name against my lips, and then his mouth burned trails of heat across my skin. He kissed the pulse under my jaw, felt it pound with his fingertips.

He smiled. Then he moved my hand over his heart and pressed it to his bare skin. I felt his heartbeat pound in concert with mine. "Me too," he murmured into my throat.

It was kissing that started a fire on my skin and blazed a path down. I writhed with the rising heat between my thighs, and I ached for his touch to stoke the flames higher. I gasped as his hand found my breast and caressed the sensitive skin around my nipple, and then moaned as he lifted me higher so his mouth could follow his fingers.

I wanted him. I wanted his mouth and his hands. I wanted his eyes to feast on me, his words to caress me, his ideas to enflame me. And maybe most of all, I wanted his arms to hold me, to make me feel safe and cherished and desired.

I pulled away, the pounding of my heart echoing in my ears. His eyes met mine and I saw heat in them, desire so strong it took my breath away.

"You're fired," he said. "Would that make a difference?"

"I … can't."

"You say that, but I don't understand." Frustration laced his voice.

"Oliver …" I tried, and failed.

He searched my face for some clue to my thoughts, but I'd worn a mask too long, and I hid too well for him to see beneath the reserve.

Finally, he nodded. "Okay." He drifted backward to put distance between us, and I mourned the loss of his touch. He inhaled deeply, then said simply, "You are beautiful. I want to make sure you know that."

I studied his impossibly handsome face, with the mouth that spoke such charming words and eyes that smiled so convincingly, and I decided, this once, to believe him. "Thank you."

He closed his eyes and smiled, as though savoring my agreement. Then he opened them again and looked me over critically.

"Okay, survival specialist, how'd you do after your ice bath?"

I chuckled. "Well, thanks to your quick thinking, you're stuck with me for a while longer."

"Even though I fired you?" he asked.

"Sorry, until the Russian is no longer a threat, you can't fire me."

"Damn," he said with a grin, "I guess you're stuck with me too."

The knots in my chest began to loosen, and I felt my heartbeat return to normal.

"Now tell me about these connections with animals you apparently have," I said, finding his chest with my feet and pushing off to float around the pool.

He stared at me in mock horror. "I bare my soul to you and *that's* what you focus on?" He sighed dramatically. "Okay, fine. I'll tell you about my pet crow, Raven."

"First, was it a pet crow or a pet raven, and second, of course you had that as a pet."

"It was a crow named Raven, and why 'of course'?"

"Just a family thing," I said dismissively, not wanting to go into the history of ravens and wolves with him then. "Tell me about Raven."

He gave me a strange look, then explained. "After Haiti, my parents finally stopped following their international NGOs, and when I was eleven, they settled near L.A. to focus on all the trendy causes with big fundraisers. Meanwhile, I was their dorky kid who liked computers too much and lived in a fantasy world of RPGs and Jim Butcher books."

I laughed. "Forgive me if I find the idea of you as anything other than the most popular kid in school completely ridiculous."

He scoffed. "I could have been a supermodel and I still would have been a nerd—because I *believed* I was. No one liked what I liked. I had no friends, and at that point, I didn't even have a nanny to pretend to be interested in me. My parents were academics and philanthropists who'd made a life out of their causes. I was an introvert who preferred the elegance of good code to the elegance of a fundraiser, and the more they pushed me to interact with people, the more I retreated, until retreating became the default."

I couldn't reconcile this version of Oliver with the beautiful man who could charm his way into anything … or anyone. "You are so easy in your skin it's surreal. You own every room you walk into, and draw in everyone you meet."

"It's purely defensive," he said, and then he sighed. "Like I said, I was an introvert, and with parents as successful and outgoing as mine are, it was either become them, or become *not* them. In my experience, animals don't care if you're popular or cool or attractive, and somehow, I was never a threat to them."

"I saw that with Grandpop's dogs. They usually go nuts with strangers, but you met them on their level, and they didn't even bother with dominance games," I said, remembering the relief I'd felt that he wasn't afraid of them.

"Yeah, well, I think it's because I've mastered the art of being the nicest guy in the room. The less threatening I was, the more animals would come to me. It never occurred to me that it would be a useful way to behave around people until I was in college and trying to figure out how to pay for the company I wanted to start. At my first meeting with my advisor, I tried out my nice-guy persona, and it must have worked, because he helped me get meetings with companies looking for new tech."

I tried to process this information about Oliver and how he put himself together. It was strange to realize it had been a conscious choice to be so flirty, charming, and easy in his skin.

"Okay," I said, "get back to the crow."

He smiled, and it soothed something in me. "Like I said, when I was eleven we were living in Southern California where my parents were fundraising to save the planet—"

"As one does," I said, trying not to be intimidated.

"As one does," he agreed with a grin. "Anyway, they were gone a lot, and I spent a lot of time up in the treehouse in my backyard watching the crows get drunk on Catalina cherries and wheel around the sky picking fights with red-tailed hawks."

I chuckled. "That sounds about right."

"Anyway, one day I found a young crow up in the treehouse,

breathing hard and trying desperately to fly with an injured wing. It took a bit for him to let me help him, but I was eventually able to coax him into a box where he was safe from predators while he healed. I kept him fed, and in turn, he decided I was only mildly offensive for a human being."

He smiled at the memory of the crow, and I wished I could have known the eleven-year-old version of him, before he became the nicest guy in the room. "I'd gone through a phase of reading a lot of Edgar Allen Poe stories, so naming him Raven was an obvious choice. I never could train him to ride my shoulder like I imagined a real raven would, but I did get him to eat out of my hand. My parents didn't even realize I had him until after his wing had healed. They couldn't figure out why this crow would dive-bomb my head every time we left the house." He chuckled, and shook his head. "And … one day, about two years later, he didn't. I never knew if something happened to him or if he just left, but I was pretty torn up that he was gone. So"—he shrugged—"I did what any self-respecting dork would do with a broken heart and access to a computer—I made myself a fake ID and got a raven tattoo."

My mouth dropped open. "You did not!"

He laughed. "I did too. Want to see?"

"Of course I do," I said, laughing at the absurdity of what he was telling me.

He lifted his leg out of the water to show me the back of his calf. There, on the muscle, was a beautiful rendition of a raven in flight, with wings extended as though coming in for an attack. It had the feel of Indigenous art, and I wasn't even conscious of reaching out to touch it until I encountered warm flesh.

"I guess it might be cultural appropriation for me to have Native American-style art on my body, but I grew up with my grandmother's stories of her year on the Navajo reservation, so I guess I just felt a kinship with the style."

"It's beautiful," I said, tracing the design with my fingertip. He held his leg awkwardly so he could see the tattoo as well.

"I usually forget it's there because I can't see it. Sometimes I'll catch it in a photo, and I'll remember the dorky kid whose big rebellious move before high school was to fake an ID to get a tattoo of a crow that left him."

Somehow, the words *a crow that left him* hung in the air after his voice died away, and I had a pang of sympathy for the boy Oliver had been.

"Do you have any other tattoos?" I asked.

He laughed. "Not a chance. This one took every ounce of bravado I had. Do you have any?" He made a show of peering around my body, and I laughed.

"No, but I've been designing one since I was about sixteen."

"You have?" He sounded delighted. "Why didn't you get it?"

"Because everyone was getting tattoos at that time, and I was having none of whatever everyone else was doing," I said, remembering the girls in my senior class proudly showing off their delicate foot or ankle tattoos.

"Why not since then?" he asked. "You strike me as someone who would do exactly what you want to do, regardless of who else is doing it."

I shrugged. "I guess there was a part of me that wondered what was really so important to me that I'd be willing to ink it permanently on my body."

"Well," he said grinning, "what's the design?"

I was surprised that it was so hard to say the words. "A wolf."

The grin on his face faded instantly and was replaced by something thoughtful and a little sad. "I think you should absolutely get it." He traced a line down from my neck, over my shoulder, and down my arm to the inside of my forearm. "Here."

My skin tingled from his featherlight touch, and he let his fingers rest there on my arm.

"Why did you want a wolf when you were sixteen?" he asked.

"Grandpop is Wolf Clan of the Selkirk First Nation, which is part of the Northern Tutchone ethnolinguistic group. He didn't really participate in band politics because he was seventeen when he moved away from

Pelly Crossing, but he raised me to respect his family's traditions, even if I chose not to follow them myself. *People's traditions*, he would say, *are part of their story. And the story of us—our deeds, our legacy—is all that we will leave of this lifetime.* Technically, because First Nations bands are matrilineal, my mom isn't Wolf Clan because Grandma Minty was white. But Grandpop has always made me feel like I'm Wolf, because he taught me his traditions and he made me realize that even if I did nothing else in life, I would still leave a story behind me."

"So a wolf represents the traditions of your story?" he asked, his fingers tracing my arm lazily.

"Yeah, something like that. And kind of a reminder to me that one day it'll be my responsibility to pass the traditions on to my kids … if I have any." I took a deep breath to quell the pain that thought brought with it. "Wolves symbolize loyalty and family though, and I guess I haven't been feeling very loyal to my family since I left the Yukon."

"I think you should get the wolf," he said quietly, his fingers still drawing quiet circles on my arm. "I'll go with you and hold your hand."

I smiled at that. "You think I won't be able to stand the pain?"

He shuddered. "No, *I* won't be able to stand that you're in pain. Holding your hand will be for me and my tender sensibilities."

I closed my eyes against the sweetness of his smile, and against this idea of something that went beyond the job. "I can't afford a personal relationship with you, even if there was a chance in hell it could work."

"What if I didn't want a relationship?" he asked with mock belligerence. "What if I just wanted us to act on the pure chemistry we've got going on?"

I sighed. "Then that's even more reason for me to keep my distance. I don't do one-night stands, I don't do affairs, and I definitely don't do clients."

Oliver seemed to chew on my words and the conviction with which I'd said them. He couldn't see the red light of my bullshit meter flashing in my head, and I turned away to look out at the river so he wouldn't catch a glimpse of it in my eyes.

"I'm wildly attracted to you, Dallas, and I don't see that going away anytime soon, but I like and respect you too much to argue with you about it." He sighed. "I just hope that if and when anything changes, you'll let me know."

"Thank you," I said quietly, hoping he couldn't hear the regret in my voice.

"You're welcome," he said brusquely. "Now, how are we going to get back to the cabin without freezing to death?"

I had just opened my mouth to answer when the roar of a snowmobile echoed off the mountain.

[30]

DALLAS

"Nudity begins with the face."

- SIMONE DE BEAUVOIR

The first second was gut-clenching dread. I could get to the rifle, but we were so vulnerable, naked in the thermal pool, that it would have been laughable if I wasn't so angry at myself. And then the next second I did laugh.

Oliver had been studying my face, maybe looking to me for a cue on how to react, and he frowned at my laughter. "What?" he demanded.

The snowmobile came closer, and the distinctive grind of its battered muffler shattered the peace and serenity of the previous hour.

"Reed," I said, looking up to the rise above the pool when the engine of his 1972 Ski-Doo Alpine cut off.

I flipped over to my stomach, and Oliver moved a few feet away in a lovely attempt to preserve my dignity. He didn't know that dignity had never been part of the equation where my cousin was concerned.

"Hey, guys, how's it going?" Reed said from the top of the rise. "Saw the frozen clothes, and I thought I'd check it out. You go in the river?" he asked Oliver.

"No, Dallas did," Oliver answered. I could hear the leftover tension in his voice.

"Dallas did?" Reed's eyebrows shot up as he turned his gaze to me. "You're kidding."

"Dropped phone, thermal stream, thin ice," I said tersely. "The pool seemed like an expedient way to warm up."

"Not to mention good for sexy times," Reed said with a grin.

"We didn't—" Oliver began.

"Client," I cut in with a glare at Reed. His eyebrows stopped dancing on his forehead, and he nodded.

"Right. So, I brought you some of your stuff from the compound," he said to me, then looked at Oliver. "You didn't have much, so I brought what I could find." Then he spoke to me again, "But I don't have any extra boots."

I stood up in the water and reached for the rucksack to pull out the towel. I dried the water off my skin as I spoke, not caring what Reed saw, and deliberately not looking at Oliver. "Give me jeans and a sweater if you've got them, and I'll take him"—I jerked my head in Oliver's direction—"back to the cabin on Bessie."

"Hang on—" Reed began.

"Clothes first, discussion later," I snapped.

Reed disappeared down the rise, and a moment later he tossed a small duffle down to me. I had pulled on the underwear and socks from my rucksack, and immediately grabbed a shirt, sweater, and jeans from the duffle. When I was dressed and wearing my parka again, I turned to Oliver, who was still in the pool.

"There's a pair of clean socks for you in the rucksack if you want them. I'm going to borrow your boots to climb up the rise, then I'll send Reed back with them when I'm on his snowmobile."

He nodded, maybe a little bemusedly, and I stepped into his boots, shouldered the rifle, and climbed the hill.

Reed walked with me down to Bessie, his aging snowmobile. "You know what you're doing, Sis?"

"Well enough," I said, not totally sure I believed myself, but willing to try.

He nodded. "I'll grab your wet clothes and bring them back with me. You get the client to piggyback you into the cabin, and we'll talk when you're in, warm, and your boots are drying. Cool?"

"Sounds good. Any chance you can check my fishing hole for burbot on your way in?"

He grinned. "Only if I get to stay for dinner."

"Deal." I smiled back. No matter how pretty my cousin was, he would always look like a mischievous six-year-old to me.

I handed him Oliver's boots, and he hiked up the snow-covered tailings mound. There were more clean socks in the duffle, so I added another pair as I waited. A few minutes later, my client was on board, the rifle, rucksack, and duffle secured, and we set off across the snow on the loudest snowmobile in the Yukon.

I followed Reed's track, saw where he'd spotted my now-frozen clothes, circled them, paused, and then shifted direction toward the thermal spring we'd found together. Reed was almost as good a tracker as I was. His problem was that if he lost interest, he walked away, whereas my perseverance wouldn't let me go anywhere until the job was done.

I pulled Bessie up in front of the cabin and turned her off. The silence was blissful, and I wondered for the millionth time why Reed didn't fix the muffler.

"He likes to make an entrance," Oliver observed, as if he'd heard my thoughts.

He climbed off the back and took the bags in while I stood up on the seat and waited for him to remember I didn't have boots. He was back in less than thirty seconds.

"You look a little like a Valkyrie," he said, looking up at me.

"Come, mortal," I said, trying to sound imperious, ruining the effect with laughter, "be my horse."

"My pleasure," he said gallantly. "My lady has only to ask, and she may ride me to the ends of the earth." He winked, I flushed, and he grinned.

"Merciless wretch," I said, as I climbed on his back.

"Mmm, I love a woman who uses 'wretch' in a sentence," he said, clutching my legs to his hips.

I tried not to hear the word "love" in what he said, and instead concentrated on the warmth of his body against mine as he knocked the snow off the boots, which he then kicked off before entering the main room of the cabin. As with his introduction to Grandpop's dogs, Oliver hadn't needed to be told to take his boots off before entering indoor spaces. He seemed to have an instinct for correct behavior, or he just really paid attention when other people weren't looking.

I stood and added wood to the stove, and then sat cross-legged on the bench while Oliver pawed through the duffle Reed had brought. He found a clean shirt, and I tried not to notice his abs, chest, and back as he changed. Tried, and failed.

He caught me looking and grinned. "I will someday wear down your reserve, milady. You shall act upon whatever fascination grips you, and I'll be your willing servant."

I scoffed. "Playing the part of a medieval knight?"

He laughed. "Mostly just stringing together words from fantasy role play games. Talking about my misspent dorky youth brings it out in me."

Reed entered the vestibule and kicked off his boots. "Speaking of misspent dorky youths," I murmured under my breath. Oliver laughed.

"What'd I miss?" Reed asked, dropping my frozen clothes on the floor by the door. "Wait, never mind. I left your fish in the snow outside. How do you want them prepped?"

"I'll do it," Oliver said, turning to me. "Can I use your knife? Mine's a little too small for burbot."

Reed's eyebrows shot up, and he grinned at me. "Nice work, Sis."

Oliver took the knife I handed him, and his eyes were on mine when he said, "She's the best." Then he winked at me, clapped Reed on the shoulder, stepped into his boots, and went outside.

$$[31]$$

OLIVER

*Raven: Symbolizing change, metamorphosis. The keeper of secrets, and
exposer of truth.*

- NATIVE AMERICAN LORE

I was into her.

I was into her, and I felt like a dorky twelve-year-old waiting for
a crow who would never come. The tight feeling in my chest hadn't let
up since I watched her fall into the river, and it had been joined by a flip-
flopping stomach after I photographed her in the thermal pool.

I took her phone out of my coat pocket and flipped to the photos.
There were about twenty of her, floating in the blue-green water, tantaliz-
ingly obscured and yet fully visible in my mind. And that kiss. A flush of
heat went through me at the memory of it, and I wanted to stomp back
into the cabin and do it again and again and again until nothing existed
but kissing her.

But I was locked out for being a client, and I could see no way in.

Two decent-sized burbot were on the line, and I took them over to the ice-covered stump that we'd used as a gutting station. Cleaning fish was a messy job, but I was happy that Dallas had shown me how to do it. I would learn anything she wanted to teach me. She was patient and thorough—that rare kind of teacher who made everything seem interesting.

Something fluttered behind me, and I turned slowly, not quite sure whether it had been plant or animal. I would have laughed, but I couldn't decide if it was funny or tragic that a large raven hopped on the snow about ten feet away from where I worked.

"'Sup, Crow." I named her in honor of my long-departed crow, Raven. I also decided, on the basis of zero evidence, that Crow was a she. I tossed her a bit of fish entrail, and she hopped forward to snatch it off the snow, leaving just a small red stain behind. I tossed her another piece, which she ate quickly. I aimed the next piece a little closer. She hopped forward and plucked it from the snow, and by the time both fish were clean, Crow was only about three feet away, watching me with a steady gaze.

"What do you think?" I asked her. "Can I prove my worth with fish?"

Crow's head tilted at the sound of my voice, and I scoffed at myself for thinking she was there for anything besides fish guts. When I bent to clean my hands in the snow, she fluttered up into the lowest branch of a naked tree.

"Later," I said to her as I wiped Dallas's knife clean and carried the gutted fish back inside.

Dallas was stirring a pot on the wood stove, while Reed chopped an onion at the table. She looked up when I came in, and the smile on her face nearly stopped me in my tracks.

"Wolf's alive," she said beaming. "Hurt, but alive."

The relief I felt at her words was almost too much to process.

"And look"—she indicated the pot, still smiling—"we have rice."

"And onions," added Reed, "and I brought you some coffee for tomorrow morning."

"Dude, you're my new best friend," I said happily.

"You'll have to do better." Reed grinned. "Dallas said she'd marry me."

"Eww"—she glared at her cousin—"I said I'd marry the *coffee*, you weirdo." She shuddered.

"I mean, it was disturbing to think you'd offer marriage to your cousin," he said, "but you're disturbing, so I was prepared to shrug it off as evidence."

"You two are deeply weird, and I have to say, I'm here for it," I said.

Dallas raised an eyebrow. "You think this is weird? You have no idea."

"Believe her," Reed added. "She once streaked through a basketball game on a dare."

"I was five, you were five, and it was Mom and Aunt Rikki's game." She snorted.

"I'm just saying"—Reed shrugged—"her nudist tendencies are legendary, as evidenced by today's bare butt in the hot tub."

"Says the man who can occasionally be found in the woods wearing cowboy boots and nothing else," she said laughing.

"I wear a hat," Reed said. "And besides, there are too many bitey things in the underbrush to go out for a barefoot piss."

"Welcome to my world," answered Dallas with a wrinkled nose.

"It's a butt-bitey world out there, but someone's got to poo in it," Reed agreed sympathetically.

I burst out laughing, Reed smirked and looked proud, and Dallas just raised an eyebrow. I had the sense that with these two, that's how it would always be.

"Let's cook those," Dallas said, pointing at the fish. "So we can get to the business of why you're here," she said to Reed.

We worked together efficiently, and when the rice was done fifteen minutes later, so were the sautéed onions and fish fillets. We talked while we ate, and I felt a little like part of the family.

"So, here's the deal," Reed began. "George and I walked the property after you guys left. The shooter was gone, but tracks put him back out to the road where we assume he parked a car."

"Did you—" Dallas began, but Reed interrupted her.

"It was a blue Honda CRV. I saw it parked near the turnoff that night, and the tire tread confirmed it."

I stared at Reed. "You could tell the kind of car from a print of its tires?"

He shrugged. "I notice things."

Dallas agreed. "Tracker brain."

"Okay, so, he drove away," I said. "Has he been back?"

"We put the word out from Eagle Plains to Watson Lake. No sightings of the guy. Ekaterina said some Russian guy from somewhere called Lake Peipus came in yesterday for knives—" Reed said.

I interrupted, "Knives, plural?" at the same moment Dallas said, "Lake Peipus?"

He looked from me to Dallas with a smirk. "You two are a comedy routine."

"Are you sure he was from Lake Peipus?" Dallas asked.

Reed shrugged. "Ask her, but that's what she said. She said the accent is pretty specific."

I looked at Dallas. "Didn't someone say the guy from ADDATA, Karpov, is from somewhere around that area?"

She nodded slowly, obviously thinking.

We ate in silence for a few minutes until she spoke again.

"I think we should head back," she said to me.

"You think he's gone?" I asked, surprised.

"No, I think he's waiting for us to return, and then he's going to try to kill you again."

"Oh"—I glared at her—"yeah, that sounds like a good reason to go back."

She rolled her eyes. "No one's going to kill you."

"I might," Reed said with a grin.

"You can't yet," she answered without even cracking a smile. "First we have to use him as bait."

[32]

DALLAS

"Maybe the significance of an event is as much about the story of it as about the event itself."

\- OLIVER

The plan was a simple one, but it required some assumptions, a leap in logic, a little bit of luck, and an epic fight.

After a meal spent hashing out the idea I'd had to trap the Russian, Reed went back to the compound to fill everyone else in on what we were doing. He was also planning to head into town for a drink and make sure some people heard we were due back from our bush camp by the next night.

My boots needed to dry by the fire, so I didn't even have to make up an excuse to spend one final night sharing a sleeping bag with Oliver. And ignoring Reed's saucy wink at us as he left on Bessie was as easy as hitting him in the back with a snowball.

After we cleaned up the dishes and made the bed, slipping into the sleeping bag together and curling up like spoons felt almost normal. Even his hard-on at my back and the arm between my breasts was comforting in a way that only had a little bit to do with suppressed lust.

Because that's all it was.

Just lust.

Telling myself that had gotten harder to do since he'd pulled me out of the river. There was something to that tradition that said saving a person's life connected you to them. I tried not to let feelings enter into my thoughts about Oliver, but being connected definitely came with feelings.

Kissing him had been all about feeling things—and not just physical things either.

But sleeping with him—actually sharing the space of sleep—that came with feelings too.

If and when we were successful in capturing the Russian, I would no longer have the excuse of "client" to keep myself away from him. At that point, the only barrier to giving in to my attraction for him would be self-preservation, my instinct for which had been slipping badly each day we spent together. But Oliver Curran and what he wanted from his life occupied a different plain of existence. Did I think he was attracted to me? Sure. Why not? I could buy the idea that he wanted sex. But sex was something I only had with people I didn't have to see over coffee the next day. In my experience, letting people in came with too many strings, and I hated it when people tried to pull them.

Oliver nuzzled my neck in the morning like a sleepy puppy and kissed me good morning with the soft peck of a friend. We used the French press in the cabin to make a pot of coffee, and I had no problem sharing it with him exactly because we *were* friends.

After coffee, we cleaned and closed up the cabin, pushed the Ski-Doo out of the woodshed, and loaded it up. I made leg shields for Oliver's boots out of plastic garbage bags, and he wore two pair of socks against the cold, but still, it was a long ride back to the compound.

. . .

We entered camp to the cacophony of dogs barking. Reed had set the dogs out on patrol all day to establish a pattern that made the Russian hesitate to do anything during daylight hours. This gave us a few hours to eat, get warm, and put the elements of our plan in place.

First on my agenda was a visit with Grandpop.

I left Oliver at the shower block and knocked on my grandfather's cabin door.

"That you, Sis? Come in."

I kicked off my boots and entered the front room, where I was greeted by the slow thump of a tail.

"Wolf!" I flew across the room and knelt by her bed, my hands skimming her bandaged shoulder carefully as I checked her body. She seemed whole, and except for the wound in her shoulder, well. I looked up into Grandpop's face, which was a little fuller and tinged with more color than it had been a few days before.

"I thought he killed her." My voice was so much smaller than I'd intended because it had to get past the tightness in my throat. Even knowing she'd survived the attack, it wasn't until I saw her that I allowed myself to let go of the residual fear from that night.

"Oh, Sis, old dogs like us, we don't roll over so easy."

I sobbed a laugh at the gentleness in Grandpop's voice, and the tears came as Wolf licked my arm. Grandpop laid his gnarled hand on my head. Fear, grief, and relief poured out of me, not just for Wolf, but for what I'd brought to my family's world, and what I'd missed of it.

"You been holding yourself together pretty tight, huh?" he said, stroking my hair.

"I guess so," I sniffed, reaching for a tissue. "You been taking your meds?"

Grandpop smiled. "Your sister's been spoiling me with sweet things, but I don't get them until I take the damn pills."

I laughed, so happy that my family was there. I got the tin of green medicine out of his side table drawer and sat on the bed to rub it into his hands.

"You got a little color back," I said, studying his face.

"It's easier to breathe when I'm not coughing so much anymore."

"Oliver said he felt normal again after about two weeks, so you should be getting better every day."

Grandpop's gnarled knuckles loosened up under my hands, and he sighed. "I thought I was done," he said quietly. "I was glad for it. There'd be times the only thing getting me out of bed of a morning was habit and the thought that your grandmother would shake her head at me and tell me to go find something to do." He closed his eyes for a moment as I massaged the ointment into his hands.

"I still talk to her every day," he continued after a bit, "tell her what needs fixing, what's starting to grow, and what the day sounded like."

I thought about Oliver's statement that his clearest experience of the world was visual, and I wondered if my grandfather got his world through sound.

"Having you all here now reminds me that living is done best when there are people to love. I hadn't been living too well in the in-between times, when you all were living your own lives."

A pang of guilt hit me. I'd made an art of staying away from the Yukon and all the memories of who I'd allowed myself to become when I'd worked as a guide. Two weeks at fish camp every summer and the odd weekend winter trip were hardly enough to sustain a relationship with the most important man in my life.

"I'm sorry, Pop. I didn't mean to be gone so long," I whispered.

"I'm sorry too, Sis. I forgot that letting go would mean missing out on time with you." He smiled at me, the deep wrinkles around his eyes reminding me of the lifetime of stories I had yet to mine from him.

"Now, tell me what you're going to do now you're back in camp," he said. "Reed's been working something with the dogs, and he's got friends in town keeping an eye out for your shooter, who he says might be Russian?"

I nodded. "If he's the same guy who went after Oliver in Chicago, he is."

Grandpop nodded. "I worked with a few Russians over the years. The men I knew were hard workers, but it was their patience I remember best. When they wanted something, they could wait for it, and when that thing was revenge, they served it ice cold, long after the crime had been forgotten."

"This isn't revenge, but yeah, the guy does seem to be playing a long game," I said. "Oliver found a tracking device sewn into the lining of his coat when we were out at fish camp."

"I'm going to guess your Russian stuck around here and waited for you to come back. It's what I'd do."

I nodded. "That's what we're thinking too. He might come tonight, or it might take a couple of days for him to come back, but we're working on a plan to trap him." I told Grandpop the outline of what we'd discussed with Reed up at the cabin, and he had a couple of good suggestions.

Then Grandpop squeezed my hands and told me to go see my mom and sister. "They've been worried about you. Worried about your client."

"It was fine. We were fine," I said.

"You know what I mean," he said gruffly.

I leaned over and kissed his cheek. "I do, and I love you. Thanks for looking out for me."

"That's what family does," he said, his eyes closing.

"One of us will be by with dinner later," I said quietly.

I bent down to give Wolf a rub behind the ears.

"Keep him safe," I whispered to her.

"You both do," Grandpop murmured.

I met Oliver after his shower. His hair was wet, and he wore clean clothes. He looked refreshed and irresistible, and I had to restrain the instinct to touch him.

"Hey," I said impulsively. "Drop your stuff in my cabin and walk with me."

"Okay," he said with a smile. "How's Isaac?"

"He looks better, like he's getting more air," I said, waiting for him outside my cabin. He dropped his bag and emerged a moment later. "And"—I grinned—"I saw Wolf."

"How's she doing?" he asked with obvious relief.

"Looks like the bullet clipped her in the shoulder, but she was alert and happy to see me."

"I'm telling you," he said threading his fingers through mine and holding up our hands, "let me do this while you get your wolf tattoo. It's time."

I exhaled, but didn't untangle our hands. "Yeah, you might be right."

"Yes!" he said happily. "Do you have someone here? Because I know a girl—"

I used the excuse of pulling gloves out of my coat pocket to let go of his hand. "I'm sure you do."

He stopped walking. "What? No. I mean I have a friend whose girl-friend is this totally badass feminist tattoo artist. She's always giving away time under her needle to raise money for causes. Her specialty is recreating parts of famous paintings, but— No, never mind. You should go with someone here."

I looked sideways at him as we walked. We were heading through the woods at the back of the property where the flat land rose up to become a hill. "Why?"

He shrugged. "I don't know. Maybe because I feel like it's tied to your family and they're all here. I know that if I had waited until I was eighteen to get my crow, I would have been living in Boston, and Raven would have been a distant memory by then. Maybe the impact of some-thing is as much about the story of it as about the thing itself."

I thought about that. "You mean the tattoo has as much meaning because it was your act of rebellion as it does because it was a tribute to the crow you loved?"

"Who says I loved the crow?" he said quietly.

I'd slowed my walk and had begun picking my way carefully through the woods. Although it was unlikely that the Russian was watching this side of the property, it wasn't out of the question.

"How could you not love it?" I murmured quietly. "You fed it and cared for it and taught it to trust you."

We emerged from the woods on a ledge that jutted out of the hillside. It blended into the woods behind it when viewed from below. I'd long ago built a shelter of sorts out of deadwood and rocks where I could sit and look out over the view of the flat land below.

Oliver's gaze wandered over the shelter. "Can we go in?"

I let him change the subject. "That's why I brought you here."

Snow blanketed the outside of the shelter, but the wood slats I'd laid on the ground inside were dry. I'd grown up in this place, and climbing into the shelter was like rediscovering the best memories of my childhood.

We sat on the wood floor with our shoulders touching and our legs drawn up in front of us as we looked out over the view. "The sky is even bigger up here," Oliver breathed.

"Look over … there," I said, pointing to the dirt road that turned off the highway. "That's the turnoff to camp, where Reed said he spotted the strange car. Now look just beyond the clearing, just over … there," I said triumphantly as I shifted my finger to the left. "Do you see that reflection?"

"I do," he said after a moment. "Sunlight on chrome?" he guessed.

"If I had to guess, I'd say that's our Russian."

He studied the distance from what was probably the Russian's car to the highway. The car itself was hidden about a hundred yards from the south boundary of camp, which meant he would have to circle around the ATCO and the long drop to get to the camper and my cabin. During the day, the dogs would alert us to a skulking human. After dark it was a different matter.

"Any point in just calling the police or the Mounties or whatever?" he asked.

I shrugged. "We could, but as far as they're concerned, he hasn't done anything wrong. Shooting a dog gets a maximum of six months in jail and a fine, and it's our word against his unless someone matches the bullet. We pretty much need to catch him in the commission of a crime."

He exhaled. "Yeah, that's what I was afraid of."

I looked him directly in the eyes. "You are not going to be in danger from him. I really don't think he's going to risk a gun again, knowing how well-armed the camp is. He'll go for close work, and that's how we'll get him."

"I may not be in danger, but if there's even the smallest chance that you could get hurt, that's what I'm having a hard time with."

I scoffed. "My job is to protect you."

He bit back whatever he'd been about to say, and instead, looked out over the view.

I studied his profile, watching the play of emotions in his eyes. "Why did you say you didn't love Raven?"

He avoided my eyes. "I didn't say that."

"You pretty much did," I retorted, turning his face to mine.

He held my gaze, and then shrugged. "I never got to keep the things I loved."

"What does that even mean?" My heart ached for the matter-of-factness of his tone.

"My parents moved all the time, following the causes. Until I was nine, the only time we went back to the States was to visit my grandmother. I'd lived in three African countries, two Southeast Asian, three European, and two Middle Eastern countries by the time I finished the third grade. Susan and John Curran are heroes of the philanthropic jet set, and they were always in high demand because they could talk their fabulous friends out of loads of money. They only had one child because even one required more care than they had time for, but I learned to be fairly low-maintenance so they didn't find even more reasons to leave me behind. I could walk away from almost any house without tears, taking just one backpack full of my stuff with each move because it was easier and cheaper to just buy new things in every new place rather than pay for packing and shipping. Not getting attached was my superpower," he added quietly.

"What about friends? Did you get attached to them?"

He looked away again, out over the view. "I made a couple of friends at first, but you know, little kids suck at keeping in touch, so it just got easier to keep it casual."

"So that's why you were content to be the dorky loner kid," I said, understanding dawning. "It's easier to leave when there's nothing holding you."

Everything I'd assumed I knew about Oliver was painted with one color. I'd had no idea there was such a spectrum of hues that made up the charming, flirty, successful man for whom everything seemed to come so easily.

And with the realization that Oliver had a default, and that default meant he would never allow himself to love me because he expected to leave, a sense of peace settled in.

"You're smiling," he said.

I leaned my head on his shoulder. "I'm happy I got to share this with you. It's the place I always go when I need perspective."

"And what perspective have you gained today, milady?"

"I just got a little freedom to enjoy living in the moment."

He bumped my shoulder with his own. "Oh really? Anything in particular you're planning to enjoy?"

I smiled flirtatiously. "Maybe." I kissed his nose and stood up to hold out a hand to him. "Come on, let's go see what Christi made for dinner."

[33]

OLIVER

"You're fired!" I shouted at Dallas.

"You can't fire me. I don't work for you!" she yelled back.

We'd gone back to her cabin after the dinner Christi made, which was the best beef stew I'd ever eaten, to wait out the sunset. When the dogs had been called in and it was full dark outside, we began to fight.

I yanked open her front door and stormed out to the porch.

"You can't just leave! Where are you going to go?" Her tone was furious.

"You were ready to drop me off at a hotel! You don't want me here," I sneered.

She glared at me. "Says the guy who never saw me until I was useful to him."

I scoffed. "You've made it perfectly clear that there's nothing here for me."

"Oh, it's on me? Leaving's your move, isn't it?" she shouted. "You leave. The nicest guy in the room has one foot out the door, and no amount of pretty words or flirty smiles warns a woman it's coming until the door slams behind you."

My heart pounded, and I forced the words out. "And what about you, with your no-clients rule? You're such a fucking tease, Dallas!" My eyes burned, and I turned away so she couldn't see. Damn it. Why did this have to be so hard?

I took a deep breath, flipped the hood up on my coat and said with my back to her, "I'll be gone in the morning."

I stalked away to the camper and stormed inside. I heard Dallas slam her cabin door, and I wanted to throw something.

"That sounded painful," Reed said from the shadows deep in the camper, and I almost jumped out of my skin. Maybe that's why my heart was beating so fast.

"Surprisingly so," I said, and it was true. Her comment about one foot out the door had hit me right in the solar plexus.

"I realize she's the bodyguard, but she's not the only dangerous one. I'd be careful if I were in your boots."

"I get it, Reed. *Client*, remember?" I was still flinching away from the words we'd hurled at each other.

I felt his gaze on me for a time before he finally spoke again. "There's more than you know at stake here. Don't turn out to be more trouble than you're worth."

[34]

DALLAS

He came out of the camper and slammed the door behind him. He trudged through the snow toward the long drop, slipping on a patch of ice and almost going down. The hood of that ridiculous Canada Goose coat was up, his hands were in his pockets, and his shoulders were hunched against the cold. He slammed the door of the big outhouse behind him, and the night went silent.

I willed myself to breathe. The fight had hit painfully close to things that felt raw and unfinished. Oliver had been affected too. I didn't miss the tension in his shoulders or the anger in his movement. He wasn't that good an actor, and neither was I.

As I watched from the window of my cabin, every predator instinct I had suddenly went on alert. A shadow, moving with liquid grace, emerged from the edge of the forest. The dogs had been shut into Grand-pop's cabin, so the shadow remained unseen by anyone but me, the tracker, watching, waiting, but it was too distant to catch a glimpse of a face. The shadow moved like an eel, slipping from shadow to shelter as it approached the edge of camp. It lurked toward the old wooden outhouse, and when it took refuge behind it, I silently exited the cabin and made my move.

I slipped along the edge of the camper, hidden from the view of the shadow, on a tracker's inaudible feet. I paused there, a wraith in the night, anticipating the moment the shadow would realize there was only one way into the long drop. And then the shadow slid around the side of the old wood building, built a hundred years ago and still, inexplicably, holding together. My line of sight was a direct one, and I held my breath as he slowly, carefully opened the door and slithered inside.

I exploded from the shadow of the camper and sprinted across the open yard while a scream pierced the dark.

It was an effective scream, a shrill scream, the kind of scream that fractured ice and caused avalanches. It echoed across the camp, and the dogs in Grandpop's cabin burst into furious barking.

I flung the door open and hurled myself into the long drop just as the Russian, fixed-blade knife in hand, reached the hooded man seated at the far end of the long drop.

"Hey!" I yelled to get the Russian's attention.

He opened his stance, back to the wall, and I could see a knife in each hand. His head swiveled between the hooded man and the tracker at the door. It was Oliver's Russian. The knife wound I'd dealt his forehead was angry, red, and identifying.

The scream stopped, and the hood of the Canada Goose jacket tipped back as Reed stood up and kicked at the Russian's hand, sending one of his knives flying out of reach. My spinning kick to his other hand just missed as the Russian lunged for my cousin with his remaining knife.

Backed into a corner, Reed leapt up onto the toilet box, dancing toward me as he evaded the slashing knife, while the ancient floorboards creaked ominously under the Russian's weight.

My own knife was tucked behind my wrist, and when the Russian spun to face me, I kicked again, connecting with his chest and shoving him against the far wall so Reed could get clear. It put us both on the same side, but the Russian would have to fight us one by one in the tight space.

Fighting wasn't our goal, however.

As the Russian lunged for me, he moved over the weak spot in the floor again, and I heard the boards groan, more insistently this time. He swung at me and I ducked right, then spun my knife out and re-opened the gash across his brow.

He bellowed and charged, slamming me into the edge of the doorway. I swallowed a groan at the sharp pain in my shoulder and ducked under his swing, slashing with a backhanded grip on my knife and driving him backward.

Reed added a kick to the Russian's ear that let me get my feet solidly under me. The Russian shook his head like an angry bear and slashed up with his knife, clipping Reed's shin with the blade.

Reed screamed again, and the sound pierced my brain.

The Russian froze for a fraction of a second, just long enough for me to jump up and send another kick to his chest. He staggered backward onto the rotted floorboards, where Reed sent a second kick to his knife hand. As Reed's foot connected, I dropped and swept the Russian's legs out from under him.

He crashed down, the boards broke, and the floor opened up and swallowed the Russian into the pit. Another bellow of rage filled the hole and blasted up through the hundred-year-old floorboards.

I stood, panting with exertion, at the edge of the broken planks, looking down at the Russian. He scrambled to his feet, cursing and spitting.

"Duck!" Reed shouted.

The Russian hurled his knife, aiming for my face. I dodged left, feeling the air move past my cheekbone as the knife lodged, point first, in the ceiling.

I glared at the man with blood dripping into his eyes from the reopened cut on his forehead, nostrils flaring with rage as he stared up at me.

"Now you're really in a pile of shit. No weapons and no way out," I snarled at him. I looked up at Reed, still standing on the toilet seat box, and nodded toward the knife in the corner. "Don't touch the knives. We'll let the RCMP do their forensics."

Reed nodded and pulled his phone out of his pocket. As he dialed, he studied the furious Russian trapped under the camp's long drop.

"That ten-year hole," Reed said, "just got, like, a whole year's deposit, eh?" He wrinkled his nose comically. "Not sure which one stinks worse, actually." Then he spoke into his phone. "Yeah, hey, Rob, it's Reed. Cool, man, how are you?"

The Russian's agitation quieted, but the death glare aimed in my general direction was fanged.

"Listen," Reed continued to his friend Rob, an RCMP in Dawson, "this Russian dude, the one we think shot Grandpop's dog Wolf? Yeah, man, she'll be okay, thanks. Anyway, so he just tried to murder me in the long drop out at Grandpop's compound. Thank God the floor caved in, because he's sitting at the bottom of the hole looking at me like he wants to eat my liver."

Reed smiled charmingly at the Russian, who growled with absolute menace.

Just then, Oliver burst through the door behind me. The look of relief on his face when he saw me was so pure it made my breath catch.

"You're okay?" he gasped.

"I'm fine," I said, heart still pounding, adrenaline still making me shake, shoulder beginning to throb.

"I almost broke when I heard the screams," he said. He looked pale and a little frantic, and I was glad that I'd made Oliver promise not to come into the long drop, no matter what he heard.

"That was me," Reed said with his hand over his phone's speaker, a proud grin on his face.

"Reed's been working on the pitch of that scream since we were kids," I explained, my breath beginning to calm. "Useful when he wants to break glass or cause temporary paralysis."

Oliver stepped inside and cautiously peered over the edge of the hole at the Russian, who was scanning his prison for a way up or out. He stepped back again when the man glared up at him and muttered in Russian.

"What'd he say?"

I shrugged and said, "No idea."

Oliver hesitated only a moment before he understood. Then he called down at the man in the pit. "What did you say?"

The Russian remained silent. Reed was still talking to Rob on the phone, so I gestured to him to keep eyes on our prisoner and then directed Oliver outside.

We walked far enough away that there was no chance of being over-heard. "He said, '*My brother will kill you,* '" I murmured.

Oliver looked startled. "His brother? But this is the same guy from Chicago, right? There was never any other guy following me."

"We need to check in with Cipher in the morning and find out what they know. For now, the RCMP will hold him until we can sort out extra-dition or deportation. You're safe at least for tonight, Oliver. Whoever his brother is doesn't know this guy's been caught."

Oliver took my hand in his and held it tightly as we walked up the steps to my porch. He started to say something, and then closed his mouth as if the words eluded him.

I stopped outside the cabin door and faced him. He looked uncertain, and not even his eyes smiled.

"Dallas, I—" he began, but I stopped him with my finger to his lips.

"Let me say something first." I searched his eyes for agreement, and he finally nodded. "I hate that we had to fight to make him believe you were vulnerable."

Whatever he thought I was about to say, it wasn't this.

"What I said to you wasn't fair, and I'm sorry. I don't want you to think I really feel that way."

"Me either." He exhaled. "I felt sick after I left here. I'm sorry, Dallas."

"Apology accepted," I said quietly.

"Apology accepted," he agreed.

"Would you like to come in for a beer?" I asked.

His eyebrows shot up. "You drink?"

I smiled. "Only when I'm not on the job."

His gaze was intent on mine, as if he wanted to be completely sure. "So, if you're not on the job right now, does that mean I'm no longer a client?"

I held his gaze and slowly smiled. "Come in and find out."

[35]

OLIVER

"Love, genuine passionate love, was his for the first time."

- JACK LONDON, *THE CALL OF THE WILD*

The door closed behind me, and Dallas turned to look at me, her gaze traveling over my face. "For the record," she said, "I'm not a tease."

I exhaled, wanting to kiss the seriousness off her lips, but she was Dallas, and no matter how much I wanted her, she wasn't mine to kiss.

"I know that," I said, trying to keep frustration out of my voice. "But you're you, and I want you, and apparently I'm spoiled, because it was a tease to want what I couldn't have. Also for the record, I've always seen you, but I needed your skills, so that's all I saw at first."

She nodded and seemed to digest that.

"Reed's coat is better on you than the Canada Goose," she said, as she kicked off her boots.

I looked down at the parka, which was functional and warmer than my jacket because it covered me past my hips, and silently agreed. Dallas bumped my shoulder companionably as she headed for the kitchen. "Come in," she said over her shoulder.

My boots and Reed's coat came off, and I stood over the wood fire warming my hands. It was a weak substitute for the heat of her skin, which was where my hands itched to be.

She opened two cans of Kokanee and brought me one. We clinked cans and drank the icy beer, our eyes never leaving each other's.

I shivered as desire for her raced through me. "Whisky would be better in this weather," I said, pretending the cold had any effect on me at all. It didn't. Not when she looked at me like that.

"Whisky has a twenty-minute lag time," she tossed out casually as she bent to add more wood to the stove. "We might be busy then," she said without meeting my eyes.

Oh. Ways we could be busy in twenty minutes danced vividly in my imagination, but then slammed against the wall of "client" that she'd been throwing up around me since we met.

Fuck it.

I set my beer down.

She met my eyes and slowly, deliberately took another sip of hers. My heartbeat pounded in my chest and uncertainty flared for one excruciating moment as our gazes held. And then she swallowed and carefully set her beer next to mine.

I exhaled and pulled her in by the waist. Her arms went around my neck. We stood that way, heartbeats separated only by clothes, mouths separated only by breaths, until finally, she ran her fingers lightly down from my cheek to my jaw.

"You have a nice face," she said with the smallest of smiles.

I'd been called all versions of handsome in my life, but somehow, hearing it from her mattered more than it ever had before.

"I like yours too," I said, in the understatement of the decade. She was beautiful, unique, interesting, fascinating—everything that was so much more than just a combination of aesthetically pleasing features.

My hands traveled up her sides and around her back. She flinched, and I froze.

"What?" I whispered.

She shook her head. "It's nothing. Just a bruise."

I searched her face for pain or reluctance or anything else to stop my hands, but there was only Dallas—and the searing way she looked at me. Slowly, so slowly she could still my hands if she wanted to, I lifted the hems of her sweater and the t-shirt she wore underneath and pulled them off over her head in one motion. My eyes stayed locked on hers as my hands went to her hips. She was naked from the waist up, and in my peripheral vision I could see her small, beautiful breasts with dusky nipples that were peaked with the cold, or maybe not the cold. I pretended more gentleness than I felt as I turned her to face the fire. I wanted to map her skin with my hands, to feel every silky inch of it under my palms.

I traced lightly down the skin of one shoulder, which I saw was red and looked swollen.

"What happened?"

She shrugged with the other shoulder. "I hit the doorframe."

I hid the angry growl behind an exhale. "Christ. He hurt you?"

I could hear the smile in her voice. "I gave more than I got."

Selfishly, possessively, I traced her skin, and goose bumps rose in the path of my hand. "Still …"

She huffed a laugh. "The hundred-year-old floorboards weren't going to go down without a fight."

"I thought Reed cut the joists," I said, aching to kiss the lines on her skin.

When we'd decided to trap the Russian in the long drop, the floor repair Reed had been meaning to do, but hadn't gotten around to, was integral to the plan.

"He did. Apparently the floor was held together by more than just wood." She turned to face me again and wrinkled her nose adorably. I laughed and kissed it, and then I couldn't help pulling her into me, one arm holding her to me while the other touched her face. She closed her eyes, and I savored the feeling of her. I kissed her eyelids, then trailed my lips down her cheeks and her jaw.

"Is this okay?" I murmured into her skin.

"No," she said.

I pulled back and searched her eyes, where I found the slightest hint of uncertainty.

"It's not enough," she whispered.

I barely stifled the groan. *My God, woman*, my brain shouted, and then my eyes went to her mouth, and I told my brain to *shut the fuck up already and kiss her*.

Finally, unable to stop the forward momentum even if I'd wanted to, I kissed her lips, gently at first, then with more pressure as her hands reached for the hem of my sweater and pulled it off over my head.

Her eyes sparked as she traced the lines of my chest, and it wasn't the cold that made me shiver as her hands slid down my stomach to the waistband of my jeans. She unbuttoned them slowly, purposefully, and my skin flushed with the heat of wanting her.

When my jeans were open, Dallas made a humming noise in her throat as her hand trailed lightly over the bulge in them. Then she unbuttoned her own jeans, slid them off with underwear and socks, and just like that, she was naked.

The fire in the wood stove lit her from behind, and the urge to photograph her was so strong that my mind scrambled to memorize the moment so I could relive it some night when I sat in the dark, desperately trying to remember every curve, every muscle, every inch of her beautiful body.

She studied me, and I realized my thoughts must have shown on my face.

"You're imagining the pictures you could take, aren't you?" she said.

"Actually," I said on an exhale, my words running ahead of my brain, "I was trying to memorize you. It's the only way to include myself—how I feel when I look at you—in this moment."

My words seemed to catch her off guard, and I hoped she wouldn't actually ask how I felt, because I wasn't sure I was evolved enough past pure, instinctive *want* to articulate it.

"Someday," I said, my voice rough as I stepped forward to take her hand and lead her to the bed, "I'll tell you about it. But for now—"

"I'm more of a show than tell person," she said, reclining on the bed, the curve of a smile on her lips as she stretched out a foot to toe my jeans, "so show me."

Her confidence in that moment was so sexy it took my breath away.

She watched as I stripped off the rest of my clothes, and her gaze spread heat over my skin everywhere it touched. When I joined her on the bed and we slipped under the duvet, I didn't even notice the cold fabric as she wrapped her naked body around mine. She looked up at my face, and I kissed her deeply, breathing in the scent of herbs and woodsmoke from her skin and hair. Her hands roved over me, exploring my skin with abandon, utterly fearless in her quest to find places to touch.

My hands tangled in her hair as I kissed her, and when I knew the taste of her mouth, I slid under the covers and kissed my way down to her breasts and her perfect nipples that were warm and tasted faintly of the coconut oil she used. Her body squirmed beneath me as I continued memorizing it with my mouth, down her rib cage, across her soft belly, and over the curve of her hips.

I traced the line down the inside of her hip, and my touch made her shiver. Her self-control was so evident in everything she did, and this tiny, involuntary shiver that *I'd* caused felt like a victory. I smiled into her skin as I kissed my way down to the intersection of thigh and hip. I lingered there, inhaling the scent of her, touching, stroking, teasing her with my mouth and hands.

I ached to be inside her.

The taste of her, the feeling of her against my tongue was every fantasy I'd had since I'd first kissed her. She writhed with pleasure, and every shiver, every twitch, every moan taught me exactly how to use my mouth to give her pleasure.

I loved her confidence. I loved that she told me with words like "yes" and "more" and "there," and when she came, I held her as the spasms shook her. Then she pulled me up to her and kissed me deeply, the flavors of her mixing together in a heady combination of musk and beer and woman.

Once she'd recovered, she reached over to her nightstand and opened the drawer. She felt around the contents blindly and finally had to lean over to find the foil-wrapped package, which she waved triumphantly. "Ah-ha!"

I laughed, and then went still at the look in her eyes when she tore it open.

She wanted me, and being wanted by this woman suddenly felt more than physical. It felt like something that mattered.

"Roll over," she said, and I did, because I was not a fool, and because she was the sexiest woman I'd ever known.

She slid down my body under the covers, and I lifted them to watch her tongue slide up my cock. She circled it, then took it in her mouth, and I had to close my eyes against the vision of her for fear of losing control. It was too potent, too powerful, and I gasped the word "condom" in self-defense.

She rolled the condom down the length of me, and then positioned herself over me and sank down. I thrust deep inside her, and we both cried out. She rocked back and forth against me, using my thrusts to grind herself on me. When she came again, I lost the thread of control I had left and my own orgasm pulsed inside her for what felt like an eternity.

After a while, she dropped down to my chest, and we lay like that, chests heaving together, still connected.

My heartbeat gradually slowed to match her breath, and I felt a band tighten in my chest as though we were bound by something tangible, something more than just the earth-shattering sex we'd just had.

Lights flashed through the window in a pattern that seemed official, and Dallas broke our connection to sit up and look out the window. I missed her with a suddenness that startled me, and I shoved the feeling away before she could see it on my face. But her eyes were fixed on the lights outside.

"Looks like we're on," she said. "The RCMP's going to need statements from all of us."

I groaned and tried to bury my head under the covers. I might have reached for her again if she hadn't slid out of the bed. I turned to watch her as she got dressed.

"You *are* fucking magnificent," I said, tasting the inadequacy of the word as compared to the woman in front of me.

She pulled up her underwear and wiggled into her jeans.

"You're not so bad yourself," she said, and the slow, sexy confidence of her smile lit a fire in my soul.

[36]
DALLAS

"Deep in the forest a call was sounding, and as often as he heard this call, mysteriously thrilling and luring, he felt compelled to turn his back upon the fire and the beaten earth around it, and to plunge into the forest, and on and on, he knew not where or why; nor did he wonder where or why, the call sounding imperiously, deep in the forest."

- JACK LONDON, *THE CALL OF THE WILD*

Reed had apparently been taunting the Russian while he waited for Rob and the RCMP to arrive, so the guy was rabid with violence when he was finally pulled from the hole, and consequently, was decidedly *not* given the kid-glove treatment by our Canadian Mounties.

It was hours before we were all finally able to go to bed, and Oliver and I didn't even have a conversation about it—we both just fell into my bed and were asleep about thirty seconds after his arms wrapped around me.

The next morning I got up, took a cold shower, and was in with

Grandpop and Wolf when Oliver knocked on the door. He looked tired and rumpled, and I wanted to smooth his hair and bring him coffee in bed. It was a feeling I resisted with every fiber of my being.

"Good morning," he said, as he came in. He gave me a small smile, but in no other way did he indicate any sort of intimacy with me, and I appreciated it.

His eyes went to Grandpop. "You look like you're getting more oxygen. How do you feel?"

"Like I've been in a lowland fog and I've just reached some high ground. It's a hard climb, but the air's clear and the view's interesting." Grandpop studied Oliver through narrowed eyes. "How about you? Heard you had some excitement."

Oliver shook his head. "Wasn't me. Your grandchildren have spines of steel. They must've gotten it from you."

Grandpop chuckled. "They got it from Araminta, my wife. That one was fearless and so sure of what was right. She never thought twice about stepping out in front of someone who needed it, and she never backed down from a fight."

"Well, Dallas has made a career of protecting people, so clearly, your wife was a great influence," Oliver said to him as he bent down to stroke Wolf's fur. She looked at him with trusting eyes, and he sat on the rug next to her bed and ran his fingers across her body.

"She made the hard choices, and she stuck to her guns." Grandpop continued. "When the girls were young, she even sent me away to make sure they stayed safe." He chuckled, but I didn't like the sound of that at all.

"What are you talking about?" I said. "I never heard that story."

"Oh, it must have been sometime in the seventies, after one of my cousins had lost her baby in the scoop."

I met Oliver's eyes and saw that he remembered our discussion of the Sixties Scoop. "Well, another of my cousins was married to a white man, so she and her kids were safe. They'd been taken off the Indian status rolls, Europeans being patriarchal and all." Grandpop shook his head, like it was something that made no sense to him.

"Did Grandma Minty's status change because she married you?" I asked, honestly surprised that it had never occurred to me to wonder.

"It did." The chuckle this time was grim. "Like I said, Europeans are patriarchal, so that meant my wife and daughters all had my status. When Araminta heard social services was doing sweeps around Dawson, she sent me back to Pelly Crossing to stay with my family until they'd checked on our house." Grandpop's expression had hardened.

"Oh, Grandpop," I said quietly. Oliver stayed silent, his fingers trailing through Wolf's fur while his focus was on Grandpop's story.

"Well, I didn't much like it, but other families would send their kids out the windows when social services came calling, so ..." He shrugged and shook his head. "We fought, but it worked. Social worker came because my name was on the status rolls, but when she saw a well-to-do white woman in charge of the house, not another word was said." He looked angry, and it was the first time I'd ever seen an expression like that in a conversation about my grandmother. "She made the hard choices, but she protected us all, and that's what counted."

He seemed to come back from his memories a little surprised we were in the room, so I stood up and kissed his cheek. "Internet's still down, and we need to go into town. What can I get you?"

Grandpop looked over at Oliver. "You heading out soon?"

The question startled him. "Pretty soon," Oliver said, darting a look at me.

"You come by before you go," he said, settling back in his bed. His gaze settled on me. "I got what I need, Sis. You go on to town, and I'll see you when you get back."

Oliver gave Wolf an extra ear rub and then stood up to follow me out.

Grandpop's story was crawling through my brain and under my skin, and Oliver must have felt my disquiet.

"Tell me about Indian status," he said.

I exhaled. "You don't ask easy questions," I said, as we got into Polar Bear. Reed had changed the tires for me while Oliver and I had been at fish camp. "Depending who you talk to, it's a legal identity, a tax exemption, a paternalistic policy, a privilege, a punishment, or the Canadian equivalent of apartheid law."

I shot a quick glance his way. Oliver wasn't as glassy-eyed as I'd expected and appeared to be chewing on my words, so I continued. "Grandpop was talking specifically about the policy that made any wife or offspring of a First Nations male also First Nations. But a First Nations woman, like Grandpop's cousin, married to a white man lost her status, which was fine when it came to protecting her kids from the scoop, but not fine when it came to cultural identity or the few legal protections we have. And it doesn't even consider the fact that First Nations societies are matrilineal."

He was silent as we drove past the dredge tailings moonscape, and I was trying to wrap my brain around what it had meant for Grandpop and my mom and aunt that Grandma Minty had basically traded on her color to deny her kids' status.

"So"—Oliver broke into my thoughts, which was honestly a relief— "you got your Indian status from Isaac through your mom, and that's what gives you your hunting rights."

"Correct. It varies by territory, but Yukon First Nations don't have bag or catch limits and can hunt any time of year."

"Nice," he said.

I scowled. "Yeah, a lot of guys say that."

"I didn't mean—"

"I don't want to fight," I interrupted, utterly not in the mood to give a classroom lecture.

I turned off the highway on Seventh Avenue, and Oliver wisely changed the subject. "Can we swing by the old place you like on our way to Mark's?"

I raised an eyebrow, but made a right on Turner Street. I parked in front of the property and let the car idle while Oliver studied the overgrown double lot. The cabin was probably a teardown, but the old wood was in good shape and could be reused, and the lot was big enough to be able to expand the cabin without losing the rare feeling of privacy on a town lot.

"Who owns it?" he finally asked.

I shrugged. "I've never done a property search. It's been empty longer than I've been alive."

"What if I bought it?" he asked.

I frowned. "Why?" I had to work to keep my voice neutral.

He shrugged. "You should have a place in town for when you visit your family."

I pulled away from the curb and said nothing while I tried to sort through the source of my budding anger.

Oliver spoke about things as if there could be a future. This was a guy who didn't do relationships, not even with pets, because he didn't do attachments. But talking about buying my cabin—that was *future* talk.

I hadn't been thinking about my future when I'd had sex with Oliver, but suddenly my conversation with Christi came back to me. The condom in my dresser was a leftover from my relationship with Ashton and probably long expired. What if I got pregnant? Was he the person I'd want to father my kid? A guy who didn't get attached. A guy who needed a bodyguard. A guy who could charm the pants off literally anyone, including me.

And then the leading edge of anger shifted to something else. Panic threatened to choke me, and Oliver must have seen something of what I felt on my face.

"I said something wrong again, didn't I?" He sounded confused and yet resigned.

"Honestly, I don't even know what you said. I mean, I know the words you used, but I have no idea what you meant." I forced my voice into a calm tone I didn't feel.

"Forget I said anything," he sighed. "I don't know what I meant either."

We pulled up outside Mark's house, and I turned to Oliver before we got out of the car.

"Listen, I had a really great time with you last night, and I really like you, but this"—I nodded at Mark's house—"is business, and as soon as we both check our email and connect with Cipher, we're going to be up to our eyeballs in business. And"—this was the part I'd been dreading—"because the Russian mentioned a brother, I'm afraid this isn't over, which makes you a client again."

I couldn't read his expression, and I wasn't sure what I expected to see on his face, but it wasn't … *nothing*. I inhaled and then said simply, "I'm sorry."

He gave a neutral nod of his head and got out of the truck. I followed him up to Mark's, where he knocked but then stepped aside to let me enter first when Mark answered the door.

"Hey," Mark said, looking like he just rolled out of bed. "Good timing. Looks like your AI's reached slime mold brain."

"No shit?" Oliver said, a look of wonder lighting up the previously blank expression on his face, and I tried not to feel hurt that the words between us were so easily forgotten.

"No shit." Mark grinned, opening the door wide for us to enter.

[37]

OLIVER

*"He felt strangely numb. As though from a great distance, he was aware
that he was being beaten. The last sensations of pain left him. He no
longer felt anything, though very faintly he could hear the impact of the
club upon his body. But it was no longer his body, it seemed so far
away."*

- JACK LONDON, *THE CALL OF THE WILD*

My own brain was very happy to switch focus from Isaac's brutal
story and Dallas and her weird panic about the house on Turner
Street to the neural network of Mark's mining rig. Getting back to my
cyber-nerd comfort zone allowed me to answer her questions with
professional detachment.

"Slime mold brain is good?" she asked in a tone that sounded
skeptical.

"Think of it as the size of slime mold, but with the ability to process a
particular thought faster than every human brain on the planet

combined," I answered, as I sat down at Mark's computer and pulled up the program that would let me see the results of its machine learning.

She watched me for a minute, but when I didn't elaborate further, she pulled out her phone and checked her messages.

"It switched from YouTube to TikTok yesterday, and I'm pretty sure your program has populated itself well enough to be operational today," Mark said.

Dallas looked up from her phone. "What does that mean? Explain it to me like I'm five."

I pulled up the video of Jennifer Jones, the activist Dallas had been protecting in Mexico. "You've obviously seen this video," I said, hitting "play" on the now famous sex tape of Jennifer, a petite white woman with dark hair, and some hunky white dude with blond hair. Jennifer's husband, Emmanuel, was Black, and their children were mixed-race and gorgeous, and that fact alone had put her in the crosshairs of some pretty nasty people. The sex tape just took it up a notch.

Dallas winced and looked away. "Obviously."

"Wait, I haven't," Mark said eagerly, leaning in. "Who is that?"

Dallas glared at him. "It's supposed to be Jennifer Jones, but it's not, it's fake."

"Who's Jennifer Jones?" Mark asked.

I answered his question. "She's the activist who became one of the faces of voting rights reform in the last election."

"I'd vote for her." Mark leered.

Dallas hit him in the arm. "Don't be gross."

"What? I'm just saying, that video gets my attention," he said, watching the screen avidly as I entered the code that would run my fake-buster.

"That's not Jen," Dallas growled, pointing at the screen.

"But it's a very good fake with no obvious markers," I said.

"What are the markers of a fake?" Dallas asked.

"The easiest to spot are lighting mistakes—lighting on a face that's inconsistent with the light sources in the room," I said, my attention on the computer. "Others include blurring at the jaw or around the mouth, hair that's too perfect—"

"Perfect hair is fake?"

"A deepfake program can't generate flyaways," I said. "This one tried to"—I pointed to the screen—but it's still not quite there. Another marker is when the person in the video is talking. Look at the mouth—it's usually just a little off in the lip sync."

"There's no talking in this video," Mark said, leaning in again. "Just a lot of moaning and panting." He dodged Dallas's shove and grinned at her. She scowled back.

"My program goes beyond facial recognition," I said. "The YouTube data sets taught it to look at movement, specifically linking certain ways of moving with height, weight, build, athleticism, body position, and age." I navigated to the code and entered a new field.

"With Jennifer Jones it's easier because there's a lot of footage of her from interviews and news pieces," I continued, as the rig ran through the parameter definition I'd just set. "This will take a few minutes."

There was a knock on the door, and Dallas automatically made a move toward it. "It's Reed," Mark told her. "He said he was coming by today."

She looked surprised. "Reed got less sleep than we did."

Mark's gaze went from me to Dallas and back again. "Oh, really." I couldn't tell if it was disapproval or teasing in his voice. There might have been an edge of disappointment too.

"Shut up, Mark." She went to the door, and I heard Reed's voice in a muted conversation with her, presumably as he took off his boots. When he came in a minute later, he was alone.

"Dallas went out to grab Cheechakos," he said, tossing a nod in the direction of the computer. "What's happening?"

"Porn, obviously," Mark said.

"Clearly," Reed said with a grin as his eyes narrowed to look at the screen. "Isn't that Dallas's client, that political activist chick?"

I nodded. "Jennifer Jones."

"She legit saved the chick's family, you know?" Reed said, as he dropped into the sofa and picked up a video game controller.

"Dal's a bodyguard, right? Isn't that her job?" Mark said, flopping onto the other side of the couch and grabbing the other controller.

"Security specialist," I said automatically, with only half of my attention focused on their conversation. The other half was on the code.

"Yeah, well, you know what happened to those game designer chicks in Gamergate?"

"Didn't an ex-boyfriend post one of their addresses online and the trolls went apeshit?" Mark asked.

"Those women got rape and death threats from every corner of the bottom-feeder underworld," Reed said. "Same thing happened to Dallas's client, except they included her husband and kids in the threats. Some guy broke into their house one night while they were there. Went for the baby. Dallas took him down, called the cops, and then hustled them all out and got them to Mexico."

"Jeez," Mark said. "That's intense."

"She spent the two months in Mexico taking care of the kids while Jennifer locked herself in a room and Emmanuel basically long-distance moved them." Reed's voice drifted away as his attention was caught by the game they'd just begun on Mark's TV monitor.

My mind was spinning on the information Reed had just casually dropped. Dallas took a home invader down? Of course she did. I finally tried to pull one of the threads of thought. "Jennifer locked herself in a room?"

Reed scoffed. "Depression? PTSD? Who the hell knows? Meanwhile, she's got little kids who are just as scared and confused as she is. Fucking clients, man." He shot me a look. "No offense, dude."

"Offense taken," I said. Maybe it was the frustration of Dallas's dismissal of me, or maybe I was sick of feeling like the word "client" was a slur, but I finally had enough. "If we're such shit to deal with, why does she even bother to take us on? She could do some other kind of work."

Reed glared at me, and Mark pointedly kept his eyes locked on the game he was playing on the TV screen. Finally, Reed shook his head. "When you're good at a thing, you do what you have to do to make money at it so you don't have to do the thing you hate. Because if you get stuck doing a thing you hate, you're just marking time between getting up in the morning and going to bed. There are things more pathetic than that, but not many."

He gave me a hard look, and I was surprised at how much he looked like his grandfather in that moment. "Dallas is the best tracker I know. Maybe as good as Grandpop, and way better than me, but I'll hurt you if you ever tell her I said that."

Mark snickered from his corner of the couch but kept his eyes on his game.

"Maybe you don't know this, man," Reed continued, "but she got so burned by catering to clients that she left us all behind, just to get away from all the shit they dumped on her."

There was pain in Reed's voice, and I realized he lost his best friend when Dallas left the Yukon.

"She told me about the moose," I said quietly.

He scoffed. "The moose was just the last straw, and not even the worst one. I'm just saying that Dallas has had to put up with way more than anyone should have to just to be able to do something she's great at, so yeah, she has boundaries, and they're there for a reason, because it seems like every time she lets her heart get involved, even a little bit, it all goes to shit."

Reed turned back toward the TV, and I watched him for a minute, thinking that Dallas was lucky she had someone who loved her so fiercely. She had several someones—her mom, her sister, and her grandfather were equally protective of her—and I had to admit, I was a little jealous of that.

The sound of the door opening and the scuff of snow being banged off of boots told me Dallas was back. I got up to meet her at the door to the vestibule.

"Can I take that?" I asked, indicating the box of fresh baked things in her hand.

"Yeah, thanks." She handed it to me so she could take off her boots, and I considered it a victory that she let me help her.

I carried the box in and set it on the kitchen counter. Dallas stopped at the computer to study the screen and looked up at me, her expression serious. "What does this mean?"

I joined her there, and then dropped into the seat to load an online photo editor. "The program identified that the face and body weren't matched, and also which photo-editing software was used—" I pulled the video into the editing software and talked while I worked. "So, even though this has been compressed and copied a million times, my software has used the markers to identify and recreate the layer …"

I hit a key, and the face of Jennifer Jones disappeared from the video, revealing a similar, but not identical, brunette underneath.

"No shit," Mark's voice breathed. I looked around to see that all three of them had arrayed themselves behind me to see the computer screen, and I chuckled at Mark's predictable response.

"No shit," I said with real satisfaction.

"Dude, you're going to make millions. Every government agency on the planet is going to want a piece of this, and they're all going to want exclusive rights," Reed said in an awed tone.

"Ka-ching!" Mark added with delight.

"I need to send this to Cipher so they can start working on getting us back into the States," I said to Dallas.

She nodded. "I spoke to Darius while I was out. He's expecting to hear from you."

I didn't dwell on the little spike of hurt I felt that she didn't wait for me to speak to Cipher. They were her co-workers, and I was just the client.

"I need to do some more work to refine the program," I said, trying to switch the gears of my brain from too sensitive to all business. "Can I pay you for the time and work on it here?" I said to Mark.

He grinned. "How about I just take a percentage of your sale."

I rolled my eyes. "Nice try. How about an hourly rate?"

"You guys should eat before you get lost in nerd stuff and forget to,"

Dallas said, as she grabbed a muffin from the box in the kitchen and headed for the door.

"Where are you going?" I asked her.

"I need to follow up with the RCMP and see if I can learn anything more from the Russian," she said, pulling on her coat.

"Do you want company?" I asked.

She shook her head. "You have nerd stuff to do. I'll check in a little later. Reed?" She addressed her cousin. "If you guys order lunch, save the receipt and I'll buy it from you."

"So it can get added to my bill," I said with a look that said, *seriously?*

It was worth it just to see her smile. "Exactly."

[38]

DALLAS

"When Achilles was a young child, his mother dipped his body in a vat of yarrow tea to protect him from the dangers of war."

- BEVERLEY GRAY, *THE BOREAL HERBAL*

Oliver stayed at Mark's to continue refining his program, and after dealing with travel arrangements, I sat in my mom's kitchen pulling dried fireweed and yarrow flowers off their stems, while Christi heated almond oil and Mom cleaned the jars. Infusing oil with healing plants could be done in the winter as long as the jars of oil were set in the window to absorb whatever sunlight they could. My stepdad called it our kitchen witchery, and working side by side on projects we could share was my favorite way to talk to my family.

"So, when are you thinking of heading back down south?" my mom asked me.

"I'm going to stick around here for a while," I said. "I'll give Aunt Rikki a break from looking after Grandpop."

269

"Really?" she asked, surprised. "Your bosses will let you take time off like that?"

I shrugged. "If they don't, I can always find something else." I was carefully not looking at her, and she knew it.

"Dallas," she said quietly, "what's going on?" She dried her hands and came around the table to sit beside me. When I didn't meet her eyes, she picked up a bundle of fireweed and began stripping flowers.

"I've been gone a long time," I finally said, "and I've missed my family."

"Do you want me to stay here with you?" Christi asked. "I don't have to go back to Calgary with Mom and Dad. I'm sure I can find something here when the tourists start coming up in May."

I shook my head. "You have things you need to do in a bigger place than Dawson City. I'll hang with Grandpop and Aunt Rikki, and maybe talk Reed into getting a place with me in town before the mine sites open up."

Silence filled the room for the space of a couple of conversations, and then Mom finally said, "I heard Ashton moved to B.C. with his girl-friend and their kid, and his dad shut down the outfitter last year."

"Good for them," I said without inflection. They couldn't see the pounding of my heart, and I wouldn't let them hear it in my voice.

"Have you truly moved on from what happened with him?" my mom asked.

"It was six years ago, Mom. I've moved on."

"Really? Because you've never talked about being with anyone else since then."

"I'm not in the habit of discussing my sex life with my mom." I tried to add snark to my voice, but it just fell flat.

"You used to be," she said quietly.

I snorted ungraciously. "I used to be eighteen too."

"What about things with Oliver?" Christi said. "He seems really into you."

"He's a privileged rich guy from Boston," I said more angrily than I meant to. "He'll go back to Chicago and find some big investors for his new code, and then he'll be off partying in the Maldives with pretty blondes. I'm not Oliver's type, and frankly, he's not mine."

George cleared his throat from the sofa, and I looked up, surprised at myself for forgetting he was in the room. But he wasn't the only one in the room. Oliver had just kicked off his shoes and come in from the mudroom. He stood frozen in the doorway.

My insides clenched and my face heated, and then Oliver pasted on a bright smile and said, "So, I've booked my ticket for the Maldives, which one of you beautiful women wants to come with me?" He stepped into the room and shook George's hand hello, then came over to kiss my mom on the cheek.

I felt like the world's worst person, and Christi shot me a look loaded with *oh no.*

"Oliver," I began, with no idea what else to say.

He held up a hand. "No worries." He looked at the stripped flowers in the bowls on the table, then at the jars of oil Christi was heating up in a pot of hot water on the wood stove. "Making potions, I see? That's cool. I just came by to say how nice it was to meet you all. Reed just brought me out to grab my stuff, because I'm probably going to be working all night at Mark's to get this program ready, and apparently," he said, glancing at me, "one of the other Cipher agents is coming up tomorrow to escort me back."

Shame burned my face, and I forced myself to meet his eyes. His face was a mask of amiability, and it hurt to see him turn his smile to my sister as he stepped forward with his arms out.

"Christi, you're an amazing cook, and I look forward to someday paying ridiculous amounts of money to eat in your restaurants." He gave her a big hug, and my throat closed as I fought back tears.

"Thanks, Oliver. It was really good to meet you. Good luck with your code, and whatever else you do."

"Mr. and Mrs. Thorpe, thank you for making me feel welcome," he said to my parents. "I know it was awkward to have a stranger come here when you were dealing with so much, and I appreciate your hospitality more than you can know."

"Take care of yourself, Oliver," my mom said, darting a glance at me.

I got up from the table and headed for the mudroom as George shook Oliver's hand again. I had my boots and coat on when he emerged. The smile on his face fell instantly, and he looked tired.

"You don't have to explain anything. Message received," he said tightly.

"I'm sorry, Oliver. You weren't meant to hear that, and it was rude and insensitive." We stepped out into the night air, and the cold hit my face like a slap.

He stopped walking with a jolt. "You know, Dallas, I just don't understand something. Why—? You know, never mind." He exhaled in frustration and continued walking.

"I was going to tell you I wasn't going back to Chicago when you got back here tonight," I said lamely.

"And were you going to tell me you don't respect me and I was just some diversion to pass the time?"

"That's not fair," I said, exasperated. "I shouldn't have even gone there with you. You're a client."

"Enough with the damn client shit!" he snarled. We were near the part of the yard where everyone parked their trucks, and he was standing next to Reed's beat-up Blazer. "Why do you hate clients so much?"

"I don't!" I spat back. "They're my job. That's it. My. Job. And I don't cross the line with clients, no matter what. So screw you and every other guy who felt entitled to any part of me. You're not."

Angry tears gathered in my throat and behind my eyes, and I turned away to brush at them as Oliver stared at me.

"You think I felt *entitled* to sleep with you?" He sounded appalled. "Do you think I hired you to get in your pants? Are you fucking high?! I didn't even like you when we first met. I thought you were some weird, buttoned-up stalker girl Cipher used to freak people out so they'd hire bodyguards."

I glared at him. "So much for being the nicest guy in the room."

He suddenly looked exhausted. He pulled open the passenger side door of Reed's truck and climbed inside. I held the door to keep him from closing it, but he didn't even try to. "I really liked you, Dallas. I *admired* you."

The past tense of his words made my chest tight.

He scoffed, seemingly at himself. "You made me feel good about myself, like maybe I didn't always have to be nice or charming or whatever the hell else you call me. Maybe I could be dorky and excited about stuff that wasn't about looking like a good investment to people who pay for what I do."

I spotted Reed coming out of the ATCO.

"I don't know what I thought could happen between us," he said, staring out the window at Reed's approach, "but I was having fun. So, I guess I should thank you for that," he said, not meeting my eyes.

"Hey, Dal, you want to meet us at the Triple J for dinner?" Reed called out as he approached the driver's side of his truck.

"No, thanks. I'm not hungry." I willed Oliver to meet my eyes, but he kept them firmly averted, so I gently closed his door as I said, "Goodbye, Oliver."

He responded to something Reed said as the truck started to back out of the yard, but didn't look at me again as they drove away.

[39]

DALLAS

"You don't make a photograph just with a camera. You bring to the act of photography all the pictures you have seen, the books you have read, the music you have heard, the people you have loved."

- ANSEL ADAMS

I met the Air North plane from Whitehorse at the little airport south of Dawson City the next morning. Seven people got off the aircraft. Two of them were my colleagues.

The expression on Anna's face was exactly what I expected it would be—wonder and delight. She certainly didn't need to accompany Darius on his trip to pick up Oliver, but I could imagine the conversation would have involved a pretty simple "yes, please" when a trip to the frozen North was mentioned. Anna was up for any adventure, anywhere, anytime.

She met me with a hug. "It's so gorgeous here!" she exclaimed happily.

Darius's greeting was much less effusive. "This place suits you, Dallas."

"It definitely shapes you," I said, as I walked them out to Polar Bear.

"So, tell me the long version of what's happened since you left Chicago," Darius said when we were in the truck and driving to town.

I told him everything that pertained to Oliver's safety and to the capture of the Russian, whose name the RCMP still hadn't gotten. Apparently all documentation he'd used, from the rental car to his flight reservations, was in different names. The veracity of any of them had yet to be determined.

"We have some news on that front," said Darius. "The Lake Peipus region was the link. It seems that Alex Karpov has a brother, two years older, named Dimitri, and Dimitri Karpov was in the Russian equivalent of our special forces for the last decade."

"Do you have a photograph?" I asked.

"It should be in your inbox," Anna said.

I unlocked my phone and handed it back to her to find. A few moments later she said, "I saved it to your photos."

"Can you pull it up?" I asked as we turned onto Seventh Avenue.

"Wow. Great photos of you," she said.

"What? I don't take selfies."

"Oh, they're not selfies, and if I had to guess," she said, handing the phone back to me, "whoever took them is way into you."

The screen was open to one of the shots Oliver had taken of me in the thermal pool. I turned it off and stashed it on the center console. "We're almost there. I'll look at Karpov's brother later."

I parked in front of Mark's house. "Oliver spent the night here working on the program. My cousin and his friend are with him. They're expecting you," I said.

Darius nodded and got out. "I'll go see where they are in the process."

"I'll be right there," Anna said. My insides twisted a little, because I knew she wasn't going to let the photos go.

Darius gave his wife a smile of such sweetness it hurt, then he turned his gaze to me. "I look forward to catching up with you, about more than just client welfare."

Anna got out of the back seat and into the one Darius had just vacated. "Air North had these wonderful homemade pastries on the flight, and now all I can think about is getting my hands on fresh bread."

I chuckled. "I know just the place."

It wasn't until we were firmly ensconced in a warm corner of Cheechakos eating chocolate croissants and drinking coffee, that she opened the conversation as unexpectedly as only Anna could.

"So, why are you pushing him away?"

I blinked at her, a little flustered, and opened my mouth to respond, but nothing came out.

"We're obviously up here because you're done with him, and based on those photos, I'm going to guess it's not because you hate each other."

"Oh, I'm pretty sure he hates me by now," I said.

Anna dismissed that statement with a wave. "That's probably just pride. Men seem to be afflicted with certain varieties that result in retreat." She studied me over her coffee. "For that matter, retreat seems to be your thing too."

"I'm not retreating." I sounded defensive, even to my own ears. "I've just spent too long away from my family. It's time to come back home for a bit."

She tore off a piece of croissant and sighed with pleasure as she ate it. I let my gaze wander to the front of the bakery where people were lined up to buy the fresh pastries. I didn't know anyone in the place, and a small part of me wanted to stand on a table and shout, "I belong here," while another part was thrilled to be anonymous in a town where everyone knew everyone's name.

"Did you ever consider asking him if he wanted to stay?" Anna finally asked.

I looked at her like she'd grown two heads. "Why would he want to do that?"

She shrugged. "I'd hang out up here in a heartbeat. And I'm not even in love with you."

"He's not in love with me."

"Those photos on your phone suggest otherwise," Anna said.

"I'm naked. They suggest temporary lust," I murmured.

"You clearly haven't looked at them closely. I admit I'm a shameless voyeur, but I only saw a couple of them, and they're full of tenderness, respect, adoration, appreciation, and yes, lust. But most of all, each one is an expression of joy. That's hard to show in a picture, but he managed it." Anna took a sip of coffee and seemed to be waiting for me to argue.

"We had fun," I said quietly, not meeting her eyes. I played with the crumbs on my plate and considered my own words. We'd had fun. It had been fun to be alone in the snow with Oliver. It had been fun to teach him how to ice fish, to clean a catch, chop wood, and cook on a wood stove. It had been more than fun to sleep wrapped in his arms, to watch the northern lights together, and to soak naked in a thermal spring with him.

Anna finished her croissant and wiped her hands. "I know that all my filters are broken, and some people find me tough to be around. But there are definite advantages to saying exactly what I think when I think it. People know where they stand with me, and I'm not a mystery for someone to guess at or fill in the blanks."

She met my eyes directly. "You don't live out loud. Your privacy is your right, but when you don't share yourself, you're not an obvious safe space for other people to share themselves with you."

"Wow," I breathed. "You don't pull punches, do you?"

She held my gaze and said wryly, "Broken filter."

"Not a safe space, huh? That's kind of crappy to hear about yourself." I exhaled through the nausea that statement had suddenly brought on.

"Dallas, they're just words. They're only as true as you make them." Anna's tone was gentle. "But if they hit hard, you kind of owe it to your-self to look at why."

I stood up and grabbed my dishes to clear. Anna did the same without comment, and it wasn't until we were back in Polar Bear that I finally spoke again.

"Remember on the boat when you said I could tell you to shut up?"

"I told you I'd shut up when you have something to say," she said with arched eyebrows. "Do you?"

Frustration made me growl. "I don't like you very much right now."

"I'm kind of an asshole, right?" she said cheerfully.

I tried to be angry with her, but the bubbly grin on her face was infectious, and I couldn't keep a straight face.

"Now," she said, "tell me about this town."

And since it was pointless to be mad about something that was basically true, I gave her a rundown of Dawson City's history, starting with the prehistoric fishing settlement of the Tr'ondëk Hwëch'in, which was overrun by gold miners in 1898 and became Dawson City, population 40,000 at its height. I drove past Jack London's cabin on Eighth Avenue, told her the legend about the Moosehide Slide, and I showed her the rec center next to Diamond Tooth Gertie's where a cache of rare nitrate films, including silent films and newsreels from 1903 to 1929, had been discovered, preserved in the permafrost, at the bottom of an old swimming pool. The Dawson Film Find of 1978 was a real treasure because that type of film was so volatile that most other collections around the world had literally set themselves on fire. I'd always felt a little bit of kinship with those nitrate films—incendiary, and able to survive because I'd been buried in Dawson.

It was possible to walk from one end of town to the other in less than twenty minutes, so driving past the Palace Grand Theater and the slanty shack—an actual slanted shack—took just a few minutes, but each glimpse of the town I'd spent so much time in brought back memories of summer Sundays, hikes up to the Midnight Dome, and volunteering at the Dawson City Music Fest.

Sharing bits of my town's history with Anna made me want to share the pieces of me that had formed here with someone who cared about the person I'd become because of this place.

There was that sharing word again.

I finally parked in front of Mark's house, but I let the truck idle while I considered what to do next. "You're coming in, aren't you?" Anna asked.

"I haven't decided," I said quietly.

She gave me a look that probably had paragraphs of "don't be an idiot" attached to it, but I pretended I hadn't seen.

"Okay, well, we're on the afternoon flight back to Whitehorse, and we'll be heading back down to Chicago tomorrow. Hopefully we'll see you before then?"

I nodded, distracted by the snow beginning to fall outside the windows. "My cousin will give you a ride to the airport."

"Dallas," Anna said in a tone of voice that made me look at her, "what are you holding on to?"

She didn't ask what I was letting go of, because I had an answer for that. I was letting go of Oliver before he let go of me. I was letting go of a job I loved to stay in a town I'd deserted, and I was letting go of friends I'd only just begun to let in to reconnect with family I'd shut out.

I didn't have an answer for her question, and I shook my head, helpless to form the words *I don't know*.

"Okay," she said softly, and then she got out of the truck and headed into Mark's house. I drove away before I could see who answered the door.

[40]

DALLAS

- DUNCAN CAMPBELL SCOTT, DEPUTY SUPERINTENDENT OF THE
DEPARTMENT OF INDIAN AFFAIRS

Grandpop was sitting up in a chair when I came in carrying a container of soup and some bread. Wolf lay on the rug next to him, and she thumped her tail at me as the other three did circles around my feet.

"Hey, Sis," he said in a much stronger voice than he'd had since I'd been home.

"Hey, Pop," I answered in something attempting good humor.

He didn't buy it.

"Pull up a chair and tell me," he said, as I set out the soup in a bowl in front of him.

I sighed. "I just got called out by a friend of mine for, I don't know, being stuck, I guess."

He raised an eyebrow for elaboration, so I tried again. "I'm thinking about staying for a bit." The eyebrow went higher, but he still said nothing. "I asked some other agents to come up to escort Oliver back to Chicago. One of those agents, my friend Anna, basically said I'm being too careful with myself and not admitting that I care about him."

"Him being the client?" Grandpop asked.

I sighed. "He's different."

"He's still a guy who hired you, isn't he?" Grandpop said, making the distinction clear.

"He became … more," I said, feeling the inadequacy of the word.

"More, huh?" Grandpop murmured, and then he was silent for a time until he finally asked, "Why are you sending him away, Sis?"

The tenderness in my grandfather's voice made my throat close, and I looked up to meet his eyes. "Because I'm afraid," I whispered.

"Are you afraid he'll come in, or afraid he won't?" he said.

I bent to Wolf, feeling the pounding of my heart in my hands as I ruffled and smoothed her fur over and over. Her eyes never left mine, and I felt as if she understood.

When I finally swallowed enough heartbeats to be able to speak again, I looked up to find that my grandfather's hand had been smoothing my own hair, like I'd been doing to Wolf.

"He's … the opposite of me, Pop. I don't know how else to put it. The pieces don't … fit."

"You know I've been on the outside for a long time," he said. "I left my family when I ran away from that school, and I just never really went back. But I was lucky. I had sixteen years of culture before I left home, and bits and pieces since then. I was there long enough to learn things like laws," he said, "meant to keep blood strong. Laws about Wolves and Ravens."

Something in my chest tightened. "You're Wolf Clan, I know."

"We"—he held my gaze—"are Wolf. You're my family, and I've done what I can to pass on what I know. That's what we do. We teach, we learn, we live."

I remembered Oliver telling me that he'd learn whatever I'd teach him. And he had learned. He'd become someone different in the Yukon. Someone I liked. A lot.

"In our culture," Grandpop continued, "we marry Ravens. Opposites. To keep the blood of our children strong."

"He's not First Nations."

Grandpop made a dismissive sound. "You, me, we've got each other, we've got our family, we've got our traditions and our history. We bring them into any family we make. Your grandmother Araminta, she was my Raven, my opposite, but she filled the places in me that were empty. Come to find out, there was a me-sized hole in her heart too."

He chuckled. "Do you know that when I met her, she was a stringy white girl with a raven on her shoulder?"

I'd heard the story before, it was family legend, but I listened differently this time, thinking about a boy with a crow that dive-bombed his head.

"She raised it from a chick," Grandpop chuckled. "That bird was something else. Came with us when we left Dawson, after Araminta and her pa nursed me back to health. Stayed with us until he got too old to ride her shoulder. Then just up and left when it was time for him to go. No goodbye, just gone."

He smiled. "I guess it's just the way of animals. People need goodbye to know they mattered."

"He's going to leave," I said quietly, more to Wolf than to my grandfather.

"Well, sure he is. You sent him away. Left him before he could leave you. But he can't come in if you don't open the door. There are spaces in both of you that need filling, Sis." Grandpop sighed, and I looked up to meet his eyes. "You're a lone wolf, trying to come home. But you need your raven, your own pack, to really find your way here."

I ran my fingers through Wolf's fur and thought about the pain I'd put in Oliver's eyes. I thought about the chance, small as it was, that I could be pregnant, and I thought about the tattoo of a crow on a boy's heart.

"You should know," he continued, "that your— that Oliver came to see me this morning."

I looked up in surprise. "He did?"

"Your cousin brought him to say goodbye." *To tell me I mattered to him*, Grandpop's eyes said.

"Oh." I exhaled, trying to ignore the fist that lodged itself under my rib cage.

"He told me what an honor it had been to know you, and he hoped I'd forgive him someday for being a client. Whatever that meant to us, he said, we should know that to him, it was the best thing he's ever been."

A sob tore at my chest and nearly made it to my throat before I swallowed it down. I got up off the floor and dusted off my jeans.

"I might be gone a few days, maybe a week or two. Will you be okay here and take your meds while I'm gone?"

"I'll be just fine, Sis. I'm feeling like fish camp is just around the corner."

I kissed him on the cheek. "I might invite a raven," I said.

"Well, I'll find something to teach him if he comes," he said with a smile.

I took a deep breath, gave Wolf another pat, and said, "I love you, Pop."

"You're good at it, Sis," he said, and my eyes filled with tears.

[41]

OLIVER

"Love never dies a natural death. It dies because we don't know how to replenish its source. It dies of blindness and errors and betrayals. It dies of illness and wounds; it dies of weariness, of witherings, of tarnishings."

- ANAÏS NIN

I sat at the window of the hotel room looking out over the snowy view of the parking lot, past a few squat buildings, and to the tree-filled mountains beyond. The lone streetlight was a sickly contrast to the brilliant pinpoints of light in the inky vastness of Yukon sky.

Anna had seemed disappointed when we boarded the small, twenty-seat commercial flight from Dawson City to Whitehorse, and she had been uncharacteristically quiet since then. Darius was friendly, but not chatty, and I realized with a shock that I missed the easy conversation of Reed and Mark.

Reed had driven us to the airport, but either I'd gotten used to his driving, or he'd toned down the speed for the Cipher agents, because we'd made it without a white knuckle in sight. I'd hugged the tall, rangy, long-haired First Nations man with the charming smile and his cousin's eyes, and maybe I put a little extra into that hug for her, because he mumbled, "She'll figure it out," before he let go.

"Thanks, man," I'd said before he left the one-room airport. "Tell Mark I'll wire him when I get back to the city."

Reed had waved his hand dismissively. "He knows you're good for it. And it's been fun hanging with you, figuring all this shit out. Maybe I'll come crash at your place in the city sometime and we can do it again."

"Anytime," I'd said, meaning it.

I'd caught a glimpse of Isaac's compound from the air as we took off, and the ache in my chest made me pensive and moody, so I kept my eyes locked on the view outside the window and tried not to think about *her*.

Thinking too much made breathing hard, so instead, I sat in a chair covered in the kind of busy pattern hotels use to hide stains, with my feet up on the windowsill, staring out at the night sky, trying not to catch glimpses of my own pathetic reflection in the glass.

And when I caught the image of her in the glass, I figured I'd just rounded a new bend in self-pity … until she spoke.

"I'm sorry."

My pulse skyrocketed as I spun in my chair. "Dallas?"

She stood completely still just inside the door of my hotel room with her hands open at her sides as though to show me she was unarmed.

"How did you— No, I don't want to know," I said, my heart slamming. I wasn't sure if it was fear or anticipation that made it so loud in my own ears, and I willed myself to sit back in my chair and wait for her to speak.

"I'm sorry," she repeated quietly.

"For breaking into my room like an assassin and scaring the crap out of me? Yeah, what the fuck?"

"For pushing you away," she said, taking a step forward.

I flinched, and she stopped.

"For not being honest."

I crossed my arms over my chest to hide my heartbeat under them.

She took a breath. "For pretending I hadn't …" She inhaled again, like the words were costing something. "That I wasn't falling for you."

"Christ," I whispered under my breath.

"Am," she whispered back, "falling for you."

I stared at her in shock and surprise and … pain, maybe. "What am I supposed to do with that, Dallas?" She was silent, and I couldn't read the expression on her face, so I pushed harder. "I'm just a privileged rich boy from Boston, right? I'm not your type, and even worse, I'm a fucking *client*."

It was her turn to flinch, and I was glad.

But the confusion and pain that fueled my tirade vanished as quickly as it had come.

"I'm tired of the roller coaster." I exhaled. "The last couple of weeks have been an endless ride of highs and adrenaline rushes and crashing lows, and I'm just exhausted."

She stood in silence, watching me, and then she kicked off her boots and sat on the floor with her back against the wall.

"What are you doing?" I asked.

"Settling in," she said.

"Why?"

"Because what I want requires patience."

I couldn't take my eyes off her, and yet I wanted her gone.

"Come here," I said.

She got up off the floor and came over to perch on the window ledge across from me. Her gaze was watchful and slightly wary.

"What is it that you want?" I asked, trying to gentle my voice so it didn't match the one in my head that snarled in frustration.

"I want"—she exhaled—"I want to let go."

"So, I'm some kind of wild fantasy for you?" I heard the edge of disgust in my tone.

She shook her head. "Not like that. Well"—she allowed a slight smile —"a little like that, but I'm not specifically talking about sex."

The part of myself that wanted to throw a triumphant fist in the air warred with the part that was done with anything as hard is this was. So I stayed silent.

"I hold myself pretty tightly," she said hesitantly.

"You think?"

Her smile was grim. "I've been more … *home* here with you than I have been since I was twenty-one."

Now she was just confusing me. "You said you come back every year." It was a small detail to zone in on, but the details mattered with her. Understanding her mattered.

She seemed to search for the right words. "I've been back, but I haven't really been *home*. Every airline ticket is a round trip scheduled for the day we get back from fish camp. My bag never gets unpacked, and I don't even have a second toothbrush that I keep in my house at the compound."

I pictured her big, yellow duffle bag tossed in the corner of her house, a few clothes spilling out of the top. There'd been cooking implements and paperbacks on the shelves, but nothing more personal than her Buck knife … and all the art she'd created. She might not have come home to the Yukon, but part of her had never left.

"So," I began, feeling around for the right words, "this is about you unpacking your bag?"

I expected her to bite back with something snarky, but she surprised me. She nodded slowly. "Something like that."

She put her legs up on the window ledge and crossed them. She fit inside the window alcove like it was built to accommodate her perfectly. She studied the toes of her socks, the cool ones that were hand knit by her aunt.

"I've been carrying baggage around with me since my guiding days, and I'm so used to hauling it everywhere I go that I forgot to notice how heavy it's gotten."

I studied the way the shadows and light played across the bones in her face. There were hollows under her eyes I hadn't seen before, and her cheekbones stood out in stark relief against the planes of soft brown skin.

Now that I'd seen her beauty, I could never not see it. Her grace and elegance were subtle, buried beneath a veneer of bossy capability. But the woman in the window had let me see her vulnerability, and she would never be anything but beautiful to me again.

"The thing with the moose on my last trip as a guide," she began quietly, "was just the water boiling."

I arched a questioning eyebrow, and a faint smile answered on her lips.

"The fable of the frog that's dropped into tepid water and stays in as the heat gradually goes up until it boils to death?" I nodded, and she continued. "Well, that was me. My boyfriend at the time, Ashton, was also a guide, and we were the best ones the outfit had. I could track anything, anywhere, and he made everything fun."

She bent her knees so her feet were under them and then wrapped her arms around her legs. It was a casual pose, but on her it looked wary and self-protective. "I was sixteen when we met, and we did everything together. Nothing felt like work, and the whole territory was our playground. We did everything from heli-skiing in the winter to whitewater rafting in the summer, and clients loved going out with us because I was the competence and he was the fun. I set up the camps, cooked the meals, guided the hunts, and cleaned the game, while he told stories and played music around the campfire and made everything an adventure, for me and for the clients. It never felt like an unequal division of labor because without his playfulness, my work was just work. It was kind of like the story about the ant and the grasshopper, except he never had to get his wood in for winter because he could charm help from anyone."

She looked out of the window, but her gaze didn't seem to focus on anything in particular. My chest had grown tighter with every word she said about the perfect boyfriend, and I waited for the hammer to fall.

"Ashton was ambitious, and when his dad, who owned the outfitter, wanted to train him to manage the business, he was more than happy to get out of the field and into the office. For the first time, guiding felt like work to me because my boyfriend wasn't there to entertain the clients, and I quickly learned that clients expect to be entertained."

She glowered at some distant memory. "The first time a client came on to me, I very nicely told him I had a boyfriend. He said, 'That shouldn't be a problem, should it?' I told him it was, and he left it at that. I didn't bother to tell Ashton about it because it didn't matter. The next time, a client tried to kiss me, and I pushed him away. He said he'd paid enough for his trip that it should be a perk. I told him to fuck off, and when we got back to town, he complained to Ashton about my attitude."

My fists were clenching, and I forced myself to relax them so she wouldn't notice. This story wasn't about me and how I felt about anything, so I tried not to be a distraction. She hadn't met my eyes since she began telling it, and she continued, staring out the window as she spoke.

"I don't know what I expected. I didn't need him to go to bat for me —I could do that for myself—but I definitely didn't expect him to give the guy an extra day of hunting for free to make up for his inconvenience." Her expression was angry. "And then my boyfriend pulled me aside and said he understood if I didn't want to guide that client out for his free day, but in the future, if I could be more accommodating, everyone would profit."

She exhaled sharply. "More *accommodating*. He must have seen something murderous in my face because he backed off and said something about a friendlier attitude, but we both knew what he meant. Needless to say, I didn't lead that client out on his free day, and I took the next two weeks off for fish camp with my family. They got an earful about clients and accommodations and Ashton, but when I went back to work, Ashton groveled and apologized and was so sweet that I took him back."

I literally had to bite my tongue to keep my thoughts about Ashton's sweetness from spewing past it.

Dallas finally met my eyes. "I stayed with him for another eight months, and I wasn't hit on again by clients, probably because I'd become so bitter and angry that no one wanted to get near me. I didn't figure out why he made up with me until later, but it was all about my First Nations hunting rights. It hadn't felt like a big thing to put an extra kill on my tag every once in a while when things were good between us …"

I just barely held back a wince at the tone of disgust in her voice, but if she noticed my discomfort, she ignored it.

"Later, when things weren't good, every time he smiled and sweet-talked and asked nicely, it was just the heat getting turned up on the pot of water."

She stared out the window again, looking at something beyond the night, and when she finally spoke, it was an echo of her normal voice. "I was pregnant when I went into that river to get the moose. Ashton and I had fought about it before I left on that trip. He didn't want kids, he said. I didn't know what I wanted, but that voice I heard—it wasn't just about me."

I held my breath, afraid of what came next.

Her eyes were dry, but there were tears in her voice. "I lost it anyway." She dropped her feet down off the window ledge, and I took them into my lap, wanting to somehow soothe away the pain that laced every word.

"Ashton—" Her voice choked on his name, and I forced myself to stay calm. "He never came after me to find out what happened when I didn't come back after that trip." Her short laugh was bitter. "He has a five-year-old kid with his new girlfriend," she said. "Blond and blue-eyed like his mom and dad."

She took a deep, shaky breath, as if to re-center herself.

"I didn't like myself very much then. Obviously, I wasn't good enough to have his kid"—anger threaded her words—"even after I allowed him to pimp my family's—my people's—hunting rights to strangers."

She finally met my eyes. "And everyone thought he was just the nicest guy."

The nicest guy. She said the words without irony, and yet I felt them like a fist hitting me in the gut.

I let go of her feet and stood up, needing to put space between us. She looked startled at my sudden motion and withdrew her feet back up to the window ledge. She watched me warily as I crossed my arms and leaned against the desk.

"I'm not Ashton," I said.

"You were for me," she said in a tone of voice I couldn't identify. "Not at first—at first you were just a client."

I bristled at the word "just" and stared stonily.

"But at fish camp, you weren't just a client. You were a playmate, a partner"—she shook her head as if in wonder—"and I thought about what it would be like to keep doing things together, to plan things, to want a … future." That wasn't the word she'd been about to say, and panic crept into my chest.

"And then I shut it all down, because I'd betrayed my family to have a future with Ashton. I'd *lost* … my family."

She'd lost a baby.

Dallas met my eyes with her own clear gaze. "I'm still living inside the choices I made all those years ago, and they've taken the shape of iron bars, punishing me for my crimes. Moving back to the Yukon, even for a little while, is a step toward"—she exhaled—"forgiveness."

I wondered if something let go with her breath. "I became someone I didn't admire or respect when I was with Ashton, and I thought it was because of who he was. What I realized after spending these weeks with you, was that no matter who I'm with, admiration and respect are on me to generate and on me to maintain, and if I can't do that, it's *my* problem and no one else's."

She wasn't still talking about the future, and these were words I could focus on. "How did spending time with me make you realize that?"

Her lip quirked in a tiny smile. "Because you're the nicest guy in the room, and I actually liked myself better when I was in your company." She winced slightly. "And that pissed me off, because it meant clients weren't the problem, and Ashton wasn't the problem."

She stared out the window, and the silence hung between us.

I finally broke it with my own memory. "My grandmother used to roll her eyes every time my parents moved us to a different city," I said. "She'd say, 'The only thing that changes in each new place is the weather, because no matter where you go, you bring yourself and all your baggage with you.'"

Dallas huffed a mirthless laugh. "Like I said, my bags have gotten pretty heavy. It's time to put them down and maybe unpack a couple," she said.

I nodded slowly. "So, this is you, unpacking?"

"Actually," she said, meeting my eyes, "this is me apologizing."

[42]

DALLAS

"Strong people are able to forgive. Superheroes are able to forgive themselves."

- DALLAS

"So, what now?" Oliver asked, his arms still crossed protectively over his chest.

I shrugged. "About all the crap I just laid on you? I don't know."

"Is there anything else?" He frowned, and I couldn't tell if it was at me.

"You mean am I going to ask you to knock me up?" I refused to let him see the flush of guilt I felt about the expired condom with those words. "Move up here and live off-grid with me? No, Oliver, there's nothing else." I gave him a small smile to soften the words. "I heard you when you said you don't let yourself love things. I know who you are, and I won't ask for anything you can't give. I just wanted you to know that even though you're way too handsome and way too charming to be real, my freak-out wasn't fair because it wasn't about you. I'm sorry I was a jerk. You don't deserve that from me, or from anyone."

I couldn't read his face, so I changed the subject.

"Quinn is working on getting the Russian extradited back to Chicago. They found security camera footage from the L train both before and after his attack on you that matches our statements, and his link to Alex Karpov makes him a person of interest connected to an ongoing blackmail and murder investigation."

"He's linked to Karpov?" Oliver asked.

I pulled my phone out of my pocket. "Darius didn't tell you?" I scrolled to my photos file and opened it to the image Anna had downloaded. I handed it to Oliver.

"Dimitri Karpov, ex-special forces from western Russia, brother to Alex Karpov, former owner of ADDATA."

He studied the photo, his frown replaced with a look of concentration. "I took video of the Russian when the RCMP officers were taking him away," I said. "You can see that it's him."

Oliver scrolled back a few photos and studied the short video clips, then replayed them a few times.

"We can get Alex Karpov on a few different charges. The challenge is flushing him out. I'm pretty sure that's why Quinn wants Dimitri extradited—so we can use him for bait."

"Bait," Oliver repeated. "Would Karpov come for his brother in person?"

"It's possible. I'd come for Christi or Reed if I thought someone had them," I said. I would come for Oliver too, but I wasn't going to say that out loud. "The trick is to convince Karpov we actually have his brother."

Oliver looked up from my phone with an expression of sly mischief. It was so reminiscent of the playful man I'd known at fish camp that I dared to let myself have a little bit of hope.

"I can do that," he said with a smirk.

· · ·

By the time we'd landed at Chicago O'Hare, Oliver's manner with me had gone back to something less guarded. The four of us had slept a little, laughed a lot, and we'd worked out a reasonably sane plan to lure Alex Karpov out of whatever hole he'd crawled into. Based on dark web traffic, the guys at Cipher thought he was back in the Great Lakes area, so we might even be able to get an in-person visit if we played it right.

Quinn had been able to open up an executive suite at The Vault, and Oliver was escorted directly there by Darius and Anna while I made my way to the Cipher building. Shane passed me on my way into Quinn's office, and she stopped me with a hand on my arm.

"I thought you were staying in Dawson City for a bit," she said, looking concerned.

"I will be," I said. "I just need to see the case close."

She studied my face for a moment, then nodded. "Cool. I'll grab Gabriel and Alex, and we'll fill you in on everything we've found to date."

"I'll be here," I said, and then knocked on Quinn's office door.

"Come," he said from inside.

He sat at his desk with a beautiful dark-haired baby perched on his lap grasping for the empty water bottle on the desk in front of them. Quinn waved me in, and the baby reached for his cuff with a grabby fist. I tried to tear my eyes away, but they wouldn't let go of the baby's beautiful face.

A face I knew.

"Dallas!" A little boy's voice called my name, and all the breath left my body as he launched himself at my legs. I hadn't seen Zoro where he'd been playing on the floor because my eyes had been so focused on his sister, Rio. I knelt down, and his arms wrapped around my neck like the little barnacle I'd known for two months in Mexico.

"Jennifer will be right back. She wanted to see you," Quinn said to me.

Zoro looked me in the eyes with a serious expression. "Mama said I could hug you. Can I hug you?"

I laughed so I wouldn't cry. "I would love a hug from you," I said, and he tightened his arms and buried his face in my neck.

I caught Rio's gaze across the top of her brother's head, and she seemed to suddenly realize who I was. Her arms reached for me, and her little face wrinkled in distress.

I kissed the top of Zoro's head. "I'm going to hug your sister now too," I said into his ear.

He promptly let go and nodded. "Rio cried and cried when you went away," he said, "but I'm bigger, so I only cried a little bit."

My eyes filled with tears. "I'm big, and I cried too," I said solemnly.

Zoro seemed to think about it for a moment, then he nodded. "That's okay, then. Mama said tears wash out things that hurt."

"Your mama is very smart," I said, as he went back to the blocks he'd been playing with on the floor.

"You should hug Rio now," he said seriously as Quinn handed me the baby and I settled into a chair across the desk from him. I smiled at Zoro, and then turned my gaze to the beautiful girl in my lap.

"Hello, Rio," I said softly.

Rio reached for my face and gurgled happily. She'd been just four months old when I'd last seen her, and nothing about me should have been familiar to her. And yet she met my eyes, and her spirit knew mine. Something tight unfurled in my chest, and I felt like I could breathe.

Quinn let me have my moment with Rio before he finally spoke. "Darius called me with the details of the trap you want to lay for Karpov," he said. "I have a few questions, but overall, I think it's an interesting plan. My biggest concern is whether Karpov will be convinced we're holding his brother."

"We'll make it personal," I said to Rio, because she held my attention in the vise grip of her liquid brown eyes. I tore my gaze away from hers to meet Quinn's granite expression. "My grandfather said Russians play a long game when revenge is on the line. For Cipher to capture and hold Dimitri Karpov will seem like revenge for implicating us in Jen's deep-fake. Revenge as a motive will make sense to a Russian. He doesn't need to know Dimitri's in official custody."

Quinn considered me before he spoke. "It's still a long shot, but not outside the realm of possibility." He watched me kiss Rio's fingers as they explored my mouth, and if I'd been paying attention I might have actually seen a smile. "Alex is monitoring Karpov. He and Jorge were able to ping his dark web activity to a location in Michigan, near where his yacht was moored—we're working on an exact location."

"I want to be on the team that goes to get him," I said.

"I need you to stay on Curran until Karpov's in custody."

Zoro knocked over the stack of blocks he'd built and was happily singing to himself as he rebuilt the tower. My eyes went back to my boss, though my attention was on the children.

"We have a two-bedroom suite for him," Quinn added, "so you can stay on him until this is resolved."

Rio reached for my nose, and I moved closer so she could grab it. "I'm not sure the client will want that," I said warily, as though speaking to the baby would mask my discomfort.

"Are you okay?" Quinn asked in a tone of voice I could only describe as concerned.

I looked up in surprise. I expected "did something happen between you?" or "what would make him uncomfortable?" I absolutely hadn't expected the owner of Cipher Security to worry about my well-being.

"I'm fine, everything's fine," I answered automatically, my eyes drawn back to the gurgling baby on my lap. Her tiny, rosebud mouth smiled so easily as she concentrated on my face.

"Dallas," Quinn said gently, "whatever you need to do is fine with us. You're a good agent, and we feel lucky to have you working with us. If you want to work on a contract basis, or part-time, or even just part of the year, we can figure it out. And while your skills are impressive and useful, it's your mind and heart that are most valuable to us and to your clients. Let us know how we can support you, and we'll make it work."

For Quinn that was practically a soliloquy. I took a deep breath to push back the lump in my throat as I kissed Rio's chubby little fist. "Thank you," I finally said, my heart aching to clutch the baby in my lap and never let go. "I'd like to take some time to be with my family through the summer. After I've gotten the wood in, maybe I'll be back?" I looked over the top of Rio's head at him.

His mouth twitched in the approximation of a smile. "After you've gotten the wood in," he said, nodding. "Sounds like a pretty tough place to live."

I shrugged. "Well, I don't know anyone up there who has ever needed close protection, so I'm thinking tough is relative."

"Point taken."

There was a knock on the door, and a lovely and dynamic woman stepped inside. Rio's face lit up like a lightbulb as she reached her hands up to her mother.

I stood to hand the baby to Jennifer Jones, my former client, a brilliant political activist, and the woman whose name and reputation had been dragged through hell and back again.

"Dallas," she said with a smile. She moved Rio to one hip and held out her other arm to hug me. She smelled like amber and vanilla, and she looked healthy and strong. Rio tugged at strands of my hair, and Jennifer laughed as she untangled her daughter's fist from my head.

"She missed you. We all missed you," she said.

"You look really good," I answered with a smile.

"I feel good. Emmanuel has me on a farm-to-table diet, literally. We left the city and have been renting a farmhouse in hill country where Zoro helps me collect the eggs from the chickens every morning. Isn't that right, bubbs?"

Zoro looked up at his mom with an angelic grin that took my breath away. "And I only broke one." He went back to his blocks as Jen laughed softly and returned her attention to me.

"I told Quinn that I want to do a press conference. I've been hanging back, healing, but also afraid to put myself on the line again. Now I'm ready, finally, to get out in front of this."

Quinn clarified for me. "Deepfake technology needs regulatory oversight. Jen is spearheading an awareness campaign in order to get the issue before Congress."

My heart pounded as I spoke to the woman whose children I had loved like they were my own. "I'm so sorry you got dragged into this again. I never would have—"

"Dallas," she said, reaching for my hand, "you weren't the one doing the dragging. If anything, you're the innocent party here, and that a deep-fake smear campaign could happen to you, a private person who stays out of the limelight, made it clear to me that this isn't an issue I can sit back on."

Jen squeezed my hand and smiled. "I'm one of those people who feels most alive when I'm fighting for something"—she looked at her daughter's face—"or someone. I'm choosing to take this on, and I'm looking forward to the fight."

I touched Rio's arm and spoke to the baby. "Your mom is one of the strongest people I know."

Jen chuckled. "From you, that's a huge compliment. You'll come and visit us at the farm?"

My throat was so tight with unshed tears that I scooped Zoro up off the floor and tickled him to distract myself.

"Hey!" He giggled and squirmed.

"Would you let me gather eggs with you in the morning if I come visit?"

The little boy flung his arms around my neck again and said in my ear, "You carry the basket, and I'll find the eggs."

Jen laughed and then turned to Quinn. "We'll be here tomorrow for the news conference."

He moved out from behind the desk and ushered Jen to the door. "We'll have a helicopter standing by on the roof to get you to the airport right afterwards."

I scooped up the blocks in one hand and kept Zoro on my hip as I followed them out of the office. We were standing by the elevator saying goodbye when it opened for them.

I rubbed Zoro's nose with my own. "I'll see you again," I said.

"You promise?" He held my face in both of his hands.

"I promise."

It was only when I set him back down and handed him the bag with his blocks that I realized Oliver was in the back of the elevator with Alex Greene. He was looking right at me with an unreadable expression. I tore my eyes away from his and blew a kiss to Rio as the elevator doors closed.

"You okay?" Quinn murmured to me as we returned to his office.

I nodded, too full of unsaid things to speak. But when I met his eyes, I found my voice again. "Thank you."

He opened the door to his office and ushered me in. "Thank *you*," he said quietly.

Shane and Gabriel followed us in, and Quinn asked for an update.

"Regarding Karpov," said Gabriel, his deep, English-accented voice sounding quietly cultured. "Alex was able to trace the signature that Oliver's program unmasked from the deepfake video of Jennifer Jones. It matches one of Karpov's dark web personas."

There was silence in the room, and I stared at Gabriel. "Holy shit. It really is him behind all of this," I whispered.

"Yeah," Shane agreed. "We knew Karpov was connected to political micro-targeting for the far right. Discrediting a successful voting rights activist is the next step up in a pretty bold game."

Quinn looked grim. "It certainly explains the initial acquisition of Curran's deepfake tech."

It took me a moment to process the information that Oliver Curran, a brilliant young programmer from Harvard, had once sold deepfake tech to a guy who had later used it to discredit Jennifer Jones, putting her family in danger. That same guy was now willing to kill Oliver to keep his deepfake-busting software from being released to the marketplace. The threads of this were woven together like my Ojibwe spiderweb, and somehow, I'd become the protector of all the children caught in it.

Gabriel tossed a file onto the desk. "Alex has also pulled every image of Karpov for the past ten years and a list of links to every known associate," he said. I picked up the file. Most of the images were from his early career in academia.

"Did Oliver know Karpov at Harvard?" I suddenly asked, noting the caption under a candid shot of a much younger Karpov giving a lecture.

He had a vaguely similar appearance to Dimitri Karpov, but was taller and considerably thinner.

Shane shook her head. "He said their dates didn't overlap."

Gabriel consulted his notes and continued. "Quimby's not talking to us, other former ADDATA staffers are either unavailable or have developed amnesia about the man, and Greg Morris, Oliver's programmer friend from inside ADDATA, has not returned our calls."

"Has Oliver been told the digital signature on the deepfake of Jen's video was linked to Karpov?" I asked.

Gabriel nodded. "Alex is briefing him."

"Jennifer will speak to the press tomorrow at ten a.m. She will outline the deepfake that was made of her and how it damaged both her credibility and her health," Quinn said. "Shane, will you draft up a press release detailing Karpov's connection to Jen's video? We'll want it ready to go as soon as Karpov takes the bait. Jen and her family are staying at The Vault, so we'll do her press conference first, and afterward we can film Oliver's statement about his technology and how it can prevent this type of thing—"

"Wait," I interrupted, "Jen and the kids are staying at The Vault?" I hadn't even wondered where they were spending the night. "Then we can't set the trap for Karpov there."

Quinn held up a hand. "We'll make sure the Joneses' floor is inaccessible."

I shook my head. "No."

"Dallas." Quinn's tone held a warning, but I met his eyes without flinching.

"No. Rio and Zoro will be in the building."

"They'll be gone by the time the interviews go live."

I shook my head. "Oliver can't stay there either. If Karpov is tracking him in any way, the kids will be in the line of fire."

"This building"—Quinn indicated the office around us—"is too heavily protected, and there's nowhere else to stage the setup where we won't put civilians in danger."

"There is someplace else," I said, looking him in the eye. "Oliver's house."

Quinn narrowed his eyes. "He's too vulnerable there."

"That's what Karpov will think too," I said with certainty, "but he'll have to get through me first."

"Change of plan," I announced, as I walked into the office suite where Oliver and Alex worked at a computer as Darius and Anna played chess. They all looked up in surprise, but my eyes were on Oliver's as I continued. "There are little kids staying in The Vault tonight."

"Right," Darius said slowly. "And we're locking down the elevators."

Oliver met my gaze. "Jennifer Jones and her kids are staying there?"

I nodded, still processing the strength of my reaction to the baby and the toddler I'd only known for two months.

He seemed to understand immediately. "I can't stay there. I'll put them at risk."

"Wait a minute," Darius began, but I interrupted when I turned to him.

"Can you and Anna help me assess Oliver's house? We want Karpov to have just enough access to get in, but not so much that it puts Oliver in danger."

Darius frowned, but nodded. "I've upgraded the security system, but as the McCallum cameras are still in place, we should be able to make something appear vulnerable."

Alex looked up from the computer screen and said simply, "Quinn doesn't use clients as bait."

I looked around the room at each one of my colleagues. "We want Karpov to know Oliver's there. He needs to see him on the McCallum security cameras moving around the house like he's totally confident in his own safety." My gaze went to Alex. "Karpov's still up in Michigan?" He nodded, and I turned to Oliver. "Then you're safe enough tonight."

Darius studied Oliver. "Are you sure you want to do this?"

Oliver's eyes met mine, and he raised an eyebrow as if to ask if I was sure.

"I won't put those kids in danger," I said to him quietly.

He nodded and stood. "I'm with Dallas." He turned to Alex. "You have enough information about my program to do a blast out to all the news outlets when I've recorded myself announcing the Facebuster auction?"

Alex nodded. "Ready for your signal. Consider recording yourself someplace that is visibly in your house. It can act as further bait for Karpov in the event he isn't actively monitoring the McCallum cameras."

Oliver nodded. "Good point." Then he turned to me. "You'll be my close protection?"

I didn't hide my relief. "Of course."

Darius sighed. "I don't like leaving you guys vulnerable."

"You did a sweep for listening devices?" I asked Darius.

He nodded. "The McCallum system is cameras only."

"Okay." We were as ready as we'd ever be. "How about you and I cook up a little dinner party tonight, with Darius and Anna as our guests?" I asked Oliver. "On the small chance Karpov leaves Michigan, he won't go in guns blazing with Cipher agents on site, and we can refine the security plan over dinner."

He smiled at me, and my stomach did a little flip. Oh, the irony. My immunity to his charming smiles was utterly smashed to bits, and now I seemed to crave them.

"Let's do this," he said.

If only we could do *this*, I thought, waving an imaginary finger between us.

[43]

DALLAS

"You have no idea how far out of my comfort zone my life actually is."

- OLIVER

We dropped our bags at Oliver's house and then walked over to the same market where he'd shopped the day I met him. It was strange to retrace those steps next to him as we chose the ingredients for dinner. We decided to make homemade chicken pot pie, and when he grabbed a baguette from the bakery, he added, "For snacking on while we cook."

And right after we bought it, he tore off the end piece and handed it to me.

"For snacking while we walk?" I laughed.

The smile on his face faded away as he studied me, and he looked thoughtful. I refused to give in to insecurity, so instead, I asked a question I'd been wondering about since the day before. "What happened to your Canada Goose jacket?"

"I gave it to Reed," he said.

I stared at him in shock. "That's a thousand-dollar gift."

He shrugged. "He can pull it off without looking like a poser. I've been told I look like a douche canoe in it."

I laughed. "That's a thing?"

"It's someone who exceeds the normal limits of pretentiousness," he said, in a completely serious tone as if reading from the dictionary.

"There are limits to your pretentiousness?" I said with a grin.

"Apparently"—he bumped my hip with his—"there are."

We entered Oliver's house and took our groceries to the kitchen. Since the McCallum system was still operational at the house, and because we assumed that Karpov was monitoring it, we let our images be recorded by that system doing normal, everyday things. That way, if we got word that Karpov had moved, we could smuggle Oliver out, staff the house with agents, and then loop the McCallum recording so it might appear as though he were still there.

We worked well side by side in the kitchen as we prepped the meal—my knife skills useful for the vegetables, his broth and seasoning skills for cooking the meat. Then I assembled the filling while he made the dough for the crust, and when the big Pyrex casserole dish was in the oven, Oliver sat down next to me at the kitchen island and surveyed the room.

"I like my kitchen," he said.

"I do too."

"It kind of puts cooking on a wood stove into perspective," he added. I didn't know where he was going with the conversation, but I had the sense it was leading somewhere definite.

"I'm sure it does," I said. "Just like I'm sure a couple of weeks in the North reminded you how nice it is to have central heat and endless hot water."

He studied me for a long time before he finally spoke again. "We're really different, you and I."

I nodded, stomach sinking, but determined not to show it. "Seems so."

"You're kind of a nomad, living out of a duffle and vacation rentals, barely unpacking the stuff you do have. You're not motivated by money or success, really. It's mostly about … I don't know, skills? You're totally, undeniably competent at everything you do, you have a rock-solid code of ethics, and you know exactly who you are. It's pretty damn intimidating, if I'm honest."

I shrugged and looked down at my hands holding a cut crystal rocks glass of sparkling water. I turned the glass in my hand, watching the rainbows play on my skin and trying not to show how that assessment landed. Part pride, part dismay, and mostly confusion, because I wasn't sure what he was saying.

"Meanwhile, I'm over here conspicuously consuming in my gourmet kitchen, unhampered by any codes except the ones I write, and living a basically hedonistic life. I don't really look beyond what I'm having for dinner except when I'm working, and then only because I usually forget to eat. I'm good at making money, taking expensive trips, and ignoring my conscience when it gets pesky. I have nomad PTSD, and I bought this house just so I could be *not* my parents. I'm basically selfish and have the survival skills of a frat boy." He scoffed at himself, but his self-assessment wasn't ironic or without a measure of pride.

Everything he said was true, and it made even a friendship between us sound, on paper at least, completely unlikely.

"I don't know how to reconcile who I am with who you are," he finally said with a sigh.

I looked up from the rocks glass and met his gaze. "Yeah," I breathed.

"Also." He hesitated, then seemed to search for the right words. "I'm not sure I want kids."

I avoided his eyes, feeling like I'd been punched. "I don't—"

"I might be too selfish for kids," he continued before I could finish. "And you should have them. I saw you with Jennifer's kids. You'd be an amazing mom. I just …" He closed his eyes and took a breath. "I don't want to be a regret."

Well, okay, then. If he couldn't see a way forward with me in his life,

I wasn't going to talk him into it. He was a grown-up, he could decide for himself. I pushed away the tiny voice that still wondered if there was a chance I could be pregnant and focused on swallowing past the pain.

The doorbell rang and the timer beeped on the oven. "Oliver"—I grabbed his arm before he could get up—"I only regret the chances I don't take. And I'm here now. This is me taking a chance."

Then I let him go and went to the oven to take out the pot pie. I felt him hesitate behind me before he headed toward the front door. The conversation was done, for now, and maybe forever.

Darius and Anna came in with a key lime cheesecake. They had spent some time in Oliver's house setting up the new security system while we were up north, so they walked in like they knew the place.

Anna admired the chicken pot pie when she put the cheesecake in the refrigerator. "Things okay?" she asked me, while Darius took Oliver on a tour of the new system.

"I'll feel better when the case is closed and he's safe," I said.

She studied me, looking for the things I wasn't saying. "And then?" she asked.

I met her questions with my own certainty. "And then I'll go back home."

Her eyes searched mine, and then she pulled me in for a spontaneous hug. "I'm dragging my man up to visit you. I want to see what this midnight-sun business is all about," she said as she let go.

I smiled. "We'll go foraging," I said. "Chanterelles, black morels, spruce tips for jelly and gin, fireweed for jam and lip balm."

"Oh yes, please!" She grinned. "Tell me when and we're there."

Then she took me around the house and gave me the same security system tour. The new system was good, and I felt confident that Oliver would be safe, at least in his own home, when I left. We met up with the guys in the living room and sat down to eat.

Changing the location of the trap meant changing the context of the plan. We'd originally intended to deepfake the Russian's face onto Darius's body to lure Karpov to The Vault, but that was pointless now.

We weren't at The Vault, and there was no way we could make Karpov believe we'd stashed his brother at Oliver's house. Therefore, we needed another lure.

"What if I just announce the auction for the fake-busting program at tomorrow's press conference, and then for the next couple of days I have prospective buyers come here for meetings?" Oliver said.

I shook my head. "We don't put civilians in the line of fire, remember?"

Oliver clarified. "Sorry, I meant to say that I would deepfake an investor meeting here. Sterling was going to introduce me to Zuckerberg, and there's tons of footage on him. I could put him in this room pretty easily." He frowned thoughtfully. "I think."

I stared at Oliver. "That's the kind of buyer you're looking for?"

He met my gaze. "Once upon a time, yeah."

"Quinn has several connections in the intelligence community who could be potential buyers," Darius said.

Oliver shook his head. "But they're not immediately recognizable to someone studying security cam footage, and I probably wouldn't meet the head of the NSA at my house."

"But you *would* meet him," I said, stunned to my core.

He shrugged. "They were on my list."

A burst of shocked laughter left my lips, and I clapped a hand over my mouth. "No shit," I whispered, suddenly intimidated by the brain and influence of the man in front of me. The man, who, for most of our acquaintance, I had only thought of as a client without really considering the actual man.

I had grown up basing my opinion of worth on how a man measured up against Grandpop. It was my default, and I was suddenly startled into revising that default into something more complex.

A suppressed grin quirked Oliver's mouth. "Been taking vocabulary lessons from Mark?"

I chuckled, and the shock eased a little. "Two words that can mean so many things."

Like *no shit*, this man is confident. *No shit*, he has no problem taking direction from a woman or crying in front of one. *No shit*, he expects his life will work out. That confidence was surprisingly hot, and I shifted my eyes to Darius and Anna just to find my focus again.

"How tall is Zuckerberg?" I asked them.

"Haven't met him yet," Oliver said, oblivious to the flush of warmth in my face.

Anna whipped out her phone and a moment later said, "Five foot seven."

"Perfect." I turned back to Oliver. "Would it help to put his face on me?"

"You look *nothing* like him," he said emphatically.

"Of course not. But in a suit, with my hair pulled back tightly, could it work?"

"I'd have to do a lot of masking, but having a body to put a head on is a more believable deepfake than pulling everything from a digital image," he said thoughtfully.

"So, can it be done?" I asked.

His answer was slow and measured as he considered me. "Yeah, I can do it."

I tried not to feel anything more than studied, but I couldn't tear my eyes from him.

"What will that solve though?" asked Darius. "Karpov's not going to come here to stop a meeting with Zuckerberg."

"Of course not," I said. "But appearing to meet with someone like Zuckerberg will make him think a sale of the program is imminent. Karpov will come here to kill Oliver to prevent the sale, and also to get revenge for Dimitri. He's got lots of motivation to make a move."

I frowned and looked around the room for his phone. "You know, maybe we don't need to deal with a deepfake at all. Theoretically, we could do this with a phone call—"

Darius was already shaking his head. "There's no audio in the McCallum security system. It has to be visual."

"And compelling enough to bring Karpov out of hiding," Anna said. "What then? What if he takes the bait?"

"Karpov gets arrested for the crimes Shane and Gabriel investigated," I said. "Accessory to the murder of a federal judge, if I remember correctly—and Quinn gets to take him down in the courts."

Darius studied me. "You realize that even having Oliver here now is a risk. But running an op out of his house will require twenty-four-seven coverage."

Oliver had pulled his laptop out of his messenger bag and was already working as Darius and I discussed staffing and coverage needs for the house. When logistics were hammered out, Darius called in to Cipher and then came back to the table.

"Karpov hasn't moved, according to his dark web activity," Darius announced. "It's still pinging from the same spot in Michigan. Quinn is sending Saahil and Avalon up there now." He turned to me. "Are you both okay here tonight?"

I darted a look at Oliver. "Are you comfortable staying here?"

"I'm fine. I'm going to be up late setting up the drives anyway."

Darius nodded and added, "Make sure windows and doors are locked, and turn the new security system on when we leave."

"Also," said Anna with a gentle elbow in Darius's ribs, "pretend he didn't just act like a big brother and mansplain basic security common sense to you."

Darius winced. "Right. Do that."

The house felt too silent after they left, as if Oliver and I were holding our breath and tiptoeing through it. I set the Cipher alarm and then went through the house securing windows and making sure everything was locked up, while Oliver cleared and cleaned dishes.

I had dropped my duffle upstairs when we first arrived, and I took a minute to unpack my toiletry bag so I could brush my teeth. When I entered Oliver's bathroom, I immediately muttered, "Damn," under my breath and left again, as though I'd forgotten something, and then I raced silently along the landing to the stairs. I very nearly flew down them to the kitchen, where Oliver was just drying the Pyrex dish.

He spun in surprise at my sudden appearance, but I motioned silence as I pulled my cell phone out and texted "911" to Darius. Then I grabbed one of the Shun chopping knives from the block and whispered under my breath, "Hide."

Oliver grabbed his own chopping knife and slid behind the open door. God, I loved a man who took direction. I hit the light and tucked myself against the kitchen wall. The only way to get to us was past the big picture windows in the living room, which afforded me a clear reflection of the staircase.

I'd gone into Oliver's bathroom expecting his scent. He'd taken a quick shower when we'd first arrived and smelled like heaven—summer in the woods—when he came down to the kitchen. I'd expected the lingering scent of him in his bathroom, but instead picked up the smell of gun oil and peppermint.

Whoever had gotten in had done it while we were eating dinner, likely through the bathroom window, which had been unlocked to let the steam from Oliver's shower out. As I watched the picture window, the reflection of a tall, slender man wearing all black slipped down the stairs. He held a gun the way a soldier did, easily, readily, and with confidence. Whoever he was, he'd had training that I couldn't ignore, especially as I was only armed with a knife and whatever element of surprise I could conjure.

I slithered along the wall to the edge, beyond which was the open living room. The intruder had disappeared from view, likely checking the small bathroom near the front door. I debated my options while I calmed my heartbeat and breathing so I could listen beyond myself. If Darius had gotten my text, he'd be back here momentarily. I didn't know if he was armed, and I hoped he wouldn't burst in the front door, or if he did, that it was loud and shocking enough to distract the intruder.

I had no sense of Oliver behind me, but I hoped he had become one with the wall behind the door. I inched forward, every sense tuned to the intruder and the moment his reflection would reappear in the window.

The lights in the living room turned the darkened kitchen into a shadowed well of safety. It was temporary, but as long as Oliver stayed hidden behind the door, he was as safe as I could make him.

There was no question in my mind about what I would do to keep him safe. If I'd never gotten to know him, if he'd remained a client with a name, a face, but no personal connection to me, I would stay tucked against this wall with my knife, doing my job as a barrier between the intruder and my client. But Oliver had become so much more to me in the past few weeks. He was my raven, and whether or not he chose to love me, I would be his wolf.

Holding my knife in my left hand, I sank to a crouch and slid my body around the corner. I was partially hidden from view by the bookcase against the wall. There was movement in the reflection as the intruder inched into view from the entrance hall. He seemed to focus on the dining table, now empty of dishes, where Oliver had set up his laptop. The hard drives were stacked next to it, their orange cases acting like a beacon drawing the intruder's attention.

He went straight to the table, and I debated hurling the knife at his back, but protection of property wasn't a strong enough legal argument for the preemptive use of force, so I waited, hoping Darius would arrive soon. The intruder was in his late thirties, blond, non-descript in a way that reminded me of the forgettable looks of the Russian. It looked like Karpov, but I couldn't positively identify him from my position crouched against the bookshelf.

He looked around and spotted the satchel in which Oliver had carried the drives, then stuffed the hard orange cases into it. Suddenly, the screech of an alarm flooded the room, and the intruder dropped down behind the desk, slung the satchel across his chest, and aimed his gun at the hall leading to the front door.

I flung my knife at his shoulder before he could get a shot off at Darius. It struck his bicep and blew his aim, but he swung around and pointed the Glock at me before I could move, getting off another shot that hit the wall above my head.

"Hey! Morris!" Oliver yelled from the open kitchen door, obviously attempting to distract him from shooting at me again.

Damn it!

I was flying through the air to knock Oliver away when the bullet hit me.

Fuck.

[44]

DALLAS

"In our culture, if someone saves your life, they cannot own it. For us, life is a sacred journey and each day is sort of a pop quiz. You try your best, win some, lose some, and then tomorrow you start over again."

- OJIBWE WOMAN

I panicked at the sound of the third shot, expecting it to hit Oliver. "Get back," I hissed at him, ignoring the searing burn in my right side. I'd knocked him to the floor of the kitchen, and now I wanted him out of the line of the shooter's sight.

But Oliver didn't get back. He hurled his butcher knife at the shooter, then lunged forward to me, apparently trying, in some misguided way, to protect me.

My side hurt, but I could still move, and I blocked Oliver as I spun to face the shooter. He was down. Darius stood over him with a gun aimed at his chest. The shooter was bleeding from somewhere—I didn't much

317

care where—and his eyes darted between Darius and the gun in his hands.

Anna was right behind Darius talking into a cell phone. The shooter's weapon was on the floor, and I stepped toward him to kick it away. He tried to grab my leg, so I accidentally kicked his face. He let go.

"Dallas!" Oliver shouted from behind me. "You're bleeding."

"Flesh wound," I said, hoping it was true. I refused to believe it could be anything else, and my eyes locked on the shooter's. His resemblance to the Russian had become clear with the rage that twisted his face into a snarl.

"I'll take the bag," I said, as I reached for the strap across his chest.

Oliver's butcher knife had sliced the shooter's arm, leaving a smear of blood in its wake. Interesting. Oliver's ax-throwing lessons had served us both well.

The shooter snarled and lunged for me. My elbow collided with his nose, effectively stopping his forward momentum, and I took the bag off him and slid it across the floor to Oliver in the kitchen.

"Quinn is calling the police," Anna said. "He'll meet us here."

Darius's gaze flicked to me and he nodded at my side. "You're shot."

I looked down at the spreading stain of blood just above my waist and lifted my shirt to look at the sliced skin beneath. Oliver sucked in a breath behind me as I probed the damage.

I refused to allow relief to cloud my professionalism. "Bullet skimmed me," I said, and then looked beyond Oliver. I hit the light in the kitchen and stepped over to the island where a piece of the granite countertop had chipped off. Then I examined Oliver. "You're not hurt?"

His face was pale, and he just stared at me as he shook his head.

"You threw a knife," I said with admiration.

"You took the bullet," he mumbled in shock.

I made a face. "I got in its way, I didn't take it."

He scoffed in surprise. "You got in the way of a bullet aimed at me."

I didn't respond because Quinn strode in with the sound of sirens heralding his entrance. He stared down at the shooter and studied him critically. "Alexander Karpov."

Karpov said nothing, but his glare burned holes in Oliver. Quinn looked over at us, and he saw my bloody shirt.

"I'm fine," I said preemptively.

He nodded, and then we all turned to Oliver, who was studying Karpov with fury. "Morris," he spat, and then he looked at me. "That's Greg Morris, the programmer I told you about from ADDATA, the one who tried to pull me back in."

Quinn looked thoughtful, then pulled out his phone and dialed a number. "Alex, run a complete background on Greg Morris, and let's find the source of the signal locating Karpov in Michigan." Quinn's gaze returned to us as he continued speaking into the phone. "No, if he's here in person, it's because there's no one else he trusts enough to do the job. The Canadians have the brother, and now we have him. The physical threat is finished, but I'll need you to get to work unraveling the tech side of this thing."

Two Chicago PD officers entered the house and descended on Darius and Karpov. The only thing I was able to say quietly to Oliver before I was taken out to an ambulance was, "Let them take the laptop as evidence. Say nothing about the drives."

A paramedic cleaned and bandaged my side where the bullet grazed me, and then Karpov, his wrists zip-tied behind his back, was brought out for treatment of knife wounds to both arms. He glared at me. I smiled back.

Oliver *was* in shock, and after statements were given, Anna took him to the suite at The Vault. Karpov was removed to the police station in the back of a cruiser. Quinn left for the station to meet the Cipher legal team and make sure Karpov was properly remanded into custody.

Darius and I stayed at Oliver's to clean up the blood and secure the house. We disabled the McCallum security system entirely and re-activated the Cipher system. Then I locked the door behind us, threw my duffle bag into Darius's Toyota Landcruiser, and rode with him to the harbor.

We sat in the dark in his vintage truck. "He had military training and was here to hunt Oliver," I finally said. "The brother, Dimitri, was better though. He wouldn't have been distracted by the hard drives." I exhaled. "He also wouldn't have missed."

"Oliver's lucky you were there."

I met Darius's gaze in the dim light of the harbor parking lot. "I think I'm in love with him."

He nodded. "Yeah."

"That doesn't freak you out? I mean it pretty much breaks every ethical code in the book."

He chuckled. "I fell for a thief. I think you need to write your own code of ethics when it comes to who you love."

I stared out into the night. "There's a bunch of reasons it won't work," I finally said.

"Are there any non-negotiables?"

I raised an eyebrow as I turned to look at Darius.

"Non-negotiables are the things that other relationships, the broken ones, teach us we don't want—as in, if you see that quality or you recognize that barrier, run the other way."

I considered everything I thought I knew about Oliver, from the charm that hid a fear of being left, to his ability to ignore his conscience even when it itched. But there was only one thing I didn't think I could compromise on.

I stared out the window into the night, and Darius let me sit in silence until I finally said, "He doesn't want kids. He thinks he's too selfish for them."

"Is that your non-negotiable? Kids?" Darius asked.

"Yeah, I think it is."

He was silent for a moment. "Have you seen him with animals?"

"He's great with them," I said, remembering the fearlessness and deep compassion he had for my grandfather's dogs.

"My guess is he's just afraid, which means for him it might not really be about kids or no kids, it might be more about whether to hide behind fear or step into possibility." He chuckled quietly. "It's amazing how many things in life boil down to that simple question. What are you afraid of, and will you be stopped by it?"

I leaned over and impulsively kissed Darius's cheek. "You are a good man."

He grinned. "You're a good woman, and if Oliver Curran is cool enough to be loved by you, he's smart enough to figure out what's important."

I got out of the truck and slung my bag over my shoulder. "Thanks for the bed tonight," I said, as Darius handed me the keys to his boat.

"It's yours as long as you want it," he answered before I shut the door.

He waited until I was on the dock and the gate was closed behind me before driving away. I passed a sleek cruiser with a light on, and a head emerged from the cockpit as I walked by.

"Hey," a male voice called. "You work with Darius."

Darius's brother peered at me in the dim light of the dock.

"I'm staying on his boat tonight," I said.

"I borrowed the last of his coffee yesterday. I'll bring you some in the morning." He looked a little sheepish.

I thought about protesting, but I was too tired. "Thanks, Reza."

"I don't remember your name," he said.

"It's Dallas. I'll be gone by eight. Good night," I said, as I stepped onto the wooden party boat docked nearby.

He chuckled as his head disappeared back into his boat. I unlocked the cabin door and made up the bed, and as I sat down with a hotel sewing kit to stitch the bullet hole in my bloody shirt, I thought about family. Darius's brother, who watched out for his boat and borrowed his coffee. Reed, my cousin, best friend, and co-conspirator, whose answer to every question about jumping had always been "how high," my grandfather, who had been willing to leave his family if that's what it took to keep them safe, and even Karpov, whose brother was ready to kill for him. They were people who had our backs no matter what. Who did Oliver have? He was an only child raised by selfish parents whose nomadic existence had left him without even friends. He had filled the hole with work and money and thousand-dollar coats and fabulous trips, and maybe that was enough for him.

It wasn't enough for me. Maybe that was my non-negotiable—family. People to teach what I knew, to learn from, and to work beside, chatting, laughing, telling stories, and sharing tasks. People who saw me, who knew me, and who had my back.

[45]

OLIVER

"...I wanted the gold, and I got it—
Came out with a fortune last fall,—
Yet somehow life's not what I thought it,
And somehow the gold isn't all..."

- ROBERT W. SERVICE, *THE SPELL OF THE YUKON*

She arrived at Cipher looking like she'd slept, which was more than I could say for myself. I was back to the familiar routine of no sleep, and when I still hadn't managed to drift off by three a.m., I got up to face the day.

I took a long, hot shower in the luxurious tiled bathroom, and thought about the tiny fiberglass shower stall at Dallas's family compound. The hot water pounded my neck as steam fogged the glass, and gradually, the hollow space in my chest began to fill with … something that felt like yearning. It was a feeling I hadn't experienced since before I sold my first program back in college.

At five a.m. I was on a borrowed laptop setting up a website platform, and at six a.m. I was at Cipher working on the big machines in the basement.

She brought me coffee when she found me there, and when she sat down next to me at the desk, the scent of her filled my senses. *She* was Dallas. There had never been another woman in my life who filled in all the missing bits of me. She was complete, and yet she completed me, and the fact that she wasn't already on a plane back to the Yukon gave me hope that I was something to her too.

"Anna said you've been here since the crack of dawn," she said, sipping her own coffee.

She didn't wear makeup, and her long dark lashes brushed her skin when she blinked.

"I miss Mark's rig. Alex made me describe the setup to him and is working on designing a heating system like the one Mark made."

"I'm actually stunned that there's anything Alex Greene doesn't know how to do," she said with a smile. I had to tear my eyes away from her lips. Her smiles came easier with me now, and I wondered if I'd been the reason she didn't smile, but maybe now, hopefully, the reason she did.

"I've been working on something I wanted to show you," I said, finally dragging my gaze away from her face. "Look." I navigated to the website I'd set up. The deepfake deconstruction of Jennifer Jones's face from the faked video played first for shock value, then as a FaceBuster tutorial, peeling back the layers of the faked face, unblurring edges, freezing animation.

I'd named my program FaceBuster, and the website included free download links to the full program for every operating system. There was a small window in the corner for "coffee money" donations, but otherwise, I'd made the deepfake-busting program open-source, and already the message boards were lighting up.

It took her a few minutes to absorb, and then she turned a stunned expression to me. "You made it free?"

I shrugged. "Can't kill me to stop it now."

"Oliver, you just gave away millions of dollars."

I winced. "Probably tens of millions. But then I would have had to come up with a bunch of causes to donate to, and that's way too much like my parents for even my impervious conscience to deal with."

She pointed to the donation counter in the corner of the screen. "You're crowdfunding?"

I smiled. "Reed's idea. I figure I still owe Mark for the rental of his mining rig, and I should probably pay Reed for his time. They're both pretty good wingmen for my sketchy business plans."

Her expression was thoughtful. "And what is that plan now that you've given away your product?"

I looked around the basement computer bank and was not inspired by what I saw. "Is there any place with a view of something more interesting than machines around here?"

She thought for a moment, then brightened. "Do you have a coat?"

I grinned. "Darius loaned me one of his."

"Come with me," she said, holding out her hand.

I took it and didn't let go.

She led me to the roof of the Cipher building, accessed from a staircase on the top floor. When she opened the door, my first impression was of enormous sky, and I was suddenly struck with the realization that I'd only ever experienced such a majestic sky in the Yukon.

Then I saw the round gas fire pit surrounded by bench seats and a glass windblock on one side. Dallas pulled some cushions from a box near the door, and we carried them to the bench facing the river. I set them up while she lit the fire, and then we settled in to watch the Chicago skyline.

Her right side was pressed against mine. "How's your battle wound?" I asked.

"Didn't need stitches, but Reed will be impressed. Sadly, nothing beats a moose goring, and Grandpop's goring wound puckered better than this one will."

Only this woman would consider battle scars badges of honor. "I was actually asking how badly it hurts," I said with a laugh and a shake of my head.

She looked surprised. "Oh. It's fine. Twinged when I hung my head over the sink to wash my hair, but it's clean and doesn't look like it'll infect."

I studied her. "Where'd you sleep last night?"

"On Darius's boat."

I had assumed she'd stayed in a suite at The Vault like I had, though I'd hoped she would have stayed at my house. I guess I should have asked her to. There were a lot of shoulds on my list when it came to her, so I began with the one that had churned through my mind all night.

An admission of weakness.

I took a breath. "I haven't felt safe since I was nine years old," I said.

"What? Why?" She was shocked.

"My parents left me behind one day, and I think I never trusted them —or anyone else—not to do it again."

She was silent, maybe waiting for me to fill in the blanks, but the terror of that time still echoed in the beat of my heart, and I stared into the fire as I said, "I probably should have told you why I was always such an asshole to you."

She hesitated, then said quietly, "It hurt."

I met her eyes. "I'm sorry."

I told her how I'd experienced her the day we met. From the first moment I saw her on the train, I'd noticed her calm confident energy. Nothing more—not her face, not her body, just her energy. And when I'd realized she was following me, her energy felt sinister, and then when she'd actually saved me, all I could do was run away. And all the carefully constructed confidence I'd built for myself had shattered.

"Every time I saw you after that, I was running away. You terrified me at Cipher"—I scoffed at myself—"and the fact that I wanted to bolt was why I was so pissed. Then there was the night of the break-in, the night we got shot at, and then especially when we fled to Canada."

I inhaled sharply to buy myself time to find the right words. "It took me a long time to build up the confidence that you call my charm. I think of it more as the shell that holds me together. Every time I bolted, my confidence took another hit." I met her eyes. "And you, with your seemingly boundless competence and skills and self-assuredness—you were there to witness my weakness."

"Oliver, you weren't weak for wanting to live." She held my gaze intently. "Giving up, giving in, that's weak. Not only didn't you give up, you fought back, and you brought your own strength to the fight."

She searched my eyes, as if willing me to really hear what she was saying. Maybe she saw my reluctance, because she changed the subject. "Tell me what happened when you were nine."

I took a deep breath and let the memories come.

"My parents had moved us to Haiti for their work with a French NGO—non-governmental organization," I began, trying to create a context that she might understand. "We lived in university housing in Port-au-Prince."

Her brow furrowed, like she was trying to place the history of the country.

"There were riots at the university, and Aristide's forces came after the students, breaking legs and beating them with clubs."

The sound of screams still filled the silent hours of my nights. They were what I tried to drown out with work. "I was out with my nanny, a pretty marketing student named Amélie. My parents had fought about her that morning. I think my dad was sleeping with her."

My memory of Amélie was of chipped fingernail polish and the smell of cigarettes, and her tears as we walked to the student union for her coffee and my Haitian pate that morning.

"I don't remember why, but I ran from her in the university square just as the police stormed in, and no one saw me hiding under a table in the café. Amélie came looking for me, calling my name, and I watched a policeman break her arm with his stick."

"Oh, Oliver," Dallas whispered. I couldn't look at her though. I couldn't stand to see the sympathy I heard in her voice.

"She fled, probably to the hospital, I don't know. I never saw her again." The image of young men and women, so big and adult to me at the time, bleeding, crying, cradling broken bones and bloody friends came in flashes of pain. Even my memory closed its eyes to the scene that I'd run from, all the way home without looking back.

"Our apartment was empty when I got back. Clothes were pulled from hangers, drawers hung open. I found out later my parents had left a note for Amélie on the kitchen counter telling her to bring me to the embassy. I didn't see the note."

"When did they come back for you?" Dallas's voice was full of pain, and the small part of me that was actually still there on the roof with her, staring into the fire, marveled at her empathy.

"The next morning," I said, feeling the crushing weight of the lonely night ease off my chest with the words. I finally met her eyes, and there was horror in them. "I know now they were probably just covering their own guilt, but when they found me they said spending the night alone was what I deserved for running away from Amélie."

Dallas's expression turned fierce, and in that moment I knew I loved her for wanting to protect the little kid I'd been. "I'm not sure I should ever meet your parents," she murmured, mostly to herself.

Her anger lifted more of the memory filter and brought me back to myself. "Ever since then, running away from anything is a trigger," I said. "I think I'm standing my ground by buying a house, putting down roots, playing the corporate dickhead game, becoming *not* my parents, but I've just been trading one kind of escape for another."

The flames in the fire pit danced against the glass rocks. I leaned forward to warm my hands, and to avoid the searching gaze of the woman next to me.

"My parents packed me up and took me back to the States after Haiti, but every time they went out to a fundraiser, I didn't sleep until they got home, even with a babysitter, because only then did I know for sure they hadn't left me behind." My tone was self-mocking, but saying the words out loud made the memories feel less powerful, more like just memories, not the story of who I was. I could almost feel a piece of the puzzle clicking into place.

Dallas's hand slid up under my coat to rub my back.

"Thanks," I said.

She scoffed. "I'm not doing it for you. My hands are cold."

I laughed and took her hand in my own as I leaned back. I kissed her fingertips and finally met her eyes.

"Feeling safe enough to sleep is kind of a big deal in my world. But here's the thing I realized when I was still awake at three this morning. The minute they put those zip ties around Karpov's wrists, I was safer than I've been in more than a month, but those nights I spent at fish camp with you, even knowing there was an assassin waiting for me somewhere out in the woods, were the safest I've felt in my life."

I took a breath to organize my thoughts. "To me, safety isn't about being protected. I'm a white guy with money in America, it's hard to be safer than I am on any given day. I think the thing that lets me sleep at night with you is a sense that …" I struggled to find the words, and then another piece of the puzzle clicked into place. "It's the sense that I *matter*. That I'm wanted, maybe even cherished a little. The sense that someone likes me for me, not for what I have or what I can do. It's trusting that someone—you—has my back."

I held Dallas's hands to my cheeks to warm them, and she smiled at my next words. "There is nothing I could do in those woods that you couldn't do a hundred times better, so those times when we talked, when I could make you laugh, when you taught me how to do things, I felt like I mattered to you."

"You do matter to me," she said quietly. "And you know, confidence can be defined a couple different ways. One of them is the feeling of self-assurance in our own abilities, and another is the trust, the belief, that we can rely on someone else. I have that with you. I trust you to have my back."

I knew how short the list of people she could count on was for her, and my pulse picked up at the faith she placed in me. "Here's the real kicker. The other thing I realized at three in the morning is that I'm still running. I'm so afraid I'll be left behind that I make sure to run away first. That bullshit about being too selfish for kids? Do you know the first thing I thought when I saw you get shot?" I clutched her hand in mine. "What if you were pregnant and you lost it?"

Her breath caught, and I turned to look at her.

"My God, are you?"

She shook her head with a small smile. "The condom worked. I got my period this morning."

"Christ," I whispered, and when my eyes filled with tears, I knew it wasn't panic that made my heart pound. I pulled her into my arms and held her until I found my voice again.

"A whole bunch of feelings just slammed into me, and none of them" —I looked her in the eyes—"make me want to run away."

Her eyes searched mine as her fingers stroked my cheeks, already stubbly with whiskers after a four a.m. shave. "Grandpop told me you visited him before you left Dawson."

I nodded. Of course I had. I respected the hell out of Dallas's grandfather.

"He told me something that hasn't left me alone," she continued. My fingers tightened on hers and she smiled. "He said I'm a lone wolf trying to come home, but I need my own raven to help me find my way."

Dallas met my eyes as she explained. "My grandmother was his raven. Maybe it was because she actually had a pet raven, or maybe just because she was his opposite, but he said they filled in the empty spaces in each other."

I held myself completely still, afraid to move in case she pulled away from me. But my heart was pounding, and I felt her words deep in my soul.

She smiled and looked back at the fire as if it held the image in her memory. "Reed dragged me over to the window to make sure I saw you feed the guts of a fish to a raven that day out at fish camp. He said you looked at home out there in the snow with that bird, you looked at peace. Peace was not something I've felt too much of since I ran away from the Yukon."

She and I had that running-away thing in common, but I didn't say it out loud. I didn't need to.

Dallas exhaled. "When I'm with you, I feel it. I feel the kind of peace I feel with my family, or making a meal with something I've foraged, or watching the northern lights dance in the night sky."

Then her hand traced my face from my eyebrow to my jaw, and I pressed my lips to her palm, feeling impossibly close to the woman I held in my arms.

"You fill my empty places with peace"—she smiled—"and play. You see things that are possible, and you make me believe they can be." She had my full attention again, and I loved the soft smile on her lips. "You said I was a nomad who barely unpacks, and I was thinking of a way to change that."

I suddenly craved her next words, though her eyes searched mine with a tinge of uncertainty. "Do you think we could both unpack in a little house I buy on Turner Street in Dawson, and we also unpack here at your house, and somewhere in all that unpacking we manage to create two places we call home?"

There it was, the final piece to the puzzle snapping into place.

"Hmm," I said, as I kissed her so softly on the lips that the sound whispered between us. My pulse quickened, and I wanted to bury my face in her skin. I resisted long enough to speak.

"Do you think we could rig my computers to heat our house, and maybe we could get a gas stove for the Turner house kitchen?"

She smiled. "I was kind of thinking of rebuilding the cabin to be just a giant kitchen with a big dining table for all the family dinners."

I hummed against her mouth as I kissed her. My body hummed with wanting her, and in between kisses, I said, "Bedrooms. We'll need a few of them."

"A few, huh?" she teased. "Why so many?" Her hands went under my sweater, and heat pulsed through me at her touch.

"Well, the kids can sleep with us for a little while, but Anna and Darius are going to need a room if they come to visit," I murmured against her lips.

She poked me sharply, and I jumped back. "Hey!"

Her fierce expression was softened by lips made wet with my kisses.

"Kids, plural? How about we figure out if we even still like each other after a summer at the family compound."

I laughed and pulled her in for more kissing. "Does that mean," I said between tastes of her lips, "I get my own seat in the long drop?"

EPILOGUE
DALLAS

"Fish camp is my favorite family gathering. It happens during the annual salmon run, and the whole family comes together to harvest the salmon and make preserves for the rest of the year. Every family has their own camp where siblings, aunts, uncles, and grandparents come together. My mom runs our fish camp, and it's very labor-intensive. You stick to a schedule of processing salmon according to what Mom or Grandma says, and doing A LOT OF CHORES! But during the downtime it's so much fun!"

\- DARCIE PROFEIT

"Man, you're making me look bad," Reed grumbled to Oliver as he passed our bucket of cleaned salmon. We sat by the river's edge, gutting and cleaning the morning's haul while Christi, Mom, and Aunt Rikki repaired small holes in the net before it went back into an eddy for the afternoon. Our law said the innards from the fish should be tossed in the water, but Oliver snuck pieces of the livers to a raven that seemed to have adopted him since we'd been at fish camp.

"Nah, you got that covered without any help from me." Oliver gave

Reed's outfit an exaggerated once-over, and I laughed. Reed wore his steel-toed work boots with the tongues hanging out like tired dogs, cut-off jean shorts, and a battered straw cowboy hat. His long hair was tied back in a piece of pink ribbon he'd scrounged from his sister, Rori, and his shorts barely hung onto his narrow hips with the tenuous help of a string salvaged from one of Minty's old aprons.

"You're just jealous," Reed said, as he slit open another salmon.

I dipped my bloody hands into the eddy to rinse off the fish guts. Then I leaned over and kissed Oliver full on the lips before I picked up the bucket of clean salmon. My own denim shorts decidedly did not hang off my hips, and Oliver's gaze burned appreciatively.

"He's not jealous," I said to my cousin. "He has everything he needs right here."

"Ugh," Reed said, making a face. "Get a room."

"We've got a tent," I said sweetly, then turned a meaningful gaze to Oliver and said, "Where you can find me as soon as I get this fish hanging in the smokehouse."

The two guys continued their back-and-forth banter as I walked up to the cabin, where Grandpop sat outside showing Rori how to bind the fletching on an arrow. She was twelve and had become Grandpop's medicine-giver for his once-a-day TB meds. He only had a month to go, and now he acted as though he'd never been sick.

I set the bucket of fish on the table in the smokehouse and went back to the front of the cabin to kiss Grandpop on the cheek. "What's next on his chore list," I murmured in his ear.

"Make him chop some more alder wood to smoke the fish. But do it after you guys make lunch. I like that sage-smoked salmon and bannock burger he made the other day."

I laughed. "Will do." Then I kissed Rori on the head as I walked past. "The salmon candy's almost done. Want to be my taste tester?"

"Yes!" She jumped up. "I'll bring you some, Grandpop. Be right back."

She followed me into the smokehouse, and I opened a jar of the long, thin strips of salmon we brined in salt and maple syrup. I pulled out two strips, dried them off, and handed them to her. "You might need to be Grandpop's hands for tying off your bow, but he's still stronger than both of us for bending the wood."

She grinned happily. "I found the perfect birch sapling."

"Take him with you to show you where to cut it," I said. I didn't want to disappoint her with the news that birch was good for tension but not for compression, but Grandpop would redirect her to a better wood, just like he'd done with me when I was her age.

I had just finished hanging the salmon backbones for smoked chowder when I heard Oliver come up from the river. I didn't have to see him to know he was there, and that sense of him had gotten stronger in the months we'd been back in the Yukon. He exchanged a few words with Grandpop on the porch, and then he came in behind me to wrap his arms around my waist and nuzzle my ear.

"Any chance you have time to slip away?"

I leaned back into him with a grin. "Only if you're up for a quickie. We're on lunch duty."

"I heard," he murmured into my neck as he kissed it. "I'm honored."

I turned in his arms and kissed him without touching him. "I'm fishy. Meet me in the tent in five."

He smiled mischievously. "I'll be the one wearing a maple leaf."

I laughed and ducked under his arm and out of the smokehouse. I took the bucket of gills and fins and dumped them into the river, cleaned the empty bucket and left it for the next round of gutted fish, then washed my hands thoroughly with the big cake of soap my mom made from fireweed and rosehips. It didn't eliminate the smell of salmon, but it definitely cut it.

Mom and Aunt Rikki were debating the best recipes for dry smoked salmon with Christi, and they all pretended not to notice me heading up to the four-wall tent Oliver and I had built at the far edge of camp.

I slipped inside to find Oliver stretched out on the double camping pad we'd laid on the floor, and I burst out laughing at the maple leaf boxers he wore.

"Told you." He grinned.

I toed off my boots, peeled off my tank top, and made sure my underwear shimmied down with my denim shorts. His eyes roamed over my skin appreciatively, over the scar above my hip, and landed on the healed tattoo of a wolf and a raven on the inside of my forearm.

As promised, he'd been there to hold my hand.

He had also struck up a conversation with the tattoo artist, a Gwich'in woman named Sarah who worked with mechanized needles and also in traditional hand-poke techniques with bamboo, thread, and ink. She had admired the raven on his leg, and had echoed it in the design she did for my wolf. Sarah wore three lines down her chin and several bands around her fingers and wrists. Oliver had asked her about an elaborate thigh piece she had visible under her shorts. She explained that the meanings of tattoos were private. They were a woman's to share when and with whom she wished. He had apologized for his ignorance, and then later found some articles about traditional tattoos which usually marked rites of passage for women.

"Come here," he said, patting our bed. He lay back, and I straddled him over his maple leaf boxers. He laughed and stroked my thighs.

"You're so beautiful," he said, as he traced the lines of muscle and tendons. His fingers found the slightly puckered scar where the bullet meant for him had nicked me, and then, as always, they made their way to the inside of my forearm where the wolf and the raven played.

He smiled as he traced their lines. "I love watching you do what you do." His eyes met mine. "You're kind of a rock star."

I snorted a laugh as my own hands traced the lines of muscle in his arms and chest. "Says the man who gave away a fortune in the name of ethics."

He grinned. "Good thing your cousin convinced me to set up the 'coffee money' donation button. It'll help pay for an awesome kitchen at the Turner house."

I leaned down to kiss him. "Good thing you don't let him convince you of much."

He laughed and spoke between kisses as his hands roamed over the skin of my back. "Like going in on refurbishing a dredge he found in an old tailings pond? Or buying the slanty shack to turn into an escape room?"

I stretched out on top of him, and he moaned in pleasure at the contact of my skin. "I'll have you know," he continued, "I'm seriously considering buying the Midnight Sun Hotel and renting it out to the production crews that come every summer."

"Oh good," I murmured into his mouth through kisses. "It'll give us a place to stash our friends when the baby comes."

He froze beneath me. I smiled into his lips, then pulled back to see his eyes. They were wide and nothing short of jubilant.

"We're pregnant?" he whispered in wonder and awe. There was no fear in his face.

I nodded. "I'm pretty sure. I'll test when we get back to town."

His arms came around me and he held me tightly, his heart pounding against my chest as his heartbeat matched my own. Then he flipped me over so I was on my back. He lay on his side, one hand supporting his head while the other traced reverent circles around my breasts and down to my belly.

Tears welled in his eyes. "I love you," he said.

"I love you, too." I reached for his beautiful face, and my thumb wiped a tear from his lashes. "I think maybe I'll ask Sarah if she'll design a thigh piece for me—different, because our cultures are different, but related. Kind of like an Indigenous sisterhood."

"She told you what her tattoo means?"

I nodded, smiling at the wonder in his voice. "And I look forward to creating mine with you."

"Like our family," he whispered again, kissing me deeply. "Together."

If history is written by the victors, it's the stories of real people that fill in the blanks.

In 2017, as I was researching the history of schools in Dawson City, Yukon for a short story I was writing, I came across a mention of a residential school there. That led down a path of investigation into the school at Carcross and the whole residential school system that Canada and various churches implemented throughout the nineteenth and twentieth centuries with the aim of the "enfranchisement" of the Indigenous population into Euro-Canadian culture.

Ironically, the term "enfranchisement" means to give the right to vote —which wasn't granted to First Nations people in Canada until 1960—or to make free, which in the case of the residential school system meant free from the language, traditions, and practices of their native cultures. First Nations children were taken from their homes and placed in boarding schools where they were forbidden to speak their own languages. They were taught English and French, and also to become Christians and farmers. The schools were a way to implement the "aggressive assimilation" that was already happening in similar institutions in the United States. The goal was to dissolve any tribal affiliation or treaty rights, and the result was cultural genocide—the intentional destruction of First Nations cultures throughout North America.

During the writing of this book, I asked my lovely friend Darcie, a talented filmmaker whom I met many years ago on the Yukon set of the television series *Gold Rush,* to give me notes, as her Northern Tutchone heritage and some of her personal stories are the basis for several facets of Dallas. Among other things, she mentioned that Grandpop and Minty would not have been allowed to keep their kids if they'd been living at the compound—off-grid with no running water and no power. That was the first I'd heard about the Sixties Scoop. I changed the timing of Grandpop's and Minty's ownership of the compound to avoid the scoop years, and then went searching for whatever I could find about those policies that were enacted from the late 1950s until about 1985.

Within the Sixties Scoop policies lies the question of "Indian status," and again, it was Darcie's personal history that illustrated the issues so well to me. The Indian Act, first passed in 1871, is a highly paternalistic and invasive Canadian law that governs status, bands, and reserves to this day. Under the Indian Act, Darcie's great-grandmother lost her First Nations status when she married Darcie's great-grandfather, a white man. The result of this was that their children and grandchildren, including Darcie's mother, did not have First Nations status. This actually kept them safe from the Sixties Scoop, but at immeasurable cost to, among other things, cultural identity. It wasn't until the 1985 passage of <u>Bill C-31,</u> which addressed some of the discrimination inherent in the Indian Act, that Darcie's mother and her siblings were able to petition to get their First Nations status restored. As Darcie said to me, "The Indian status in Canada is a very contentious thing. It was based on racism and assimilation, but it also in many ways protects our identity and still honors a fraction of the treaties made, including some inherited rights as Indigenous people in Canada."

I didn't come close to scratching the surface in this book of the extensive and too often tragic history between the First Nations people and the Euro-Canadians. I hope you'll do your own research, and even better, find the stories told by people who lived and live it every day. Those are the voices that fill in the blanks between the pages of the histories, and those are the lenses through which the larger truths can most often be seen.

Oliver's story of a bout of tuberculosis caught from his grandmother is my own. My grandmother did indeed spend a year on a reservation in Arizona when she was young while her father recovered from it, which is how she was exposed to it. The description of the four-drug cocktail and the Department of Health's management of the treatment protocol are accurate.

All the facts that Oliver and Alex Greene spout about DeepFace, the various facial recognition programs, and deepfake technology are absolutely real. Every time you tag a friend in a photo on Facebook, you're teaching their AI to recognize that person. The more I research modern internet technology for these books, the more I wonder whether the benefits of social media—the connections created between people—outweigh the costs to privacy and truth. For me, the connections still win, so for now, you can find me in my "secret" reader group on Facebook, Kick-Ass Heroines, or on Instagram, where I never post photos of my food.

ACKNOWLEDGMENTS
FOOD AND GRATITUDE

"My perfect evening is spent with people I love—husband, friends, family—sharing good food, great wine, and interesting conversation."

- APRIL WHITE

They say a food blogger could hide a murder confession in the text leading up to the recipe and no one would ever find it. Knowing that to be true isn't going to change the fact that I'm about to write some pretty serious lead-in text. No murder confession, but instead a confession about all the people and food that inspired and supported this story.

There are not enough ways to say thank you to my lovely and remarkable friend Darcie. She shared her history and stories with me, gave me glimpses into her rich cultural traditions and into her own life experiences as a Canadian First Nations woman. She answered my endless questions, and most importantly, provided feedback, insight, and reactions to the way I depicted Dallas's world. I took absolute creative license with the details Darcie gave me, so any missteps, mistakes, or misrepresentations are completely my own. I could not have written this book without Darcie's generosity, wisdom, and kindness, and I send special thanks to her mother, with whom she consulted as she read my early drafts.

The ramen that Oliver makes is based on the extraordinary ramen my friend Olivier (pronounced the French way) makes at his restaurant Toki Underground in Washington D.C. Olivier shared his recipe with me, warned me that ramen recipes tend to be long, with a few ingredients that may be hard to find anywhere but online, and gave me permission to include it here. P.S. The real Olivier may or may not resemble the fictional Oliver in my head.

TONKOTSU RECIPE (serves 2) from Toki Underground

SOUP
 2 KG (5 lbs) pork bones (femur)
 2 KG (5 lbs) pigs feet
 8L (about 2 gal) water

TARE (soup seasoning)
 250ml (1 cup) water
 10g (2 ½ tsp) Salt
 30g (2 ½ tbsp) mirin
 20g (1 ½ tbsp) sake
 15g (3 ½ tsp) bonito flakes
 10g (2 ½ tsp) kombu

TOPPINGS

CHASHU
 400g (1 lb) pork belly
 15g + 15g (7 tsp) ginger, sliced
 ½ white onion (whole, peeled)
 2 crushed garlic cloves
 250g (1 cup) soy

40g (1/3 cup) brown sugar

30ml (2 tbsp) sake

2 green onions, roughly chopped

ONSEN EGG

2 fresh eggs (room temp)

5g (1 ¼ tsp) baking soda

GREEN ONIONS

50g (4 tbsp) thinly sliced

TWO PACKETS FRESH OR DRY RAMEN NOODLES OF YOUR CHOICE

METHOD

This will take some good timing. You'll start the night before to have the finished bowl ready for dinner the following night. While the soup is cooking, you will prepare the chashu, tare, and onsen eggs. This is the basic recipe for Tonkotsu, but you can add any other toppings you'd like.

DAY BEFORE

1. Place pork bones and feet in a pot and cover with water. Refrigerate overnight.

DAY OF (morning): SOUP

1. Discard water and replace with 8L fresh water. Bring to a simmer on the stove over med/high heat and skim off any scum periodically as it rises to the surface for the first 2 hours.
2. With a lid on, continue cooking the bones and feet, replacing the water to the original level as it evaporates for the next 2 hours. Stir the broth occasionally, making sure the bones/feet

don't sit at the bottom and burn. Remove the lid and cook for approx. 4 more hours or until reduced to desired thickness.
3. Sieve out the solids from the broth into another saucepan and set aside. Keep warm.

DAY OF (while the soup is cooking): TOPPINGS

TARE

1. Bring water, mirin, sake, and salt to a boil and remove from heat. Add the kombu and bonito and set aside to cool. Place in a sealed container in the fridge.

CHASHU

1. Place the pork belly in a saucepan with enough water to cover it along with the ½ onion and 15g of sliced ginger. Bring to a simmer on a low/med heat and cook for approx. 30 minutes, skimming off any scum that rises.
2. Meanwhile, place the soy, sake, sugar, garlic, and ginger in another saucepan. Bring to the boil and remove from the heat. Place in a separate container to cool.
3. Remove the belly from the saucepan and cool in an ice bath. Save the cooking liquid. Remove the belly from the ice and pat dry.
4. Add the cooking liquid to the soy mix in a 1:1 ratio. Put cooled pork belly and 2 tablespoons of the soy mix in a Ziploc and marinate for at least 4 hours in the fridge. Save the remaining soy mix for the onsen eggs.

ONSEN EGGS

1. Bring a small saucepan of water with the baking soda to a boil. (Baking soda will help the egg separate from the shell

when peeling.) Add your two room temp eggs and cook for 6 minutes.
2. Meanwhile, make an ice bath in a small bowl. As soon as the eggs are cooked, remove to the ice bath and cool completely.
3. Gently crack the egg shells on a flat surface and peel. Put the eggs in a container and cover with the cooled soy mix leftover from the chashu and refrigerate.

ASSEMBLING YOUR BOWL

1. Bring your pork bone broth to a simmer over medium heat.
2. Slice the pork belly to desired thickness and gently pan fry on each side.
3. Bring a medium pan of water to a boil (big enough for your two portions of noodles), and cook your noodles according to manufacturer's guidelines (dry noodles will take longer to cook).
4. Place a spoonful of tare in a bowl and add the hot broth. Taste, and if you need more seasoning, add more tare to your taste. Remove noodles from the water and drain well before adding to your bowl. Add pork belly chashu, onsen egg, and scallions and enjoy! OISHI!

My husband, Ed, has worked in the Yukon Territory for much of the last decade, and our family has spent many school breaks in Dawson City. He loves the "frozen North," the people there, the traditions, culture, and the environment. He is a visual storyteller, and so many of his stories painted the backdrop for this one. The details about Dawson City are from my summers spent there, and if you ever have the chance to visit the Yukon, you'll understand what I mean about the big sky. I first tasted the vanilla-brined pork chops that Oliver makes at a mining camp where we stayed one summer. Jen, the amazingly talented camp cook, shared the recipe with me, and now I use the spice rub for everything.

VANILLA-BRINED PORK CHOPS

FOR THE BRINE:

- 4 cups water
- 1/4 cup kosher salt
- 1/4 cup brown sugar
- 1 tablespoon vanilla extract
- 1 star anise, broken into pieces

FOR THE SPICE RUB:
(You'll have extra left over)

- 2 tablespoons sweet paprika
- 2 tablespoons brown sugar
- 2 tablespoons kosher salt
- 2 tablespoons freshly ground black pepper
- 1 tablespoon dry mustard
- 2 teaspoons ground cumin
- 2 teaspoons ground coriander
- 1 teaspoon dried thyme
- 1/2 teaspoon ground cinnamon

INSTRUCTIONS:

- Combine all of the brine ingredients in a mixing bowl and stir until the sugar and salt are dissolved.
- Place the pork chops in Tupperware or gallon-sized Ziploc. Add the brine and refrigerate for 12-24 hours (a day ahead is best).
- Combine all the dry rub ingredients in a bowl and reserve.
- Remove the chops from the brine and dry them well, sprinkle each chop liberally on both sides with the dry rub, and let rest for a few minutes at room temperature while you heat your grill or cast iron pan to medium-high heat.

- Depending on the thickness of your chops (and the strength of your grill), cook them for 4-6 minutes per side (even longer for thick chops) until just cooked through (internal temperature 125 degrees F).
- Let rest on a cutting board tented with foil for about 6-8 minutes before serving.

And finally, the chicken pot pie that Dallas and Oliver make together is my family's ultimate comfort food. I Frankensteined it during our year at home when COVID-19 closed our schools and in-person everything was cancelled. It will forever be associated with pantry staples, stretching meals across days, leftovers for lunch, and family time together.

CHICKEN POT PIE

HOMEMADE(ish) BROTH:

- Boxed chicken broth
- Celery/carrots/onions
- 1 package of chicken thighs
- Curry/turmeric/cumin/salt to taste

INSTRUCTIONS:

- Bring the broth to a simmer, add vegetables, spices, and chicken thighs. Simmer, covered, for 20-30 minutes until the chicken is cooked and pulls apart easily, spice to taste.
- (Note: brining the chicken thighs for 12-24 hours in a water/salt mixture in the refrigerator results in *significantly* more tender and flavorful meat.)

FOR THE POT PIE:

- Diced celery/carrots/onions (mirepoix)

- Diced potatoes (Yukon gold is best)
- Oil or butter to sauté
- Frozen peas (optional)
- Shredded chicken thighs (see above)
- 1 cup of hot chicken broth (see above)
- 1 tablespoon flour
- ½ cup of milk
- Frozen pie crust, puff pastry, or tinned biscuits (you can make your own pie crust, I'm just not that talented).

INSTRUCTIONS:

- Pre-heat the oven to 450 (or whatever the bread product you're using requires).
- Sauté the mirepoix and potatoes for about 5-8 minutes while you shred or chop the cooked chicken thighs (see above).
- Add in chicken and any frozen vegetables.
- Add whatever herbs or spices appeal (thyme, curry, turmeric, salt, pepper all work).
- In a separate vessel, whisk the hot broth and flour together, then add the milk.
- Pour into the vegetable/meat mix. Stir to combine.
- Then either transfer the meat/veg mix into a Pyrex dish and cover with pie crust/biscuits/etc., or if you're lazy like me, do all the sautéing in a cast iron pan so you can just cover with the pie crust and put it directly into the oven.
- Bake for 15-ish minutes until the topping is golden brown.

And just like any meal prepared with love, the ingredients that went into this book deserve special attention. To my editor, friend, saver-of-sanity, compatriot-of-college-apps, dog-walking partner, denizen of driveway drinks, and the best spy I know—Angela Houle, *thank you*. To the women who kept me sane in 2020: Angela, Korry, Edith, Kate, Nicole, Rebecca, Jess, and Maria, I love you. To Penny, Fiona, and Brooke, you are absolute rock stars, and I am in awe of your talent, generosity, and that extra thing you have that makes you remarkable people. To my moms, Helga and Valerie, and my sisters, Tania, Laura, and Linda, you are stuck with me, and I could not be more honored to claim our kinship. To my dearests, Heb and Natasha, I miss you. My loves—Ed, Connor, and Logan—you are my life, my hopes, my dreams, and my passion. And to Darcie, Rikki, the real Dallas, Dan, Nicole, Rebecca, and Jes, thank you for your wisdom, your instincts, your generosity, and your truths. You may never know how valuable your hearts and minds are to me, but I know, and I honor you for the gift of them.

THE RAVEN AND THE WOLF

A few years ago, I wrote a short story about Isaac and Minty called *The Raven and the Wolf*. That story won the Gold Nugget Prize for original fiction in the Dawson City Authors on Eighth writing competition. When I decided to set *Code of Ethics* in the Yukon, I realized it would be a perfect backstory for Dallas's grandparents. You can find *The Raven and the Wolf* on my website, and while you're there, take a look around at my other Smartypants Romance books, and also at the time travel action/adventure/romance and historical mystery books I've written. There are a couple other award-winners among them that I'm pretty excited about, as well as a link to Isaac and Minty's story, *The Raven and the Wolf*, at AprilWhiteBooks.com.

APRIL WHITE has been a film producer, private investigator, bouncer, teacher and screenwriter. She has climbed in the Himalayas, lived on a gold mine in the Yukon, and survived a shipwreck. She and her husband live in Southern California with their two sons, dog, various chickens, and a lifetime collection of books.

Facebook is a solid source of distraction for her, and therefore, her Facebook page, April White Books, is usually the first place to find news, teasers, quotes, and excerpts from her books. She also has a secret reader group on Facebook, called "Kick-Ass Heroines." If you'd like to get in on some of those conversations, you can request an add here: Kick-Ass Heroines.

Instagram is probably her favorite social media site because she finds so much inspiration for her plots and characters among other people's photos. Follow her there for books, travel, and the occasional profound observation.

Goodreads is another place to find her lurking around the stacks and spying on her friends' reading habits. Become her Goodreads friend so she can see what you're reading, too.

Marking Time was the 2016 Library Journal Indie e-book winner for Young Adult books, and was chosen by Library Journal for national inclusion on both the fantasy and young adult SELF-e Library Select lists on Biblioboard, The whole series is also available for libraries nation-wide through Overdrive, and April is very happy to participate in any library (or bookish) events to which she's invited.

$$* * *$$

Website: https://www.aprilwhitebooks.com/
Facebook: https://www.facebook.com/AprilWhiteBooks/
Goodreads:
https://www.goodreads.com/author/show/6570694.April_White
Twitter: @ahwhite
Instagram: @aprilwhitebooks

Find Smartypants Romance online:
Website: www.smartypantsromance.com
Facebook: www.facebook.com/smartypantsromance/
Goodreads: www.goodreads.com/smartypantsromance
Twitter: @smartypantsrom
Instagram: @smartypantsromance

<u>Green Valley Chronicles</u>

<u>The Love at First Sight Series</u>

<u>Baking Me Crazy by Karla Sorensen (#1)</u>

<u>Batter of Wits by Karla Sorensen (#2)</u>

<u>Steal My Magnolia by Karla Sorensen(#3)</u>

<u>Fighting For Love Series</u>

<u>Stud Muffin by Jiffy Kate (#1)</u>

<u>Beef Cake by Jiffy Kate (#2)</u>

<u>Eye Candy by Jiffy Kate (#3)</u>

<u>The Donner Bakery Series</u>

<u>No Whisk, No Reward by Ellie Kay (#1)</u>

<u>The Green Valley Library Series</u>

<u>Love in Due Time by L.B. Dunbar (#1)</u>

<u>Crime and Periodicals by Nora Everly (#2)</u>

<u>Prose Before Bros by Cathy Yardley (#3)</u>

<u>Shelf Awareness by Katie Ashley (#4)</u>

<u>Carpentry and Cocktails by Nora Everly (#5)</u>

<u>Love in Deed by L.B. Dunbar (#6)</u>

Dewey Belong Together by Ann Whynot (#7)

Hotshot and Hospitality by Nora Everly (#8)

Love in a Pickle by L.B. Dunbar (#9)

<u>**Scorned Women's Society Series**</u>

<u>*My Bare Lady by Piper Sheldon (#1)*</u>

<u>*The Treble with Men by Piper Sheldon (#2)*</u>

<u>*The One That I Want by Piper Sheldon (#3)*</u>

<u>*Hopelessly Devoted to You by Piper Sheldon (#3.5)*</u>

<u>**Park Ranger Series**</u>

<u>*Happy Trail by Daisy Prescott (#1)*</u>

<u>*Stranger Ranger by Daisy Prescott (#2)*</u>

<u>**The Leffersbee Series**</u>

<u>*Been There Done That by Hope Ellis (#1)*</u>

<u>*Before and After You by Hope Ellis (#2)*</u>

<u>**The Higher Learning Series**</u>

<u>*Upsy Daisy by Chelsie Edwards (#1)*</u>

Green Valley Heroes Series

Forrest for the Trees by Kilby Blades

<u>**Seduction in the City**</u>

<u>**Cipher Security Series**</u>

<u>*Code of Conduct by April White (#1)*</u>

<u>*Code of Honor by April White (#2)*</u>

<u>*Code of Ethics by April White (#3)*</u>

<u>**Cipher Office Series**</u>

<u>*Weight Expectations by M.E. Carter (#1)*</u>

<u>*Sticking to the Script by Stella Weaver (#2)*</u>

<u>*Cutie and the Beast by M.E. Carter (#3)*</u>

www.ingramcontent.com/pod-product-compliance
Lightning Source LLC
Chambersburg PA
CBHW051203190726
48288CB00006B/1781